# Praise for *Leaving Tuscaloosa*

I've been there. I worked on the *Tuscaloosa News* in the early '70s, and I can tell you flat-out that Walter Bennett has got a real gift for capturing time and place, and an absolute genius for creating his larger-than-life yet totally believable characters. *Leaving Tuscaloosa* is deeply moving, disturbing, haunting, and important. With vivid, muscular prose and great scene development, this fast-paced novel picks up speed until it truly embodies Bennett's phrase, "Time's freight train" hurtling down the tracks with its inexorable roar—bringing a new era of integration and change into the Deep South. I could not put this one down.
**Lee Smith,** *On Agate Hill, The Last Girls*

Above everything else, *Leaving Tuscaloosa* is all story. Of course, the characters are terrific, the setting is authentic, and the book is important because it explains what we need to know in the modern era. But more than anything else, like all excellent novels, its story is absolutely compelling. From the moment some teenage white boys are involved in a prank that kills a respected member of the black community, the book is unstoppable. As the crisis spreads, as the threat of violence builds, an entire era of American life comes alive. Compelling, important, and haunting.
**Craig Nova,** *Cruisers, The Good Son*

In *Leaving Tuscaloosa* Walter Bennett skillfully reawakens those days when segregation/integration seemed the core problem of the world. Rich character development and strong scenes of action make this novel an absorbing experience for the reader, whether Southern or not.
**Elizabeth Spencer,** *The Light in the Piazza, The Southern Woman*

Like Isabel Wilkerson's prizewinning nonfiction work *The Warmth of Other Suns*, Walter Bennett's gritty novel, *Leaving Tuscaloosa*, uses multiple points of view to deliver a recollection from that horrific era in American history that led to the migration of thousands of African Americans out of the Deep South. The characters ring true, and their fateful collision in the early 1960s must not be forgotten. This book should have a spot on college reading lists in political science, history, public policy, and sociology, in addition to its rightful study as a work of finely crafted fiction.
**Georgann Eubanks,** *Literary Trails of North Carolina*

A cliff-hanger cut from real historical drama, this story broadens the picture of the civil rights trail and situates us in the midst of the freedom movement, portraying the harsh realities of the color line and the battle for human dignity. The author's rich story-telling walks you into the sounds, sights, racial fears, and tensions between the dual worlds of blacks and whites and portrays the courage of ordinary people and their refusal to submit to a repressive social order. It is a vital format for preserving and passing on the historical narrative that children of this generation don't come to know. Civil rights history is a story of American history and culture and of the relationships between the races which comes across in a gripping way in *Leaving Tuscaloosa*.
**Dr. Karyn Trader-Leigh,** *Diversity Consultant, KTA Global Partners, LLC*

# Leaving Tuscaloosa

A Novel

Walter Bennett

*To Kathleen —*
*Thanks for all*
*The help & best*
*wishes —*
*Walter*

FUZE
PUBLISHING LLC.

Fuze Publishing LLC
1350 Beverly Rd.
Mclean, VA 22101

www.fuzepublishing.com

Book Design by Pam Chastain Design
Cover Illustration by Jim Jarvis/West Side Studio
Map Illustration by Laura Berendsen Hughes

Library of Congress Cataloging-in-Publication Data
Bennett, Walter
Leaving Tuscaloosa
Control Number: 2012939346

ISBN 978-0-9849908-3-2
ebook ISBN 978-0-9849908-2-5

Printed in the United States of America

First Edition

To Betsy

*The past is never dead. It's not even past.*

William Faulkner
*Requiem for a Nun*

*We entered the [village of Chief Tuskaloosa] and set it on fire, whereby a number of Indians were burned... so that there remained not a thing. We fought that day until nightfall, without a single Indian having surrendered to us—they fighting bravely on like lions. We killed them all, either with fire or sword... so that when it was nearly dark there remained only three... [They] shot their arrows at us... We killed two of them.... The last Indian, not to surrender, climbed a tree that was in the fence, and taking the cord from his bow, tied it about his neck, and from a limb hanged himself.*

Relation of Luys Hernandez De Biedma
Soldier in the army of Hernando de Soto
To the King of Spain in Council—1544

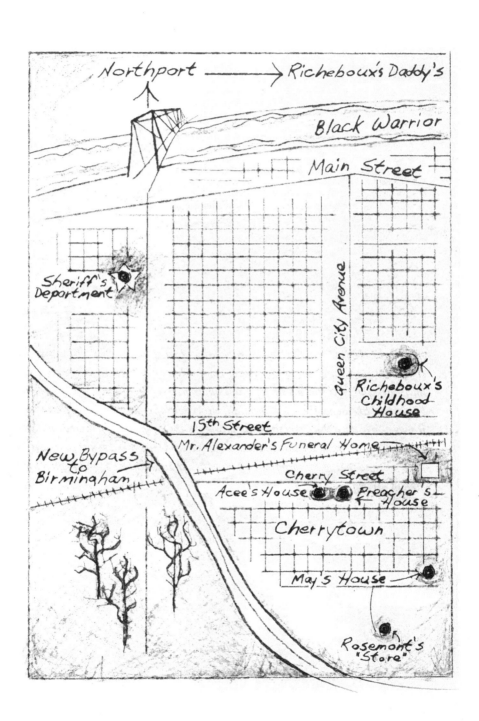

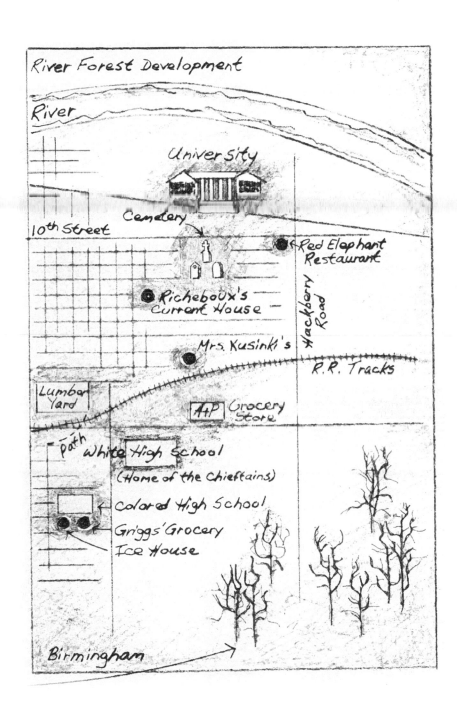

River Forest Development

River

University

Cemetery

10th Street

Red Elephant
Restaurant

Hackberry Road

Richeboux's
Current House

Mrs. Kusinki's

R.R. Tracks

Lumber
Yard

A+P Grocery
Store

Path

White High School

(Home of the Chieftains)

Colored High School

Griggs' Grocery

Ice House

Birmingham

June 1962

# The Town

The town sits atop bluffs that drop to the river in broken ridges of sweet gum and pine. Indian villages once flourished along these banks—Choctaw, Chickasaw, and Creek—long since erased by the picks and spades of white men—red-faced Scots-Irish farmers; pencil-fingered planners; hard-jawed traffickers in iron and coal; and African slaves. They hacked it, trampled it, tilled it, and mined it until all traces of the ancient life were gone, save the occasional arrowhead, turned by a plow, and native spirits, whispering at nightfall among the river's shoals and eddies.

Now it is an ordinary town. Streets run straight. Buildings are glassed and square. Stoplights change from red to green.

Late Friday afternoon: the angle-iron sign atop the First National Bank building makes its last stand against the thinning sky. Streetlights pop on, reflect off the old streetcar tracks. Office blinds draw shut. Shop doors close. Circling swifts funnel toward chimney tops too old to serve the fireplaces that support them. The town is a mausoleum draped in plastic flowers: half of it a monument to the past, the other half tacked on.

In neighborhoods off Main Street, where the old families live in their old, clapboard houses, the long, wide porches dim to shadow. The last screen door slams. Magnolias darken to silhouettes of black and green. Hands flit over florescent-lit stoves and Formica countertops.

A turned head, a call up the stairs: "I need some help down here."

Red-painted toe nails dry on the ledge of a second-story window. Cigarette smoke wafts through the screen. "There in a minute."

"O.K., no dance tonight."

"But Mama."

"Now!"

Away from the business district and old neighborhoods, University Avenue winds along the bluff, parallel to the river. It dips past old mansions, beer parlors, and pool halls, then rises toward the vast lawns and blocky buildings of the University. Across from the white-columned President's mansion, the Denny Chimes have bonged the six o'clock hour. Fraternity houses feed KAs, Phi Delts, and SAEs, bound for dorms and sorority houses for dates with Tri Delts, KDs, and sweethearts from high school. Nearby spread the working-class neighborhoods. Plumbers, painters, salesmen, and teachers wash off the week in the bathtubs and shower stalls of shot-gun houses crowding the willow oaks and asphalt grid between the University and the white high school on 15th Street, home of the Tuscaloosa Chieftains. The men folks will help with the dishes, feed the German Shepherd out back, settle in for an evening of penny-ante poker, Crazy Eights, or TV: Andy Griffith, *Bonanza*, Friday night fights at ten. The women will bathe the kids, catch a smoke on the porch, talk to neighbors.

"They're hiring out at Barnhardt Chemical; I'm thinking about applying."

"What?"

"Secretary."

"I'd think twice, honey. I worked out there when Hank was in Korea. The smell gets in your clothes. And the men try to, too."

"Well, I could use a bit of the latter around here."

Then it's off to bed. Some people have to work on Saturdays.

These are the white people. Their lives run as straight as the streets of Tuscaloosa, as regular as the stoplights. It's been this way for years, every Friday night, from the mansions downtown, to the hard-luck houses of working-class neighborhoods, to the lush campus of the University, to the molded concrete balustrades of the football stadium. Cards shuffle, black-and-white TVs flicker off walls, pool balls kiss and drop into pockets off green felt tables, college kids sway together in front of Negro bands, playing the old sing-along songs. They are happy; they get what they expect out of life. They do not hear Time's freight train, clacking down the track.

Ten blocks away, across the lumberyard and railroad tracks in Cherrytown, the colored section, the train runs every night. There, too, the streets are quiet except for a couple of liquor houses where men gather in yards to drink and talk in the light of coal oil lanterns. Card games pick up on porches and in rooms around back. There are no magnolias here—mostly elm, privet, and mulberry, scraping the edges of tin roofs, pulling the last ounce of green from swept dirt yards.

In the unpainted houses people finish supper, move onto porches to sit and talk. Women rock slowly, wave hand-held fans. Men bend forward from ladder-back chairs, rest their elbows on their knees, and smoke. The air smells of lard and custard pie. The talk is unhurried. Cigarette smoke hangs under the porches, drifts into the yards.

"Preacher Gryce finally going down to talk to Rosemont."

A swing creaks and stops. Hand-held fans pause, start again.

"'Bout what?"

"'Bout shutting down Rosemont's juke-joint, I reckon."

"Rosemont ain't gon shut that place down. He makes too much money."

"Police gon shut him down if he don't quit selling liquor to white boys."

"They ain't gon shut nothing long as he keeps up his payments to Deputy Starnes."

"Still, Reverand Gryce going to talk."

"Reverend Gryce's got the Spirit—no doubt 'bout that. But with Rosemont, talking's 'bout all he gon do."

———————

John Folsom Gryce shuts his screen door, steps onto the front porch, and runs a toothpick through his teeth to remove the last shred of his wife, Ludy's, baked chicken. Galluses hanging from his broad shoulders drape loosely about his waist. The night air is so heavy he could lift it in his arms. Sounds of the neighborhood drone through it—folks talking on porches, Aubrey Bryan's saxophone, next block down. Even the tree frogs sound like they're underwater. He pulls the toothpick from his teeth, examines it between the thick ends of his thumb and finger. A little blood on the splintery tip. He snaps it in two and flicks it over the rail.

Rosemont Greene's liquor house is the last place he wants to go on a Friday night. It'll be full of drinkers, carousers, and fornicators—the very sort of goings-on he spends most Sundays preaching against. Still, he promised Sister Waites he would go talk to Rosemont about her son, Raiford, who's into some civil rights business out in the county. She's scared about Raiford. She ought to be. Raiford's trouble. And Rosemont's mixed up in it somehow. And not only that but John Gryce promised God a long time ago he'd talk to Rosemont about that liquor house. And God's waited long enough.

Behind him the clink of silverware falls silent where Ludy has been gathering the supper plates from the table. He knows where she's standing without looking—right there in the door leading from the kitchen to the front room—with the plates in her hand, watching him through the screen.

"John."

"Yes."

"What time you coming back?"

"When I finish."

"That won't be long, you counting on help from Rosemont."

Ludy taps a fork against a plate to get the food off. "He killed that man, you know, went to the penitentiary for it. Say he 'bout cut his head off with a razor."

"That was over thirty years ago. Besides, I'm not the one who's gon do the talking. God is."

"Rosemont listens to God even less than he listens to you."

"He ain't heard what God's got to say."

Preacher Gryce finds the chain to his gold Elgin watch and flips open the lid: 6:20. He can take his time walking down there—time to think, open his heart to the word of God. He hooks his galluses in his thumbs and pulls them over his shoulders.

"Bye, Ludy."

"Speak the truth," she says.

———

Acee Waites stands in his usual spot at the Red Elephant Grill, frying burgers for white folks. His thin hands are swollen from the heat, fingertips numb to the first knuckle. Happens every night about this time when the heat and grease get to them. When he was small, coming out of church with his mother, Preacher Gryce knelt before him and took Acee's hands in his. Huge black hands, big enough to sit in. Acee'd never thought of skin shades before that, other than brown and white. But next to his, Preacher's hands were so dark they seemed to come from another age. Acee's skin looked depleted, leeched of the earth's richest minerals.

Preacher turned Acee's hands palm-up. "Artist's hands," he said and nodded up at Acee's mama. "Careful in their work."

He tilted Acee's chin up and looked him in the face. "Question-asking eyes," he said. "Best way to find God."

When Preacher had examined Raiford the same way a couple of

years before, all he'd said was, "You're a good boy, son. A strong boy. Take
care of your mama and family."

"Yessuh," said Raiford.

Raiford tried until their daddy left, and after that he tried even
harder. Then one day Acee woke up and Raiford was gone. He was in
the neighborhood, he was other places around town, he'd moved to
Birmingham and then to Atlanta. When he came back, he told their
mama he was old enough to live his own life. "No," she said. "You just
into devilish things."

And now this civil rights business he's running out in the county.
Jumped the rails altogether. Messing in stuff that's sooner or later going
to bring trouble down on everybody.

Acee scrapes the spatula over the surface of the grill, pushing a
puddle of grease before it. Behind him Annie and Lugenia's arms and
hands work like snakes, cutting onions and tomatoes, tearing lettuce,
slicing buns. They hum hymns together, one picking up where the other
leaves off, then picking up the words—"across that ri-iver; blessed Lord,
blessed Lord." Beyond the screen door next to the stove, dust builds
in the restaurant parking lot as carloads of teenagers come wheeling
in from the Friday-night streets. The city's slow hum builds toward
midnight.

His mama told him before he left for work that Preacher Gryce
was headed down to Rosemont Greene's liquor house to talk about
Raiford. Preacher Gryce watches over Sister Waites and her two sons.
The crackers have already thrown dead cats and skunks in Raiford's yard
and shot into his trailer. And Raiford's only been at it a couple of months.
Preacher Gryce don't want Raiford's business bringing trouble down on
Cherrytown like they had in Anniston, Birmingham, and Montgomery
with whites beating up the Freedom Riders. Preacher Gryce confides
these things in Acee. *You got to know the times. You got to know what
people can stand. You got to move when God tells you.*

Got to. Preacher has Acee in his beam, sees the makings of a
leader in him, model for the community—the "Lord-is-calling-you"

thing. And that's got ahold of Acee, too. That's weighing him down just like his brother is. Preacher, with his hopes and dreams, Raiford with his trouble-making, hang about Acee's shoulders like a dead man's arm.

Acee starts flipping the burgers, pressing them into the grease. Raiford's his own God. Moves when *he* wants to, goes by how much *he* can stand. Raiford knows the times, and far as he's concerned, the time is now. Like that convoy of mule wagons, patched-together cars and pick-ups he led up the old Montgomery Highway to the County courthouse to register colored voters last week, sheriff's deputies trailing behind, stopping their cars to talk, laugh, and smoke when the caravan halted to change a tire or a radiator boiled over on somebody's twenty-year-old Ford. Or the rallies at one of the red-dirt-stained, country churches to protest the sharecropper system. Or the hand-drawn placard Raiford planted on the courthouse lawn, showing a black man on his knees in chains and a fat, white man with a whip standing over him.

It gets a little worse every time. And it doesn't help that Raiford's companion in all of this is a white woman, come down from somewhere up North—a skinny, middle-aged lady with black hair, wiry as a Brillo pad. Some say they sleep together. Doesn't matter whether it's true. The talk alone will still get you killed.

Acee glances down at the opened buns Annie and Lugenia have laid out on the counter next to the grill for him to slip the burgers on. They lie there, spongy-white with their mouths open, plastered in mustard and mayonnaise, all but smiling up at him. It passes like a shadow through his brain that the cool, white buns are white folks; the burgers popping and curling black around the edges on the grill are colored—the ones feeling the heat, the last traces of red life burning before his eyes to a charred, dead gray.

It's the kind of thought Raiford would scream out loud. *When you gon get out the white man's kitchen and fight for yourself, Acee? Fight for your race? When you gon quit listening to Preacher Gryce and his Jesus talk and think for yourself?*

Acee slips yellow slices of Velveeta on the meat patties and taps the edge of the spatula on the grill to shake off the dripping cheese and grease. Out the screen door, around the light over the stoop, insects bat the naked bulb. Cars keep pulling into the lot. Kids get out, laughing and yelling—high-schoolers, college kids—all white. The warm wood of the spatula handle feels glued to Acee's sweaty hand. He taps it again, stares through the greasy mesh of the screen door.

Over in Cherrytown his girlfriend, Resa Robinson, sits on her porch, waiting—that oval of amber deep in her eyes; the ends of her hair brushing her neck, framing the harp-like bend of her jaw; hands resting in her softly shifting lap. Resa and Raiford used to go together, couple of years ago before Raiford took up his "cause" and took up with the white woman as well. Somewhere in Resa's eyes, a light still glows for Raiford. And maybe it's that, or maybe it's something else—the Preacher's hopes for Acee, the community's watchful expectations—but where Resa is concerned, something is in the way. It causes Acee to trip over himself, keeps him from getting as close as he wants. Close as he needs. It's like he's always reaching for her, through a screen door, over houses and rooftops, a hand with its fingers spread toward the blank face of the nighttime sky.

The burgers are burning. The plastic-looking cheese runs off the edges and spreads in soapy bubbles on the grill. It doesn't matter. The crowd pouring into the Red Elephant Grill eats so fast they don't taste it anyway.

———

Beyond the screen door where Acee works, carloads of white teenagers wheel into the restaurant parking lot, slide to a halt in orderless rows. Dust rises, tires spin, mufflers blare and die. Girls with boyfriends wait for their doors to be opened, step daintily in loafers and flats onto the gravelly dirt. Skirts swish. Bobbed hair and wide patent-leather belts catch the restaurant's fluorescent glare. The boys move in stiff-hinged angularity. They shift about, fumble at cigarettes, lean against car trunks and fenders, ankles crossed in black loafers and white socks.

In the far corner of the lot Richeboux Branscomb slouches against an old Mercury, long, muscular arms folded across his chest. His head tilts forward. A disobedient swatch of honey-colored hair all but hides his face. Mem Cohane stands facing him. Her hair is the same color as his, but clean and cut short; her face sharp and intelligent. She leans forward on her toes and stretches her neck toward him as she talks, then rocks back onto her heels, throws her arms into the air, kicks the dirt between them.

A black '55 Ford with chrome-lined fender skirts and mud-flaps rumbles to a stop next to them. The driver grins out the window, revs the engine, and gives them a blast of his new glass-pack mufflers. Mem backs up a step to lean against the car next to Richeboux and puts her hands over her ears. The driver cuts the switch. The engine chugs and dies. A thin boy with pale skin and dirty-blond hair, combed into a ducktail, gets out of the passenger side. His face is lit in a permanent grin. A second boy gets out of the back. He, too, is grinning—but it's more of a smirk. His wiry red hair is pasted into a flattop with petroleum jelly. His face is red with bloodshot eyes. A madras shirt drapes his belly. The driver is the last to exit. He shakes his tousled hair as if to get dirt out of it, rests his palm on the car roof, and pops his fingers against the metal in time with a song in his head. He smiles over at the boy and girl.

"Hey, Richeboux. You wanna come with us after the dance? Jamie and Ellis went down to Uncle Rosemont's after school and got some beer."

The girl whirls and brushes past the loungers around the Ford.

"Hey, Mem," says the thin one with ducktail hair. He uses his fingers as a comb to sweep a swag of hair from his forehead. "No big deal. You can come, too." He turns to the others and grins—even wider.

She shoots a glance over her shoulder. "Go jerk off. That's about all any of you are good for." They watch her ass switch up the restaurant steps and through the swinging glass doors.

"Richeboux, how come you still messing with her?" says the fat one. "Jew girls are too high and mighty."

Richeboux looks up. "Shut up, Ellis."

"Anyway," says the tousle-haired driver, still keeping time on the roof, "You coming with us or not? We're planning to take a little cruise through Cherrytown."

———————

At the police station, two blocks from the courthouse downtown, Chief Deputy D. Sugarman Starnes rests his thin legs on his desk, reads the evening paper, eyes squinting through smoke from a cigarette smoldering in his ashtray. The dispatch radio is on the shelf behind him, telephone within reach to his front. The whip handle he carries wherever he goes lies next to it across a worn, leather-bound Bible. His hand automatically rubs his bad leg. It starts hurting this time every day. He's got two extra cars on the streets tonight. It's Friday, nearly a full moon, and you don't want to get caught short. Besides, there's a graduation dance at the high school. Bound to be an extra wreck or two.

It's right there on page three of the paper: that colored boy again—Raiford Waites—out in the county, raising hell with the colored preachers and sharecroppers, telling 'em to "rise up, throw off the white man's burden." Got 'em talking about a strike against the stores downtown, threatening to drop their sacks and walk out of the cotton rows. Thinks he's Moses, leading the Israelites out of Egypt. Hell, in the Navy they'd have had his ass in the brig long time ago. They'd have thrown him to the sharks.

Starnes quits rubbing his leg. The ache starts again.

*Son of a bitch!*

He lets the paper drop across his knees. From atop the row of filing cabinets across the room, the mangy, stuffed wildcat he shot in Sipsey Swamp five years ago stares at him with its glass eyes and fangy grin. Starnes glances down at the paper. The name, "Raiford Waites," pulses up at him. Might be good idea to check in on Mr. Waites and that Yankee white woman he's been hanging around with. Starnes's best deputy, Darryl Culp, is in one of the extra cars. Starnes taught Darryl everything he knows, and Darryl will know how to handle this: pay a visit to the old trailer Waites lives in, soft knock on the door, checking on complaints from the neighbors—the usual excuses. Maybe catch him and that Yankee white woman going at it. Could arrest him for that alone.

He slides his feet to the floor, picks up his whip handle, and taps the butt gently on the desk. Then he turns and flips on the switch to the dispatch unit. It squawks and screeches, settles into static.

"Hey, Darryl—you there? I got a little errand for you."

# Rosemont (Razor Blade) Greene

"God is restless tonight." First thing John Gryce says when he walks in
here. Like he just been had a talk with Him. Now, what am I supposed
to do with that? Things always restless 'round here on Friday night.
That's how I make a living. And God ain't been nowhere around this
liquor house on no night, far as I can see. And that's fine with me.

　　And Preacher John Gryce ain't been here either, whole time he's
been in Cherrytown. Lord this, Devil that, talking me down in that
church of his that's near 'bout gobbled up every so-called Christian in
the neighborhood. But this evening down the road he come, walking
up out of the night like a prophet amongst the heathens. With every
step, silence come with him. Right on up the porch, past my customers,
laughing, drinking, and making out on each other—the married, the
unmarried, the 'bout to be—and smack on through the screen door.
Folks grinding against each other on the dance floor let go and back all
the way to the wall. Time he's in the door good, ain't nothing moving or
making a sound but the juke box, blinking lights and blasting out that
new song by Etta James—*Something's Got a Hold on Me*. Something got
a hold on Preacher, too. He takes off his hat and stares at the box a good

minute, like the fire blazing through his gold-rim glasses can strike it dumb.

I ain't moved from my seat at the far end of the bar. I set here most nights I'm open 'cause it gives me a good view of the place and keeps me out the way 'less trouble starts. Got a thirty-six-inch ball bat behind the counter and a .38 in my pocket to take care of that.

Soon as Preacher lays eyes on me, he walks right on back to where I'm setting, tips his hat toward a couple of women hanging 'round me this particular night, then delivers himself of his pronouncement 'bout the restlessness of God. He says it loud to beat out the music from the box, but Etta's song ends about then, and he sounds like the voice of God Himself.

I touch the rim of my new Panama, turn toward the bar mirror and try not to grin. Miss Nancy and Miss Pearl sidle their way on up the bar, start talking to Marcus who's giving me a asking look 'bout whether he should keep pouring drinks or start hiding the bottles.

"I doubt God spends much time here," I say.

Gryce ain't taken his eyes off me. "God goes wherever man goes. Even if the devil's there."

I look him straight in the eye. "I ain't seen *him* round here, either."

"Then you ain't looking."

I been knowing this talk was coming, and I done already got tired of it. I cross my leg on the stool, pick a fingernail at that notch on the bar where one of Bailey Bridewell's wife's bullets hit two years ago when she come in here and tried to blow his head off.

"You got your place. I got mine. I ain't messing with you. Ain't no call you come marching in here, messing with me. You done already scared my customers out of half a night's fun and me out of half a night's makings."

He takes his hat off, drops it to his side, commences to look about like he's memorizing the place and fixing to take down the names of everybody there.

"What you want?" I say.

"To have a little talk."

"I ain't even studying 'bout shutting this place down. If that snake-headed Deputy Starnes cain't make me do it, I'm right sure you cain't."

He shifts his hat to both hands and starts to turn it in his fingers like he's counting inches 'round the brim. His fingers big as some men's arms. "That's not why I'm here, Rosemont. It's more important than that." He looks down at that turning hat, purses his lips. "In private," he says.

First time he ever call me by name. I 'bout fell off the stool.

I motion over to Marcus, wiping glasses like mad behind the bar. "Watch 'til I get back and turn that juke down a beat." I nod toward the hallway that leads to the room in back I do my business in.

Gryce ain't more than a step behind me. I unlock the door, pull the cord on the overhead bulb, which gives a pop and goes black. I put a match to the coal oil lamp sets on my work table and pull up one of the straight-back chairs from against the wall. He's still standing there, hat in his hands.

He pretty much fills up any room he walks into, 'specially one as tight as my office room. I'm nearly six foot, and he's a good half foot taller. When he looks down at you through them glasses, he looks even taller. Gray-haired, big-boned man, back and shoulders still strapped with muscle where he used to work the boiler room over at the University coal plant. Wrists too big for his shirt sleeves. Forehead hard as the rocks I used to break in prison. People say I got a deep voice, but his comes rolling up off the floor. Makes the walls shake.

I take a seat on an old army cot I keep in there for Bailey when he gets too drunk to walk home, set my hat down, and pull out a smoke. I offer him one, kind of grinning. By then he setting in the chair like he's got a rod down his back, hands on his knees, eyes blazing even in the weak light. I lean forward on my elbows, spit a flake of tobacco to the floor, and look up at him.

"Well, we private."

"What's Raiford Waites planning next?"

"I don't keep up with Raiford."

He shakes his head. "Not what I hear." He inclines himself 'bout a inch in my direction, waving off the cigarette smoke. "Look here, Rosemont. Things have started happening around here—serious things. You know it, and I know it. And I know you are connected to 'em." He leans back in the chair and looks at me like he's done hit me with something I wasn't ready for and he's waiting to see if I'm gon flinch.

He leans forward again, even closer now. "God guides me, Rosemont Greene, and I know when I'm looking at a man who stands in the center of things."

I reach under the cot, pull out the ashcan, flick my ashes, then blow another long breath of smoke and look right back at him.

"I ain't in the center of nothing."

"You make liquor, buy liquor, and sell liquor. You got as many people down here juking on Saturday night as I preach to on Sunday. You pay off the police so you can run this place and sell beer to white boys. And God knows why you do it, 'cause far as I know, there's no profit in it, but you give money to Raiford Waites so he can carry on all that civil rights stuff out in the county."

"All I know 'bout civil rights is I ain't never had none."

He watches me a minute and gives me that slow, shaking head. "You know what I'm talking about, better than I do. But in case you're a little behind, let me give you an example. I went to see Raiford myself night before last because his mama, Sister Waites, asked me to. She's sick to death over it. He's about taken over a little church out near Layton Crossroads Store. Poor farmers in there, just like you and I used to be, sweaty old hats in their hands, overalls still dusty from work. A couple of white students from the University or somewhere, sneaking about, passing out papers to the congregation. Got one right here."

He reaches in his back pocket and pulls it out. Somebody had done wadded it up once, but I could still read it. "SLAVERY NO

MORE! BOWING TO THE WHITE MAN, NO MORE! Demand Your Rights! Demand Your Birthrights! Demand Freedom!"

"Sounds like Raiford," I say.

"And he was saying the same thing from the pulpit. Pastor just standing there like Raiford was the Prophet Isaiah, preaching to the Israelites. Yelling it. 'You 'fraid of the white man? Let me tell you 'bout the cracker white man: he's 'fraid of you. Get up out from between his rows of corn and cotton; stand and finish the fight that's started. Don't say 'tomorrow.' Don't say, 'Well I got my crop to plant and get in.' It ain't your crop you planting. And it ain't your life you getting in."

His head's shaking again, but his eyeballs stay on me. "That white woman that thinks she's a princess, standing next to him, nodding at every word. Raiford's got the touch; no doubt about that. Had that audience 'uh-huhing' and 'yes-siring.' I tried to talk to him after it was over. He just turned and walked away."

Gryce sets back in his chair and studies me a while. "Now tell me, Mr. Rosemont Greene: how long you think it's gon take before people start getting killed over talk like that, houses and churches start getting burned? I saw a car and two pick-ups with white men in them drive past that church while I was there. They weren't police, either."

I get up and go over to the window that looks out on the back parking lot. Big, round moon, bright enough to make you blink, rising over the woods at the lower end of my weed patch. Almost grinning at me. Feel like I'm caught in the middle—big round-faced preacher on one side, moon on the other. Ain't a place I like to be.

"How's whatever Raiford up to interfering with you?"

"Don't you know what I do?" he says.

"Yeah, you the man claims he talks to God, trying to run the neighborhood."

He jumps up out the chair and slaps that hat against his trouser legs. I flinch. I don't like a man moving that fast behind me.

I turn and we stand there a minute, nose-to-nose—well, more like my nose to his Adam's apple—then he sets back in the chair, starts turning that hat again. "Sit down," he says.

I ain't sure why, but I do.

"This ain't between you and me. God's calling you, Rosemont Greene. You best listen."

"Calling me to what?"

His face sags 'til I can see the bones in it.

"I held Sister Waites, crying in my arms when Acee was sick and her baby girl died. I don't want to do that again. I don't want Deputy Starnes and his men rolling into the streets of Cherrytown in the middle of the night, knocking down doors and knocking heads looking for Raiford or anybody they think works with him. I don't want the Klan anywhere near here. I don't want to be holding a bunch of funerals I don't have to hold."

"What's all that got to do with me?"

"You're the only person in Cherrytown that has any control over Raiford."

"Hell I do. Don't nobody control Raiford but Raiford."

"You pay his way. He's getting support from somewhere."

"Folks up north pay his way. That skinny Jew-looking lady you seen at the church, hangs 'round his trailer on the river, pays his way."

He heaves a sigh like he's just come off a full shift and 'bout to start another one. His voice drops about ten notches, takes on that low-toned, parlor-room sound. "Rosemont, I'm asking you, man to man: work with me on this. Talk to Raiford. Tell him what I just said. He's lost his righteousness if he ever had any. But he's Acee's brother. He's got a heart, just like you do."

I'll admit—Gryce is 'bout the only person I know can make me dodge a look.

"You know what's happening in Atlanta, Birmingham, Mississippi. We've been lucky. But if Raiford keeps this up, people are going to get hurt right here in Cherrytown. People he should care about. God only knows how it will end."

"Maybe end in folks finally getting some rights," I say. "That's my kind of righteousness."

He stands up again and takes a step to the window. The moon done 'bout cleared the pines except for a jagged edge along the bottom. Gryce raises up that big hand and stretches his fingers out like he's taking a measure of it.

"I know about rights," he says. "And God does, too. They're coming. I have His word on it."

"Now that's where we disagree," I say. "They ain't coming 'less we reach out and take 'em."

"Like trying to pull down that moon," he says.

He puts his hat on and gives me that eye-of-God look.

"Think about what I said." He pauses a second in the doorway and says in the lowest voice he used all night. "Think about what God says. There's a time, and there's a Time."

I listen to his feet going on up the hall. Something jerks me out the chair to the doorway. "Yeah, there always gon be a time—someday. You call yourself the leader. How come you ain't leading?" I 'bout half-whisper the last part. He keeps right on walking. Time I get to the bar and dance room, he's through the front door, halfway down the porch steps. Everybody still backed up against the wall, watching him go.

Marcus slips out from behind the bar, plug the juke box back in.

# Richeboux Branscomb

Richeboux rests his arm in the open rear window of Andre's '55 Ford, takes nervous puffs on his Marlboro, blows smoke into the Alabama night. The busted springs of the car seat grind into his butt about where his coccyx splits his cheeks. Andre's glass-pack mufflers rumble beneath him.

The three heads in the front seat flicker in and out of silhouette in the oncoming headlights. He's seen them in the same order from his back-seat corner so often that it's like watching an old-timey movie. Andre's the driver—"Fireball," they call him, after Fireball Roberts the race car driver—thick, scissor-chopped hair, the same little boy's head that perched above the seat-back in front of Richeboux in grade school. "My nice boys," the teacher used to say. She rubbed their heads, messed up their hair, as she walked down the aisle between the desks, tapping her leg with the ruler.

Jamie Higginbotham ("Einstein"), National Merit Scholar, rides the hump in the middle—greasy ducktails, big ears, head and neck like a rooster hung upside down. The large blue vein that courses down the middle of his forehead pulses with excitement when he talks. It carries the cunning for the whole group—and the crazy ideas, too.

Ellis Burt rides shotgun. Fat cheeks hang from the barber-trim of his waxed red flattop, and jiggle every time his head whacks the door frame when Andre makes a turn. Oozing beer sweat through the faded madras stuck to his old woman's shoulders. Richeboux's been with Ellis since first grade, too, long before Ellis's voice cracked with cigarette coughs and meanness. Ellis was the one who usually felt the whack of the teacher's ruler after she'd rubbed Andre's and Richeboux's heads as she walked down the aisle. You could hear him sniffling for the next half-hour.

Jamie fiddles with the knob on the radio, changing stations. Squeak, squawk. He likes the twangy stuff by skinny white guys like himself—Don and Phil, Gene Vincent. Thin lips work over his slick teeth like a slide rule. He hits a blues station with Bo Diddley and another with Bobby Blue Bland.

"Hey, man, give us some white music! All they got on these stations now is this banshee stuff."

"Not banshee, Einstein—soul," says Andre. He drops his hands from the steering wheel and imitates playing a guitar. "Bo Diddley was a gunslinger... dilly-dilly-dilly-dilly, dal-ly!"

"Watch it, Fireball. Keep singing that crap and you'll start to change color."

Richeboux flexes the muscles of his forearm, feels them rise and fall against the hard edge of the windowsill. His fingers want to grip a baseball like he did last year when he was the best pitcher on the Tuscaloosa High team. "Chief Tuscaloosa," they called him. If he hadn't quit, he'd be down in Montgomery right now, pitching the Chieftains through the state playoffs. And these assholes would be on their own to screw up the evening however they want to. He should have said "No," when they tried to talk him into all this: "You gon be a pussy, or you coming with us?"

There's a fifth member of the group, sitting across the cave-like back seat from Richeboux: Ronnie Raitano. "The Worm," they call him.

Mouth open in its half-grin, lips stretched across the wires bracing his teeth. His dad's a big-shot scientist at the chemical plant upriver. The family moved south from New York City last summer. Ronnie's got a twin sister who's a real knockout, looks like Annette Funicello from the old *Mickey Mouse Club* on TV. Every guy in school wants to get in her pants. "Hell," said Andre. "Worth giving him a shot at hanging out with us. You know what they say about northern girls."

So Ronnie's been worming his way into the group ever since. Caught up to them as they were leaving the high school dance. "Hey, you guys headed out? Hey lemme go; I got beer money." Ronnie's a natural. It's the Yankee in him, Ellis says. They train 'em to worm up there.

Ronnie leans across the seat, taps Richeboux on the arm, whispers. "Hey, Richeboux, where're we going?"

Richeboux takes another drag, watches the old working-class houses slip by with their single-bulb porches and pinched-in yards— like his own house, not more than four blocks away. Andre's tires rumble across the railroad tracks. A right turn at the high school will put them on the road to Cherrytown.

"Beats the shit out of me."

Ronnie leans forward, both hands gripping the back of the front seat. "Come on guys, where we headed?"

Andre steers with one hand hanging over the wheel. Gives his shoulders a shrug.

Jamie is still fiddling with the radio. "To do some shit."

Andre makes the turn at the high school. The gym lights are out. The dance is over. Teacher-chaperone cars pulling out of the lot.

Three blocks farther on, they pass the old clapboard store that marks the boundary between white Tuscaloosa and Cherrytown. Bars on the dirt-streaked windows. Old man Griggs owns it. Rolled-up shirt sleeves. Thick fists on the countertop. Skin on the knuckles like a hide stretched to dry. The colored folks buy their groceries there. During ten-minute breaks at the high school, Richeboux and his friends pile into cars and haul themselves down to Grigg's Grocery for Honeybuns and Cokes. Signs for Old Golds, Chesterfields, and chewing tobacco hang over the porch. A new bright-blue Pepsi sign lights the dark window.

"Cherrytown," says Ronnie. "Are you guys serious? Man, I never been at night. I hear it's hot stuff!"

The last of the streetlights blinks across Ronnie's face. Something in the eyes—the dim light of fear—betrays the forced wide-mouth grin. Richeboux's tendons tighten. Punch Ronnie right in his braces; bang Ellis's beer-soaked head against the door post til it cracks; strangle Einstein's chicken neck. He needs that baseball in his hand. He crooks his fingers into the shape they'd be in if he were about to throw a fast ball, turning it, feeling his nails dig into the seams.

The road grows dark without the streetlights. The image of the Pepsi sign shrinks to a blue point in his brain.

He takes a sip of warm malt liquor, returns the can to its niche between his thighs on the brown-and-cream woven-plastic seat. The gassy smell of beer rises from between his legs and the empty cans at his feet.

"Hey Andre!" Ronnie's all but yelling now. "Take it up to ninety and do a bootleg when we hit that turn to Cherrytown. Scare the hell out of 'em. They'll think we're the po-leece."

Richeboux works himself deeper into the corner between the back of the seat and the door.

"Whyn't you cut it down," he yells to Jamie.

Jamie turns to look at him, blue vein pumping away. "What's the matter, Chief—you nervous?"

"No. I'm tired of you twisting that knob like it's your dick."

Richeboux's been to Cherrytown a bunch of times in the daytime to buy beer at Uncle Rose's. But, like Ronnie, he's never been at night. He's heard things: knifings, shootings, fights over women. He's seen boys and young men from there, walking the roads at night, headed uptown to the Bama Theater and once there, climbing the stairs to the balcony with dark, quick-legged girls in swaying skirts. The muscles in the girl's calves flex with each step. Soften and flex. And the boys' arms seem even stronger than his. He hears they fight with ice picks and razors. He's seen the two stubby fingers of Rosemont Greene himself, rumored to have been cut off in a knife fight over a woman. And when colored people are together having fun, like the boys and girls climbing the stairs at the Bama Theater, they don't seem to give a shit about the white/colored stuff. It's like the old rules have vanished. He flips an ash out the window. Around him the darkness has picked up a steady, silent beat.

They pass the colored high school, which sits on the last paved road leading into Cherrytown. Across from it, the old ice-house and ramshackle row houses slip by in the darkness. At the T intersection, Andre cuts right onto the gravel road that will take them to the turn onto Cherry Street, smack through the heart of the colored section. Rocks click against the oil pan and hubcaps. Andre reaches across Jamie and turns off the radio. There are parties going on in a couple of the houses, men standing under a kerosene lantern hung in a tree in front of one of them, drinking beer. People on the porches. Lonely yellow bulbs from the houses that have electricity and oil lamps from the houses that don't glimmer through branches of mulberry and privet. Smells of cooking smoke, honeysuckle, and warm, packed earth ride the night air like burnt molasses. And there's that other smell, too, of powdered flesh, bare feet, and sweaty armpits—folks who live close to the earth. They walk on it, dig it, plant it, and shit in it. Colored shit smells different, his grandfather once said. Stinks more. He doesn't believe that, but there is that odor of wild, dank earth. It makes him want to open the car door, drop to all fours on the ground, and put his tongue to it.

A group of men drinking beer on a corner turn their heads to watch.

Andre eases around the turn onto Cherry Street.

Ellis raises his head from its slump against the door, waggles himself awake. "Hey, we're there—fucking Congo central." He opens his rhino-like mouth, lets out a long burp, and grabs the dashboard. "This is the road the slaves lived on on old man Cherry's plantation. Used to be whipping post in the middle of it."

Ronnie stirs, bends forward to rest his forearm on the back of the front seat. A whistle comes through his braces. "Uh, yeah. But before that it was an Indian trading path, remember? Alabama history class. Choctaws, Creeks and stuff."

"Red, brown, black," says Ellis. "All the same to me." He bumps Jamie's shoulder. "How many eggs we got?"

"Five. Four whites and a brown. Who wants one?"

"Integrated eggs," says Ronnie. "What you bet the brown one's got the biggest pecker."

Ellis turns in his seat. "Naw, I got the biggest dick in Alabama."

"You *are* the biggest dick in Alabama," says Andre. He downshifts past another group of black men gathered under a lantern hung from a tree limb in front of what looks like a deserted house. They watch the car pass and turn toward the house, mumbling to each other.

Ellis wipes his runny nose with the back of his wrist. "Gimme one. I'm gonna nail one of these bastards."

"No!" says Andre. "You threw half the carton already and haven't hit shit. Even missed the stop sign."

"O.K., how's 'bout Ronnie?" Ellis keeps his eyes straight ahead as if he's just dropped a rattlesnake into the back seat. "Whatchu say, Worm-man. You gon pussy out again?"

Richeboux stares harder out the window, as if the effort will pull him into the soft, swirly night. Why do he and Ronnie always wind up lumped together—the ones who don't throw the eggs, the ones who didn't fuck the fat, ugly, married woman Ellis brought to the drive-in last Halloween? Ronnie sits quietly, one leg cocked over the other. His Marlboro stands straight up from the tips of his fingers as if he's afraid he'll spill the ashes.

Jamie stretches his arm across the back of his seat and holds the open carton toward Ronnie. His grin outshines the puny light from the dashboard.

"Come on, Worm-man, take an egg! They're kosher."

"I don't do kosher, man. I'm an Italian Stallion—pizza, pasta, and pussy." Ronnie trying to make a joke is like a cat trying to shit a football. He stares at Jamie with his wiry grin, takes a puff on the Marlboro, coughs a ball of smoke.

"Never ask a big-city boy to do anything that takes balls," says Ellis. "Waste of fucking time."

Richeboux's girlfriend, Mem Cohane, was born in New York, too. Half Jewish, his mother says, as if that should put an end to it. First in their class, "most likely to succeed"—all that stuff. That picture of her in this year's annual—thin tennis-player arms pressing a load of books to her chest, that stretched-forward look as if on tiptoes, gazing toward her future. He thinks of the thighs that match those arms—sort of like the calves of the black girls at the Bama Theater—muscular, tan, leading to the damp place between her thighs that beckons him like opened fruit. He shuts the image down—can almost feel Ellis leering at it.

Ronnie keeps coughing. Richeboux takes the cigarette from Ronnie's fingers and flips it through the window. Outside, the street has grown quieter. The smells are more mixed and muted. Shadowy people rock in swings on a couple of the porches. A chained dog barks. The silhouettes in the front seat blend into the darkness. The Ford's engine gurgles along, floating them through the swampy night.

Jamie is back at Ronnie again. "Come on, Italian Stallion, take one."

Ronnie reaches for the egg, touches the brown one then sets it back to get one of the whites.

Andre slams on the brakes to dodge a cat, or was it a rat, running across the road. The rear wheels lock. The treadless tires slide in the gravel. The four passengers grab seats and door handles to hang on.

"Aw shit, Andre!" Jamie's shaking raw egg from his hand. "You broke 'em. You got egg all over everything."

"Yeah, me, too." Ronnie rubs his hand on his jeans. "It feels like jism."

"I ain't gon squash some cat in the middle of Cherrytown," says Andre. He glances back at Ronnie. "What the hell's jism?"

"It's cum, Fireball," says Ellis. "That's Yankee talk for cum. Hey, Einstein, don't wipe it on me."

Jamie closes the carton and pulls it back to his lap in the front.

Ellis drums his thumbs and fingers on the dashboard, bopping, grooving, keeping time to whatever is in his squared-off, razor-trimmed head. "Any left?"

"The brown one," says Jamie. "The Nee-gro egg."

Ellis punches Andre's shoulder. "Thanks a lot, Fireball." He's patting his thighs now, rat-a-tat-tat. "Whaddya see, Andre?"

Andre glances over his shoulder at Richeboux. "Hey, how 'bout the strikeout king? Come on, Chief. You ain't thrown an egg all night."

Ellis hangs his arm over the back of the seat and looks at Richeboux. The short sleeve of the madras shirt rides up his fat, freckled arm. "Yeah Chief. You the baseball man—how come you ain't thrown yet?"

Ronnie scoots toward the middle of the seat, drapes an arm around Richeboux's shoulders. "Best pitching arm in the state."

"Yeah," says Andre, glancing in the rearview mirror. "'Til he quit."

Ellis's tongue rolls in his mouth like a catfish. "'Til Coach Talbert kicked him off the team."

Richeboux pushes Ronnie's arm away. "I quit."

Ellis turns back to the front, reaches across Jamie and thumps Andre on the shoulder. "Come on Fireball, find us a good one to throw at. We ain't had a good target all night. Find us one of those high-stepping bastards."

Andre flicks Ellis's hand away.

"Yeah," says Ronnie. "When you see them in their own neighborhoods, they act different. You ever notice that? It was like that in New York. Like they own the place."

Andre drops the speed of the Ford. "Hey, we got one. Couple of blocks ahead. Big sucker. Got his back to us."

Ellis takes the carton from Jamie, reaches back over the seat, and shoves it under Richeboux's chin. Richeboux stares down at the empty slots of the carton, smells the cardboard and raw egg. *Poke Ellis's nose right now, hear it crack, and splatter blood all over Andre's car.*

"Come on Chief Tuscaloosa. Let's see if you still got it."

# John Folsom Gryce

Preacher Gryce wipes his face with his bandana. Gnats buzz around his head—he's been swatting them ever since he left Rosemont's. And that half-smile on Rosemont's lips as they talked a few minutes ago—that's been buzzing around his head, too. Rosemont is more than smart: Rosemont is a dedicated man. Before tonight, all he's heard about Rosemont was liquor, gambling, jail, and the police. Paying off this person; cheating that. Pistol and razor man. But something else was there tonight, a quietness that seemed quick and ready to move.

And the business with Raiford. Rosemont is right about that. *Don't nobody control Raiford but Raiford.* That look in Raiford's eyes down at the country church two nights ago when Preacher tried to talk to him. Preacher's seen that look before—out by the river when he baptized Raiford and his younger brother, Acee, five years ago. Acee was fourteen, Raiford seventeen. "You waited too late on both these boys," he told their mother. "'Specially Raiford." But the baptism took with Acee, took to the point that at the moment he raised that boy from the water with his arm under Acee's back, he had a new disciple, and pretty much a substitute son too. It's been a blessing these last five years, watching

Acee walk the line toward Jesus. The community's got its hopes in Acee. But something about Acee has started to drag on Preacher Gryce's mind. There's that slight tremor he feels under his palm when he rests it on Acee's shoulder, as if a muscle is twitching to pull free.

The baptism didn't take with Raiford. Anger over his daddy leaving had already made him hard as a cooter shell. The water of life poured right off. Preacher can still see the shiny drops spray from Raiford's hair as he shook himself free and started his march toward the bank. His own voice hurled from his lungs like a clap of thunder: "Raiford Waites! God ain't finished with you yet!"

Raiford stopped dead in the water. Everybody around him—the preacher and those watching from the bank—held their breath. Raiford turned, jaws clinched, eyes blazing. It was a look the preacher had never gotten from a black man. The river's current pulled at Preacher Gryce's vestments, unsteadied him. He righted himself in time to watch Raiford stalk to the bank and march away through the parting crowd, his mother wailing behind him.

Preacher Gryce had thought: *Maybe He ain't finished with me, either.* Because it wasn't God that failed Raiford Waites; it was John Gryce.

And it felt that way tonight with Rosemont Greene.

He waves the bandana at the gnats and takes a deep breath. He can taste the dust. It never settles in these thick, muggy nights. For the first time this evening he hears the night sounds around him—a rustle of leaves in the treetops along the road, the whir of crickets and tree frogs, the lonely strains of Aubrey Bryan's alto sax from his back porch. Music John Gryce does not approve of, which stirs him anyway. That's what comes from visiting Rosemont's.

That was the problem wasn't it: he didn't have the spirit of God in him when he walked into Rosemont's. He just thought he did. Vainglory is the worst kind of sin—especially in a preacher. *Man claim he talks to God, trying to run the neighborhood.* It was a rebuke, powerful as any given by the Prophet Jeremiah. That's who Rosemont reminded him of tonight, because Jeremiah had that quality of getting down inside you, taking your own voice, using it as a judgment against you—"thy own backsliding will rebuke thee." Rosemont rose up off that cot when John Gryce left, stepped right out in the hall behind him. *You the leader. How come you ain't leading?*

He bends forward with his hands on his knees. The shape of his shadow blots the light of the moon. He plants his feet more firmly in the roadside clay, and begins that reflexive bend in his knees to kneel and pray. But he stops halfway down and rights himself. It's not right—here in the open in front of his neighbors' houses. He passed some porch-sitters a few houses back, gave them a nod and "Good evening." And beyond that, he does not know what he would say; for the first time in years, he's does not know what to ask God.

Ahead of him, down the road, his porch light shimmers through the leaves of a large maple tree. That's where he needs to be—home with Ludy, tell her all that's happened, watch the wisdom light her face, listen to her words, and then talk to God quietly in his own way. Might as well face it: things have changed. That twist in time he's been dreading is here.

He straightens and arches his back. The saxophone has stopped. So have the tree frogs. No, they're still there. But another sound is drowning them out. Not thunder nor the dying echoes from dynamiting over at the quarry north of town—not on Friday night. It's a car engine, a low rumbling he's not heard before—not around here—and he knows every car in the neighborhood.

He wipes the bandana across the folds of skin on the back of his neck, stuffs it back in his pocket, and starts walking. Probably some out-of-town folks, headed down to Rosemont's.

The rumble grows louder. Whoever it is is not headed to Rosemont's. They've passed that turn. They're on the road behind him. Mufflers. That noisy kind that sounds like the pistons are stumbling over each other. Maybe somebody in the neighborhood got Bailey Bridewell to put on a pair. Not smart for a colored man. The police notice things like that. Anyway, he'll find out who it is, soon as they pass. He's got to get home. Ludy will be wanting to go to bed, and he's got to tell her what's on his mind. 'Cause this thing with Rosemont tonight was a big thing. He can feel it growing in him with every step he takes. She'll want to hear all about it. But mainly she'll want to know what the inside of Rosemont's place looks like on a Friday night.

# Richeboux Branscomb

Jamie and Ellis strain forward, elbows resting on the dashboard.

"Damn, he *is* a big one," says Ellis. "He's on Andre's side, though. Richeboux's gotta switch seats with Ronnie to get him."

Andre starts gearing down. Richeboux drinks off the rest of his beer, releases a soft, warm burp, drops the can to the floor. He turns and faces backward, places his hands on top of the back seat and makes a bridge with his body so Ronnie can slide under to the other side. The beer sloshes in Richeboux's gut. He lowers himself into the seat behind Andre and rolls the window all the way down. His eyes feel glassy. Maybe the night air will blow the beer buzz from his brain. Ellis's eyes are still on him—like his daddy's used to be when he was a toddler, trying to take a pee.

Ronnie takes the carton from Ellis, holds it tightly to his chest.

The Ford growls along, not more than fifteen miles an hour. A thumping comes to Richeboux's chest. The sounds and smells of the night disappear.

The man is fifty feet ahead, walking in the same direction they are headed. Dark suspenders criss-cross the white shirt on his oak-like back. Long forearms swing from the rolled shirt sleeves. He is bent slightly forward as if lost in thought. Yet, there's an ease about him that Richeboux gets in his own body when he's walking loose and free. He can almost feel the man's movement in himself—an elasticity between them.

He wrestles his upper body out the window, plants his butt on the sill, and clamps his left hand around the door post. His other hand reaches back for the egg, his palm itching to feel the hard roundness of a leather-stitched baseball. But it's not a baseball. It's got that smooth, oblong shape to it, that feeling of suspended interior weight, like something alive. Like the yellow yolks that jiggle every morning when his mama slips the sunny-side-ups from the spatula onto his plate, their tender pupils waiting for the fork.

He grinds his butt deeper into the sill for balance and curls the hand with the egg up and behind him across the roof while Ronnie grabs Richeboux's legs and braces his own feet against the door. The throw will be a wicked twist across Richeboux's body. He shifts to lessen the strain.

"Careful, Big Chief," says Ronnie. "You're pulling away."

He could have avoided this whole thing, stayed at the high school dance with Mem, told Ellis and the rest of them, "Not tonight—got other plans." A little nod toward her in the gaggle of girls on the edge of the dance floor, and she'd take it from there—a step back from the group, that quick cock of her hip as she gave him that "let's-do-it-now" look that even Jamie, "Mr. Einstein," admires. It would have been all he needed to say. But their eyes were on him, waiting. Just like Ellis's are now: are you a pussy-whipped chickenshit, or are you coming with us?

Richeboux cocks his throwing arm, rests his elbow on the roof. Ronnie wraps his arms tighter around Richeboux's legs. Richeboux's left wrist trembles, torqued to the door post. His other hand is as steady as it was in those games he won on the dusty red-clay baseball diamonds across the state.

The engine turns slowly, each cylinder recording its piston's rise and fall. The man's pace slows as well. His head dips slightly. His hand rises to his hat brim. He will turn in the next second, an acknowledgment, a quiet "Good evening." It crosses Richeboux's mind that this man is a leader of some kind—preacher, funeral home director—those are the big shots in the colored world, at least so he's heard. Something in the proud, straight back; the slow, certain walk.

The wrist that holds the egg flinches and stops. Richeboux readjusts his fingertips—the disappointing lightness of the thing, its thin delicate shell. His second flinch does not stop—a snake striking from the car roof in a great swoop across his body. The egg leaves his fingers in wobbly flight. Not the whizzing trajectory of his fast ball, no perfect oval, no white blur narrowing to a perfect point. But it hits— pow!—just behind the ear, a perfect throw, a sound so loud that for a second Richeboux wonders if he's cracked the man's skull. Pieces of shell explode. The slimy drip begins. Richeboux pulls his arm backward for balance. The roof gutter of the car digs his elbow, giving him a numb, funny-bone feeling. He clamps harder on the door post to keep from falling, flings his throwing arm back across the roof, scratching for a hold.

The tall man grabs the spot behind his head. His hat and glasses fall as he drops to his knees, then to all fours. He begins to feel around for them in the dirt and grass. Richeboux has the crazy idea that if he could just leap from the car, hand them to him, and jump back in, they could get out of there before the man turns his head.

Andre jams the gas pedal to the floor. The Ford lurches and stops, lurches and stops.

"Damnit, Andre!" Richeboux screams through the front window.

Andre revs it until all cylinders are hitting and pops the clutch. The car booms to life. Tires spin. Gravel sprays like shrapnel.

Richeboux's sweaty hold slips on the door post. The fingernails of his other hand screech across Andre's polished-to-a-shine enamel. And for an endless second, his upper torso swings out backwards over the road. The tops of trees, barely hiding the nearly full moon, flip upside down. Will his head bounce? Will he, too, be left sprawling in the ditch? Flying gravel stings his cheek and temple. Dust fills his eyes. He clings with his calves to the door, locks his ankles under Ronnie's armpits, trying to do a free-handed sit-up, willing himself back into the car. He loses it, swings back out as the Ford catches full traction. His flailing fingertips brush something—weeds, a bush, the man's face or recovered hat?

Jamie and Ellis lurch over the back of the front seat, grabbing at Richeboux's belt, arms, and T-shirt. A sharp pain rakes his back as they pull him into the car across the window ledge. His temple bangs the door post. He fights to catch his breath, spit the dust from his mouth. And what was that he heard as the man's knees went down—a shout, a curse, a stifled cry of pain? Like the spring before in the play-offs, when he hit that tough-faced boy from Montgomery with the blond spit curl—the state batting champ. And then that long half-hour of mumbled silence until the ambulance came and they finally got the boy on the stretcher. Just lying there, the spit curl hanging limp over the bloody temple where the ball hit.

Ellis is pounding the seat-back. "Damn, what a throw!"

Jamie's grinning and dripping spit, cackling his rooster like laugh. "Fast-ball, Brass-ball, Big Chief Branscomb!"

Ronnie whirls to look out the rear window as the car speeds away. "Holy my Jesus," he says. "He's chasing us."

"Damn! He is," says Ellis. "Look at that son of a bitch run."

Jamie's cackle breaks into a guffaw. "Ohhhh shit! It's gonna get wild. Watch out, Andre! Dead end!"

Andre hits the brakes. "Fucking overpass!" Cuts the wheel to the right. The car slides to a sideways stop against yellow sawhorses where the new bypass splits old Cherrytown off from the more upscale colored homes running up toward Stillman, the Negro college. Dust rolls through the car. Richeboux and Andre crank their windows up. Above the sagging roofs and treetops, Richeboux can see the silhouette of the elevated four-lane hanging over the backyards of houses. Must be like living under a drag strip.

A numbness feeds into his arms and legs. With the window up, the car feels tighter, its interior shrinking. The side of the door presses his arm. This is his last chance to run—to jump out right here, while Andre is stomping his dying clutch, trying to jam the car into low gear—straight into one of those squares of darkness between the houses. He looks toward the great shadow of the overpass, imagines himself hidden there, bent over, hands on knees, catching his breath. Then off to wherever—to *not here*—to *alone*, to Mem. But his legs won't move. His feet feel nailed to the floor.

Andre finds the gear, guns the Ford into a rutted driveway. Sprigs of privet rake the side of the car with a high, screeching noise. Andre hits the brakes. In the middle of the dirt yard, moonlight illuminates a rusty white tricycle with a twisted wheel. Richeboux's little sister, Leigh, had one just like it before she got sick. Short, fat legs, pumping the pedals. When she died, his mother took it with all her other toys to the Warrior River Bridge and dropped them, one-by-one, in the water. Richeboux's grip tightens on the armrest. The memory shrinks to a distant cry in his heart.

Andre backs out, jams the Ford into first again, and heads back up the street. The man is coming straight at them, his chest high and his head back like a sprinter at the tape. He clenches something in his hand, grabbed along the way—a piece of limb, a pipe—as if he's carrying it to the next man in a relay. Richeboux falls back in his seat, turns his head to stare out the side window at the dust-filled night. *Damn! What would make a man do that—pick himself up from that ditch, grab a stick or whatever, and run at a car full of people?*

Andre hunches forward, hands clamped on the hoop of plastic and chrome. Ellis bounces up and down as if pumping speed to the car. "Hit him! Hit the son of a bitch."

Ronnie whispers, "Jesus H. Christ, Jesus H. Christ." Above it all Jamie's wild donkey laugh.

The man's white-shirted chest fills the entire road. The thing in his hand rises and falls in the headlights. Andre brakes hard and cuts right, dropping a rear wheel in the ditch. A galvanized mailbox flattens before them. Richeboux, on the other side of the car, ducks anyway. The man spins as the car swerves, dodges the left front fender, then whirls as if around a pivot. The arm with the object in it swings in full arc. Richeboux can see only the silhouette of the thing, dark and cylindrical. The centrifugal weight of it pulls the man outward, picking up speed as it comes. Richeboux is locked in one of those dreams where the frantic muscles will not move. He waits for the iron bar to disintegrate the window next to him, crush the bones of his cheek, shatter the arm he throws up to block it. An explosion of glass sprays over him and the interior of the car. His ears register the metal-rending thud as the pipe whacks the door post behind Andre's head. The arm that swung it, a heavy freight train of an arm, pulls back through the shattered window as the car speeds past. An unbuttoned white shirt sleeve, spattered with blood, hangs across the man's wrist. The pipe, now bent, drops from the windowsill, bounces off Richeboux's shin, and clatters among the beer cans on the floor.

For a split-second Richeboux is sure the tip of the metal grazed his chin. He puts his hand to his face. Blood. But shards of glass have done it. That retreating hand, the large brown fingers—the strength in them could smash anything. And before that, before the swing even, the man's face in the bouncing headlights as he began his whirl—ablaze with anger, but something else in the quaking eyes and clinched muscles of the chin that is fighting like hell not to be shown. Not fear—not in this man. Nor sorrow. But shame. The man knew who he was after; it was all meant for him, Richeboux. He gives a swipe at the pieces of glass on his lap. Ronnie squirms himself into a kneeling position on the back seat so he can look out the rear window. Richeboux does the same.

The man leans forward in the middle of the road, hands on his knees, breathing hard. Then suddenly he straightens, throws his fists in the air, and screams at the moonlit sky.

Ellis's fingers claw at the dashboard. "Shit, Andre! Get back on the road!"

Another mail box goes down. They finally hit a culvert that bounces them onto the roadway.

"Fucking Fireball Roberts," yells Jamie. "Fucking demolition derby!"

"He's still coming," whispers Ronnie.

Ellis cranes his fat neck backwards across the seat. "Son of a bitch!"

Richeboux smells the secondhand motor oil in Andre's engine running hot, burning grit into the cylinders. He fumbles to pick the bloody splinter of glass from his cheek.

The man's shadow moves ghostlike through the dust, winks past the yellow porch lights coming on in the shacks along the road. Screen doors bang. A man shouts from one of the porches, starts clambering down the steps. The chained dog starts to bark again. A couple others join in. Richeboux feels the scene begin to spin, tornado-like, as if the crazy night is pulling him from the car, settling him on one of the porches among the staring colored people. From there the scene passes before him—the running man with his righteous, resolute face, the flying dust and gravel, and Richeboux in the car with his elbow hanging out the window from his half-empty self, his face as blank as the headlight that just went out on Andre's car.

They slide the next corner and head out of Cherrytown. A couple of blocks ahead is one of the honky-tonks. A group still stands under the homemade streetlight. It's grown—maybe a dozen black men, half in the yard, half in the road, drinking beers, smoking, and talking. They fall silent, watch the car approach. Andre slows down to squeeze by. "Roll up the windows!" says Ellis. He slides down in the front seat. Jamie and Ronnie roll up the remaining windows that work and hunker. Andre lowers himself enough to peer over the dashboard. Richeboux gets that feeling again: locked in with no way out. Sweat mixes with the blood on his cheek. His hands press together between his knees. The stink from the empty beer cans grows stronger. He sucks for air through the smashed window. His pulse keeps time with the knock in Andre's engine.

The black men in the road part slowly toward either side. The Ford creeps among them. By ones and twos the men drop their beers to their sides and watch the car. Ronnie is bent double, hands behind his head, whispering, "Jesus, Mary, and Joseph, get us out of here. Jesus, Mary, and Joseph...." Ellis and Jamie are out of view in the front seat. Richeboux balls his fists against the woven plastic seat, presses himself harder into the corner. A tremor runs in his arms. He will not duck. If they throw at him, he will not cower.

The men's pupils follow the movement of the car.

"Easy does it, Fireball," says Jamie from somewhere below the dashboard.

One man's look is more of a glare. He is tall, dark-skinned, with steady eyes and arms longer than Richeboux's. And something is missing in the quiet, broad face—that look of holding back, the stutter of hesitation and fear. What is there, instead, Richeboux immediately recognizes—an anger that cuts your insides like a knife every day.

The tall man bends from the waist, looks at them through the windows of the car. "What you want, white boys? Ain't no pussy 'round here for you." He straightens into a pitcher's stance, raises the arm with the beer.

Jamie's peeks over the windowsill. "Hit it!" Andre rises in the seat. His foot slams the gas pedal. The car coughs, does its stutter and lurch. The engine's knock is now like a hammer, whacking from inside. Richeboux's heard of cars throwing a rod. When they do, they stop don't they? The car lurches again. The motor catches and revs to life. The knock becomes a ripping noise under the hood. They fishtail in the loose gravel of the road. The tires catch, and they are off toward the turn that will take them out of Cherrytown.

A beer can whacks the top of the trunk and ricochets off the rear window behind Richeboux's head, spewing foam across the glass. Richeboux jerks around to look. The tall man with the wiry arms leans toward them in the middle of the road. Dust boils around him. He shakes his fist, gives them the finger, yells something Richeboux can't hear. That man could drive a baseball through the side of a house. He is still there, yelling, pumping his middle finger up and down, as he blurs into the darkness through the foamy streams of beer.

Nobody says a word until they're back on the hard surface and across the tracks.

Ellis pushes himself up. "Damn. You see the arms on that sucker threw the beer?"

Ronnie rocks back and forth, still mumbling about Jesus, Mary, and Joseph, hands still clasped behind his head.

Richeboux breaks a remaining spike of glass from his windowsill. "Why don't you shut up, Ronnie."

Ronnie turns to Richeboux. "I wasn't scared any more than you were."

Richeboux stares at nothing out the window.

"I wasn't," Ronnie says.

Richeboux slams his fist into the side of the door.

Andre eases off the road under a streetlight and shoves at his door. It's stuck from where the pipe hit the door post and crimped it forward. The pipe's imprint is a good inch deep. The post is bent and torn slightly from the roof. Andre grunts and shoves, finally he gets the door open, and gives a crying moan as he gets out of the car. "Aw, man, it's wrecked," he says.

Richeboux gets out along with the rest of them. His legs are shaky. He stuffs his hands in his jeans pockets.

Jamie, Ellis, and Andre begin to check the car. Ronnie bends forward with his hands on his knees and starts throwing up.

Richeboux takes a step backward onto the pavement of the road. Aside from the smashed window and bent door post, there are dents and scratches on the front bumper, grill, and left side mirror where they hit the mailboxes, and a curved scar on the trunk where the beer can hit.

"Frigging demolition derby," says Jamie.

Andre spits. "It's not funny, Einstein."

Richeboux walks to the closest rear tire, kicks the loose hubcap back into place. "We should have stayed at the high school."

Ellis leans into the car through the open window and fumbles about on the front floorboard for a beer. "You're the one who threw the egg, Chief." He takes the church key from his shirt pocket, pries open the top of the beer, takes a swig, and looks over at Andre. "It wadn't my idea to turn down a dead-end street."

"Shut your fat mouth, Ellis."

"I'da run him down."

"Bullshit!" Andre's hands hang at his side, elbows slightly bent, fists closing.

"Fireball, my ass." Ellis takes another gulp of beer. "You couldn't even keep the car in the road."

Andre takes a wild swing. Ellis throws the beer can. It glances off the side of Andre's head and sprays beer over the rest of them. He turns to run—that little duck-and-scoot thing he does—but Andre has him by the back of his shirt and rides him to the ground. They roll in the weeds beside the road, Ellis squalling, kicking, throwing his arms, Andre whacking at whatever parts he can get to.

Jamie and Ronnie move to separate them. Richeboux turns and starts up the road toward the high school where he left his mother's car. He will not think of the egg he threw. He will not remember the day he whipped his fastball at the batter from Montgomery, the way the boy's knees buckled and he dropped like a sack of stone. It was that same feeling again tonight, the same motion of wrist, arm, and shoulder, where his brain seemed wired to the ends of his fingers. Whip! Release! And it was there, that last-second buzz across the inside corner, that lightning snap against the black man's skull. *His* knees had buckled, too, and down he went. But he did not lie there and wait for an ambulance. He got up and looked the thrower in the eyes. That face, the look of a wounded God in it, coming at them through the headlights.

Somewhere inside Richeboux a door quietly shuts. He trudges on through the night air. It's like walking underwater.

# John Folsom Gryce

He could always run. Like one of those mid-August, dead-summer Alabama winds, the half-blood Choctaw grandmother who raised him said. Like the ten-point buck he saw jump a split-rail fence one cold day on the black-belt farm where he was raised, chestnut fence, maybe ten rails high; or the cottontail his two beagles chased when he was nine years old, out of a brush pile behind his daddy's garden, down the dirt road toward the house with the wide porches where the white people lived, with him hauling the old shotgun, almost keeping up with the rabbit for a quarter-mile or more.

Then he rounded the corner of that old stable, and there stood the white man, Mr. Coleman, spraddle-legged in his faded too-big-and-too-short overalls. A pile of split wood was at his feet, a two-bladed axe in his hands. Just stood there, looking at him and his rusty shotgun, at the scrambling, yelping dogs, and the rabbit darting from the road, across the thick-planted salad patch and into a dark stand of pines.

He'd started walking then—something about the way the man watched him, the axe hanging at the ends of his long arms, patches of gray hair cropped by his wife's scissors sprouting from his head, and below that, eyes set like marbles in a face so gaunt you felt you could see through the ruddy skin to the bone. One of the hands holding the axe was missing half a finger.

He'd seen the man before but mostly when his daddy was around and the man was handing out orders about what to do about the place—what land to break, what stumps to pull, what fields to plant. And it was always as if he, John Gryce, wasn't there, or was there but barely seen in the frame of the now-faded memory. But he remembered that day with the dogs and the rabbit, because for a brief moment he had been in the center of the frame, suddenly and squarely, as he slowed to a stop by the corner of the stable, lowered the shotgun, and let it hang in front of him like the white man held the axe, not daring to follow the rabbit and the dogs across the rows of late-November collards and mustard greens.

The white man's stare said nothing one way or the other, but it had stayed on him the rest of his life—long after he finally got the nerve to turn and head back up the road toward his own house, the shack at the juncture of four cotton fields; long after his daddy died and he'd started working the white man's land for him—plowing it, hoeing it, chopping it, discing it, dropping his sweat down the stingy, red-clay rows; long after he'd said goodbye to his grandma, left home, joined the army, gotten his two years of college at Stillman, worked the sawmill and the turpentine plant, fallen into a deep-flowing current of love, married Ludy, had kids, and taken up preaching and working the steamy nights in the boiler plant at the University. Long after he'd gotten his own church and his kids had grown and gone and his oldest boy had died on an icy, wind-scarred mountain in Korea and Ludy had nearly died of the grief. Long after he'd learned how to give love and receive it, and how a black man like himself—and a black woman, too—need at least a taste of it or they will die of the hate. That stare had stayed with him. And it had interrupted something in his coming to be a man, so that the picture he had of himself was fragmented. The pieces would not fit together.

So he'd given up on that. He was who he was, and he would use what he had to become an instrument of the will of God. He would give wholeness to his community, to other people.

And that's all he'd been about, really, on this visit to Rosemont's—save the community, understand the changes coming, find a way through them for his people, follow the way of Jesus to brotherly love. Love is the answer. Make it a habit. Spread it where you can. And that's what he intended to do with the car creeping up behind him, soon to pass. Nod and tip his hat: politeness is part of the ministry of love. A little gesture that invites a gesture in return. That's where unity comes from.

And that moment of exchange was almost upon him, but something eclipsed it, a shadow from that disembodied day in his youth when he rounded the corner of the stable and saw the white man with the axe. That feeling was there again: of being in the center of the frame. And he turned—or started to—when he saw the flashing arm and felt the egg explode behind his right ear below the hat band. He was on his knees even before his hand reached his head and felt the slimy shame of it, running down his neck, soaking his shirt collar and suspender strap.

He knew it was white boys even before he found his hat and glasses, looked up, and saw them pulling the thin, muscular one back into the car with his T-shirt riding up his back. And something about that—the naked, almost girlish shape of the boy's waist and ass as it swayed out over the road—brought to his mind the length of iron pipe in the ditch in front of him that he'd seen a hundred times or more as he passed this way and never thought twice about it. So there was that extra three-to-five seconds as he felt about in the dirt and grass for it, and then he was up, just like that, and running straight down the road after them like he'd chased the hounds and the rabbit that day when he was nine. His legs were pumping. He felt again that quick spring and strain in his tendons, the heat building in his calves and thighs under his light summer slacks. And there was another look driving him now—not the white man's soul-killing stare—but Rosemont's soulful, challenging eyes. *Out of the pulpit, preacher, and into the street.*

And then they stopped, as of course they had to with the new bypass blocking the way—pitiful white boys, thrashing about in their dumb laxity from God, cranking their souped-up, run-down car around, finally getting it headed back in his direction.

He kept straight for it—dust-streaked windshield, grinding gears, spinning shafts, half-bald tires working the gravel. The two headlights bounced and swayed on the road. They blinded him for a split second. He whirled—didn't know what else to do—just missed the left front fender of the Ford and then brought himself back around, swinging the pipe like he was knocking down a house with it. He didn't aim but saw the window before he hit it as well as the face behind it, pressed backward into the seat, eyes and mouth wide open, then squeezing shut as the face turned and the arm went up to ward off the blow. The whack of the pipe against the door post all but shattered his arm before he let it go. The motion of the car dragged his wrist back across the window's jagged sill.

He stopped at the end of his whirl, half bent over, hands on his knees. Pain throbbed in his wrist and cut hand. Blood soaked into his trouser leg. He glanced up. The car's front end dipped back into the ditch and pulled its underside along the bank. White boys, so stupid they couldn't even run a car out of a ditch.

It was the third mailbox, cut down like a shock of late corn, that did it: got him going again, arms swinging, thighs pumping. He lurched to keep himself from falling as his feet caught up with the rest of him. Marguerite Haskell's mailbox: he'd put it up for her one Saturday, ten years ago from parts he'd salvaged at the boiler plant. That flattened mailbox and hearing the car's oil pan scrape over the culvert. Maybe they would lose it—crash on either side of the road, the whole carload of them—and then there they'd be, sprawled in the middle of *his* neighborhood. White boys in the middle of his frame, caught in the stare of a black man's eyes.

But they hit the next culvert and bounced out of the ditch and steered clear of the one on the other side. He could see the taillights shimmy in the road as the driver fought for control on the loose surface. He kept running, even as they made the next block and the next, slid the corner, and headed up the road toward the two beer and gambling houses he's been trying to shut down for the last five years. And he never made it to the corner or even down the first block, just felt a lightness in his arms and legs as he passed his own house, an airless feeling of leaving it behind with Ludy there waiting, a slight betrayal of his own heart. He knew for certain then that this was it: he would die here on this dark road, chasing these numb-brained, heart-dead white boys. The pain stabbing his chest had been there from the start, biding its time somewhere in his armpits or groin.

His knees did not buckle. The lower half of his body simply vanished. He sprawled in midair. He lost track of his arms and legs, and experienced a fleeting moment of regret that didn't really attach to anything—certainly not the present moment—but vaguely to his entire life. He hit face-down in the road. His nose and chin bounced, then settled. The pain in his arm and hand was back, but it didn't seem to matter. And it occurred to him how strange this was: to be lying here with a mangled hand in the middle of a road he'd walked over in one direction or another at least a thousand times. He'd never thought of lying in it, getting down in the dirt, smelling it, tasting it, breathing it. And that's what was missing now wasn't it—the breathing. It was coming harder and harder. And why wouldn't it with those blows from the axe sinking deeper and deeper in his chest?

## Acee Waites

The smells of the Red Elephant grill are all over him—hot iron, sizzling fat, the seared flakes of meat he's scraped into the little trough on the front of the grill, still cooking into crisp, black cinders. And the ammonia, from where they clean the floors and countertops every night after the place is closed—cooked in with the rest of it. It gets inside him like a chemical fire.

Half an hour ago he thought he was finished for the night. And then the fat man, Sonny Hucks, comes sidling up, stands across the grill, staring down at the burgers, working up his I'm-sorry-but-there-ain't-a-thing-I-can-do-about-it look. Hard to pull off on a pink, bulldog face, punched out of shape from years of boxing in the dirty little rings around Alabama. The beetle-sized mole on his eyebrow bobbed like a cork. "Looks like you gon have to stay on awhile, Acee. Jimmy ain't showed up, and there's a party over at the high school. They been pouring in here like head lice all night."

Jimmy is Hucks's nephew—worthless and lazy as Hucks—and he just decides not to show. Sorry, white-ass bastard.

"Damn, Mr. Hucks. I been at this grill over eight hours. I'm tired."

"Don't cuss me, boy. I cain't help it. We got more'n we can handle. Ain't nobody going home early tonight."

Early, hell—it's almost midnight. "My shift s'pose to be over at nine."

"Well you can forget nine tonight, so keep cooking. You'll git paid for it."

Laughter and the cooler air of the dining room poured through the swinging doors as Hucks turned and made his exit.

Acee runs the spatula across the grill like he could dig a groove in it. He can feel Annie and Lugenia at the counter behind him, frying the fries and building the burgers from the buns and meat he slides over to them on a pie tin that never gets washed. He bets they didn't even look up when Hucks was in the room. Acee worries them. They want him to stay quiet—don't argue with Hucks; don't mess with white folks.

But he's already stretched tight tonight over Preacher and Raiford. Annie and Lugenia see it—the muscles in his back locked so hard he can barely move his shoulder blades. Just one mistake—drop a burger, spill grease from the lard can on his clothes—and it will all break loose. They don't like cussing, either. He taps the spatula on the edge of the grill, turns and smiles at them. Their hands move quickly over the lettuce, tomatoes, and buns, not missing a lick.

He leaves a new round of burgers to thaw at the edge of the grill and slips out the back screen door onto the stoop for a smoke, get Sonny Hucks out of his mind. The stoop is packing crates laid together. Grass grows between the slats. Every time Acee steps on it, he expects it to collapse under his feet. He shakes a Kool from the pack he keeps rolled in his T-shirt sleeve, and lights up. The exhaust fan from the kitchen hums. He blows the first drag of smoke toward it and watches the jet catch the smoke and blast it into the night. Moths whack the bulb over his head. One of those clumsy, brown-shelled bugs lands on his neck above the T-shirt. He brushes it off. The night has cooled from the ninety-degree day, but the humidity is still there, hanging in the branches of elms and willow oaks around the parking lot. Not a breath of breeze. A small cloud drifts by the moon. The muffled sound of distant thunder. It's hard to calm down when the air clings to you like burger grease. He takes another a drag on the cigarette. His hands feel like fried pork.

Across the parking lot, a Mercury pulls in, one of those turtle-backed '50 or '51s like his daddy used to have before he left to wherever he's gone. This one is maroon with clay-smeared whitewalls. It crawls over the gravel lot, through the ragged rows of parked cars, and pulls up under a streetlight. A boy and girl get out, jawing at each other. She slams the door and heads across the lot toward the restaurant. He rests an elbow on the car roof and watches her retreating back and the ticktock of her rear end.

"Can't you just listen for once?"

"To what—more bullshit about why you are never where you say you'll be?"

He shuts the door and lunges after her. "Hey, I'm sorry. I said it a hundred times."

"You're always sorry, but you're never there."

There's something familiar in the boy's voice, something strained, that tries very hard. And there's something in the way he moves, too—a shifting slouch, leaning slightly from the waist, like a boxer expecting a blow. He steps in front of the girl, turns to face her, and pretends to weave and dodge as she tries to step around him.

She stops dead, folds her arms, and glares at him. He moves aside and lets her pass.

Acee exhales another long breath of smoke toward the exhaust fan. Yeah, it's Bo, the kid Acee used to play with when they were little. Reachboo, Rishboo—something like that—was his real name, but everybody called him Bo. He was about Acee's age, and he lived across the lumberyard. They played together the summer Acee got over his diphtheria—pretend games about Indians, an idea they came up with together, but Acee can't remember why: he'd barely heard about Indians except for talk in his neighborhood about Preacher Gryce having Choctaw blood. They formed their own tribe with Bo's little sister. Bo's mother took the three of them on a picnic to the Moundville State Park where the Indian village used to be. Nervous lady with deep worry lines pinched between her eyebrows. Took up for Acee when the guard wouldn't let him in the Indian museum.

But Bo's daddy put a stop to him and Bo. Got after Acee one day when Acee was waiting for Bo at their usual meeting place on top of one of the stacks of lumber. Bo's daddy showed up instead—a broad-shouldered, thick-in-the-middle man with eyes that hit like hammers. He wore khaki work pants, dirty at the knees; brogan shoes; and a white shirt streaked down the front where he'd wiped his hands on it. Acee slipped back from the edge of the lumber stack and scrunched down in the middle.

"I know you there, boy. Go on home. Richeboux ain't playing with colored no more."

Acee looked around at the tops of the other stacks of lumber, maybe fifty of them, and it seemed like the only people left in the world were him and that white man.

"You hear me, boy? You go on and git before I find the boss man and get those dogs on you."

Acee slipped down the far side of the stack of lumber and took off running, past the other stacks toward the gate on 15th Street and the path beyond it through the woods to his house. The colored workers straightened from their work, glanced at each other, shook their heads. Acee could feel them watching as his bare feet sped over the dirt and sawdust. And he felt the eyes of Bo's dad on him, too—all the way home.

So, it's been quite a while since he last saw Bo. But that's him for sure. Same eyes flickering their cautious signals of apology and hope. He grabs for the girl's arm as they start up the steps. She pivots away from him. The madras skirt twirls from her waist as she darts inside. Her quick, tan feet, wedged into the sharp V of her black flats, barely touch the floor. The energy she and Bo carried between them from the moment they stepped out of the car vanishes with her.

Bo flops down on the front step, droops his head, and lets his forearms dangle from his knees. And for a moment, it almost returns: those days when Acee would walk into Bo's yard, catch him in his dreamy state as he sat on the front steps with his chin propped in his hand or in the porch swing, legs dangling, eyes fixed on the floor—just before Bo turned his head, his face breaking into a grin.

*Hey, Acee.*

*Hey, Bo.*

*Acee, listen! I know a place we can...*

But the girl is back outside on the restaurant stoop, hands on her hips, standing over Bo. She moves up behind him, rests her knees against his shoulders. The flounce of her skirt hangs about his neck. She starts mussing his hair.

"Come on," she says. "I won't bite... not yet."

Acee could use some of that. That's what he'd planned to do when he got off work—catch up with Resa, make up for lost time. He hasn't seen her in two days. But he's here, now, 'til midnight, working the grill. He looks down at his hands, spreads his fingers, flips his cigarette into the gravel beyond the stoop. Half a mind to walk away from here, find her—she's probably at her aunt May's house—tell her he's thinking about joining the army, which he probably won't do. But it will get things started, bring that bitchy pout to her cheeks, the blaze to her eyes. After that, it's like working the torch on his metal sculpture in the shed behind his house—with a little pop of flame warming to a soft, quiet blue. Turn it up slowly, keep talking—"Oh, Baby... now, Baby." Feel the heat start to rise. Move in closer, work his hand over her neck and shoulders, then ease down her back to where it rises toward the soft round places. You can hear the flame hiss then. Feel her start to melt. She likes the light touch. Soothe the outside to heat up the inside. And when you do, it's like jumping into fire.

But he's stuck for another two hours on Sonny Hucks's grill. Bo and the girl have gone inside, and he might as well do the same.

So he's back in the greasy steam, flipping burgers, laying on cheese, when he hears the call from the shadows beyond the screen door he's just walked through—barely loud enough to beat the noise from the exhaust fan.

"Hey, Acee!" It's his cousin Terry. What the hell's he doing here? And how did he find it? Terry gets lost walking across his own yard.

Acee steps back outside under the cone of yellow light, the spatula dripping in his hand. He squints into the shadows down the side of the building. Terry's body leans like a bent stove pipe against the back wall of the Red Elephant next to the overfilled garbage cans.

"What?" he yells over the hum of the fan.

"It's your mama. She said tell you to come home. Raiford's done got in some kind of trouble."

"What kind of trouble?"

"I don't know. But the police been there, looking for him 'bout a hour ago. Must have been a dozen of 'em."

Acee shuts the screen and turns back to the grill. It was bound to happen, whatever it is. And it's going to mess with his life, which is messed up enough already.

"Come on in here and tend these while I talk to Mr. Hucks."

He leaves Terry at the grill, goes through the swinging doors into the brightly lit dining area. There's Bo again, leaning on his elbows across one of the tables in a booth near the back, trying to talk to the girl he came in with. She's turned in her seat, yapping with a bunch of girls in the booth behind, turns back to him and slaps his hand off her knee under the table. Acee crosses the back corner of the dining room, enters the tiny hallway leading to the storage pantry and Mr. Hucks's office, and knocks on the door.

"Who is it?"

"Mr. Hucks, I got an emergency at home. I need to talk."

"Goddamnit," Hucks says. Chairs scrape beyond the door. One falls over backwards.

Acee stands with his hands on his hips and stares at his feet. More chair scraping. A woman's giggle. At least half a minute passes. He looks back at the panel of the door. "Mr. Hucks?"

"Wait a second."

A thin finger pushes up the hook-latch. Acee shoves the door open. Sonny Hucks is behind his desk in the broken swivel chair like he's been there all night. A skinny blond waitress they call Wayne, who's been working there only a few weeks and who can't be much older than Acee, backs away from the door, straightening her hair. She leans against the side wall with her hip stuck out and watches Acee walk in.

"What are you staring at?" she says.

"Nothing," says Acee.

She gives him a smirk. "I don't care what anybody out there thinks—especially you coloreds."

"Shut up, Wayne." Hucks rests his forearms on the edge of the worn metal desk and stares at Acee. His hair is messed up like somebody's had her fingers in it. A yellow-gray lock of it hangs above the twitching eyebrow.

"What you want, Acee?"

Another step puts Acee at the edge of the desk. The room is so small it feels like the walls are caving in. He takes a half-step back and crosses his hands behind him. "I need to go home, Mr. Hucks. There's trouble at my house. My mama's done sent for me. My cousin Terry's here. He can work the grill 'til you close."

"What kind of trouble?"

"Something 'bout the police looking for Raiford."

"That boy's been asking for trouble since he left working here. What's he done this time?"

"I don't know, Mr. Hucks. Mama just said come home."

Hucks throws his arms up in a hopeless gesture, pushes back in his chair, and looks over at Wayne. "What you grinning at?"

She leans her ass against the wall, braces the sole of her foot part way up it so that six inches of knee and thigh show, and nods toward Acee.

Hucks runs his eyes up and down her. "What you think I should do?"

Her knee waggles back and forth. "You're the boss. Whatever the hell you want."

Hucks looks back at Acee. "Well, if you don't know what your brother's done, there ain't much you can do 'bout it, is there?"

"Mr. Hucks. I b'lieve this is serious."

"Maybe it is—maybe it ain't. But what you gon do if you go home? Your people are there; they can handle it. I got to have you here, Acee. We overloaded. Jimmy's sick or something. I don't know nothing 'bout your cousin."

"He can handle a grill. He's grilled before."

"Don't matter," said Hucks. "You the grill man, and I need you here. That's why I pay you more than the rest of 'em back there. Now get back to work. You can leave when we close."

Hucks rocks back in his chair, puts his hands behind his head, and stares at Acee as if counting the seconds. Acee glances toward the door, turns back to the fat man. "Mr. Hucks, I ain't never asked you to take off but once before and that was for my granddaddy's funeral."

Hucks rocks forward, drops his forearms on the desk, and looks at it as if he's talking to it. "Boy, didn't you hear me?"

"Yeah, I heard you, Mr. Hucks. But I need to go."

Hucks jerks his forearm back and sweeps it across the desk like a boom. A railroad spike paperweight and empty coffee cup slam against the plywood panel wall.

"Boy! You come busting in here like you own the place, telling me you got to go home and you don't even know why. You ain't got more'n another couple hours. Now get back out there on that grill."

He could run, scoot off down the hall, get his ass back to the grill like Hucks says.

"I mean it," says Hucks. He looks Acee dead in the eye. "I ain't got time for this bullshit."

Acee turns his head toward the waitress. The smirk has

straightened to a tight-lipped grin. A fidgeting animal hides behind those slow, lazy eyes. He turns back to Hucks.

"You got time for that."

Hucks's chair slams against the wall. "Boy, get the fuck out of here!" He starts around the desk toward Acee. The waitress scrunches toward the corner.

"I'm gone," says Acee. He turns and bolts out the door, jerks off his apron, and drops it to the floor of the small hallway. He re-crosses the corner of the dining room with Hucks right behind him. "You ain't walking away from me, you sonofabitch."

Customers stare from the tables. The girl with Bo looks startled— that quick, cat-like part of her—as if she might leap to all fours on the floor.

Acee pushes past a couple of white waitresses coming out of the kitchen with plates of food. "Well 'scuse us!" says one of them.

Hucks catches him in the doorway between the dining room and kitchen, grabs a fistful of Acee's T-shirt, rips it at the collar. One of the swinging doors hangs open; the other one whacks Hucks in the side. They're still in plain view of the people in the dining area. He lets go the back of Acee's shirt, grabs the front of it, and slams Acee's back into the open swinging door. With the other hand he jerks Acee's belt and pants front halfway to his Adam's apple. Acee's on his tiptoes, his balls pushing the seams of his jeans. A dull ache spreads to his belly button.

"Boy, don't you *ever* talk to me like that. I'll fix you so you can't walk straight."

Hucks's smell is a mixture of onions, hair oil, and unwashed skin. His knuckles are jammed into Acee's belly. His other hand twists the top of Acee's T-shirt. Acee's breaths come faster. His arms hang at his sides as if held down by weights. But his forearms find their strength. He raises them and pushes back, hard, against the fat man's chest.

It's like pushing a fire hydrant. Hucks grunts and rams back against him, jamming Acee tighter against the door. Acee's chest flattens, his ribs bend. He can see the white boy, Bo, standing at his table, watching them. One arm and hand are out as if keeping the girl in the booth. The skinny waitress is there, too—without the smirk now—and the other two waitresses he brushed past stand with their mouths open, still holding the trays of food. One of them moans, "Oh, my God." The white girl grabs Bo's arm, looks up at him, mouths words. Acee looks back at the fat man.

"Turn me loose, Mr. Hucks."

The moaning waitress drops her tray of food. Glasses break; ice cubes skitter; plastic plates bounce and clatter. A saucer, dripping banana pudding, rolls across the dirty planks, bumps over a strip of aluminum, edging the linoleum, and wobbles to a stop against Hucks's planted foot.

Hucks glances down at the settling saucer and then out into the dining room where at least half the people are now on their feet. He looks back at his fist, gripping Acee's shirt, releases it and the pants he's holding with the other hand as well, and slowly backs away. He has a confused look on his face, as if he's not real sure how he got there.

Acee takes a breath and looks around the kitchen. Terry closes his gaping mouth and glances toward the screen door. The spatula drips grease onto the floor. Acee reaches and touches his arm. "Set it down. We're leaving."

"What?" says Hucks.

Terry wipes his nose, looks at the sizzling, smoking burgers and then back at Acee. "We ain't gon finish these?"

"Let 'em burn." He shoves Terry toward the door. The spatula clatters to the floor.

"Lawd have mercy"—Annie and Lugenia groan at the same time from the burger-making table, shaking their heads. Hucks lurches to block Acee's way.

"Come on, Acee. Wait just a damn minute!"

But Acee is already around him and out the door.

"Boy, you got a lot of damn nerve."

The screen door slams. Acee keeps pushing Terry into the logjam of parked cars.

"You leave here tonight, you ain't coming back," Hucks yells from the stoop.

"Keep walking," says Acee.

"I ain't sending you no pay, either. You leave here with all these orders to fill, you can starve for all I care."

They're at a trot now, threading their way among the cars. Hucks won't follow; he'd never catch them if he did. Besides, he's the only one left to work the grill.

The ache from Acee's testicles has migrated to his thighs and groin. If he thinks about it too hard, he'll puke. He reaches to grab the back of Terry's shirt. "You bring Travis's car?"

"Naw, man. I caught a ride up Sixth Street."

"I reckon we're walking then."

"Running, more like it. What you do to make him so mad?"

"Interrupted that skinny waitress sucking his dick."

They reach the sidewalk and make fifty feet before he stops. "Wait up a minute." He steps behind a bush in someone's yard, undoes his belt to loosen his jeans, and rests with his hands on his knees. The ache in his balls begins to ease. His wrists and forearms are trembling. "I just ask him to take off. I asked real nice, too."

"Well, you off now. You off *for good.*"

Acee straightens slowly. He can see the look in his mama's eyes, waiting for him when he gets home. *What you gon do, Acee?*

They're off again, headed uptown. It's a three-mile walk home, and the first half of it is through the heart of Tuscaloosa's oldest white neighborhoods with their willow oaks and white-framed houses. Well-tended shrubs muffle the city's noise. Silence lurks in the shadowy yards, wraparound porches, and darkened windows. Terry and Acee keep up the pace for another couple of blocks, then slow to a fast walk. Acee whirls from time to time to look back. Sometimes cops slow their engines to an idle and creep up on you. Acee keeps his voice just above a whisper.

"How's mama?"

Terry's pace slows even further. "She ain't doing so good."

"It's that stuff Raiford's been messing with. I'll bet he pulled a sit-in or something."

"I don't know what Raiford be up to."

Scattered drops of rain start to fall. Terry stretches the back of his T-shirt over his head.

"Preacher hurt, too."

Acee stops. "Preacher?"

Terry keeps walking. "Fell in the road or something. Bunch of 'em carried him to his house. Then the police come. I ain't heard no more 'bout it."

"Damn," says Acee.

They detour beneath trees to make use of the shadows. Terry whispers even lower. "You reckon the police is after you, too? They get going good, sometime's they arrest everybody."

"I ain't done nothing to be arrested for."

"I ain't neither," says Terry.

Rain drops tap the leaves above them, drift through the streetlights to spot the concrete. The pulpy smell of the paper mill has worked its way down river and lies on Queen City Avenue like the breath of a disease. It works its way into their hair and clothes, reminds Acee of his sister's long illness and his own—in bed late at night, fighting his fever, smelling the yellow smell of the paper mill, waiting for her to die. Near the Catholic church, with its shadowy arches and high, pointed windows of stained glass, the first cop car passes, catching them in the open between the shadows of two giant elms. The cops look at them, the driver leaning across the seat to get a better view out the passenger window. He straightens in his seat. The car zooms into a screeching bootlegger's turn and rocks to a stop in the opposite lane. The cop grinds the transmission into first, guns the engine, pops the clutch, and the tires smoke their way back up the avenue, straight in Acee's and Terry's direction.

But they are already running, across the shadowy church grounds, down the back alley between the chapel and church hall across Oak

Street, and into the crowded maze of houses beyond. Dogs bark from backyards and side porches. All they have to do now is jump the right fences, stay away from the wrong dogs, mind the sound of a car screeching to a stop, the slamming of car doors, the searching flashlight beams. Within a quarter of a mile they cross the railroad tracks, make their way through the woods and across the creek, and slip into their own neighborhood. They are home free when they get this far.

They move on down Cherry Street. Lights and oil lamps are lit everywhere—unusual for this time of night. There's a crowd at Preacher Gryce's house, spilling out onto the porch and the misty yard. Some wave as Terry and Acee pass.

"Y'all heard about the Reverend?"

"Naw," says Acee. "What about him?"

"Died. Right out there in the road 'bout two hours ago."

Acee stops, looks down the empty road, past his own house which also has its lights on and people in the yard. The road smells of dampened dust. Where porch lights filter on to it, bits of gravel sparkle in the rain. Preacher walked that road day and night. Acee remembers the broad shoulders and swinging arms, the fedora tipped forward, the face lost in thought but ready to smile.

"Died?"

"Yeah. Chasing a car full of cracker white boys, hit him with a egg. Heart attack, I reckon."

There's a couple of flattened mailboxes half a block down. Grass flattened and scraped clean along the edge of the ditch.

"Where's Resa?"

"Ain't seen her all night."

Acee starts walking. Terry stands and watches him go. By the time Acee reaches his own yard, the rain has wet his head and shoulders. He can make out his mother's words among the snuffles and tears.

"Lawd, he was the most unlisteningest child. You couldn't tell Raiford a blessed thing. But he ain't done what they say he has. I know he ain't done that."

# Richeboux

*He stands sideways on the mound. His arms are loose. The ball turns easily in his hand. From his viewpoint above his left shoulder, the route to home plate is long and bare, narrowing to a point at the end. The field is smoky. Moths flit in the stadium lights. The fans watch him with zombie eyes. Championship game. The teams are tensed in their dugouts; bat boys crouch on one knee. His coach stands behind third base, hands cupped to his cheeks, screaming a silent scream. Brush him back, he'd said ten seconds before when Richeboux came out to the mound. You ain't gon beat this cocky bastard throwing ninety-mile-an-hour strikes.*

*This cocky bastard, this batter his teammates have been talking about all week, who beat them twice during the regular season with three doubles and a home run, who has the highest batting average ever in the state. "We're counting on you, boy. You got the arm. Burn the hairs off his chin. Scare the shit out of him. Take him out of his game."*

*His own face fades in and out of the frame, Indian-streaked face with the school colors, done especially for this championship game—red on cheeks and forehead, a broad black stripe down the middle of his nose from hairline to chin. The eyes are not there—only black-rimmed sockets. His thumb and fingers close on the ball; fingertips find their purchase on the seam.*

*He can feel a pitch before he throws it, loses himself completely in the act about halfway through the wind-up, just before the power kicks in. He knows the ball's arc, curve, and speed the moment it leaves his fingers. He can hear the smack in the catcher's mitt before the ball gets there. All his stuff is good, but his fast ball is like a comet from his hand. Fire burns up from his legs, shoots through his arm and shoulder. He usually doesn't have to put it close to scare them. But this batter is special. Richeboux's been waiting for a second shot at him since April.*

*He will not look at the batter, hunched over the plate. He will not look at the waiting catcher's glove. He will not look at the plate. It's the space he wants, and he knows where that is—six inches from this boy's face and brain. His body begins its slow tilt backward, the leg rising for balance then twisting his torso to its pivot point. His pitching arm uncoils to the empty place in the sky where it all begins. The other arm stretches fulcrum-like toward the plate. The body hurls forward. The hand with the ball whips past his ear, driving the pitch like a nail into that tiny space, locked in his mind's eye.*

*It all comes back now—the rush in his body, the un-flexing of his wrist, the sudden emptying of fingers, the "umph" of his breath at the end. The noise from the crowd vanishes. He watches the ball turning, spinning, blocking his view of everything beyond.*

*At what point in that action and movement did he know that it would all go wrong—that this batter would stand his ground, would not move far or fast enough, that something was not quite right in his grip on the ball—a nick in the leather, a raised stitch in the seam, the scrape on his fingertip in the release—that told him this pitch would miss that space in his mind. This pitch was going straight for the batter's head.*

———————

His moan wakes him, the fading echo of a whack, a sickening thud on a skull. The pillow smells of sour sweat. He rises to his elbow on the mattress and flops onto his back. A warm blade of sunlight cuts across his neck and chin from the edges of the window shade he never raises. He is here again, staring at the swirly patterns of mildew on his bedroom ceiling. The naked bulb hangs above him on its twisted cord—a daily reminder of something he hasn't done, something he can't quite identify. Every morning he has the urge to leap up and smash it.

And there's something else this morning—a hint of that familiar ache in his pitcher's arm, a feeling that something has receded into the darkness he's just waked from. The Montgomery batter sprawled behind the plate. The boy's cap upside down in the dirt. A big brown hand rising to the spot behind the ear as the colored man dropped to his knees. That man got up, found his hat, and put it back on. That man came after him.

From the kitchen down the hall comes the clank of an iron skillet on the stove, the metallic scrape of a spatula, the smells of bacon and coffee that have been there since he first awakened but which he has just now noticed.

"Richeboux, breakfast."

He pushes himself out of bed, starts to look about in the half-light of the room for his clothes.

"Richeboux, do you hear me?"

The jeans are on the floor, egg stains on the lap. He throws them on a pile of dirty clothes in the corner his mother keeps nagging him to wash. He pulls last night's T-shirt over his head. The smell of Mem Cohane is all over it, a dopey mixture of sweat, perfume, and Clearasil. It mixes with the nickel-like odor of his own body. Something about the evidence of her still being there, cooked into his clothes eight hours later, makes him want to fall to his knees, wrap his arms around her tight little ass and thighs, bury his head in her lap, run his fingers over the hard bones of her face. All the things he didn't do when they made out last night. He throws the T-shirt on the pile in the corner and rummages the basket of clean clothes his mother set in there Monday night for him to fold and put in his drawer—one of her old make-him-feel-guilty tricks.

She is still at the stove when he gets to the kitchen. Same flowered bathrobe with its unmended underarm tear. It embarrasses him how old it is—most of the fuzzy little balls have worn off—but mainly the way it clings to her hips, round and softened by age but still shapely. The bounce is there when she walks—he can't help but notice it. That spring in her toes. And his stepfather, Arnold, creepy little ape-man, grabbing for it. Why did she marry a man like that, put up with his shit, let him mess with her?

Like he did two weeks ago when she made the mistake of saying that the thing she enjoyed most in the world was a quiet night and a good book.

Arnold had sprung from the couch and flung his beer against the wall. "Fuck these goddamn books."

"But Honey, I didn't mean you. I meant when there was nothing else to do. I meant when you are gone."

The asshole started hauling books from the shelf, sending them crashing to the floor. Her begging him, grabbing at his arm. "Honey, please!" The rip in the underarm of her robe as Arnold shoved her off. Her exposed knees and thigh as she crumpled to the floor, flesh with its tiny blue veins, swaying from the bone. More crashing books, then the shelves. Breaking glass. The frantic look she gave Richeboux as she grabbed the sofa arm and pushed herself to her feet. He'd started for the bastard but she quickly moved in front and placed both hands against his chest.

"No, Richeboux. I'll handle it."

He took a step back, fixed his stare on her, then stormed from the room—down the hall to his bedroom and slammed the door. And there was the light bulb, hanging from the ceiling, waiting.

Richeboux swings his leg over the back of the kitchen chair, slides into his seat at the chipped enamel table, and stares at the toast and four strips of bacon on the plate in front of him. He will not look at her as she stands before him—the back and shoulders, bearing quietly their years of patience and pain, the jiggle in her hips and in the flesh under her arms as she uses the spatula to work the eggs.

"Your father called. He needs you to be on time. He's got to meet someone else by noon."

"What's it to you?"

"Don't be that way. I don't need it this time of morning."

He clenches his fist on the table. She grabs a hot pad, stoops to get a grip on the skillet, straightens, turns, reaches across the table, and scrapes the eggs into a steamy pile on his plate, all but burying the bacon. Scrambled this morning instead of sunny-side-up. A sign she's pissed about something.

"So, you're not talking?" She stands with the empty skillet drooping from her bony wrist, a smirky twinkle in her eyes—a vaguely warm and familiar invitation, carrying its equally vague accusation. "Where were you last night?"

"Over at the high school."

"Doing what 'til almost two a.m., if I may ask?"

"It wadn't two a.m."

"Yes, it was, Richeboux. I was wide awake, waiting for you."

"Well, we went somewhere afterwards. I don't have to tell you everything I do."

She glares at him as she uses the spatula to scrape the egg residue from the iron bottom. He starts eating, washing down the bacon, toast, and eggs with big swallows of milk.

"It's that Jewish girl, isn't it—whatever her name is. Mem, the one whose daddy owns the jewelry store."

"She's not Jewish."

"Richeboux, she's a Jewess. Her daddy was Cohen or Cohn or something like that before he changed his name to Cohane."

"Who cares if he changed his name. I wish I could change mine."

"Hush that!" She sets the skillet in the sink, turns the tap on, and leans away from the hiss of steam. "When you change your name, Richeboux, you're hiding something. That man is hiding his past. And so is she. You can count on it."

"Who cares. I'm not gon marry her."

She scrubs at the skillet with a Brillo pad, washes it under the tap, sets it in the drying rack. A lock of gray-blond hair, loose from its bobby pin, sways across her forehead.

"It's none of your business anyway," he says.

"Watch your mouth!" She turns from the sink to face him. "Your daddy might not give you this job, you know. He didn't sound very sure about it on the phone this morning."

"So?"

"Well, you could show a bit more enthusiasm for it. You *could* do that." She reaches up with both hands to pin the hair back in place, opening the bobby pin with her teeth and talking at the same time. "What if this doesn't work out? What are you going to do then? You'll have to pay rent here. Arnold's made that clear."

"I already pay rent here."

"Less than two months total since Christmas. I paid the rest."

"Yeah, well, I shouldn't have to pay rent in my own house. Nobody else does."

"Well, that's the way it is here. So you'd better make plans for it."

He uses the fork like a trowel, shoveling in his food. She continues to look at him. "What did you think you were going to do when you got out of high school?"

"I was planning to go to college."

She pours coffee from the percolator on the stove, blows the steam off, and takes a sip. "Richeboux, you can still go to college. You'll just have to work some of the time." She rests her rear against the countertop, drapes one arm across her waist and sips her coffee. "Anyway, that's between you and your dad." She sips her coffee—waiting, always waiting.

"Why do you think he changed his mind?"

"I don't know."

"Is it because you quit the team?"

"I don't know."

She continues to sip. He refuses to look back, finishes the eggs and drinks off the rest of the milk.

"I hear his office is real nice. I hear she decorated it for him."

Richeboux drops his fork in the plate, glares at it and then at the table. "Where's the paper? I want to read the sports."

"Your stepfather took it. He always takes it on Saturdays. You know that."

"Yeah, I guess I do!" He shoves the chair back, grabs his plate and fork.

She slides down the counter to allow him to get to the sink and then turns and reaches to place a hand on his shoulder. The slept-in smell of her rises above the smell of bacon grease hardening in the worn porcelain sink.

"Richeboux, honey, be polite. It's not that hard to do, and you need this job."

He dips beneath her touch, drops his plate and silverware in the sink, and turns on the spigot.

She sighs, sets the coffee down, takes off her apron, and hangs it on the back of the kitchen door. Then she grabs her coffee and walks out of the room. It feels as if the air in the room leaves with her. The heel of his hand presses against the cold lip of the sink. He looks up at the window, his vague reflection in it.

She yells from the hallway, "Be back by noon. I need the car. I've got things to do."

"Where're the keys?"

"Wherever you left them last night. I haven't used it."

He gets his milk glass from the table and starts washing.

"Did you hear me?"

"Yeah, I heard you." He washes his plate, silverware, and the spatula and skillet, sets them in the rack, and wipes off the kitchen table. He pulls a box of baking soda from the cabinet over the stove, wets his finger, sticks it in, and comes out with enough to brush his teeth, which he does with his finger, over the sink. Then he finds the car keys on the end of the counter where he threw them the night before.

She pokes her head through the bedroom door. "Back by noon!"

---

The morning air is clean from last night's rain. He crosses the Black Warrior River toward Northport, over the high bridge that runs from the center of town. It's where he, Jamie, and Ellis threw the M-80s into the water over a year ago and sank a man's homemade plywood boat. Ellis got away before the cops came—chickenshit bastard that he is—but Richeboux and Jamie got arrested. And Richeboux's dad went to court with him.

The bridge's angle-iron railings slide past.

He was leaning on the down-river side of those railings when they dropped the firecrackers. Watching them hit the water was like the sea battle in *The Sands of Iwo Jima*, except the spray from the river was yellow-green from the chemical plant upriver. They never heard the boat coming. And then Ellis threw the whole string of the remaining M-80s, all lit from the same fuse, and they watched it fall, twisting, tumbling, sparking in the air. The bow of the boat emerged from the shadow of the bridge. The huge firecrackers landed mid-section and rolled, spewing sparks, toward the rear. The man let go the hand throttle as if the outboard had caught fire and leapt up, tap-dancing toward the bow over the hissing fuses. Ka-Blam! Ka-Blam! Ka-Blam! The boat started sinking, even as it began to circle. The man shook his fist at them before he went over backwards into the water. "Assholes," he yelled. "Assholes!" until the water gurgled his scream.

Richeboux could not let go of the bridge railing. The bow tipped upwards and slid under with the man thrashing in the water. Jamie gave Richeboux a tug. "Come on Brass Ball. Holy shit! Fucking Titantic, man. Fucking Pearl Harbor." On a nearby barge men ran along the deck with grappling poles and life preservers. Richeboux tore himself from the railing and headed for Jamie's Cushman scooter. Jamie stomped the crank peddle like mad. Not a sputter. Ellis was gone, out of sight off the other end of the bridge. The cops got the two of them, pushing and pulling the Cushman, with Jamie still stomping at the crank.

He'd figured his dad would be pissed, but the old man seemed O.K.—young men feeling their oats, that kind of stuff. "You gon have to work it off," he'd said. And Richeboux did, though it took him the whole summer to do it, working on his dad's grounds crew on the golf course, cleaning up around the new houses, saving up for what they guessed would be a fine, court costs, and to pay his share of the man's boat.

Late in August they drove to court—night court in the old courthouse downtown. It had felt good for a change, having the old man on his side, all dressed up in his blazer, tie, and wing-tips. He could look like a big shot when he wanted to. A warm breeze blew through the open window of his dad's new Pontiac, tickling the hair on the back of Richeboux's neck where he'd failed to get the haircut his dad had told him to get. He rubbed his hand on the leather seat and thought of the times, two or three years before his parents split, when he and his father drove the old pick-up out to his grandfather's place on the Coosa River to check trot lines for turtles and fish. His father joked a lot then, let him sip a little beer or bourbon—whatever he was holding between his legs on the seat—even slid over and let him drive when they got off the main road. But that evening on the way to court, there was the smell of aftershave where bourbon used to be. The fine ridges of bone on his father's face, the heavy eyebrows he reached for as a baby, were lost in country club fat that glowed in the light of the Pontiac dash. There were no jokes, not even a hint of a smile.

At the courthouse his father and Jamie's old man started sweet-talking the police and the man from the boat. "Maiden voyage," the man had said. "Took me a year to build it, and them boys blew it up it just for the hell of it. I mighta been killed." The man's family was there, including his cousin who was on the City Council.

Richeboux's dad knew the City Council member. Shook his hand like they were old friends. Took him aside and talked to him. And his father had stuck with Richeboux through the meeting with the D.A.: "Y'all don't need to worry about punishment. I'll take care of that. Richeboux's just got a few things to learn. He's already earned a bunch of money to pay for this. He'll earn more if he needs to. Mr. Cherones will get his boat back, better than the last one. I guarantee it." Everyone went along, and for the first time since his dad had left them, Richeboux felt as if a part of him had come back home.

As the brass-studded doors of the courtroom swung shut behind them, Richeboux paused, waiting for a pat on the back, a nudge of some kind, maybe even a hug—"How 'bout that, son—have I got the touch or what?" But the old man whirled, grabbed him by the shoulders, and slammed him against the marble wall. The ridge of wainscoting cut his spine. A hand, heavy as a board, smacked him across the face. His father had never hit him before. Richeboux's arms flexed to ward off the blow, but he dropped them. Tears brimmed, ran to his chin.

His dad glared another second, turned on his heels, and slammed his way through the revolving door to the outside. Richeboux wiped his face on the sleeve of his windbreaker, glanced down at the snot on the light-beige nylon, took a deep breath, and followed. The night court crowd, gathered in the hallway, looked up from their huddles to watch him go.

His dad was unlocking the car by the time Richeboux got to the courthouse steps. He tried to speak, but the words hung in his throat.

His father put one foot in the car, rested his arms on the roof and open door, and looked at him. "I have to come down here and bow and scrape in front of all these people to get you out of a mess like this. Kiss ass with a washing machine salesman over a pissant plywood boat because his cousin's on the City Council. Boy, don't you know how the world works? You know how hard I've had to bust my ass to get respect in this town. Don't you ever pull anything like this again. Ever!"

His father got in and slammed the door. The starter screeched; the engine roared. Tires squealed as the old man backed from the parking space and zoomed off down Main Street. Richeboux stood at the top of the worn granite steps and watched him go. The man with the boat and his family shook their heads and "tsk-tsked" as they brushed past, headed to their cars. He watched them leave in the same direction as his father, then started walking home.

———————————

Now he turns his mother's Mercury off the Northport bypass, through the brick gate with the wrought iron "River Forest" sign bolted against a curved wall of cream-colored bricks. Traces of red clay, washed from construction sites, stain the base of the sign, the new asphalt, and the concrete curbing. He hates this whole scene—the rambling, ranch-style houses of brick, glass, and stone bordering the golf course; the perfectly tended lawns; his father's fancy office off the 15th green; the colored-boy caddies, hauling bags of clubs and bourbon up fairways behind laughing, dirty-joking golfers. And the grounds keepers—like he'd been the two summers before—off somewhere, working out of sight. Well, at least he won't have to do that anymore. He's done his time hauling fertilizer and re-sodding greens, working like a redneck farmer, making a fairyland for rich fat-asses to chase little white balls.

He finds a parking place next to his dad's baby blue Chevy El Camino in front of the "River Forest—Main Office" sign. He's been hoping, halfway, that the old man won't show—that something has come up at one of the home construction sites to keep him away, or maybe that he's just forgotten about it—it's happened before. Not likely today though, since he called the house to be sure Richeboux would be on time. Mud is spattered all over the El Camino, even the windshield. Why can't he get a real truck, like the old Dodge they used to check the trot lines?

The office door is of varnished oak with a carved magnolia blossom framed in the middle. Richeboux turns the shiny-gold knob and steps into a flourescent-lit foyer. Everything smells new—the glue from the carpet, fresh paint, a lingering odor of sawn wood. Tracks of drying red mud lead across a light-gray carpet past an expensive-looking secretary's desk. From an open double-doorway at the end of the hall comes the impatient tone of his father's voice. "Uh-huh, uh-huh. Same bullshit I heard last time. Look, Dwight..."

Richeboux follows the mud tracks down the hall and halts in the doorway. His dad is in his leather swivel-chair, turned away from his desk to face out a wide bay window toward a green where a foursome is putting out against a backdrop of sweet gums and cedars. The men have on trousers of bright green, deep rose, and madras, set off by white polo shirts with gold crests on them from the club pro shop. His father holds a phone to his ear while he cleans his nails with a silver letter opener. "I understand, Dwight. But we cain't drop this thing 'just like that.' There's a whole bunch of money tied up in it; you can't walk away from thirty-thousand dollars."

Richeboux taps against one of the panes in the glass office doors.

His dad keeps it up with the "uh-huhs," as he turns, glances at Richeboux, and nods toward one of the matching armchairs in front of the desk. Richeboux slides into it, stretches his legs out along the deep carpet, and looks around the office. Nothing new except a Chamber of Commerce award for "Businessman of the Year," framed in gold and now on the wall with the other two. The bronze statuette of two bird dogs flushing a covey of bobwhite still anchors the front of the big mahogany desk. Richeboux has always admired it. His dad used to bird hunt when he lived with them. But his mother would never let Richeboux go near liquor and guns.

Color photographs of his father and his new wife are on display around the room—golfing shots, vacations at the beach, one of them on the deck of a fishing boat with big, ocean-sized spinning rods in their hands and a giant fish of some kind hanging between them. "To Brad, Love Marianne," is scrawled in a lazy hand across one corner, as if she's done it with her fingertip after a long night of champagne. She doesn't look relaxed in the picture, though, as if she's slipped into a room where she doesn't belong.

There is the eight-by-ten of her children, too, on the credenza next to the fish picture—all three of them, smiling at the camera, dressed up in their Sunday clothes. The "new" family. He might as well give it up. It's a done deal, as his father used to say.

There are black-and-whites of him and his sister, also on the credenza—five-by-eight studio shots taken when they were children before the separation. Maybe a year before Leigh's leukemia. His mother keeps a similar one of Leigh on her night stand at home, and whenever Richeboux looks at it, he sees death biding its time in the shadows around Leigh's eyes. The eyes themselves plead with him from the center of the black-rimmed frame not to let her go, or at least to follow her to wherever she is. He avoids the picture. In fact, he's quit going into his mother's bedroom at all, now that it's hers and Arnold's.

His dad reaches across his credenza, and retrieves the morning paper. He tosses it across the desk toward Richeboux, jabbing at the headline with his finger.

### Policeman Murdered.
### Search Underway for Negro Suspect.

Richeboux scans the story.

*Darryl Culp, a deputy with the Tuscaloosa County Sheriff's Department, was shot and killed yesterday while attempting to serve an arrest warrant at a mobile home near Taylorsville. The suspect is a 22-year-old, Negro male, Raiford Waites... arrest stemming from a cohabitation charge with a white woman.... Culp, father of two young boys... shot twice in the chest... pronounced dead at Tuscaloosa County Hospital... manhunt underway.*

The article goes on to say that the sheriff's office had received numerous complaints about the trailer in the rural part of Tuscaloosa

County. It had become a gathering place for whites and coloreds involved in recent integration efforts. Some of the cars observed at the trailer had license plates from as far away as Ohio and New York.

His dad "uh-huhs" through the receiver a couple more minutes, tells Dwight to meet him at the bank on Monday, and hangs up. He sits with his hand on the receiver and glances up at Richeboux. The auburn hair on his thick wrists has a tended look, brushed by sun and success.

He shakes his head. "You can't make money by being a chickenshit."

He gets up from the chair, goes to a small refrigerator on the Formica counter in a corner of the room, and pulls out two Cokes. "Want one of these?"

"Yeah."

His father opens both bottles with the opener attached to the counter and pokes them in Richeboux's direction. Richeboux takes one and gives it a sip. The Coke pings in his nostrils and on his tongue. He rubs it against his upper teeth and straightens in his seat.

His father nods toward the paper. "That's him, isn't it?"

"Who?"

"The boy they're looking for—Raiford what's-his-name. He's the one brought his kid brother across the lumberyard to play with you when we were on Deering Place. A.C.? Something like that. Anyway, look where his brother's got himself now. I told your mama not to let you play with colored. There's a wildness in 'em."

"Might be," said Richeboux.

"Well, this boy's good as dead. Shoot a cop around here, that's all she wrote. Even if you're white."

His dad nabs the bottle caps off the floor, flips them into a small sink on the counter, swings himself back into the swivel chair, and lifts his feet so that the dirty soles of his work shoes hang off the corner of the desk. The khaki pants ride up, revealing white work socks and an inch of heavy, tanned calf. He and his new family have a swimming pool at home. He takes a swig of Coke, runs his free hand over the burr of his haircut, and looks at Richeboux. A belch puffs through his lips.

Richeboux turns the wet bottle in his hand. "I come to talk about the job."

"We'll get to that in a minute. How's your mom?"

"All right, I guess."

His dad releases another burp. "She didn't sound so good on the phone this morning. She and what's-his-name have a bad night?"

Richeboux darts his eyes around the room again—the fat furniture, oak credenza, and pictures of the new wife and kids. He puts the brakes on his eyes to avoid the photo of his sister. Acee had a sister who died, too—not much more than a baby. Diphtheria or something. He looks at his father. "I don't know."

"I expect you can count on it with an asshole like that."

His father inclines toward Richeboux, and looks from under his burnished-blond eyebrows. "He doesn't hit her, does he?"

"I've never seen it."

The old man studies him for a minute, swigs the Coke, sets it down and reaches for a pack of Winstons resting by a silver-plated Aladdin's Lamp lighter. He drops his feet from the desk to the floor, rests his elbows on his knees, shakes out a cigarette, and lights it. Then exhales a long breath of smoke and stares into the carpet. "Richeboux, don't you still owe me some money on that boat y'all sank?"

"Naw. I paid every cent of it."

"You sure 'bout that? I haven't checked it lately."

"I paid you every cent of it—last Fall, before Christmas."

His father turns his head and looks at him. "O.K., don't get in a crank about it. I'll get Sandra to check it when she comes in Monday." He turns back to stare at the carpet and takes another drag on the Winston. "That asshole and his dip-shit boat." He shakes his head and looks up at Richeboux. "Well, what's your proposition?"

"I come to talk about the job."

"I know that. What kind of job you got in mind?"

"You said if I needed a job after graduation to come talk about it."

"Yeah." His father purses his lips and floats a smoke ring into the air, a trick Richeboux admired when he was little. "But I'm asking what your proposition is." He waves the smoke ring away. "What kind of job can you handle?"

"I don't know. Work around the office, I guess. Carry messages. Help sell houses. Learn how things work." He pauses. "Stuff like that."

His father swivels the chair, leans forward with his elbows on the desk, and rests his chin on the heel of his cigarette hand. Smoke drifts up the side of his head. Out the window a jiggle-bellied golfer in madras pants has just made a putt and is doing the shimmy, waving his putter in the air.

"You ever sold a house?"

"No."

"You got a realtor's license?"

"No. I didn't know you had to have one."

"How 'bout carpentry. Ever done any of that?"

"Just 'round the house, helping Mom."

"Plumbing? Electrical work? Brick masonry?"

"No." Richeboux feels himself up against the courthouse wall again.

"Ever poured any concrete?"

"No, I ain't done any of that." He takes a deep breath. "There's other things to do around here. I thought you said you'd give me a job."

The old man lowers his head, scratches his forehead with the tip of his thumb. "No, Richeboux. What I said was to come by and talk to me when you made up your mind about college and if you couldn't find a job somewhere else. Have you looked anywhere?"

"Not really. I thought you'd give me one."

"How 'bout college. What are you doing about that?"

"I'm not going next year."

His father raises his eyes. Richeboux thought this had been settled long ago through his mother, the messenger.

"How come?"

"I ain't got enough money. I'd have to work all the time."

"Aw, bullshit! Lots of people work while they're in college. You'd have had a full scholarship if you hadn't quit the baseball team." His father jams the cigarette into an ashtray, gets up from his seat and turns his back on Richeboux to stare out the window. "You shouldn't have quit the team, Richeboux. I still haven't heard a good excuse for that."

"Me and Coach didn't get along."

"Yeah, I heard that one. But it doesn't wash. Lots of people don't get along with lots of people. But they don't give up a chance for a college scholarship—hell, maybe even a big league career—on account of it. That was just plain stupid."

"I guess I'm stupid then. I thought—"

His father whirls, places his fists on the desk, and leans on them like the front end of a horse. "Damnit Richeboux, look around you. How do you think I got this office, built that golf course out the window there and the houses around it? When I was your age, I was working my ass off, learning a trade—carpentry, plumbing, electrical. Wasn't even thinking 'bout college." He flings his hands in the air. "You act like everybody owes you something, like you can just waltz in and decide whatever it is you want to do—stay on the team if you feel like it, go to college if you feel like it, get your old man to find a job for you. I ain't running a charity here. I got other people to take care of besides you."

He turns back to the window, stuffs his hands in his hip pockets.

Richeboux pushes himself from the chair. Maybe he should just walk out and leave like the bastard left him on the courthouse steps.

"Well," the old man says, "we can always use somebody on the grounds crew. You can do that, I reckon. Take that old International truck out there, clean up the sites after the carpenters." He turns to face Richeboux again. "That's what I've got to offer you. You want a job with me, you got to start at the bottom and learn as you go. That's the way I did it; and that's the way it is in this business. Be out here Monday morning, soon as you graduate. When is that—next Friday, Saturday, Saturday night?"

"Week from Sunday."

"Where, down at the high school?"

"No. Foster Auditorium at the University." A tremor creeps into his voice. He swallows, locks down every muscle in his face.

"O.K. Start the Monday after that then. Get here by seven o'clock. Check in with Sandra out at the front desk. You remember—Miss Tilley. She'll tell you where to go."

His dad places his hands on his hips and looks at him as if he's waiting for him to do something. Just like his mama.

"All right," he says.

The foyer carpet springs under each step, hurrying him out the door.

# Acee

Fog hangs low over fields of newly turned earth as Acee, Terry, Acee's Uncle Travis, and Elton Brown, Acee's boyhood friend from up the street, head back to Cherrytown in Travis's old Hudson. They've ridden the county back roads all night, trying to find Raiford before the cops do. It was a long shot, but it was worth it to Acee to get away from the weight of his mother's head, wound in its tight, gray braids, weeping on his chest.

Terry drives while Acee fades in and out in the back seat. His neck and shoulders hurt from straining forward all night to watch for police cars and trucks full of white men, reaching across the front seat to cut off the one working headlight whenever they saw a vehicle coming because Terry couldn't remember to do it. Then Terry would ease the Hudson down some farm road or into the edge of the woods.

The colored cabins they visited along the river all looked the same—sagging porches, tin roofs, dripping rain. They climbed the front steps, knocked gently on the doors. People came, half awake and scared. All of them had been visited by the police. All claimed they rarely saw Raiford. Two held shotguns while they talked through open windows.

"Come here once, handing out a paper 'bout some kind of union for the colored. Had that white woman with him. I told him, I said, 'Boy, don't bring her down here no more. You leave that white woman and them papers alone.' It was bound to happen."

"What was bound to happen?"

"Whatever they say he done."

An old woman spoke through a cracked-open door, face deep-Africa black, eyes afloat in oil, voice hollow as an empty well. "What he want to come down here, stirrin' all this up fuh? He and them white people, carrying on, talking 'bout equal rights and such. They ain't none of 'em ast us about it—did we want it in the fust place."

Elton pushed his way to the front: "Old woman, how long you aiming to live like a slave?"

"Boy, what you know 'bout slavery? I was bawn in slavery. This ain't slavery. Slavery a whole lot worse'n this."

They backed off the porches into the dirt yards, and moved on down the road to the next cabin. It was close and damp in the car from the muggy air and their soggy clothes. They rode through the wet night until finally even Elton gave up arguing. Terry turned the Hudson out of the last muddy yard. The people faded back into their watchful darkness.

Preacher would have known how to talk to these old-timey, land-tilling people. A thick arm around a bony shoulder. "Brother" this; "sister" that. "We gon make it ain't we? We been traveling this road a long time." Preacher had lived their story. And not having him there was like half the night was missing and tomorrow could never come. *He's gone*, Acee kept telling himself. And as the night wore on, he finally started to believe it. Sadness slipped up behind him and wrapped him in its arms. Acee gave up trying to pull them off.

And he had felt Raiford's goneness, too—from the empty night, the endless swamps and bottomland forests where Raiford did whatever he did in those very yards, on those very porches. Raiford had that way of taking on everything around him; pinning you down, making you listen and squirm. It dwelt in him like a restless goblin.

Yet, it was Raiford that got him and Bo together. Raiford met Bo when he rescued him from two Dobermans that had him treed up a stack of lumber. That was back when Raiford cared about folks, tried to help 'em—Mama, Uncle Travis, neighbors—made it his job to watch over Acee. When Acee got over the diphtheria his sister, Annie, died of, Raiford took him across the lumberyard to visit Bo. Acee's legs were still weak. It was hard to keep his balance in the scattered pieces of lumber and mushy sawdust. He fell, knocked his breath out, and got a splinter in his hand. Raiford helped him up, put his lips to Acee's palm, and sucked the splinter out. He wiped Acee's hand clean and sang the choo-choo song their mama used to sing to them and Annie before Annie died.

> *That little black train's a-comin'*
> *It's comin' 'round the bend,*
> *It'll take you home to Jesus,*
> *Where you can find a Friend.*
>
> *God loves all the children,*
> *And children love our Lord.*
> *He's got that train a-waitin',*
> *If you just climb on board.*

The windshield wipers Terry has forgotten to turn off squawk back and forth. But what about Raiford now—the restless, angry Raiford? As they rode up and down the back roads on this slippery, dripping night, did he, Acee, really want to find him? What would Acee have said to him if they had, sitting in the dark in some deserted shack along the river with the white woman hanging on to him, misty moonlight shining through an open door onto the pistol in his lap? And from Raiford's cornered and defiant eyes the same question: "What you gon do now, brother—keep pretending or follow me to the next step?"

It's the white woman who seems to have upset the country people the most. Upset his mother and Travis, too. He'd overheard an argument between them and Raiford late one night after he'd gotten home from his shift at the Red Elephant and gone to bed. Raiford had slipped into the house for something, and his mama and Travis got out of bed and argued with him about his white woman and the goings-on in Taylorsville. Their voices rattled through the beadboard walls.

"It just ain't right," his uncle kept saying.

"Who says it ain't right? Some rat-faced white man down at the courthouse?"

"God says it ain't right. It's a 'bomination to live in sin with a woman, black or white."

"God let us live like dogs for three-hundred years. God don't tell me what to do, 'bout women or nothing else."

"Aw, Raiford!" said his mama. "Child, what has gotten into you? Listen to Preacher Gryce, son. Take it to Jesus. Jesus is the answer."

"Reverend Gryce's a fool," said Raiford. "Jesus is a white man's god. When y'all gon understand that?"

"You blaspheming now," said Travis. "Lawd have mercy." His voice wobbled like an old wheel.

But his mama's voice got calm for a change—that old tone he and Raiford used to hear when they were little, before his sister died and her nerves went bad. "You're risking it all, Son. You could be a king. You could be like Preacher Gryce. But you're sacrificing everything. And before it's over, you're going to hurt a lot of people."

"Let it come," said Raiford. "Let the whole temple burn. It's run by crackers and thieves. That's where the abomination is. I ain't gon crawl through life being a white man's nigger. If a black man's gon live, there ain't but one way to go."

"Going to hell," said Travis.

"Going to your grave," said his mother. "Sure as I'm looking at you."

———

Dawn has fully broken by the time Acee, Terry, Travis, and Elton make it back to Cherrytown. Acee stands in the half-light of his kitchen and stokes the iron cooking stove with firewood. His mother snores in the next room. Travis, Terry, and Elton sit silently at the rusting chrome-and-Formica-topped table behind him. Acee pulls the iron skillet from the nail on the wall. The knots in his muscles won't let go. Neither will the empty ache in his stomach nor the hollow feeling in his chest. Acee works the stove out of habit, stuffing in kindling, laying the strips of fatback in the skillet, and shoving them aside when they leak enough grease to fry the eggs.

He uses the spatula to kick the grease from the fatback over the eggs, leaving the yolks soft and runny the way Travis and Terry like them. He slides the finished eggs from the skillet onto a platter along with the crisp fatback and some light bread he's toasted on the stove top and takes his seat. The smells have made him even more hungry than he is tired, but sounds of boots scraping the planks of the front porch stop him before the first bite. A loud rapping rattles the latched screen door. He lays his fork beside his plate.

"Aw-Naw!" says Elton, his mouth open to his loaded fork. He closes it, shakes his head, and drops the fork to his plate.

Travis looks at Acee, that tremble back in his eyes, as if it's Acee's fault and Acee has to deal with it. Terry gets up with his plate and scurries out the back door to eat on the stoop. The banging at the front door keeps coming.

"Open up! We ain't got all morning."

"Tell the motherfuckers to get a warrant," says Elton.

Acee stands, rests his fingertips on the table. Before he can take a step, Terry comes peddling backwards through the back door, still carrying his plate. A big deputy is right behind him. It's like a mountain has walked into the room, eyes squinting from under a rockface of forehead. There is no neck; the head runs straight to his shoulders from the skinned fringes of his hair cut. The gun belt creaks like a harness. At the end of a massive freckled forearm hangs a nickel-plated .38.

The deputy's thighs spread to a braced stance at the center of the room. A second man steps from behind him like a trainer walking a bulldog on a leash. There's no gun that Acee can see, but he holds loosely in his thumb and fingers what appears to be the knob handle of a bull whip. He has a shriveled, old-woman look—pooched belly, caved-in chest, and a face with creases so deep the razor can't reach the dark hairs within. A crescent-shaped scar borders one of his mica-like eyes. "D. Sugarman Starnes, Chief Deputy," is etched in the brass name plate over the western-style shirt pocket.

Acee drops back in his seat. Terry keeps backing toward the corner between the stove and the wall. The back of his knees hit the wood box. He flops down on the chunks of rough-split pine. His lips are open, spit about to drip. "Eeow!" he says as his underarm brushes the stove top. His plate of food clatters to the floor. A flake of greasy, white egg, dotted with specks of pepper, slides down the toe of the Chief Deputy's black boot.

"Clean it off," Starnes says. He takes the cigarette from his teeth, flicks an ash, and looks past them toward the front door. "Tossie, y'all come on in here. Kick it in if you have to."

Terry licks the burn on his arm and starts rubbing it. Starnes taps the whip handle against his leg.

"Boy, didn't you hear what I said?"

Terry drops to his knees amidst the spilled food, uses his shirttail to wipe the boot, and scoots back to the wood box.

Starnes raises his eyes to the three of them around the table. The eyes seem mismatched, one lazy, the other—the one bordered with the scar—taking in more, speaking before the lips do.

"Awright, where's he at?"

Acee clenches his fists, digs his fingernails into his palm. Behind him wood rips as the other deputies kick the front screen door free of its latch.

Elton flicks his tongue to wet his lips. "Who you talking 'bout?"

Starnes leans foward, jabs the butt of his whip handle a foot from

Elton's face. "Who you think I'm talking about? Get them hands on the table where I can see 'em."

The tobacco flakes pop and burn in the cigarette smoking from Starnes's fingers. The fingers are fat at the knuckles and taper softly toward the nails like those of a dainty white lady. It's as if the parts of him have been stitched together from the leftover parts of others.

He picks a flake of tobacco from the tip of his tongue. "And stand up when I'm talking to you."

Acee, Elton, and Travis all rise. Terry tries, falls back on the wood box, and finally makes it to his feet, still rubbing his arm. Mashed flakes of egg dangle from the knees of his jeans.

Starnes clears his throat. The fat deputy's mouth widens to a grin. He takes a sideways step out of the way as Starnes opens his arms, preacher style, flops his head back, and pins his eyes to the ceiling. The black men flinch. The room gets smaller and hotter. The fat deputy's grin gets bigger. Starnes's shadow falls cross-like on the table. He squeezes his eyes shut as if in prayer, sucks air through his hairy nostrils, expanding his chest, then breathes out slowly: "Gather ye near, children, that ye may learn to fear me. I have words to teach you who I am." The arms lower. He returns the cigarette to his mouth, rests his fists on his hips, looks squarely at Acee.

"You know where that's from, boy?"

"Bible, I reckon."

"Bible, he reckons." Starnes winks at Flat Top. Flat Top grins wider, takes a step back. Starnes's shoulder jerks and wrist flexes. The whip handle slams onto the table like the strike of a snake. Plates and silverware clatter. Every part of Acee jumps. Travis grabs his chair to keep from toppling. Terry starts a bubbly moan.

Starnes's gaze is back on Acee. "You the smart one—is that right?" The cigarette is burned short now, causing his eyes to squint. "There's always a smart one." He lowers his head, shakes it slowly back and forth, and looks back at Acee. "Let me tell you something, boy— you get smart with me, I'll lock you up forever. You understand? You'll flat disappear. Your mama'll be crying in the bed over two lost sons."

Acee feels for the wall behind him, presses his butt into the beadboard.

"Raiford don't live here no more," says Travis. His napkin is still stuck in his shirt collar and bobs under his Adam's apple. His pupils are locked in a horizontal quiver. His tongue slides nervously over the inside of his lip.

Starnes looks at Travis as if he hasn't been worth the effort before. "I know he don't live here. I want to know where he's at."

Acee takes a breath. "We don't know where he's at, and that's the God's truth." His lips press shut. He shouldn't have mentioned God to Starnes. "We ain't seen him in over a month."

Through the door behind him, his mother argues with the deputies in her bedroom. "Y'all done tore the house apart last night. Ain't that enough?"

"Shut up 'fore we jerk you out that bed." They open closets, shove furniture, and stomp through the house. One of them slams out the front door and heads around the house, checking underneath, checking the shed outside.

"We in here, mama," Acee says.

"I been up all night over this. I can't stand no more."

Acee backs a step toward the door to the living room.

Once again the Chief Deputy moves reptile-quick. The butt of his whip handle jabs Acee's chest. "Boy, get back in here!"

Acee gulps for air, resists grabbing his chest where the whip handle hit. The ticks of the cooling cook stove explode in the air. Its burned-iron odor mixes with the body heat in the room. The big deputy cocks his pistol. Metal, hitting its groove, clicks in every vertebra of Acee's spine. He raises his hands, palms outward, and eases back to his place at the table. Both of the men are looking at him now. The deputy's thumb is still on the hammer.

"There you go," says Starnes. "Now you getting the picture."

Acee lowers his hands to the back of his chair.

In the next room, his mother's voice is faltering, about to cry. The stove ticks slower. Starnes drops his cigarette to the linoleum, snuffs it with the sole of his boot, and jets the last lung-full of smoke through his nostrils. He leans forward, braces himself on the tabletop with his fists. The whip handle clunks against Travis's plate. His voice lowers to a graveyard whisper.

"Now, I'm 'bout to tell you boys something you need to know. That deputy got killed yesterday was a friend of mine—as good a man as ever walked this earth. And we gon find the man that killed him." He bows his head. "So help me God." The fist holding the whip handle tightens. "And when we do, God help him and whoever's been hiding him."

He straightens, lets his gaze slip from face to face. "That's aiding and abetting, which I expect y'all know about. You burn for that same as murder." He glances down at Travis's plate of uneaten food, shifts the tip of his whip handle away from the greasy eggs. "You'll look 'bout like that piece of fatback on that plate there."

He stretches his neck, strokes the sides of his Adam's apple with his thumb and fingers. "Now I'm gon ask you one more time where he's at. And if you know, you better tell me."

The other deputy widens his spread-legged stance. "Come on Shug, let's take 'em downtown. Me and Tossie'll make 'em talk."

"Nawp, I ain't there yet. I'm gon let 'em think on it." Starnes drops his eyes to the floor and then back to the men. "But we getting mighty close."

"Officer—" Travis's voice is shaking now. "We don't know where that chile is. We truly don't. Like Acee said, we ain't seen him in a *long* while."

One of the searching deputies—a skinny man with a farmer's tan and a growth on one side of his face—leans through the door to the kitchen and shakes his head. "He ain't here, Shug. We done checked everywhere. They ain't even cleaned up the mess from when we was here last night."

Starnes keeps his eye on the three men. The big deputy glances toward Starnes. His goofy grin has returned. "Let's go, Shug. This whole place smell like last night's pussy."

The whip handle smacks the tabletop again. Travis's plate breaks in half. "Otis, don't use that talk around me!"

Flat Top backs up a step, uncocks his pistol and returns it to the holster. Starnes nods toward the living room door. The big deputy shoves past Travis. Starnes is close behind, favoring a game leg and rubbing it with his hand as he walks. Starnes pauses in the threshold and nods toward Acee. "It gets mighty dark down in that jail. Couple of weeks ago we hung two men on the same rope. Like to kicked each other to death to see who was gonna die first."

The shadow of a smile crosses his hant-like face. Then he's gone. The front screen door slams. Boots clatter down the porch steps. Travis pushes his chair back and rushes to the bedroom to check on Acee's mother. Elton starts to fork in his cold meat and eggs. Terry opens the lid to the wood stove, pukes in the coals, and wipes his mouth on his wrist. He stares at the rest of his food, scattered at his feet.

Acee nods toward his own plate. "Take mine."

He walks onto the back stoop, jams his hands in his pockets to stop them from shaking. Through the screen door behind him, he can hear his mother still crying, Travis trying to soothe her. Her moans take the air he breathes, slip past him like wounded animals into the yard.

Under a chinaberry tree in the far corner, early morning sun lights the clapboard sides of a small shed. The deputies have left its door open. A quiet darkness waits inside.

The shed's floor is packed dirt the color of burnt motor oil and littered with car parts, rusted tools, and other scraps of useless metal, scattered about like the car graveyard they passed early that morning in a clay field west of town. In the middle of the mess is a greasy wood stool, spotted with burn marks, and beside it, a scratched pair of army-green welding tanks, from which hang a hose, torch, and battered pair of goggles. Within an arm's reach from the tanks is a structure of intricately fused pieces of scrap metal that roughly resembles a tall man, bent from the waist. Acee halts in the doorway and lets the gray light come in around him.

It's been four months since he worked on his sculpture—a sleety day in February that turned to cold rain, freezing on the trees. The Red Elephant was closed, and he had the whole day to spend on it. He put on three layers of clothes and brought a small coal oil heater from the house. By late afternoon, he'd finished welding the last of the larger pieces of the frame: fire pokers and truck springs for legs; torso from sheet metal, pulley wheels, and angle iron; wrists, hands, and fingers from ice hooks, strips of metal, and steel cable. He turned off the torch, slumped back onto the stool, and contemplated what he'd done. It felt like he'd built a skyscraper. But the human shape was there, roughly formed, and there was something else: the slightest intimation of life— that curious bend from the waist he had not planned, the arms open and extended in half-gesture toward the floor.

*And on the seventh day, He rested.* Acee was too tired to smile and too tired to keep Raiford's words from winging back to him: "You wasting your time. Ain't nobody gon pay for nigger art."

Acee set the torch on the floor, peeled off the goggles and gloves. "Well," he said, "I've done all I can do."

Then he remembered the box of copper wire and cable he, Terry, and Elton had stolen from a power line work site. They'd hidden it under old lady Haskell's house, who boarded up her crawl space to keep snakes out. He took the remaining half of the ice hook with him to pry off the boards, and brought the wire back to the shed. That's when the scary part began.

Adding the bright burnished copper was like setting the statue on fire—combusting the broken pieces of iron and steel to life. He could feel the heat run up his wrists and arms as he ran the coils from the statue's fingers and hands, around the elbows, and through the neck to the drooping head with its tin face, dotted with washers and shavings. He'd stayed at it all night, wrapping the wires behind the sockets of the eyes, running strips of them across the gash of mouth, tracing them down the jaw line, past the base of the throat to the empty space where the heart would be. And there the twisted ends of them hung. The heat left him; the fire began to die out.

Sometime during the night sleet started again, popping on the shed's tin roof as he slumped on his stool, head-down, half-asleep, the soldering iron hanging in his hand, bits of wire and drops of solder all about him on the dirt floor. And the sensation hit him that the statue had moved. It began as a dream and came on so fast he'd burned his ankle with the tip of the iron when he jumped from the stool and stumbled back against the shed wall. The form stood dead still before him, its new veins of copper catching the thin morning light. The two-by-fours he'd used as supporting braces were in place, but there was that feeling—a look about the newly lined eyes and mouth—that the statue had a mind of its own, which was wise and touched with mirth—and that it had slipped back into its posture a second quicker than Acee's eye.

After that, Acee stayed away, tried not to even look at the doorway of the shed, tried to make what was in there an empty space in his mind.

---

But now, after Starnes's visit, an empty space is where Acee needs to be. He kicks his way through the litter, takes a seat on the stool, rests his elbows on his knees, and looks at the statue. It has taken on even more majesty since the last time he saw it. He is reduced to a soul lost in the wilderness, a fumbling man who has unwittingly created a god he does not understand but yet is bound to worship.

He reaches forward, touches his fingers to the cold metal. The muscles in his thighs flex, and an old feeling comes back: a suspension between fear and joy he used to get in Preacher's office behind the church when Acee would make his afternoon visits. Preacher would sit behind his desk with his elbows on his knees and talk. On the wall behind him hung the huge angle-iron cross he and Acee made together when Preacher first taught Acee how to weld. Preacher's words ran on and on. Acee's thoughts wandered, but Preacher's voice called them back until, sooner or later, it took him to where he knew they were headed all along—to "the *real* Jesus," said Preacher, the one who dwelt in cotton rows, shotgun shacks, and saw mills with the Negro race—not the white man's starry-eyed Jesus, walking in lush gardens under a blue sky with a lamb in his arm and a flock of them at his feet. During their last visit, Preacher had stopped talking in mid-sentence, raised his head, and looked at Acee.

"He's here," he said. He held up his hand as if to bid silence. "Kneel with me, son."

Preacher came around the desk to kneel beside Acee on the faded oriental rug, a hand-me-down from a white church downtown. Above them the angle-iron cross seemed to grow larger and heavier. Preacher said a prayer for Acee, his family, and his future, and about the strength needed to carry the burden of black people.

"Oh Lord, call this young man," said Preacher. "He's got the spirit; give him the will."

Acee kept raising his eyes, glancing around. He didn't feel Jesus's presence. He'd never thought about what a black man's Jesus might look like. Preacher's prayer went on and on. Acee lost track of the words, but they settled like a blanket on his shoulders. And that blanket has gotten heavier every day, until it feels like the weight of a thousand years.

And that's what the statue feels like now—Preacher bending over him, the gesturing arms calling him into them, into the statue itself to become Preacher's new flesh, to open his own arms, and take up Preacher's work with his people.

Acee retrieves his welding gloves, leather apron, and baseball cap from the peg by the door, retakes his seat, and rests his hands on his knees to ease the tremor in his arms. The tanks wait like obedient soldiers. The morning is fully awake. Birds chirp in the trees. The temperature is already rising. He places a hand on a cold, rounded shoulder of one of the tanks, unwinds the hose, and slips on the goggles. He turns the brass valves, puts on his gloves, and reaches for the striker at his feet. Click—pop! A small yellow flame appears at the end of the nozzle. He adjusts it to a spike of iridescent blue, then cuts it back into a hissing blue-white jet. The awakening day, the birdsongs, disappear. Already he can smell the skin searing from the metal. He adjusts himself on the stool, and reaches for a filler rod from the coffee can at his feet.

On top of the pile of scrap metal in a corner of the shed is a shiny plow blade—the last piece of scrap metal Preacher gave him. Preacher probably followed that blade down a thousand furrows behind the swaying rear end of some white man's mule. Acee fetches the blade and holds it before him. It is triangular, with a point and two other winged corners, and is sculpted concavely to peel up soil and turn in into rows. Years of use have dulled the point and corners into rounded projections that seem to stretch the blade from its center.

Acee rubs his fingers over the soil-polished metal. Some part of Preacher remains in the curve of that blade. He holds the blade up to the statue, turning it this way and that to see where it fits. The open space is waiting for it, right there in the center where the heart would be. He wedges the blade into place among the metal guts and ribs and starts the first bead of the morning along the blade's shiny edge. In spite of the tears in his eyes, he runs the bead in a perfect furrow, without a speck or bubble. The line of metal glows like lava spewed from the center of the earth.

# Richeboux

Richeboux parks the Mercury in the corner of a dirt lot behind the A&P across from the high school. He gets out and heads across the lot toward the weed-choked ditch, separating the lot from the railroad right-of-way. His mother will bitch at him for being late getting the car to her, but tough shit. He's got an hour maybe—at least forty-five minutes.

He jumps the ditch to the tracks and stops to look in both directions. Late-morning sun gleams off the tracks. The air is dense in the right-of-way's closed-in depression. Scrags of sweet gum, cedar, and pine shoot up along fences that separate the tracks from people's backyards. The whole place smells of baked rocks, steel, and creosote.

To his left the tracks pass a row of apartment buildings before their long sweep around the lumberyard to the station. Mem will be headed down those tracks soon in that very direction, on her way to her fancy New England college. Mem, who is so sure she knows where she's going with her life, who rubbed her body against him last night in the back seat of his mother's car until the hot jet of cum pumped against his stomach, wetting his blue jeans and underwear. He felt her sureness then. Making out with her has that effect—reminds him of who he is and where he is with his life—or where he isn't. And what will he do about that, once she's gone?

He turns down the track and starts walking. Ahead of him a break in the bank-side brush leads from the right-of-way to the back yard of Mrs. Kusinski's duplex apartment, his teacher and tutor in English when he was on the baseball team. Yearning pulls him toward it like a spear embedded in his chest. A luscious agony sets in. The thought of her, lolling about in the darkened apartment among her books, with a rumpled dress on, has his dick pressing the front of his jeans. It seems like a defeat. He's lost control of his body, and he's not even at her door yet.

It happens in her class, too, when she leans her butt against the eraser tray beneath the blackboard and lets her eyes wander toward the window. Her voice trails off. She picks up a book from her desk and starts to read aloud—Poe, Whitman, or her all-time favorite, Dickinson, the old maid from Massachusetts. Her head falls back against the board's chalky surface as she finishes a poem or even before, if she's reciting by heart. The dreamy look gets dreamier. A black low-heeled shoe drops to the floor. The stockinged arch of one foot begins to rub up and down the calf of her other leg. He can almost hear the silky sound of it. He's heard some of the other guys snigger when she does that and has tried to join them, but he can't quite pull it off. Because he has the feeling—had it from the first time he saw her do that—that the whole act is for him. He has to cover the front of his jeans with his books just to get out of the classroom.

He swings himself over the heavy black ties, trying to get things under control and stops when he reaches the hole through the fence. Once again he glances up and down the tracks. The ribbons of glistening steel all but hum in their waiting for the noonday train. He imagines where it will go—across the blank-eyed fields of Mississippi to the soothing sounds of New Orleans. The erection starts to ease. He jumps the ditch, scrambles up the bank and into the shady back yard.

The yard is empty. The line of identical back stoops, with their assortments of drying mops, house plants, and barbecue grills, sleepy and quiet. He walks quickly to her back door, number A-12. The usual pile of yellowing newspapers and magazines is in a wood-framed box on the stoop, weighted down by one of those old-timey irons you heat on the stove. She picked it up at a yard sale. For sure she doesn't iron with it. The dresses she wears to school are wrinkled and overworn. It's books she cares about. She reads even more than his mother does.

He knocks softly on the screen door. His gut is wound around itself. A woman closer to his mother's age than his and even smarter than Mem. A sleeping tigress who has the power to maul, leave wounds inside.

He doesn't hear a sound until the door cracks. And there she is, in the same pea-green linen dress she wore to school yesterday with its drooping pockets and big white buttons down the front. She's been lounging about in it, probably hasn't taken it off since he last saw her leaving the high school with a double armload of books on her way to her car. She's pulled the wide white belt from its loops and dropped it somewhere. The dress hangs like a curtain over her body, inviting him to feel in the warm, breathing dark to find her.

Seeing her face here, away from school, makes him feel like he's stumbled through a door into some parallel universe. Her features disorient him. They are hard and soft, lazy and kinetic. The hawk-like face is framed by swoops of copper hair, gathered to a ragged haystack at the back. A couple of damp strands hang loose over her lady-like temples as if protecting them from the rest of her. The whole mess is held together by a large tortoise-shell clip. And those deep, dark eyes— caves leading to the shadowy places where she lives and hides. He wants to dissolve into her pupils, find out what's inside. But the black opals only reflect himself back to him.

She was born in some European country he can never remember the name of where her father was connected to the military—a mysterious figure, she says, gone from home a lot. There's a rumor at the high school that she's a Communist because of her foreign accent and a voice, deeper and more man-like than any woman he's ever heard—that and the fact that she left her classroom for a year at Columbia University and came back with crazy ideas about how to teach. They are all equals, she says, striving together to discover the divine. She treats them like college students. And it pisses him off that he wishes he could act like one for her but has no idea of how to pull it off.

She gives him a flickering look before turning and leading him through her tiny kitchen into the living room. Her bare feet thump the linoleum and swish across the living room carpet—strong feet, used to being naked. Bright strips of sunlight trim the drawn window shades. The air hangs, dead as a soiled shirt. A smell of cat urine comes from a litter box. She doesn't clean the place. No wonder her husband's never home. He's an army officer—colonel or something—traveling around the South, inspecting ROTC programs. They are separated, she says, and he assumed that meant they were getting a divorce. But she'd told him "no" the only time he asked. "We're separated in body and spirit, and we'll stay that way. I will not run my life by someone else's rules."

A lamp with its shade tilted stands at the end of a couch where she's been sitting, casting its light over a dozen books and magazines, scattered on the couch and coffee table, and two empty wine glasses and a coffee cup that have been there awhile. A dead-looking white-and-orange cat stretches on the cushions among papers he recognizes as the year-end themes from his English class. She required them to choose a novel from a list she gave them and write a critique. He'd written on *The Scarlet Letter*, a book she'd suggested to him, for some reason he couldn't figure at first. But the more he read, the more the repressed lust in the novel ate at him. She had known exactly what she was doing. His paper is in there somewhere—a piece of him, laid open. Maybe it's the one under the cat's belly, lifting and falling like an old bellows.

She twirls herself back onto the couch with one leg tucked under her and lets the other hang off the edge. Her toes widen and close—a habit he's noticed before. She plants an elbow on the armrest and rests her cheek in her hand. The dress divides across her knee to the first button. A large scar that she says is from her childhood, where her father accidentally slashed her with a saber while practicing, runs across the tightly stretched skin of her knee. The healed stitches are large and clamp the line of the scar as if done by wire. They remind him of the seam on a baseball. He wants to rub them with his thumb, feel with his fingertips the hollow behind her knee.

His erection starts again. He looks for a place to sit. Books are everywhere.

She nods toward the chair closest to the couch. "Just push them to the floor."

A couple of books land with their pages open. She glances at them and back to him—that half-smile that recognizes their mutual embarrassment.

"I've been reading D.H. Lawrence. Have you ever read anything by him?"

"No." A panicky feeling hits. He glances at the snoring cat. The feeling comes back of being in a lair. That force inside him that drives him, that she hooked to pull him here, it may die in the shadows of this room. And what will be left then?

She has on her teaching look. "Well, you should try reading Lawrence. He has much to tell us about the joy of life and how to find it. In fact, he would be a good author to read in counterpoint to *The Scarlet Letter*." Her fathomless gaze rests on him. A slight smirk breaks around the edges of her mouth and eyes. "You know, the book you did your paper on."

"Yeah, I know."

She slides the corner of one of the books from under a paw of the sleeping cat. The title on the front says *Women in Love*. "Here, let me read you something." He grips the arms of his chair, balances on the edge of the distance she is about to put between them. She flips backwards through a bunch of pages, pauses, and flips some more. His heart wobbles in his chest.

"Listen to this." She smiles as if she's about to hand him a present, then lowers her head to read. A strand swings loose from the frazzled bun on the back. His peter pushes harder at the front of his jeans.

> *They climbed together, at evening, up the high slope, to see the sun set. In the finely breathing, keen wind, they stood and watched the yellow sun sink in crimson and disappear.*

> *To her it was so beautiful, it was a delirium, she wanted to gather the glowing, eternal peaks to her breast, and die. He saw them, saw they were beautiful, But there arose no clamour in his breast....*

As she reads, he focuses intently on the dip between her forehead and the sharp bone of her nose. The dangling foot, with its short, wide toes, bounces unconsciously. She reaches to gather it and tucks it under her. It starts to flex back and forth across the rough fabric, making a swishy sound. The cat stretches, recurls itself, and goes back to sleep. He tries hard to catch the last of the passage—something about the woman embracing the evening and leaving the man standing there with an icy wind blowing through his heart.

She drops the book into her lap, stares at it, then fixes him in her not-quite-there look. "How does that make you feel?"

"Kind of weird, I guess."

"Hmmm... yes. It does." She lowers her head. "Did you like it?"

"Yeah." He rests his elbows on the arm of the chair and stares at the floor. "Yeah, I liked it."

"What did you like about it?"

"I don't know. The part about climbing the mountain and the sunset, I guess." He interlaces his fingers, flicks one thumb with the other.

"What about the people? Are they are in love? Do you think they'll wind up together?"

"I got no idea."

She gives him a hurt expression. "You're certainly in a rosy mood."

"I don't know *what's* happening with those people," he says. "I ain't read the rest of the book."

"Try 'haven't,'" she says. "'Haven't read.'"

She pulls a paper from under the stack the cat is sleeping on, opens it, and flips through the pages. There's a lot of red writing on the back where she's penned a long note to him. He feels light in the chest. He'd tried so hard to write that paper the way he figured she wanted him to. "Look inside," she'd said. "Find the artist within." All bullshit!

She stops turning pages near the end, folds them back on themselves, and begins to read in deep tones, certain of every sound they make.

> *I think this story is a real tragedy because Hester and Dimmesdale gave up in the end. They let other people decide their lives. That's what the A was all about. It was a brand from society. Hester wore hers where people could see and Dimmesdale hid his. At the end they had a choice: they could tell society to kiss their butts, or they could keep on trying to make everybody accept them, which wasn't going to happen. I think what they did was stupid, mainly Dimmesdale, because he was too dim to see what the choice was. So what happened was that they lost each other and society, too, because he was too chicken to stand up for what was right.*

She drops the paper into her lap and looks at him. "This story made you angry, didn't it?"

One of her favorite caricatures of him: the angry young man.

"I wadn't angry. I just thought it was stupid to let a bunch of prissy Pilgrims tell you how to live, cast spells on you, and all that."

"Was what they had done wrong?"

"It wadn't wrong enough to go around all droopy for seven years and then just give up and croak like the preacher did. It wadn't worth spending your life, walking around with a big red A on your chest."

"How about us, Richeboux. Do you think we have a scarlet letter we're trying to hide?"

So this is where it was headed from the start. He'd been wondering what she was up to. Usually she doesn't waste time—just shuts the door, leads him to the couch, and pulls him down to her. But today she's been leading him into something else. He feels trapped again.

"I don't. I don't know about you."

She turns her gaze to the window shade with its outline of light. "We all do, Richeboux. The question is what we do with them—our scarlet letters—or what we let them do to us. That tough way you talk in your paper; that don't-tread-on-me attitude, that anger is a foundation for courage." Her eyes are those of a furtive animal, one that cowers in the dark. "I envy that, Richeboux—you and Hester. You are braver than I."

He shifts in his chair, starts to cross an ankle over a knee, then drops his foot back to the floor.

"Yeah, she had guts. I'll give her that."

Her head bends toward her lap. Wisps of hair that didn't quite make it into the gathered haystack brush the back of her neck, which is taut and strong. A careless fingertip crawls beyond the dress's edge and starts a slow circling of the scar on her knee. "So, what are your scarlet letters if they don't include us?" She catches herself caressing the scar, slides the hand, palm-up, to her lap, and lifts the other arm to let it rest along the back of the couch. The dress slides over gentle hillocks of breast. It occurs to him that she has nothing on under it.

"Richeboux?" Her eyes are on him now. "How about when you hit that boy on the other team with the baseball?"

"Naw. Why would I feel guilty about that? It's part of the game."

"Because you meant to do it."

"Coach told me to."

"He told you to pitch close to him is what you told me."

"Same thing. I ain't perfect. Anyway, I quit."

"How's that different from what Dimmesdale did?"

He spins himself out of the chair and heads out through the kitchen, focusing on making it to the back door. He pauses with his hand on the knob. Behind him the apartment is so silent he can hear the cat breathing. He goes dizzy for a moment, tightens his grip on the knob. So this is it. This is how it will end, as if it never happened. He pulls the door open and starts out.

"Richeboux, darling." The words hang in the dead air of the room. A sob grabs his throat. He grits his teeth, swallows it.

"Come back, please."

He clings to the knob. He'd pull it out, lock and all, if he could. "Please."

The grip loosens. The door shuts. She is as he left her, but a sadness has seeped in that engulfs the whole room and him with it. She moves as if it takes a great effort and begins to push the books, papers, and magazines off the couch to the floor. The cat yowls, lands with a soft thump on the carpet, and trots off down the hall with his ass showing and his tail arced in the air. She looks up and pats the seat.

He's hard before he makes the distance to the couch. He folds his leg under him and faces her with one arm draped along the back of the couch. He feels wedged in his blue jeans. She takes his hand, leans toward him, and guides his palm inside the top button of her dress onto her chest, just below her clavicle.

She gasps as if his touch has made an incision. Her breathing quickens. Her eyes search his, a slight, frantic movement from right to left, piercing everything he's built around his life. "What do you feel?" she whispers.

He's barely able to manage the words. "Skin. Pulse, I reckon."

"It's life." She clears the phlegm in her throat. "It beats in you and me."

His hand will either wither or explode under the moist pressure of her palm. Her heart thumps out at him. The skin of her chest grows hot. She flicks a finger at the corners of her eyes.

"Would you rather feel that life or die like Dimmesdale and the young man in Lawrence's novel, unable to feel the blood in the sunset, feeling instead the wind cut through his clothes?"

"I don't know." He wishes he could find a mountain crag to hide in like the one she read about. The words gust out of him: "I want to be with you."

She moves his hand down her dress, slips hers away to undo the top button, then pushes again, guiding his palm down the bones of her chest to an erect nipple. It scrapes his palm like the tip of a tongue.

His hand is trembling. She reaches back with her other hand and pulls the pin from her hair. Ringlets of copper uncoil about her neck and shoulders. She leans back, unwinding her legs, and pulls him down between them to her chest and stomach. His dick becomes more hers than his. This is it. This is where the agony that leads him here turns into something very large that he does not understand. He feels lost in it, drifting aimlessly to wherever it leads. He wants to reach for her in that airy space, rip off her dress, fuck her and all her sadness, feel her warm wetness close around him.

A shudder runs over him. He buries his head in her hair, the sticky tangles of it, splayed around him over the musty arm of the sofa, and weeps in gulping sobs.

"It's O.K.," she says. She's sniffling, too. "Darling, it's O.K."

She tightens her hold. His tears flow onto her neck, across the straining veins of it, and seep through her hair onto the slick, worn fabric of the couch. Her hand slides from his back, snakes its way down his side between their stomachs to his crotch. Her fingers are the only thing moving now. But they are certain and quick. Her sharp teacher's knuckles rub his erection as she begins undoing the belt buckle to his jeans.

## Acee

Acee lies on his side on the cot in his room, adrift on the foggy
sea of half-sleep, shivering in the vague knowledge that he will wake to
a world even more chaotic than the one he just left in his dreams. And
Preacher will not be there.

There is a sense of someone else in the room. He cracks his eyes
and blinks at the light. Resa is curled on the cot Raiford used to sleep on,
not more than three feet away. Her hand props her head as she reads an
old *Look* magazine Travis brought home from the funeral parlor where
he works. A drooping raven's wing of hair hides most of her face. Below
the wide rolled cuffs of her dungarees, the muscles of her calves rest
against each other like sleeping animals.

She's used to Acee watching her while she pretends not to see.
He's not sure how that works, but there's a suspended silence about it, as
if he has arrived at the edge of a pool, its surface still and waiting. He can
dive in without making a ripple and be soothed in the cool, dark water.

He wants to say something, but faces from the shacks they visited
along the river last night peer out at him from the receding fog of sleep.
He rubs his eyes with his thumb and fingers, brings them into focus

on the slow rise of her hip, its quick drop to her pinched waist, and the strain of her breasts against the front of her halter top. But it is the hidden part he wants to see: the dark-honey cheeks; the quick sable eyes; the intelligent lips, waiting to speak.

She raises her head to glance at him, then returns to the page. "How are you doing, Baby?"

"I'm fine. How long you been here?"

"'Bout an hour."

He rolls onto his back and stares at the ceiling, wondering where his mama and Travis are, what he and Resa can get away with without being heard. The thought is like a dog slinking through a gate that should be shut, and the fact that it's open fills him with sudden guilt, perhaps even blasphemy after what has happened with Preacher and Raiford. He pushes it all away, shoves it back under the dark cover of sleep he has just thrown off.

She is so present in the room, so here in the leisure of her body and intensity of her mind that it's almost as if the night's horror didn't really happen. His mind can leap over it, back to the image of himself standing on the Red Elephant Grill stoop before Terry brought the news, thinking of her, staring in her direction over the dark treetops and into the back-lit purple sky.

She is studying him without looking—he can feel it. The invisible fingertips tracing his body for signs of grief and anger. He welcomes the feathery touch.

"Where were you last night?"

"Over at Sister May's."

Sister May is Resa's aunt, best friend, and so pudgy you can't tell where her body ends and her arms and legs begin. Resa spends her nights over there, waiting for Acee when he has to work.

"I'm sorry, Baby. I told them to tell you where I was. I didn't hear about Raiford and Preacher 'til early this morning."

There it is, out in the light: Preacher—the empty space in his chest and beyond the walls of his house, spreading through the lonely streets of the neighborhood.

"Come over here," he says.

She drops the magazine, rises from her cot in one motion, sits beside him on his, and trails the backs of her fingernails across his forehead. Her head lowers gently to his chest as if she's listening for his heartbeat.

"I'm so sorry, Acee. Preacher loved everybody. But next to Ludy, he loved you the most."

He raises a hand, lets it fall onto her back, and caresses it lightly through the thin cloth.

"I need you," he says.

"I know," she says. "I should have been here last night."

"No. I mean I really need you. I need to get inside of you, get all this other stuff off me."

She pushes herself up, leans over him on her straightened arms. His hand slips to her waist. So soft! He slides his other hand up her thigh over the rough, stretched threads of dungarees.

She stops him. "Acee, we can't. Your mama and Travis went over to Preacher's house to pay respects over an hour ago. They'll be back any minute."

"Mama and Travis get to talking and visiting, they liable to be there all day."

A quick smile lights her eyes, almost a teasing laugh. It beams out at him in spite of her pressed lips and slowly shaking head.

"Please," he says.

She sighs, turns her head to look out the window over his bed. Light through the milky glass bathes her face. Every time he sees it from a different angle, it's as if he's seeing it the first time and there are qualities there, unidentified—neither spirit nor animal—waiting patiently to be found.

"Your mama doesn't like me, Acee. What are we going to do if they catch us?" She turns from the window and looks him in the face. "Besides, I've got something I need to tell you. It's from Rosemont."

"Uh uh. Not Rosemont. I ain't gon do that now. Come on. They ain't gon catch us." He smiles, nods his head toward the window. "I been in and out that window to hide from Mama a bunch of times."

"Lord," she says, gets up slowly and unbuttons her jeans. Then once again, in one quick motion, she drops them with her panties to the floor and straddles him. Her back is straight. She holds on to the window ledge and looks down at him with eyes that not only accept his need but own it. She bends toward him, begins to move, strong and slow, over his hips.

His breath has a grave like odor, risen from the dead of sleep. He tries to hold it as he reaches beneath her to unbuckle his pants. She raises on one knee to give him room. The smooth flesh of her thighs brushes his knuckles. He wants to turn his wrists and grab two handfuls of it, open her legs, bend, and put his mouth to her, bury his face there. But Resa wants it slow and easy, the way her bow slides over the violin she studies in school. He kicks his pants to the floor and places his hands on the tops of her hips as she settles back over him. She does it carefully, working him in deep.

"Awwwwwh," she says. "Awwwwwh!" She lurches forward onto her arms, looking him in the face. A wildness rises in her as if a demon has broken loose. Her back arches. Her hips flex. The old army cot squeaks. Its feet scrape the worn pine floor. Her face sags toward him. The veins in her neck swell and throb. She begins to moan in long, aching notes. Their soft vibration fills the room.

Acee doesn't make it to the end. It's been a while, and the pull of those soft relentless hips is more than he can stand. He hangs on, feeling the slippery ache in his penis as she works over him, watching the abandoned look in her eyes. She leaves him in the end, goes off to some place of her own. She never apologizes for that, and it always brings on a moment of panic in him—that left-behind-and-alone feeling. But today it's different. Today he rises with her in weightless ecstasy to a place of openness and freedom. They hang there, suspended in the nothingness of it, as he watches her pull the last spasms of pleasure from him. And suddenly he is seeing beyond them both, the two bodies on the cot, the elevated sweet emptiness of their spirits, to something beyond that is waiting to be formed. And he thinks: if this isn't love, it's the closest to it he's ever been.

She bends forward, pressing her body against him, squeezing him between her thighs.

"Acee, oh Acee," she says. "You take me there, Baby. It's so easy. It's too easy."

He drops his arms, palms open, to the cot, and lets her hold him. It's like the scattered parts of him have been gathered back from the exploded night before. The tweet, tweet, tweet of a cardinal in the bush below the window finally comes through to him—loud, clear, insistent. Other sounds of the neighborhood rise as well—two women yelling back and forth as they walk up the street, children arguing over where to play softball. The road. That's where he and Raiford used to play it. She releases him, steps to the floor, and reaches for her panties and blue jeans.

"Acee, I've got to deliver the message from Rosemont."

"'Bout what?"

"Somebody wants to talk to you."

"Who?"

"Didn't say. Just somebody wants to talk."

It's the Raiford business, sliding like a snake through a knothole in the floor. It's tangled in everything—his love for Resa, the beauty he just felt in her, the moment of freedom it brought from the jungle of his life, filled with stalking tigers and demons.

Acee rolls his head back and forth on the pillow. "Aw naw. I don't need this."

Resa tucks in the tails of her halter top, straightens her jeans, and picks at a loose thread around the pocket. She gives it up and looks down at him. "Well, that's what he said."

"Sounds like bullshit to me."

"I can't help what it sounds like, Acee. I'm just relaying the message from Rosemont."

"How come he didn't tell me himself?"

"I don't know. Maybe he was busy. He's my uncle, Acee, and he helps me pay for college. So when he asks me to do a favor, I try to do it. He knew y'all were out last night. He hasn't got time to go all over the county, looking for you."

"Yeah, well I ain't got time to walk all the way out to his place and hang 'round there, waiting to talk to somebody I don't know."

Acee wants a cigarette, but his mama won't let him smoke in the house since Raiford almost set it on fire, smoking in bed. The ceiling comes back into focus. The wallpaper is so dirty you can't tell what color it is. There's a pee-shaded stain in one corner where Raiford threw a beer can when he was arguing with their mother. It's like someone threw a shout against the wall.

Resa sits beside him on the cot, strokes the inside of his wrist with the tip of her finger as if searching for a soft place to stick the needle in.

"You know what it's about. Somebody knows where Raiford is. He's trying to get a message to you."

"It's that white woman ain't it?"

"Rosemont didn't say."

"It's her. She the only one knows where Raiford is."

"How you know that?"

"I just know."

The softball game has started in the gravel road in front of the house. Shouts from the children drift through the thin walls. "Say hey, man! Say, hey. Put it in there. He can't hit nothing."

Raiford used to pitch to him out in that same road—high looping pitches that floated in toward his swinging bat with Jackie Robinson's name written on it. It was the only bat they had in the whole neighborhood. Raiford had stolen it from somewhere—white boys, he said—but Acee suspects it was from colored. What would white boys be doing with a Jackie Robinson bat?

Resa's hands grip the edge of the cot. She slides one bare foot up and back on the floor. "That white girl he lives with is probably the one that set him up."

"Are you mad about her or worried about him?"

She jerks her head toward him, eyes flashing a razor's edge of anger.

"Shut up, Acee."

He encircles her wrist with his thumb and fingers, rubs across the taut tendon with his thumb.

"Naw, she wouldn't do that. They hate her much as they hate him."

"She's white," says Resa.

"Yeah, she's white. That's got a lot of people upset, including you, Mama, and Deputy Starnes."

She twists toward him, lowers her body onto his, works her hands beneath his back until her fingers meet at his spine. The soft mounds of her breasts spread like yeasted dough over his chest. Her head nestles under his chin. Soft, moist breaths puff his neck.

"You can't save Raiford," she whispers. "Nobody can save Raiford but himself."

This is the part he dreads—lingering evidence of the deep feelings she had for Raiford, her matter-of-fact certainty that she knows Raiford better than he does and can tell him what he needs to know.

She raises onto an elbow, runs a fingertip down the bridge of his nose to his cheek, then traces the line of his jaw as if she's imprinting the message in his brain.

"Only Raiford," she says. "And it may be even too late for that."

He brushes the wing of hair back from her temple.

"I got to try," he says. "Mama and Travis are looking at me like it's all my fault."

"You didn't shoot that policeman."

The shouts of the children playing baseball have gotten louder, busier, an argument over whether someone was safe or out.

"No," he says. "Would I—if it had been me instead of him?"

"You don't have to worry about that. You didn't, he did. And what's more, he got himself in the place where he had to." She raises up further to look out the window toward the kids.

"So, what are you going to do?" she says.

"Going to Rosemont's I reckon."

She pushes herself off of him, stands with one foot on the floor and her knee on the edge of the bed. The crotch of her jeans is wet with the dark stains of their love-making.

"I got to go home and change," she says.

An even more distant look has come to her face. He reaches toward her, lets his fingertips stroke the back of her thigh and behind her knee. A tremble runs in the flesh of her leg.

"You don't have to go," she says.

"How 'bout that thing Preacher used to say, 'bout being your brother's keeper?"

"Acee, look at me. Preacher is dead. Cracker white boys killed him. You got to figure this one out yourself."

She turns back toward the window. It feels to him as if she's drifted through it.

"Make something of yourself, Acee. Go to college. Learn your art. Get a trade."

The rims of her eyes hold tears. He hasn't seen her cry since her father died. He reaches for her hand.

"What about me and you?"

Her gaze falls back on him. "Acee, what do you think I'm talking about?"

# Richeboux

Richeboux rides shotgun as Andre follows the gravel road leading to the driveway to Ellis's Uncle Woodrow's farm. The Ford's front end shimmies. The three remaining windows are down to air out the beer smell from their ride the night before. A rattle from where they jumped the culvert in Cherrytown registers every dip and bump in the road.

Richeboux fingers the radio. Hard to pick up the good Birmingham stations out here in the county. "Ronnie coming?"

"Bringing his own car. Ellis and Jamie went to Birmingham for something. Might be late."

"Whose gun is Ronnie gon borrow this time? He can't shoot for shit."

Ellis's Uncle Woodrow lets them come to his rag-tag farm to kill hawks and crows. "Kill all you want," he says. "Hate 'em worse'n niggers." Woodrow's nearly seventy, missing half a leg from WW I, and bad to drink. Spends most of his time sleeping it off on a pallet on his back porch. He hates colored people even though he used to be common-law married to one 'til she got fed up with him beating her, cut him across his chest and down his arm with a butcher knife, and disappeared with their baby somewhere over the Georgia line.

Richeboux and Andre pass the house of Woodrow's closest neighbor—old man Heck Chittum, a colored farmer and preacher, and the daddy of Woodrow's former wife. A stack of tin cans sits in his front yard a good twenty-feet-high. Richeboux's mom showed him a story about old man Chittum and his cans in the paper a few months back. Been picking them up along roadsides for over twenty years. Say's he's saving them for his old age. The paper said he's already over a hundred, but you can never tell with colored people.

"Make nice target practice," says Andre.

Richeboux looks back as they pass. Old man Chittum is in his side yard, chopping tomatoes and peas—a short, shriveled man whose skin looks like the outside of a cured ham. He rises from his work, leans on his hoe handle, and watches them pass. A big sign next to the pile of cans reads: "Mount Ararat is Where it's at: Build Your Mountain for the Coming Flood." Andre leans across Richeboux and sticks a middle finger out the window. "Fuck you and the flood, too." He overshoots the turn. They slide sideways into Woodrow's driveway, throwing dirt and gravel until Andre downshifts to second and gets traction.

Richeboux gets a shabby feeling every time he steps onto Woodrow's place. It's like a faded photograph from the Depression—overgrown fields, outbuildings collapsing under masses of honeysuckle and Virginia creeper, a ramshackle shotgun house with one side caved in from a giant pine that fell in a storm and never got moved. A three-legged stool and worn-out car seat provide the porch furniture. What's left of the tin roof is streaked with rust. And the moldy stench from the outhouse around back clings to everything.

Richeboux gets out of the car, lifts the twelve-gauge Fox Sterlingworth from the back seat, and breaks it open to check the twin chambers. He's had that drilled into him by his father since his grandfather gave him the gun on his twelfth birthday. It's the only thing his grandfather ever gave him, but it's a lot. "One of the finest shotguns ever made," his daddy said. "Wonder how come he decided to give it to you?"

But the main reason Richeboux breaks the shotgun is that he likes to handle it—the tapered walnut grip; the slip of metal on metal as the gun hinges in his hand; the soft click of the shell ejectors; the scent of powder and gun oil from the deep hollows of the barrels, and that final, tight "Snap!" when he clicks it shut. Except for a baseball, autographed by his coach and the team after he pitched a shutout against Shades Valley as a sophomore, that shotgun is the only property he owns. Every time he opens and closes it, it becomes a little more his.

Andre hauls a Browning automatic from his trunk, jams two handfuls of shells in his pockets. He and Richeboux drift over to a side of the yard under two red oaks with a sway-back shelf nailed between them. Woodrow uses it as an outdoor wash stand. A worn sliver of Octagon soap is stuck to a slimy, whitish end of the plank. The chipped enamel pan he uses to bathe from is on the ground. Richeboux can imagine the old fart standing there with his overalls down to his knees, washing his chest and belly and scrubbing his private parts with one of the rags hanging from the other end of the plank. It doesn't do much good. Woodrow smells like rancid fat. Snuff runs down his chin. Long tufts of gray hair shoot from his ears and armpits. He doesn't even wear underwear in the summer time.

Andre fiddles with his gun, opening and shutting it, blowing lint from the chamber. Richeboux rests his rear against the edge of the bench, shakes out a Marlboro, and lights it. Andre waves the smoke away.

"How come you took up cigs again? If you hadn't quit the team, you might have gone to the Dodgers or Yankees or somewhere."

Richeboux points the Sterlingworth at an imaginary bird. "You my daddy, now?"

Andre gives him a shove. "Naw. I'm your buddy."

They start sighting and clicking triggers at targets about the yard—sleeping hounds, scrawny cats, the diseased-looking chickens, pecking at each other's sores. The rusting carcass of an old steam-driven, steel-treaded tractor sits half in the field and half in the yard. Richeboux drops the barrels of his shotgun when his sights hit it. Like shooting an antique. He starts over, tracking across the front porch to the old washing machine on the ground under the roof drip.

Ronnie pulls into the yard in the car his father lets him drive only in the daytime—a red '59 Buick with chrome-trimmed, rocket-like tail fins that stick out at forty-five degrees. Ronnie swears they actually lift the car off the ground if you get above 100 mph, which Richeboux is pretty sure Ronnie has never done.

Ronnie gets out without shutting the door, leans on the top of the Buick and begins tapping the ignition key on the enameled roof. He's got on his shit-eating grin, that I-know-something-you-don't look. Richeboux can never figure whether it's part of Ronnie's worm thing—a come-on to make them want him in the group—or a smirk at them for keeping him on the outside.

"That colored man died," he says.

Andre lowers his bead a notch, keeps one eye on Ronnie and the tapping key. "What colored man?"

"The one Richeboux hit with the egg. He died."

Andre lets the shotgun hang at the ends of his arms, glances at Richeboux, then back to Ronnie. Richeboux slackens his grip on the Sterlingworth, takes the cigarette from his lips, and flips it into the yard. A couple of chickens dart toward it as soon as it hits the ground.

"How do you know?" says Andre.

"Our maid was supposed to come to work today because my grandmother's coming to visit. But she couldn't come because he was her preacher and she's in some ladies' group at her church. She had to help with his body and stuff."

Richeboux turns, presses his thighs into the edge of Woodrow's washboard, and stares across a field, asprout in sweet gum and pine saplings. The pine tops gleam in the sun.

Andre raises his gun toward the sky again and clicks the trigger.

"Pow!" he says and lowers the gun. "That don't mean nothing. People die all the time."

Richeboux can feel Ronnie's eyes on his back, hears the squeak of excitement in his voice. "No. It's the same guy. She said he died in the road last night—the one we were on. She said some boys tried to run over him."

Andre lowers his gun again. "That's a bunch of crap. We didn't try to run over him. He was chasing us."

An odor of Octagon soap rises from the washboard, a pukey smell that clings to Richeboux's throat as if it was a bathtub drain. He tightens his hold on the grip of the Sterlingworth, clicks the safety on and off with his thumb, glances toward the path that leads around back of Woodrow's shack. The bastard is probably back there now, asleep on his pallet, a half-full bottle within reach. A dead colored man wouldn't mean shit to him. "Hell, who cares! Here, boys, take a little swig before the big hunt. It'll help your aim."

He turns to face Ronnie. The key has stopped tapping and rests point-down on the roof. There is no grin now but in his eyes that hopeful look that he and Richeboux are secret buddies, bound by an instinct the others don't have: *we knew something like this would happen.*

Richeboux's voice comes out too loud. "Lots of people walk that road. Could of been anybody."

"Damn right," says Andre. "Anybody! Center of Cherrytown. Folks are all over the place. I pass a dozen of 'em every time we go to Uncle Rose's for beer."

Ronnie shrugs, shuts the door to the Buick, walks over to Andre's open trunk.

"You got my gun?"

"Your gun?" says Andre. "Sure, Ronnie. Help yourself to *your* gun."

Ronnie takes an ancient-looking single-barrel from Andre's trunk, and joins them at the wash bench. He fiddles with the gun until Andre reaches over and flips the lever that breaks it open.

"I betcha it was him," Ronnie says. "It all adds up."

Richeboux spits into the dirt yard. *Why don't you shut the fuck up, you know-it-all Yankee.* "Nothing adds up!"

"Yeah," says Andre. "Go back to grammar school, Worm Man. You don't die from getting hit by an egg."

Andre moves down the bench, closer to Richeboux. An old comfort comes with him. When they were buddies in the first grade, they swapped spend-the-nights, slept together in the warmth of each other's bodies.

Ronnie leans the old shotgun against the bench, stuffs his hands in his jeans pockets. "I never threw one."

"Right," says Andre. "You were too chickenshit as usual."

"You didn't either, Fireball."

"I was driving, Ronnie."

Richeboux pushes away from the bench and walks past Ronnie to Andre's car. He reaches in the front window, grabs a box of Remington number six shells off the seat, and sets it on the roof. He breaks the Sterlingworth and shoves in two shells, clicks on the safety, and jams ten more of the plastic and brass shells into his jeans. The shells make a tight wedge in his pocket, like this morning at Mrs. Kusinski's when she pulled him down to her on the couch: the unbuttoned dress sliding from her thighs as he settled between them; her fingers undoing his belt, groping for him; that feeling of drifting into their nowhere land, a lost, foggy heath, with her standing on one side and him kneeling on the other.

He gives his head a quick shake and starts toward the path leading to the rear of Woodrow's shack. Andre falls in behind.

"Maybe we oughta wait for Ellis," says Ronnie. "It's his uncle."

Richeboux and Andre keep walking.

Ronnie crams shells into his jeans, spilling half of them on the ground. "Hey, wait for me."

Behind them Ellis's old Chevy rattles into the yard. It was all black until Ellis brush-painted the fenders yellow. The swipes of the brush are still visible. Andre and Richeboux turn with their guns under their arms and watch Ellis crank open the door to get out of the car. Ronnie catches up to them and stands with the single-barrel cradled in his arms like a dead body he wishes he could drop.

Ellis shuts the door and goes into the back seat for his shotgun, mumbling something about Jamie's having gone to Bessemer to get dynamite. "Bobby told us about a man up there who'll sell us some."

Bobby is Ellis's thirty-year-old half-brother who lives out on the Tombigbee River below Demopolis, cruising timber and running trot lines. Ellis got drunk one night and bragged that Bobby was a member of the Klan.

Richeboux braces himself into a spread-eagled stance. The voice in his head straight-lines to a hum. He looks about at the pecked-bald yard, rotting buildings and machinery, the whole crumbling place. He's got that urge again—to get out of here, away from his so-called buddies, away from this stinking place with its nervous, squawking chickens.

"What the hell's Einstein gonna do with dynamite?" says Andre.

Ellis stuffs shells into the feed of his twelve-gauge pump. There's a reddened cheek on one side of his face and a touch of black eye on the other where Andre's fists landed last night.

"Hell, it's graduation. We gotta do something. Jamie wants us to meet him at the Red Elephant tonight. We can figure it out." He pumps the barrel grip to seat the first shell. "Could be he's got his eye on old man Chittum's pile of cans up the road." He turns and grins. The black eye is a little yellow, as if it is starting to rot. "Make one hell of a show." He kicks the car's rear door shut and starts toward them to catch up. "Let's go kill some crows."

Ronnie takes a step back to let Ellis pass. "The guy we hit last night died."

Ellis turns. "What guy—the one on the road?"

"Yeah, the one Richeboux threw the egg at."

"Naw, he didn't," says Andre. "Ronnie's full of it."

Ellis gets that little shake in his pupils that comes when he's on the trail of something. Richeboux throws the Sterlingworth's barrel onto his shoulder, hangs his wrist across the stock, and turns to resume his walk toward the field behind the house. Find some crows—point, aim, and blast away, watch the bastards fall.

"Damn," says Ellis. He reaches out, gives Richeboux's shoulder a shove that rocks him off his stride. "Fuckin'-A, Chief!"

Richeboux shoves back. "Don't push me, Ellis."

Ellis ignores the shove. "Hell, I bet it *was* him. He was running his ass off. Probably had a heart attack right there in that road. Slambam, another one down!" He pauses and stares at Richeboux.

Sinews tighten in Richeboux's wrists. One good poke at that fat nose would drop Ellis like a sack of shit.

Ellis grins and turns to look at his uncle's shack. "Old Woodrow's gon love this." He shoulders his gun and starts toward the back porch. Andre shoots a glance at Richeboux and does the same.

Ronnie's got the single-shot hanging in front of him, bumping it with his thighs as he rocks back and forth. "Maybe we ought not to be spreading this around."

Ellis yells back over his shoulder, "You're the one spreading it, Worm Man."

Ronnie glances at Richeboux. "You coming?"

"Yeah. In a minute."

He stands with the shotgun on his shoulder and watches Ronnie follow the others. His chest is tight. He sucks in a breath but can't make it go as deep as he needs it to. It was the same way at the state play-offs the night he hit the batter—everyone rushing toward the fallen boy: umpires, parents, the Indian Chief mascot with his tomahawk and mane of feathers, even his own coach. Richeboux's teammates had walked in from the bases and outfield like robots, staring past him at the lump of arms, socks, and uniform, crumpled at home plate. He stood there on the mound, exposed, clumsy, unable to move. The stadium lights seemed to brighten around him, turn the grass on the field from green to white. The rub of the seams from the ball he'd just thrown tingled on his fingers.

He forces himself to look toward the far end of the field, lined by a dark stand of oaks and pines. Beyond the trees the early summer sky seems to stretch forever—over the place where he is standing, over the rolling fields and pine bottoms between him and Tuscaloosa, over the shacks and houses along that empty street in Cherrytown. The white shirt and strong back, face down in dust and gravel. The whole scene of the night before has vanished into time, but it's still here. He drops his gaze to the polished stock of the Sterlingworth, feels the gun's leaden perfection hanging at the ends of his arms.

The voices of the others drift from over by Woodrow's back porch, trying to wake the old man. Woodrow mumbling, reaching for his bottle; Ellis, snatching it away. "Naw! Come on Woodrow. We got something to tell you. You ain't gon believe it."

The familiar caw! caw! caw! comes from overheard. Richeboux looks up. A band of crows is attacking a red-tailed hawk. The hawk circles slowly, unable to fend off the swooping crows. His screams peal over the field, a desperate sound, scratching the tin sky. Richeboux holds the gun in both hands, feels his legs start to steady themselves, his body come back. His grip on the Sterlingworth is stronger. The tip of his finger rests on the trigger guard. He could do it—swing the stock, fit it to his shoulder, aim, and shoot—one perfectly coordinated motion. Fast as he used to zoom a baseball. And whatever—crow, hawk, dove, quail—is a goner, dropping in that dead half-arc from the sky. He's the best shot of them all by far, and the fastest. He can hit a bird in full flight at seventy-five yards. He can hit anything.

# Resa Robinson

Raiford knows how to get to a woman. It's the way he looks and the way it works on you—soft, quiet eyes; sleepy lids; dark, mysterious face biding its time for you to make the first move, which you know has already been made. And he has that breathy voice, like rain steaming off a hot pavement, like he's whispered a secret to you and is about to tell you an even deeper one. And both of them are about you. It sets you at ease at first—that is, in a nervous kinda way. Then that voice starts to crawl on you. And the eyes do, too. The coals behind them start to glow. And before you know it, the heat from those coals is in you. And there's only one way to put it out.

'Course I wasn't but seventeen when it started, but I was old enough to know better. I'd been around boys before. I'd heard all my life from Mama what messing with boys could do to you. All that talk she stuck on me slid right off the wall the minute I got around Raiford, along with every stitch I had on. It was like I'd never heard a word of it.

Preacher Gryce preached a sermon once about getting what you want and how, lots of times, it's more than you bargain for. That's the way it was with Raiford. He ate up my life. I wasn't thinking about school or college or saving money for it. I was just thinking about Raiford and giving him what he wanted. Mama despised him. She said he was a "back-breaker," which I think means he'd break a woman's back in bed and then leave her hanging the rest of the day. That's what it felt like, like he'd sexed all the want out of me and left me hanging, still wanting more. Some girls think that's the way it's supposed to be. But after he moved out to that trailer in Taylorsville and started the organizing, I got hold of myself. It all came down the day I caught him and that white woman sneaking in the back of Rosemont's store, Raiford following her up the steps, clocking the movement of her skinny ass. I waited for him that night in the out-back room at Aunt May's house we used to make out in. He walked in already taking his shirt off, like it was business as usual. Threw it in the corner, started for the bed, and then saw I wasn't on it.

"I'm over here," I said.

He turned and looked at me. This was before he let his hair grow to that afro, and he could still get that little-boy look on his face.

"What's a-matter with you?" he said.

"You messing with her and come around here, trying to mess with me?"

"Messing with who?"

"You know *who*—that bony white bitch, older than my mama."

"Mess with who I want to."

No more little boy look then—jaw set, eyes pinning me to the wall. He shook his head and got on his knees to pull the hat box he kept his extra clothes in out from under the bed.

I pushed myself off the wall and stood over him. "Mess with who you want to, you ain't touching me again."

The hat box was hung on the bedsprings, but he finally pulled it out, squatted on his haunches, and started to untie the string holding the lid on. Of course the way he was going at it, he yanked it into a knot.

I should have known better, but something in me wouldn't stop. I gave him a shove with my foot that rolled him on his back.

"You hear me?" I said. "You turned white."

He came off the floor with the back of his hand and knocked me against the wall so hard I didn't know whether the wall would break or me. I saw stars for a second, then slid down to the floor and sat there with my legs splayed out. By the time I got my senses back, he was standing over me with his fist balled. It was like a wild animal had broken loose. I started to get up, but I knew he wouldn't help me. So I just sat there bent forward with my hands holding my ankles, lips dripping blood on the floor.

"Get out," I said. "And don't come back."

He didn't even take the hat box.

"Good gittin'," said Mama. "You done saved yourself a lot of misery." And I knew she was right, but that part of me that wouldn't listen, not even to my own voice, wanted Raiford back, misery and all.

Anyway, seeing Raiford and the white woman go into Rosemont's that day told me something about Rosemont as well: he is mixed up in whatever it is they are up to. White women don't go to Rosemont's. No woman if they're worth a damn. Mama asked Rosemont once what he did with all that money he makes selling beer to white boys. He said he used it to pay off the police and gave the rest to the NAACP. He keeps a lot of it, too, because he had plenty to help send me to college. But that NAACP thing surprised me—doesn't sound like Rosemont. So I wonder: has he really started trying to help his race or has he got something else up his sleeve?

Rosemont wasn't studying about the NAACP when he was young. He was wild, had a way with women like Raiford does. When I was little, he did some time in the penitentiary in Montgomery for killing a man. He's tall, with arms and wrists he can snap like a whip. And he'd fight quick as you could spit. That's how he lost those fingers on his left hand, cut off down to the second joint. Trying to hold a knife blade a man was going to cut him with. "What did you grab the blade for?" I said. "'Cause," Rosemont said, "he had hold of the other end." Rosemont won that house where he runs the store now in a three-day poker game over at Bailey Bridewell's garage—well, junkyard is more like it. Of course, what Mama calls Rosemont's store is really not a store. It's a liquor house pure and simple is what it is.

Which is why, before we walked down here today to meet with Rosemont and the white woman, Acee had never been here. It's not that he dislikes Rosemont. He's just not the type to spend his hard-earned money on liquor and gambling. Acee's Preacher's man. Reverend Gryce pretty much took over raising him after Delentha left and Raiford moved on to other things. Built Acee's first bicycle from parts of his children's bikes who'd left home. Organized a Boy Scout troop for Acee and his friends called the Cherrytown Troopers because the white Boy Scout Council, or whatever it's called, wouldn't let them in.

So I'm not surprised when Acee comes to a dead stop at the bottom of Rosemont's front steps and looks up them at the screen door from the porch to the main room like it's the door to Hell. Then he looks back at me—a sort of pleading look, like if I tell him one more time he doesn't have to go in to that meeting, he might finally listen.

I let go his hand. "Acee?"

"Yeah?"

"You wouldn't turn around now if I begged you to."

"Naw," he says and looks back at the screen door.

It's like watching a hound dog caught in a thunderstorm. Back bent, head bent, sliding his hand up the rail, raising his feet to the next step like he wants to kick out the riser. He gives me one last look and a half-smile before he shuts the screen door carefully behind him, like maybe no one will notice he's there.

I wait around a minute to be sure he doesn't come storming back out. The sun is hot as a cookstove, and the air feels stuffy under the big oak trees in Rosemont's front yard. I head on around back to find a shady spot on the stoop where Rosemont does most of his selling beer and liquor to folks who're not supposed to be buying it, like the Police and white boys. It's also next to the back shed room where Rosemont talks business, and I figure that's where Acee's meeting with Rosemont and the white woman will be. Maybe I can hear some of it through the wall.

The dirt parking lot behind the store is quiet except for the cry of a circling hawk above the treetops that rim the weeded field beyond the lot. It's one of those hawks that sounds like a puppy crying.

I take a seat on the stoop, bounce my foot, tapping my heel against the wood support post, and try to imagine Acee sitting there in that room and how caught he will be—in the brother's-keeper thing and in the pull-and-tug between Rosemont and Preacher. And then there's that other thing about Raiford and me, sitting like a ghost in a tree, which has got me to feeling kinda guilty.

I let my heel tap one more time against the post. "And then there's me"—I whisper.

The hawk's crying drifts beyond the trees, and my mind goes with it, swirling with thoughts about me and Acee. There's a fire burning behind Acee's eyes, just like there's one behind Raiford's. But Acee's fire burns low, draws you in like a warm stove draws you into a room in winter. You want to slip in through those eyes without him knowing and cozy up to it. And the thing is, while Acee knows that flame is there, he doesn't understand what makes it burn. Which is another reason he's caught. And that's the one I can help him with.

## Rosemont Greene

I knew Acee'd be coming when I sent word, even if he don't like coming here. Acee's steady. He ain't like Raiford. He does what he thinks he's got to do. Been that way all his life. I knew their daddy, Delentha Waites. Delentha more like Raiford, always mad about something. And look like, the older he got, the worse it got, 'til finally he shot a man dead right there on Cherry Street in front of Allen's store, arguing over who owned a spare tire—and not a line of tread on it. He hit the road after that. Left Cissy, both them boys, and that baby girl, sick and near 'bout dead. Ain't nobody seen Delentha 'round here since.

I got the white woman, Miss Leone, setting in the back room, waiting. Acee knows she's here, he's less likely to come. And then, I ain't sure 'bout Resa. If she comes with him and sees that white woman, she's liable to jerk Acee out of here. I reckon it's all got to do with that old business 'tween Resa and Raiford, but whatever it is, I ain't got time to mess with it.

Acee comes through the door with that slow, sure-footed gait of his, turns and guides the screen door quietly back into place. Now who in the world but Acee Waites don't let a screen door slam behind him? Everything Acee does is like that: smooth and careful, like he's building something ain't never been built before and he's gon get it just right. His mama's got a picture of him and Raiford when Raiford was 'bout ten and Acee seven. Raiford's got that beaming face, arms slack at his sides, happy to be in the picture. Acee's hanging back, studying the camera. Hands in his pockets, hiding them nimble fingers, always itching to reach for something. Eyes cast halfway to the ground. Mind off in another world, trying to figure what his fingers want to reach for.

He sticks his hands in his *rear* pockets this time and stands there just inside the door, glancing about the tables and dance floor. Like his friend, the preacher, I reckon—looking for the Devil. Ain't no Devil this morning. Preacher must have scared him out last night.

I'm at my usual place at the end of the bar, counting up how much liquor we got, how much beer. We ain't got it, I send Marcus to that old root cellar where I keep it hid, 'cross the field behind the house. Some of Starnes's boys in here Thursday morning, took over five cases for a party they're having down on the river. Almost left me short. They got their share for the month now. I ain't paying 'em no more, I don't care what Starnes says. Acts like he owns this place. Come in here this morning with a bunch of 'em, waving a shotgun. Got me out of bed, yelling at me 'bout where Raiford's at. "I ain't got no idea," I said. I didn't, either—leastways not then. Starnes's got a wire in him over Raiford. You could see it in his eyes. Threatened to shut me down, like that's gon put the fear of God in me. He says that 'bout once a month. Shut me down—where they gon get their free beer?

Acee sees I ain't moving, and he comes on back to where I'm at. Marcus behind the bar, cleaning and stacking glasses. Acee don't even say "Hi" to him even though they been in school together. Marcus knows what's going on. He drove the white lady over here.

I lay my pencil down, look up at Acee.

"You ready?"

"For what?" he says.

I study him a minute. He keeps looking about the room.

"I doubt you are," I say. "But come on back. We'll see."

He lowers his head and follows me down the hall to my meeting room off the back. Miss Leone is in the same chair I gave her when she come about a hour before, setting there like she ain't moved a muscle. The room I added off the back is a corner room. It ain't got but one window, and I generally keep it covered. What little light is left, laying 'cross her face so you can see the shadows and angles in it. It's one of them sharp, bony faces, like if she moved it too fast, she could cut you with it. Hair blacker than mine. It's chopped and cut, too. But you talk to her for a while, and you don't see none of that. 'Cause smack in the middle of her forehead—you could put your finger on the spot—is where her brains are at. And they're the sharpest thing she's got.

She follows Acee with her eyes when he comes in, the same way she stares at me, like she's chasing the thoughts in your mind. I don't like nobody watching me like that. She don't say nothing. Just sits there with her hands folded in her lap, talking to herself maybe, or talking to the Lord. But she don't seem like the Lord type.

"This Miss Leone," I say. She gives that half-smile. Best she can do, I reckon. Acee sets down on the cot I keep for Bailey Bridewell's sleepovers. Lowers himself real slow like he's keeping himself ready to jump up and leave.

Miss Leone holds out her hand. "Acee, I'm Diana." She has a raspy voice, 'bout half whisper like her voice is wore out. Marcus says she hisses like a possum in a trap, but it's more like a flour mill to me, like everything she says is being sifted.

When Acee don't take her hand, she lets it drop.

"I've come from Raiford."

Acee is bent forward with his elbows on his knees, eyes studying the floor. "Where's he at?"

"He's alive, which is a miracle. He needs your help."

Acee's head drops half a foot.

She's sets up straight, hands gripping the side of the chair, like if he tries to leave she can cut him off.

"Acee, can you help him?"

Acee rests back on his elbows on the cot and splays his feet out. The back of his head bumps the wall. "What's he want?"

"He *needs* you to get him a car."

"Where'm I gon get a car?"

She looks up at me. "Raiford was hoping Uncle Rose could help with that."

Have mercy! Why in the world is Raiford messing with a skinny, high-and-mighty bitch like this? I bend and give her a hard squint. "How come you wait 'til now to ask me that? I ain't running a car lot."

"Raiford said you had an extra one or two you rent sometimes." She turns back to Acee, calm as you please. "You could drive it."

Acee glances up at me like I'm the one brought in the crazy woman. "Drive where?"

"New York. If you can get Raiford up there to me, I can take care of him. He'll never get a fair trial down here with these murderers and cracker-heads..." She starts to go on, but then stops herself. Looks up at me and back to Acee. Ain't no doubt about it—I can see it in her eyes: she's wound up over Raiford. And she ain't afraid to push where she got to push to help him, either.

"How old are you, Miss Diana?" I say.

"Please don't call me *Miss* Diana. I'm thirty-seven. What difference does it make?"

I hear the back screen door open and footsteps pass us, headed up the hall toward the front room. I crack the door open to check. It's a white boy I seen before, coming for beer. Tall, nervous-looking. Got a chip on his shoulder. I step out in the hall, yell to Marcus.

"Get him what he needs, and get him out of here. Starnes's all over the place."

"Yassuh," says Marcus.

The white boy freezes right there in the hall like he don't know what to do.

I shut the door and lock it. "Customer," I say. "One of those dumb-ass 'cracker-heads' you talking about." I shake out a couple of my made-up roll-your-owns and offer them to her and Acee. They shake they heads. She probably don't approve of smoking. Looks like she don't approve much of anything. I light up anyway. Her knuckles done got white gripping the edge of her seat.

"You'll help, won't you?"

I smoke slow and think slow. That's what keeps me out of trouble.

She nods at Acee. "He's your brother," and then at me, "and your friend. You're the only chance he's got." Like she gon claw her way into my skull to make me say it.

"When he got to have it?"

"Now. The police are everywhere. They've got bloodhounds. I heard them before daylight this morning." She gives a little shudder. The hardness in her face starts to crack. For a minute I think she's 'bout to cry.

Acee's looking at the floor, twisting his fists into the bed.

"Acee?" She's still in that whisper, but it's more pleading this time.

He runs his tongue over his bottom lip, like he has to wet it to talk. "I'll drive him, if Rosemont gets the car."

I expect her to least say thank you, but she just lets her shoulders sag and bows her head.

"Where you want the car?" I say.

She wipes away a tear.

"I don't know. We'll get word to you by early morning. Raiford's moving around. We'll find the best place to meet. Raiford says it's best to leave at early dawn toward the end of the deputies' night shift. They're tired and marking time 'til the next shift takes over."

Her eyes dart back and forth between Acee and me like she's finally corralled us into the deal and is shifting about to keep us from jumping the fence. I think she's mostly worried 'bout Acee. She knows something's bothering him, something between him and Raiford. She's on that like a fox on a scent.

Acee sets up and looks her in the eyes for the first time. "He shoot that police officer?"

She leans forward with her elbows on her knees like a man and looks him dead in the face. "He didn't have a choice. Two weeks ago they broke in his trailer and tore it up, searching for God knows what. They've left him messages in the mailbox threatening his life, thrown dead cats in the yard. They even follow me when I go to the store. The night this happened, they smashed the lock and kicked the door open. No knock, no nothing." She draws a breath and presses her lips together. "Bastards!"

She better's than any lawyer I ever had. I shake the ash off my cigarette and rub it out against the sole of my shoe. "Was you there?"

She whirls like I just threw a brick. "I never slept there. Ever."

Acee gives a long sigh and looks up at me. "You gon get the car?"

"I'll have it by midnight," I say. "It needs tires and a water pump. I'll get Bailey Bridewell over here working on it 'fore he starts his Saturday night drunk."

Acee pushes himself off the bed. His shadow falls 'cross her face from the light 'round the window cover. "Tell him I'll be there. I'll be where he says."

"We'll get you word through Rosemont."

She stands up proud and quick and sticks out her hand again to Acee. The ends of her hair sway 'cross her earlobe, which has a brass earring dangling from it with some kind of Jap or Chinese writing. A tip of her hair sticks at the corner of her mouth. I think of her as a woman for the first time, and it grabs something in me. I catch her eye, and I can see she knows all about it.

"Thank you," she says.

Acee just stands there. She reaches and takes his hand.

He lets her hold it a minute, then pulls it away and shoves past me, out the door. I glance back at her.

"I'll be back. I'm gon make sure it's clear for Marcus to take you where you need to go. In the meantime keep this door locked. Never know who might come down here."

She nods, looks tired all of a sudden, like she's done put in a hard day.

I follow Acee down the hall toward the back door. Soon as we're out of earshot of Miss Leone, I take hold of his arm, hand him a cigarette. He lights mine and his.

"You ain't got to do it," I say.

He clicks the lighter shut, talks while he'd blowing smoke. "Yeah, I do."

"Get somebody else. Let Terry go. He's always bragging 'bout how good he can drive."

Acee shakes his head. "Terry ain't got sense enough to find Raiford in daylight."

"I can hire somebody," I say.

"Naw," says Acee. "I got to do it."

I hear Resa's voice out near the loading stoop talking to somebody sounds like a white woman, jabbering away. I don't allow no white women down here. Leads to all kind of trouble.

I keep Acee behind me, ease up to the back screen door. It's a white girl 'bout Resa's age. The white boy who came in to buy the beer is there too, leaning on their car.

Acee steps up to the door. "That's Bo," he says.

"Bo?"

"Yeah," says Acee. "Used to know him."

"Well tell him to take that gal and get on out of here. Don't, I'm gon run 'em off."

# Mem Cohane

"Omigosh," I say to Richeboux, as soon as we pull into Uncle Rose's back lot. "That's her, Resa Robinson the colored girl I met at Y Camp in D.C."

"Shit," he says and gives me another you-better-stay-in-the-car-like-you-promised look. He turns the car toward a space at the far end of the lot like he doesn't want to be too close to Resa or Uncle Rose's store.

But I'm not putting up with that crap now that Resa's here. I'm out of the car yelling to her before it even stops, which of course ticks him off. But what else is new? I've been after him since we first started dating to take me to Uncle Rose's. He and Jamie and the rest of them are always whispering about it, but mainly it's what the adults say—parents, teachers, even our minister—that it's evil and filthy, like if you go down there, you'll catch a disease. Which can only mean one thing: people are having fun.

Richeboux jumps out of the car and yells, "Hey!" But by then I'm giving Resa a big hug, which I think kinda caught her by surprise.

We were like sisters at Y Camp. It was a special camp for kids from all over the country who had been chosen because of our high "social skills"—at least so they said—but it was really to get white and colored together and teach us to get along, which being high in social skills, most of us already knew. I couldn't believe it when I learned she was from Tuscaloosa. I mean, here was this smart-looking colored girl and we'd been going to high school four blocks from each other and never met.

I liked her right off. She had a sassy way about her that reminded me of me. I liked her name, too: Resa Robinson—like a tennis star. She was suspicious at first, but she finally agreed we could room together after I badgered the head counselor into letting us switch. We'd sit cross-legged on the bed and talk about school and camp stuff, and I kept trying to wheedle out of her what it was like—I mean, her being colored and me white. There were some silences over that where she just sat and picked at the bedspread. So I'd back off and start over with the easy subjects. We liked some of the same music, mostly colored singers like Sam Cooke and The Shirelles. She didn't like Johnny Mathis, who she said was mostly white. She said Elvis was O.K., but she wouldn't be caught dead with one of his records. I finally worked up to boys and asked her if colored boys made out and kissed like white ones. She got off the bed, stuck her fists on her hips, and looked at me. "How would I know! I never kissed a white boy and don't plan to."

Well, that showed me one difference between us, because I didn't feel that way about colored boys. I mean, why go all the way to Y Camp, three-hundred miles from home and not try something new? So, I finally talked her into introducing me to two colored brothers from Kansas City, Lamont and Trenton Olenhatch. They were nice but shy, and Resa said if I wanted to learn how colored boys kissed, I was probably wasting my time with them. But I kept after her, and we finally teamed up with them at the last night's dance. Toward the end, Lamont and I sort of paired off to go our own way. He was the darker one in color and personality. Like there was something smoldering in him he hadn't quite figured out—or maybe he had and didn't want you to see.

Anyway, unlike his stuck-up brother, he at least kissed back. He was nervous the whole time we were making out, like a horse about to bolt. He kept glancing around even though we were in the shadows a long way from the dance hall. It took some work to get him to pay attention to what was going on. He had a scholarship to Columbia University. It's one of the places I got into when I applied last fall.

Resa and I promised we'd still be friends after we came back to Tuscaloosa, and I meant it because I really believe in integration, and how else can you get it started for the country and even the world if you don't do it yourself! We talked on the phone a couple of times, but then school started and we kind of quit. I don't think she wanted to talk anymore. It upset me a little. I thought we had made friends for life.

Anyway, what luck to find her at Uncle Rose's—a real chance to patch things up. But I see right off it's not going to be that easy. After our hug, she steps back like she's not quite sure what to do.

Richeboux saunters up with his hands in his pockets and his head turned sideways, looking at the ground. I introduce them. He grunts and nods his head.

I smile at Resa. "Mr. Congeniality."

I have to remind myself about Richeboux when we're around other people. He acts shy, but mostly he's just moody. I saw that part of him the moment he walked into homeroom our junior year. My boyfriend, Rankin Gaillard, had left for Princeton that fall, and I'd never paid much attention to Richeboux before. He skulked about the school with those long arms and loop of dirty-blond hair that he has to keep swiping back into place so he can see where he's going. The James Dean look. He wouldn't even cut it when Coach Talbert told him to—just tucked it under his cap. Maybe it was because I'd been reading *Wuthering Heights* the summer before, but seeing him swagger into homeroom that day with his head down and that lost and gloomy look on his face grabbed me. Heathcliff, trudging in off the Yorkshire moors, as if he lived in a secret place and came out of the shadows to go to school and if you messed with him, you might wish you hadn't. Which, of course, just made me want to mess with him more. I'm not talking about sex so much but the dark, brooding thing. Like leaping from a cliff in the middle of the night. And I haven't found the bottom yet—there might not even be one—but I decided that whatever was down there, I would help him out of it. I'm pretty good at that sort of thing. But it's kind of sad: he's got his mind made up to keep a chip on his shoulder about everything, including me—that and hang out with his idiot friends, who will probably wind up in some fraternity at the University, watching TV in their underwear, crawling around on all fours, and throwing up.

It's not surprising that Richeboux hangs out with them. His mother and stepfather are just pitiful. Get up, go to work, complain about colored people, watch TV, go to bed. So I *do* want to help him rise above that—expand his mind, appreciate art and stuff, meet new people whose main goal in life is not pool and pinball. But he just gets moodier if I push too hard. I think Richeboux is afraid of something back in that shadow where he lives. I'm just figuring that out.

So Richeboux goes into Uncle Rose's for the beer, and that's when Resa and I really get to talk. She asks me about Lamont. The truth is I wrote him a couple of times and he wrote back, but then Mama found out and made me stop, which irked me big-time because she and my father are always talking about how the races are equal. "If they're so equal," I said, "why can't Lamont and I be friends? He's going to the Ivy League." Mama did that thing where she bends down, looks me in the eye, and shakes her head like she's trying to shoo a bumblebee out of mine. "Honey, it's not that simple. You'll have to trust us on this one."

Bull crap.

"Lamont's fine," I say to Resa. "But I think he's found a new girlfriend in Kansas City. He and I are just friends."

"Yeah," she says. "I expect that's best."

Anyway, the more Resa and I talk, the more I notice that her mind is wandering. She keeps glancing up the back porch steps toward the door. I was about to just come out and ask her when Richeboux comes back with two cases of Colt 45 Malt Liquor, which I refuse to drink because it tastes like formaldehyde. He walks right by us, puts the beer in the trunk, and stands there with his thumbs hooked in his jeans as if I'm supposed to drop everything and just hop in the car.

"She's my friend," I say. "We're talking."

He slams the door, leans against the car with his back to us, pulls a cigarette from behind his ear—more James Dean—and lights it. I turn back to Resa.

She has her arms wrapped around her upper body, sort of hugging herself, looking across the lot toward the woods at the far end.

"Resa, what's wrong?" I say.

"My preacher, friend of mine and Acee's, died last night."

"I'm so sorry." I try to give her another hug. She doesn't hug back, so I just let her go.

"How did he die?"

"Out in the road a block from his house. Some people tried to run him over with a car and he had a heart attack."

"Why would they do that to a preacher?"

She gnaws her lip and glances at the back steps again like she's expecting somebody.

"They were white," she says.

"How do you know?"

"People saw 'em."

I slam my palm against the side of the car. "Rednecks!"

Richeboux jumps. "Hey! This ain't your car."

Resa steps back like she can see a fight coming and doesn't want any part of it.

I say it as much to Richeboux as I do to her: "I bet it was some of those goon-heads from the high school who spend all day bumming cigarettes from each other out on the smoking court." I watch the back of Richeboux's neck, daring him to turn and look at me.

"Maybe a bunch of river rats from over at County High," he says. "They come over here 'cause there's nothing to do in Northport."

"All I know is they were white," Resa says. She glances at

Richeboux when she says it like regardless of who did it, he's partly to blame. Which to me didn't seem fair. I mean Richeboux *is* gloomy, but he's not hateful or mean.

"So," I say. "How about your boyfriend? Was the man who died his preacher too?"

"He was more than that. He was like a daddy to Acee. Wanted him to make the best of his life, be a preacher like him."

I glance back at Richeboux. He's resting his forearm on the roof of the car, scratching at a chip in the paint with his fingernail, his brain whirring out a Morse Code: "Shut up and get in the car!" (O.K., maybe I shouldn't have gotten out after I promised I wouldn't. But how was I to know that Resa would be here? I can't predict the future.)

I start to tell Resa goodbye when a colored boy about our age comes out on the porch with a man who acts like he owns the place and must be Uncle Rose. I know right off who the boy is. He's the one who got in the fight with Sonny Hucks at the Red Elephant last night. I turn to Richeboux.

"That's him."

Richeboux is staring at the boy too. He told me after we left the Red Elephant to go parking that the two of them used to play together when they were little. The boy looks kind of dazed, like it hasn't all sunk in yet—the stuff about his friend, the preacher. He takes a drag on his cigarette and flips it into the parking lot. I glance back at Resa. She's staring at me.

"You know Acee?"

"Yeah," I say. "We saw him last night at the Red Elephant Grill. The owner was being real mean to him. I think he got fired or something."

"Says he quit." She sighs. "But in the end it's the same thing: he's out of a job."

I think about hugging her again, but Resa looks hugged out for the day. She's got her arms crossed in front of her.

"He's your boyfriend?" I say.

"He's my sweetheart. He's my Baby." Her eyes get all misty. I catch my breath. *She's falling in love with him right before my eyes. So that's what it looks like. It just oozes out of you.* I never thought of it that way. I remember that sometimes in Y Camp, when we were alone together in our room and she was talking about boys or her friends at home, her body seemed to become more alive, more *present,* like I could feel the heat in it spreading across the mattress from her to me. A brightness came to her eyes, and her muscles seemed more fluid and relaxed. Next to her, my body felt empty and dry.

"Come on," says Richeboux. He jerks his door open. I all but stamp my feet. He ducks his head and gets in the car.

"Bye," I say to Resa. I grab her hand and hold it, and she doesn't seem to mind. In fact, she seems a little relieved. Acee whispers something to Uncle Rose and comes on down the steps. He's shorter and darker than Lamont, but he's got arms and wrists as strong as Richeboux, and he seemed pretty tough when he and Sonny Hucks were pushing each other last night.

Well, no way I'm going to leave now. Not with a chance to meet the boy of Resa's dreams.

Richeboux starts the engine and leans across the seat toward the passenger window. "Mem." He says it in a quieter, non-Richeboux way.

Acee stops beside Resa. She looks up at him, and her look spreads bright and wide like one of those slow-motion pictures of a rose breaking into bloom. One hand drops to her side and starts fiddling for his fingers. She wipes her eyes with the heel of the other.

I start to get a little misty myself—that sort of flood-rising-behind-your-eyes feeling—but I manage to swallow it down like I do when it happens with Richeboux.

She squeezes Acee's hand.

"Acee, this is Mem Cohane, the white girl I told you about meeting at Y Camp."

I offer my hand, and he just looks at it. Shy, I guess, or maybe it's because Richeboux is here and he doesn't want trouble. The white/colored thing again.

"We saw you at the Red Elephant last night," I say. "Sonny Hucks ought to be arrested."

Acee's eyes are the deepest I've ever seen, opaque shades covering oceans of wonder he's just beginning to explore. You can almost see the ship on the horizon. He lowers his head, turns to Resa, then back to me.

"That ain't likely."

Richeboux is back to cussing under his breath. Acee and Resa stand there, holding hands and looking at me as if Richeboux is proving what Acee just said. Embarrassing!

I step back and look in the passenger-side window toward Richeboux and then back at Acee. "I think you two already know each other," I say. "You used to play together."

"Long time ago," Acee says.

Resa gives him a nudge. "Well at least say 'Hi.'" She looks at me like we are watching two kindergartners trying to take a pee, waiting to see who will go first.

Acee bends forward with his hands on his knees. "Hey, Bo," he says. It's the first time I've ever heard Richeboux called "Bo." People used to call him that until his mother put a stop to it.

Richeboux finally leans across the seat. "Hey, Acee. How you been?" No smile. No nothing.

Acee steps up to the window. "I'm all right. How you doing?"

"I'm all right." Richeboux straightens up, grips both hands on the steering wheel, and stares out the front window with the muscles in his jaw tense—blaming it all on me.

Uncle Rose is still on the porch smoking, with a curious look on his face like we're a movie he started to pull the plug on then decided to let run awhile.

Acee bends sideways to look in the window at Richeboux. "You still living over 'cross the lumberyard?"

Richeboux hangs his wrist over the steering wheel and leans across the seat toward Acee again. "Naw, we moved. We're over near the University now."

"That's good," said Acee. "Too much noise over there. That saw runs all night."

"Yeah," says Richeboux. He straightens back up, looks down at his lap as if he's lost something there. "I used to hear it."

"Sounds like a hawk screaming," Acee glances back at me and Resa, straightens, and takes a step back.

"Yeah," says Richeboux. He taps a knuckle on the front window. "Come on Mem, we gotta go."

"All right!" I slip past Acee and get in the passenger side. But I stay on my side of the car this time.

"Bye, Resa," I say.

"Bye," she says.

Uncle Rose walks down the steps to where Acee and Resa are. The three of them watch us pull away.

As soon as we're out of Uncle Rose's yard, Richeboux stomps on the gas. His knuckles are white on the steering wheel, and we bounce in and out of the ruts in the dirt road from Uncle Rose's to Cherrytown.

I let him stew. We finally get back on pavement, and the big silence sets in, which lasts all the way back to the school parking lot where I left Mama's car. It's like we're in a vacuum, drifting farther and farther away from each other across the seat. I think back on Resa taking Acee's hand, and look down at mine, lying open in my lap. She has the quickest fingers. Just reached out and grabbed him and wouldn't let him go.

# Richeboux

Richeboux's Mom is on her knees in one of the flowerbeds by the house when he and Mem pull into the driveway. Same place she is every Saturday. Something about the bowed head and bent shoulders, the frantic working of arms and elbows, pisses him off. She's got on one of Arnold's old shirts, tied at the waist, and a pair of baby-blue pedal-pushers with stains across her butt where she's wiped garden dirt from her fingers or Arnold has been grabbing at her with his. She stands and stares at Richeboux. A digging trowel hangs in one hand; the other hand jams into a fist on her hip.

"You're late."

Richeboux gets out, slams the door shut, and starts toward her with the keys. His mother's eyes dart from him to the car pulling in the driveway behind him—Mem Cohane in her mom's big mint-green Cadillac. He's praying Mem will not roll down her window, but it's like praying a dog won't bark at a snake or the tide won't come in. He can hear the glass slide down behind him over the hum of the engine. He leans his butt against the front of the Mercury, crosses his arms, and waits for them to get it over with.

"Why, good afternoon, Miss Co-hane." Part of the fight between them is to see who can fake the most politeness.

Mem leans across the seat to the passenger-side window. "Why, hello, Mrs. Branscomb!" loud enough for the neighbors to hear. It's his father's name. His mother hates it.

She turns her glare on him. *You see what I mean,* her look seems to say. *She's a smart-ass Jewish bitch.*

He tosses her the keys.

"What did you and your father decide this morning?"

"Nothing."

She continues to stare.

"I got a job."

"What kind of job."

"Any kind of job. It's what you wanted idn't it?"

"No, I want you to grow up and be a man instead of riding around in Miss Co-hane's make-believe car." She sets her lips and flicks a look toward Mem and the Cadillac.

Across the yard Arnold is on a ladder against a tree, nailing up one of the signs he collects from wherever he can find them—this one for "Sweet Scotch Snuff." There must be a dozen other signs about the yard, from Johnny, the bell-boy, selling Chesterfields to a blond, blue-eyed Mabel, selling Pabst Blue Ribbon Beer, the bottle held to her cheek as if she's about to stick her tongue in it. His stepfather thinks the signs are a big joke, but they shout over the colors in his mother's flowerbeds: stupid people live here.

Richeboux nods toward Arnold. "At least she doesn't collect junk."

"Out of here!" His mother throws up the arm with the trowel, pointing it out the driveway. Her lips are quivering. She gives her head a quick shake as if to empty it of something and turns back to her flowerbed. He's barely in the car before Mem is gunning it backwards out of the driveway.

"Watch it!"

The rear of the Cadillac bounces into the road with a big scrape. Probably broke a muffler loose. She hits the brakes. The car rolls about on its springs. She throws the shifter into "Drive." Rear tires squeal on the scaly concrete. Arnold yells at them from the ladder. His mother is back on her knees at the flowerbed, jamming the trowel at a clump of wiregrass.

Mem's jaw has that determined look she gets when she's playing tennis, shifting her weight back and forth from one leg to the other, waiting for a serve. "Who cares," he says. "She's just pissed off 'cause you drive a nice car. You should have ignored her." Mem slams on the brakes as soon as they're out of sight of the house and gets out to stomp around the car so they can switch drivers. His mother wouldn't want him driving that Cadillac anymore than Mem's mother would.

They haven't gone half a mile before Mem turns to face him, pulls one leg under her, and rests her arm along the back of the seat.

"What kind of job?"

"What?"

"The one your daddy gave you—what kind of job is it?"

"I don't know—a job with the company."

The hand resting on the back of the seat near his shoulder slides back and forth over the grainy leather, stops to pick at a seam.

"Full-time?"

"I guess."

She lets her head drop. "Richeboux, you need to go to college."

"I don't need to do anything."

"Yes, you do. If you want a future. If you want to do something besides hang around here in this stupid town with your stupid friends."

He hits the brakes and whips the car onto the shoulder of the road. It happens so fast he doesn't realize he's out of the car until he hears the door "thunk" behind him. Like the hatch on a submarine.

He heads up the side of the road in the general direction of the Red Elephant restaurant where he was supposed to meet Jamie, Ellis, and the others ten minutes ago, bringing the beer, which he now realizes is still back there in the Cadillac's warehouse-sized trunk. They switched the beer from the Mercury to Mem's car when they picked hers up at the high school.

Behind him the passenger-side door opens. Her hand slams down on the roof.

"Richeboux, get back in the car!"

He stuffs his hands in his jeans pockets, keeps walking. He'd like to ball them into fists, hit something. The gnats buzzing around him. The thick summer air that feels like a bag over his head. Fuck college! Fuck Mem and her college! Fuck his father and the stupid job he offered! Fuck his mother and Arnold the asshole. Fuck his whole fucking life.

To his right the bank drops off sharply toward a chain-link fence around a gravel-dirt yard full of stacks of bricks and cinder blocks. Barbed wire runs along the top of the fence. He'd like to rip that down, wrap it around something, wrap it around his own neck.

"Richeboux, please!"

She slams the passenger-side door, stomps around the car, gets in the driver's side, and pulls out into the road. The big V-8 purrs behind him, tires popping on the heat-bubbled asphalt. The scene from the night before comes with it like a creeping cat: the slow growl of Andre's Ford as they eased up behind the colored man; the man's shadow slipping down the moonlit road; the quiet movement in his back as he walked. How could that straightness and power be gone—vanished into nothing?

Richeboux's foot snags on a kudzu vine that has crept up the edge of the embankment and across the shoulder of the road. He pitches forward but manages to catch himself and stops dead still. His body wants to lurch in all directions at once.

She's alongside him now, one hand draped over the wheel, leaning toward him across the seat, calling through the open passenger-side window. "Richebooooo, Richebooooo...." That teasing smile is all over her face—the same one she lures him across the car seat with when they go parking. A whiff of the air-conditioning brushes his arm. Behind her, a car honks and swerves to pass. He starts walking again.

She lets the car pass, then cuts around in front of him, dipping the front of the Cadillac over the edge of the bank as she slams on the brakes. An image flashes to him of the car continuing over the edge, front end dropping into the jungle of kudzu, the bumper catching, and the whole thing flipping onto its roof against the chain-link fence. He used to have that same image of his father—those nights long ago when his sister was dying and his father didn't come home. Now the image brings a rush of satisfaction that slams into heart-rending regret. The rear of her car is still in the road. She puts the shift lever in park, jerks up the brake, and leans in his direction.

The teasing is gone. She's trying the let's-be-sensible look.

"Richeboux, get back in the car. Let's go somewhere. Over to the cemetery, down by the river."

They were at the cemetery last night after leaving the Red Elephant. Usual stuff in the back seat, rubbing all over each other, him licking her nipples and crotch, her hand pulling his dick. Where was the colored man then, lying face down in the road? He has a vision of the man's neighbors—other large, broad-backed men—hoisting the man by his knees and arm pits, hauling him off the road to somebody's front porch, feet dangling, fingertips brushing the ground. Women watching, that startled, unbelieving look, hands over their open mouths, palms pressing the sides of their faces.

Across the brickyard, willow oaks covered in the the yard's white dust stand shoulder to shoulder like zombies from his dream. The musty odor of last night's rain rises from the grass and moldy ground beneath his feet.

"You're not stupid, O.K.? I'm sorry I said that about your friends." She's on her elbow across the seat with her head twisted up at him. She tries a smile.

He jerks the door open, gets in, and stares ahead. What if she puts it in "Drive" and takes them both over the bank? She gets the gears confused all the time, especially when he and she have been fighting. "D," "R," and "P," for God's sake, how complicated can it be for a straight-A student? She backed into a car parked behind her in the student lot last year after one of their hallway spats. Pushed it right over some guy's Cushman motor scooter.

"Go wherever the fuck you want," he says.

A pick-up carrying a lawn mower and garden tools is stopped behind them. The driver sits and honks his partially shorted-out horn, a spine-scraping bee-bee-bee-bee-beep that won't stop. Richeboux turns to his right so he can see. A red-headed guy about his age sits with his arms wrapped over the steering wheel, and pokes a gaunt, freckled face back at him. The guy leans across the seat and shouts out the passenger-side window. Richeboux yanks the handle, throws the door open. Mem grabs his arm in both hands.

"Richeboux!"

He'll have to drag her out with him. He swings his leg back in, shuts the door. She slides her fingers down his forearm to the back of his hand, tries to interlace them with his. He jerks his hand away. She backs up the Cadillac, and eases out into traffic. The honking stops and the driver guns his truck around, fish tailing as he lurches past, shooting them a raw, freckled finger.

---

Halfway down the white-pebbled drive that runs through the cemetery, they park and get out. Richeboux leans back in through the passenger-side window, fishes through her purse on the front seat—keys, hair brush, extra berets and bracelets, ballpoint pens, note-covered bits of paper, make-up kits, pencils and pens—and finds the pack of Kents next to the tampons.

Maybe *that's* the problem. If so, it started after last night.

He shuts the door, pulls out a cigarette, and throws the rest of the pack toward her across the hood.

"Didn't anyone ever tell you it's impolite to mess in a woman's purse?"

"You're not a woman."

"Eat shit, Tiny Tim." It's another part of her tease—about him having a smaller peter than other boys, when, in fact, he suspects she thinks the opposite, though he's pretty sure it's all guesswork. So it's Tiny Tim or Mighty Mouse, depending on the mood she's in or the mood she wants to get him in.

He lights up, tosses her the lighter across the wide, flat hood. She catches it, flicks the fly-wheel, lights up, and blows smoke sideways like Lee Remick in the movies. She leans her butt against the fender with her back to him, throws her arm behind her head and pushes her hair up to cool the back of her neck. Joanne Woodward in *The Fugitive Kind*, a movie they saw last week. She picks up the moves fast.

The smoke from their cigarettes rises against a dark backdrop of cedars lining the far side of the cemetery and fades to dirty gray against the evening sky. Two tall obelisks rise from a bordered plot in front of Mem—the tallest stones around them. They carry the name, Bibb, in large, raised letters. There used to be a Bibb who was governor. Richeboux's mom claims he was a distant cousin. Different from the New Orleans side of the family where Richeboux's name came from. Mostly thieves and fishermen.

His sister, Leigh's, grave is in the other cemetery across the river near Northport—a red clay hillside with the topsoil scraped away where wire grass would barely grow. All they could afford, his father said. In the funeral parlor, the purple shadows around her eyes and temples were pasted over with whatever they use to cover things like that. Her eyes were closed like the hinged eyes of a doll. After her funeral, he lay awake at night and imagined her in her coffin with the make-up gone, her eyes clicking open, staring at the coffin lid.

Chimney swifts dive and swoop, catching the evening's harvest of bugs. Even at night, when he and Mem are parked here, he's heard the swish of wings past the open car window. And now he can hear the murmuring voices of colored men over in a corner beyond rows of tombstones, talking as they dig a grave. What are they doing out here digging a grave on a weekend?

It can't be *his* grave, though. No colored buried here.

Mem lowers her head into a stifled cough. "Richeboux, why are you so angry?"

"I'm not angry."

She swishes her hair as if to brush him away—that trick she and his mother have of staying one step ahead in an argument, outside of it and in it at the same time, controlling how it goes.

"You ride around in your mama's fancy car, trying to tell me what I'm supposed to do with my life. You can't even stay in the car when I ask you to 'cause you got to pretend you're friends with niggers." She whirls and glares at him. The air between them evaporates as if a flame hit it. She hates that word. He wonders if the gravediggers heard it. Words like that carry.

She turns and resumes her Lee Remick pose, one arm across her waist, the elbow of the other resting on it, holding the cigarette at chin level. The charm bracelet her parents gave her for Christmas slides from her wrist and hangs on the muscles of her forearm. The charm he gave her—the Indian head with feathers, Chief Tuscaloosa—anchors the chain.

"I don't know why we keep going out, anyway. You don't care about me or this town or anybody in it." A tremor tiptoes through his voice. "Maybe it's a good thing you're leaving."

"Maybe it is."

Silence rings in his ears, a dizziness combined with the sharp pricks of nicotine. *Cut the veins, get it over with.*

"You brought it up, Richeboux. What do you expect me to say?"

"I don't expect you to say nothing. Why say anything if you don't give a shit?"

She whirls again—a stark, lost look he's never seen before—and then jerks back to the way she was, cradling her elbows. "I do give a shit, Richeboux, but I don't know why." Her voice breaks over the last phrase. She throws her cigarette at the ground, grinds it out with her foot. Then her whole body slumps. One hand rises to her cover her face. He's never seen her cry before. Never imagined she could.

He watches her across the broad plain of the Cadillac hood, his body weighted by the slump of her shoulders. The murmurs of the colored men have stopped. Acres of tombstones wait for the fall of evening. The two obelisks seem undressed against the sky. He starts around the front of the car in her direction.

She sniffs back tears. "You won't give us a chance, Richeboux. You try to kill everything."

He stops at the center of the grill, rests a hand on the V-shaped hood ornament. The cigarette burns near his fingers. He lets it fall to the ground. She's within reach if he will lean forward. That back, with its long, springy muscles that arc her body against the seat when he has his head between her legs, shutting out everything except the soapy mound before him. They do it as if some force between them pushes everything else aside so they can get at each other. The same force that is pushing them apart right now, pulled them like magnets last night on this very spot. And it seems like such a long time ago.

"That's not true," he says.

"Yes it is, Richeboux. You're trying to kill us right now."

"You're the one doing the killing. You're the one leaving."

She turns to face him. "Yeah, you keep saying that. So I guess that's it, huh? We just get it over with. To hell with us. To hell with everything." Not even trying to wipe the tears.

He moves to her, takes her hand, places his other hand on her shoulder. She folds her arms wing-like across her chest as he pulls her to him. Her head falls under his chin. She shudders. The wiry muscles go slack. Her weight gives into him. The hot, damp smell of her hair rises against his face. His gaze runs down the gravel drive to the open cemetery gates they just drove through. Somehow the view settles him—the wrought-iron spikes of fence, lined with Arbor Vitae; the white entrance columns, musty with mildew and soot from exhausts; and the road, spilling out onto 10th Street. This is the very heart of

Tuscaloosa. Or it was until last night in Cherrytown. Since then the tidy map in his mind has stretched to unknown spaces. Streets no longer go where he thought they did or end where they used to. It's so wide and deep and it's changing so fast. He's falling and tumbling in it.

"That colored boy, Acee—me and him were close when we were little."

She releases a moist sigh. "I know. You told me last night after Sonny Hucks tried to beat the hell out of him."

"What I said was we used to play together."

She bends away from him, looks at his face.

"I can read between the lines, Richeboux. I couldn't carry on a conversation with you if I didn't."

He lets her go, leans his butt against the car beside her. "I knew his brother, too. The one the cops are after."

"A.C.'s brother? The man they're chasing all over the county? That's A.C.'s brother?"

"He used to bring Acee to my house to play."

She rests a foot on an edge of the concrete bordering the plot where the obelisks are, as if she's testing it.

"Richeboux, if they used to be your friends, why aren't they now? It's not like they've changed color."

"That was a long time ago. I didn't know better."

She sighs again, crosses her arms. "Maybe you knew better then than you do now. I mean, when you were little and all. Before all your goony friends came along."

"Leave my friends out of it. They're none of your business."

"They are if they make you act stupid."

He slams his fist into the door of the Cadillac. Pain shoots to his elbow.

I'm sorry," she says. "O.K. I promised. I'm sorry."

*Yeah, you're sorry, but it's what you really think.*

The cedars across the cemetery have darkened to almost-black. The swifts swirl in a tightening circle, chirp in their frantic way as they seek a chimney before the sun goes down.

She rocks back and forth on the foot, braced against the border to the grave. "I tell you what the cops ought to be doing instead of chasing A.C.'s brother. They ought to be after those white boys who ran down that man in the road in front of his house last night."

The sound of the cars passing on 10th Street grow louder. The cemetery gates with their gold-tipped wrought-iron spikes come back into focus. He can almost hear the heavy clank they make when they close.

"What white boys?"

"The one's who killed Resa's and A.C.'s preacher. You heard Resa talking about it when we were at Rose's. Rednecks from County High you said. Or maybe jerks like Ellis and that crowd that hangs around between classes, telling dirty jokes on the smoking court."

She scuffs the sole of her shoe against the cement border. "The police are real good about chasing down colored people. They never go after the white people that murder them."

"It wadn't murder. He fell in the road." Somewhere in his brain, water drops tick-tock in a puddle. The ripples spread. "At least that's what she said—your new girlfriend. He died of something else."

She pushes her butt off the car, turns to face him.

He could start walking now like he did back there on the side of the road half-an-hour ago. Just head down the cemetery driveway and out the gate. Lose himself in the traffic on 10th Street. Cut across the stadium parking lot through the rows of fraternity houses.

"Richeboux."

"Yeah."

"Look at me."

Gravels crunch as she shifts her feet to a lock-kneed stance.

"I want to see your face."

A strip of chrome on the Cadillac grinds his tail bone. He straightens, rests the backs of his thighs against the round curve of the fender. Beyond the gate the cars are passing back and forth. Some have their lights on.

"Were you there?"

"Naw!" He says it too loud. "I heard about it from Ronnie and the rest of 'em. It was some guys from County High."

"You and Jamie and Ellis and Ronnie and Andre and who else? You all left the dance together."

"What of it?"

She turns away from him, leans back against the car. "You need to go to the police."

"About what?"

"Whatever happened."

"You just said they don't care about colored people. Gimme a cig."

She pulls the pack from the pocket of her skirt and sets it next to her on the roof. He grabs it without looking at her, shakes one out and lights it.

She's at a whisper now. "Richeboux."

He tries to make smoke rings like he's seen his father do. Her mind is everywhere around him. He's snared in it.

"I really, really hope you weren't there."

"I wadn't."

She whirls, snatches the cigarettes, tosses the pack through the open window onto the seat, and gets in. She braces her hands against the steering wheel and pushes herself back hard into the seat.

"Shit!" she says. "Shiiit!" She shakes the wheel, slams her foot into the brake pedal and glances up at him. "I'm getting out of here. I'm supposed to be home. It's daddy's birthday, and Mama's giving him a party."

———————

The colored men are walking toward the gate, carrying their digging tools, as he and Mem leave the cemetery. The younger looking one holds the pick lengthwise across both shoulders, his hands dangling over the handle. They are sweating and laughing, their ribbed undershirts white against their dark skin and smeared with streaks of red clay. They aren't much older than he is. Beyond the gate, along the curb, sits an old, faded-blue Chevrolet coupe with the trunk taken out and a wooden bed built in to serve as a pick-up. Where are they headed now? Probably to Rose's or one of the liquor houses he, Jamie, and the rest passed last night after they made the turn into Cherrytown. They probably know Acee. Probably knew the preacher, too.

Mem drives toward the Red Elephant Grill through the University campus. Twilight has settled upon the tended grounds of the Gorgas Library and the evergreens lining the driveway running up to the luminous white front of the President's mansion. The air-conditioning is on. Above it he can hear the tones of the Denny Chimes striking seven o'clock in descending volume as if fading from reality. A soft panic sets in. He presses his fingertips together, flexing them until the knuckles pop. If he lets himself go, he and everything he sees around him will sink down some dark hole and vanish forever. He turns his head to stare out the window. Perfectly spaced willow oaks clip by, their gnarled roots fighting for space between the curb and sidewalk, cracking upward through the concrete. They seem to mark his progress. Toward where? Because he's headed somewhere. He's been headed somewhere since last night when he threw the egg at the colored man. He's going faster and faster. And he has no idea where it is.

And she will not be with him.

In the Red Elephant Grill parking lot, Mem stays in the car while he opens the trunk and hauls the beer over to Jamie's car. He untwists the wire that holds Jamie's trunk closed and lifts the beer in, one case at a time, placing it among the tire irons and other scattered tools and next to a long wooden box labeled "Danger: High Explosives." *We gotta do something*, Ellis said. A new fear thumps the back of Richeboux's skull. He turns back toward the Cadillac. She's braced in the seat again, eyes straight ahead, hands clenching the wheel. Waiting for what? *Goodbye?*

*Goodbye to what?* He walks over to the car. She lets go the wheel and rolls down her window.

"Guess I'll see you on Monday," he says.

"Where are you going, Richeboux?

"I don't know. Probably spend the night up at that old hunting cabin Jamie and Ellis use. Drink some beer."

"Is that all you can think of to do on Saturday night?"

He shrugs.

A glow from the streetlight behind him allows a grayish view of the side of her face, the shadowy outlines of nose, lips, and jaw. When they make out, he likes to run his fingertip along the sharp edge of her jaw all the way to her chin. She arches her neck for him to do it. Richeboux imagines he's defining her. But that's not it. She's merely letting him feel in the dark, joining her in worshipping who she is.

She slumps forward, rests her forehead against the top of the steering wheel.

He takes his hands from the window ledge, steps back from the car, throws them in the air. "What else you want me to do?"

She raises up, slips the lever into "Drive." The tail fins of the Cadillac slip past like dolphins headed out to sea. She guns it as she turns onto 10th Street. Gravel sprays. Sparks fly as the rear bumper catches an edge of curb. Her daddy's birthday party. Big deal. He can't remember the last time there was a party at his house—of any kind.

# Acee

When his baby sister died, they didn't let him see the body. But he's seen other dead bodies—his grandmother's and Garnett Bradley's, the five-year-old deaf boy down the street, killed by the train. Just standing there on the tracks, looking in the wrong direction, sucking his thumb. There was a big crowd of people at Garnett Bradley's funeral, but when Acee's mama led him to the front of the church to see the body, they seemed to vanish, leaving Acee alone, peeking over the edge of the casket. It was like standing at the mouth of a dark cave with an invisible monster inside—like Little Garnett must have felt with the ground shaking under him before the train hit: alone, knowing something big was coming but not knowing what it was or what it would do to him.

*That little black train's a-comin' 'round the bend. Take you home to Jesus...*

But Little Garnett's body didn't look lonely; it just looked gone. Now it's Preacher's body waiting in a casket down the road in Mr. Alexander's funeral home, and Acee is shrinking toward it with every step he and Resa take.

Their neighbors move ahead of them down Cherry Street. Along the road, branches of mulberry and elm droop in the sun. The yards and houses are empty. Resa has her fingers interlaced tightly with his. If it weren't for her, he too would feel the ground shaking.

He cannot imagine Preacher lying in a coffin. The hands alone seem too big for it, hands always moving or ready to move. Acee could not keep his eyes off them when he and Preacher were alone in Preacher's study. The strength in them never seemed to sleep. The voice in them called Acee to serve, promising to take his hand and never let it go.

But he's got to put all of that out of his mind for now to help Raiford. He forces himself to imagine the night ahead, and what he sees mostly are empty spaces—the long hours waiting for the night to enter the dead zone, slipping off to Rosemont's to pick up Raiford and the car, driving eastward on the lonely back roads Rosemont has promised to map for him, the car picking its way down the lonely avenues of hardwood and pine. He can already hear the valves clicking in the rebuilt engine of the car Rosemont will give him, picture his own torso bent forward, arms wrapped around the steering wheel, peering into the darkness for the first glint of daylight off dewy fields. How will he know when he crosses the Georgia line? And where will Raiford be when he's doing all of this—under a blanket on the floor, locked in the trunk?

The funeral parlor is full by the time they get there. People spill into the yard, the men in black suits and white shirts with handkerchief corners spiking from breast pockets, the women in swatches of red, yellow, lavender, and mint green; hats of purple, blue, and black. They hug, murmur, nod. The men shuffle, drop their gazes to a spot of ground between their feet, seeking a refuge from the moment.

Resa's hand squeezes tighter. Acee looks about the yard at the mowed grass and clipped hedges. It's the only yard in the neighborhood that looks like a rich person's yard. Acee's Uncle Travis works here, washing and dressing corpses, helping to move the caskets, driving the hearse. But it's Terry who cuts the grass twice a week with Mr. Alexander's push mower. Mr. Alexander is the only black man in town with more money than Rosemont, but he doesn't spend it. The funeral parlor is the old colored schoolhouse. The hearse is a hand-me-down from a white parlor downtown.

Elton Brown and some of the crowd Acee used to hang out with stand off to themselves in a corner of the yard, murmuring, smoking, exchanging glances as they watch him pass by. He's not a part of them now. Preacher saw to that by making him the "chosen one." And on top of that he's got Resa. They drooled over her even before Raiford had her. Resentment flashes in their eyes. Acee's Sunday suit—another hand-me-down—moves loosely on his shoulders; the outgrown shirt and borrowed tie are like a noose around his neck. People say, "Hey, Acee," as he and Resa make their way toward the door, shake their heads, place hands on his shoulder, tip their hats— "Evenin' Miss Robinson." One woman he barely knows, smelling of roses and cooked collards looks him in the eyes, sorrow like a spirit across her face. She wraps the wattles of her arms around his neck, weeping, pulling him into her bosom. "You his baby," she says. "You the one he helped to raise." He wants to feel this woman's warm blanket of love settle about him. But he is smothered by it.

Resa gives him a tug. "Come on, Baby." They go with the crowd through the funeral home doorway into the jammed room with its water-stained ceiling of acoustic tile. Folding chairs are arranged in rows like church pews. The plank floor has not seen a drop of varnish since the days when it was the floor of the school. People who can't find seats stand about nervously. A pedestal fan oscillates somewhere toward the front, mixing the heat from overdressed bodies and the strong confection of perfumes. His mother and Travis are up there, probably with Preacher's family, seated near the casket. To his left, over by a window, a woman cries softly, "Lawd, oh, Lawd." Other women dab their eyes. Ahead down the aisle is a large bank of flowers—red, yellow, and pink roses; bosomy chrysanthemums; jutting gladiolas in purple and white, cut from the yards in his neighborhood. The reds and pinks seem to shout over the others, adding to the heat of the room and the clamor in his head.

He and Resa work their way to the front. Folks standing in the aisle part to let them pass. They reach the head of the aisle before he knows it. The top half of the casket lid with its shiny gold quilting, yawns open like the lipless mouth of a sea creature. The thought of it slamming shut gives him a start. Mr. Alexander stands at the foot of the casket, preparing to bow. A smile of sadness is fixed to his face like a clip-on tie. He is a dapper, hunched-shouldered, vulture of a man. His delicate fingers, laced limply before him, seem whiter than the rest of him, as if bleached out from years of embalming people. A line of mourners files by the casket, looking in, shaking their heads. "What a shame, what a shame." Acee steps aside as a short, thick woman lets herself down onto her knees by the casket, raises her tear-streaked face toward the ceiling. Her cheeks glisten in the glow of the crooked-neck lamps bending over the casket head.

Resa steers him away from the casket toward the first row of folding chairs to say "Hello" to Preacher's family. She lets go of him and kneels before Preacher's wife, pulling her down into her arms, holding her, stroking her back, calling her name softly, "Ludy, Ludy." Acee's mother sits next to Preacher's wife, staring at the yellowing wall beyond the casket. Her hands grip her worn patent-leather purse, upright in her lap, its strap drooping across her knuckles and the white handkerchief clenched in her fist. Something about that grip on the purse, the way her back looks clenched, too, not quite touching the metal of the chair, angers him. She's held that posture since she sat down, waiting for him to see it, demanding that he see what it's all done to her—his father's leaving, his sister's dying, and now Raiford and Preacher. It's Acee's fault simply because he's the only one left. Except Travis, of course. But Travis is part of the accusation. He sits beside his sister, his hand on her arm, looking up at Acee with watery, big-baby eyes, reflecting their little lights of blame.

Acee hears his own voice come from far away. "How you doing, Mama?"

She turns to look at him. "What you think, Acee?"

"I'm working on Raiford, Mama."

She squares her shoulders, rolls her gaze back to the front. Travis's eyes have not moved.

Acee reaches out, puts his hand on her padded shoulder. Wisps of hair from the braids wound tightly around her head brush his knuckles. He hasn't hugged her in years. Probably she doesn't want him to. His sister died and he didn't, and he's got his father's short stature and nimble hands, which to her signal untrustworthiness and deception. He is beginning to understand why she has adopted suffering as the signature of her life—the bent shoulders, the moan waiting quietly behind her eyes. They've all slipped away—the things she built her life upon. Maybe he should have been more patient with her, taken the risk, tried to hug her anyway. But that would break the seal on his sister's grave, release the sorrow they both try to hide.

Acee slips his hand from his mother's shoulder, backs away, nods toward Preacher's wife. Resa takes his arm and turns him toward the people passing by the casket. They fall in at the back of the line.

The line inches forward. Mr. Alexander reaches out, places a hand on Acee's shoulder, gives a sad-faced nod of the head. Acee nods back, fixes his eyes upon the strip of linoleum tacked to the floor under the casket, its faded roses cracked and split where they ride over the warped planks. Folds of maroon shroud, hiding the pedestal bearing the casket, drop halfway to the floor. His eyes follow the folds upward to the casket rim.

Preacher is sunk into the quilting as if he is melting into it. What used to be his full, brown face is withered to powdery gray, more like smoked meat than a man's skin. It sags from his cheek bones, caves at the temples, all but disappears into the dark sockets of the eyes. The lips threaten to slide apart over his false teeth. The knuckles and fingers, interlaced across his chest are more plastic than flesh. His graying hair has been stiffened with something plastic-like as well.

Acee's gaze runs down the torso to where the bottom half disappears beneath the closed half of the lid. He imagines the trouser legs of Preacher's Sunday suit—a thick winter suit they picked out for some reason—empty except for the bare bones of Preacher's legs, skeletal feet flopping out of the cuffs in shoes of cracked black leather.

Acee releases his breath slowly. He feels the urge to move on, follow the other mourners, but his feet do not move. His eyes will not leave the shrunken body. His thoughts are frozen, trapped within the cold metal walls of the coffin. It is not what remains in the coffin that bothers him; it is what is gone. There is no lingering aura of Preacher's quiet strength, no trace of warmth from a body that once burned energy like a locomotive.

That day when he and Preacher knelt to pray in Preacher's study and Jesus came—or, at least Preacher felt Him come—Preacher's voice was soft but heavy with the strength of his faith. It vibrated the room, ran like a current through the planks of the floor to Acee's knees and took hold of him so completely that he fancied the Visitor's breath on his neck. All of that has vanished now—the current of strength, the energy it brought to Acee's body. What lies before him is a corpse, withering into the puffy squares of quilting.

*When death comes, it takes not only the person who dies, but the parts of others he carried with him. It leaves them with a residue of themselves.*

Acee glances at Resa, sees the question in her eyes. He lets go of her hand, places his on the rim of the casket, bows his head, and leans forward on his straightened arms. Resa's arm circles his waist. "Easy, Baby." The man behind Resa—a man who once knew Acee's father— steps forward, places a hand on his shoulder, lets it slide down to grip him by the upper arm.

Behind him he can feel the mourners, sitting silently, watching. Their grieving eyes, the guarded hope in their tear-stained faces, hang like chains from his shoulders. Their silent voices whisper in his ear— that Preacher's strength has not vanished but lives in him. *You got the gift; you got the call. Help us get back up. Tell us how to go on.*

His arms start to shake. A moan from deep inside blubbers through his lips. Resa tightens her grip, but his knees buckle. His eyes and head roll back as he and Resa go down together, knees thudding on the floor. The rest of his body follows, bone upon bone.

From a point in the sky high above the funeral parlor, he can see the entire neighborhood. In the yards and on the porches, people are gathered, looking up at him. He searches among them for Preacher, standing with his head and shoulders above the crowd. The people shake their heads, turn their eyes to the spot in the road where Preacher died. Acee looks up and down the road. It is empty in both directions, but one end of it runs on forever, stretching beyond the houses and trees of the neighborhood, past the vacant lots and street signs. At the horizon, its gravel-gray color morphs to a narrowing band of gold. The land it traverses morphs as well, from green, to gray, to purple. And at the point of the road's disappearance, walks a figure, a black speck of a man, who neither turns nor looks back as he disappears over the rim.

Acee jerks his head as the fumes of ammonia hit his nostrils. The soft muscles of Resa's thighs, bent at the knee, cushion his head. His tie is loose, his shirt unbuttoned at the neck. Slim, cool fingers grip his chin while someone waves the ammonia bottle before him. Hands hold his arms. Mr. Alexander's white boutonniere comes into focus; then the swirls of red and purple in his tie with its rhinestone clasp; then the slack, tan face and thin lips, bordered by the even thinner, black mustache. The lips murmur something about raising Acee up, getting him into a sitting position.

Mr. Alexander gets to one knee, gives a nod to the others holding Acee. The hands work at once. Resa rises with him, locking her arms under his and around his chest. The fat lady who hugged him as he entered stands behind the others, pumping a clover-shaped fan as if it will raise the dead. They walk him toward a folding chair on the front row next to the aisle. Its metal seat, with its shellacked-over, chipped gray paint, is cold to his butt. His fingertips remember the cold edge of the coffin.

Mr. Alexander is on his feet, reassuring everyone, restoring things to the way they were—the way they are supposed to be. "He's all right,

Sister Waites, he's all right." His mother is somewhere beyond the circle around him, moaning through gasps of breath. Travis is next to her, echoing everything Mr. Alexander says.

Resa squeezes herself into the chair next to him, places her hand on his wrist. "You O.K., Acee?"

His lips stick together, but he manages to mumble, "Yeah."

"Just stay where you are," she says. "Just sit for a while."

"You right, Miss Robinson," says Mr. Alexander. "Let him sit, let him breathe. In a minute we'll take him outside to the sunshine."

The fat woman fans harder. An ache rolls like a howling ball around his skull. Resa's arm nestles about his shoulders. He closes his eyes, and lets his head fall into the crook of her elbow.

The people who have helped him drift away.

Acee draws a breath of gratitude and settles deeper into Resa. His arms are loose in his lap, his feet are splayed on the floor. Sleep whispers in his ear. In the gray light of his mind, an image rises, slowly defining itself as if congealed from the silence around it until it speaks in the hard, bright form of his statue. Every part of it except the copper wire that Acee and Elton stole from the power company is a piece of steel or iron saved by Preacher over his lifetime, treasures given to Acee as one passes on chipped arrowheads of truth. The statue bends over him like a giant shadow, its metal arms, legs, and hands serene and unmoving except for the silvery glow of the plow blade he welded as the heart this morning. The statue bends closer, speaks in a whisper:

"You have completed me," it says. "Now the real work begins."

Acee's hands reach out, fumbling the air around him for his welding torch and goggles. Resa shakes him. Her arms are around his chest again, pulling him back from falling forward from the chair.

"Acee?"

He sits back, holds onto the front edge of the chair, shakes himself out of the dream.

"Acee. You all right?" She squeezes the back of his neck, makes him look at her. There is a claim of ownership in those dark, caring eyes.

She knows the meaning of his dream better than he does and she wasn't even in it—was she? He wants to ask her about it, but he can't make his lips work.

Mr. Alexander offers a wet folded wash cloth. Resa nods, "Thank you." Mr. Alexander bends forward, puts a hand under Acee's jaw, takes a close-up look at Acee's eyes.

"He ain't quite back yet, Miss Robinson," he says. "Put that cloth to his head. It'll cool the fever in his brain."

The cloth's coolness sinks in. "I'm O.K.," he says. "Just got a little dizzy."

Mr. Alexander gives them both a smile and walks away. Acee's breathing eases. The cloth warms against his skin. He puts his hand over Resa's and pulls the cloth away.

"Let's go," he says.

They rise together. She lets her arm slip to his waist, runs the tips of her fingers under his jacket and into his rear pocket. It's the first time she's ever done such a thing in front of people, especially his mother, who thinks Resa's a whore because she's gone from Raiford to him without stopping between. He leans into her, feels the movement of her hips against his as they start up the aisle

People turn in their seats to watch them pass. A rectangle of sunlight waits beyond the front door. People mill about on the steps and beyond, casting long shadows across the lawn. Like the shadow of his sculpture with its glints of metal, stretching across him in the dim light of the shed with its open, beckoning arms. His step feels lighter. It's the way he felt at his baptism when he was nine years old, and the preacher lifted him from the muddy river back into the daylight. He could breathe again. He could breathe free.

He and Resa pass among the groups of people, adding their shadows to the others on the lawn. "You all right, Acee?" More pats on the shoulder. More clasps of his hand. "I'm fine, I'm fine." He and Resa finally break away. Down the sidewalk and beyond the ditch he and Resa will have to cross to reach the road, stands Rosemont Greene with his hands jammed into his rear pockets. His eyes squint in the smoke from the cigarette hanging from his lips. He looks at Acee like they are the only two people in the yard.

# D. Sugarman Starnes

It's still hot out on the highway—like working bottom-land cotton—and it's almost 7:00 p.m. Starnes has the patrol car door open, one foot on the ground, one elbow on the roof, cleaning his nails with his pocket knife while he watches his deputy Otis Coely work his way down a twelve-foot bank to check a carcass in a tangle of briars and honeysuckle near the creek. Probably a wasted trip, but you never can tell. They smelled it nearly a hundred yards back. Starnes can hear the flies buzzing.

They've searched shacks all the way to Eutaw, down past the Hale County line. They've run the pine barrens, canebrakes, and river banks with police dogs and bloodhounds. Starnes, Otis, and two highway patrolmen tore the killer's trailer apart, threw his clothes, his Communist-looking books, his busted furniture, his nasty mattress and sheets into a pile in the yard. Starnes'll go back and burn the whole thing—trailer, junk, and all—when he's sure he doesn't need any of it for evidence.

He's had calls from Birmingham, Selma, Opelika, Huntsville, and even Meridian, Mississippi, saying they thought they had a boy that looked like this one. Nearly beat whoever it was to death in Opelika.

But soon as Starnes got on the phone, he knew every one of them had the wrong man. Still, he sent a deputy over to Meridian with a picture to take a look—the high school graduation picture they took off the mother's dresser when they searched her house early this morning while she blubbered in bed. Had his purple graduation robe on, flattop hat with the gold tassel—real prideful look, like his head was in places it wadn't supposed to be.

Hanging out with a white woman. What kind of whore is she, coming down here, stirring up trouble, trying to find herself a buck? Probably left a husband somewhere, a family even, so she would run around in coon country. He's never seen the bitch, just got her description. Tall. Skinny. Jew-lady. Oscar Hopewell said she talks like she's from New Jersey. Said she sashayed in and out of his store like she owned the place.

Reminds Starnes of his own mother. She was a sashayer too. Strutted about the tiny house they lived in near Marion with his Daddy's mama, like she was too good to be there. Fought with his grandmother over just about everything and refused to help take care of his Daddy in the wheelchair after he started messing himself. "No account, a'tall," his grandmother said. "Miss high-and-mighty. Treat a wounded veteran like that." So his mother just up and left the day after Starnes's fifth birthday. His Daddy never said another word about her. Like he'd known when he came home, crushed from the waist down from where that caisson ran over him in France, that sooner or later, she would go. Probably gone in spirit even before the old man got out of the hospital in Washington, off whoring somewhere.

Otis has slipped in the kudzu covering the bank and rolled the rest of the way down like a keg of molasses. The lights went out on Otis about five hours ago. He's a bull when he's hassling folks, which is why Starnes likes having him along, but he can't take a long night without sleep. That's what happens when you carry all that weight. Now he's sitting on his ass with his legs spread in front of him, trying to figure out where he is.

"Get up, goddamn it!" says Starnes. "I ain't got all day to stand out here in this sun."

Starnes rubs the ache in his leg. It's always there, but today's made it a whole lot worse. This manhunt is starting to eat at him. Time's running, and he knows that the longer it takes to catch a man, the harder it gets. He wanted the bastard in jail by now or his dead body in the back of a pick-up truck. Doesn't much matter which—it's gon work out the same way sooner or later. He has no idea how this boy got from where he was to wherever he's hiding at now. They've had cars from three different counties searching everywhere they could find. They had at least a dozen cars on the road down here last night—and that was only the police cars. Must have been half-a-dozen other vehicles running around, too—some of them carrying five or six men.

"Deer," Otis says. "Lord, he stinks."

Starnes closes the knife, slips it in his pocket. Too good to be true in the first place. Even if the boy had died last night, he wouldn't smell that bad. Starnes looks back at the two highway patrolmen from Montgomery stopped in their cruiser on the shoulder behind, shakes his head. The cruiser pulls onto the hard surface and stops next to him.

"Where next?"

Starnes looks back toward Otis, still standing there by the creek, thumbs hooked in his belt, staring at the carcass like he's tempted to poke a finger in it.

"Hell if I know," says Starnes. "Y'all go on home, get some sleep. We'll start things back up in the morning. What motel you staying at?"

The two patrolmen look at each other.

"Stay at my place if you want. My wife hit the road long time ago. Got a pallet, extra bed."

The patrolmen are grinning now. "We got a place," they say. "Over near Cottondale."

Starnes waves them on. He knows where they're talking about. Widow lady over there will fuck anything walks in the yard.

He wouldn't touch a woman like that. Never has. Fact t'business, he hasn't touched a woman in over twelve years. Never liked it much when he did. Something nasty about it. Like sticking your dick in a catfish. His wife got mad and left him when he arrested her sister for cussing and blowing cigarette smoke on one of his deputies at a roadblock and license check. Ornery bitch. Whole family was like that. Took their boy with her when she left. Heard they were in Florida somewhere. Mama's boy by now. She'll make a queer out of him. None of it matters to Starnes. He'd quit messing with her long before she hit the road. Hasn't missed her a day since.

"Get on back up here, Otis," he says. If he doesn't stay on Otis's ass, he'll stand there in the sun and bloat up like that deer.

Not like Darryl. Darryl was smart. Come from that Culp family down near Demopolis. Family made a lot of money in the timber business. Some of 'em been Sheriffs, game wardens, all sorts of things. One of 'em ran the docks down at Mobile. And Darryl had that something extra about him. Starnes saw it soon as Darryl got sworn in. Took over training him. Practically raised that boy to be a deputy. Best one he's ever had. Best shot, too. And Starnes can't figure how a snake like Raiford Waites got him. Must of had his guard down. Darryl never quite had that nose for meanness like Starnes, that extra edge. Never had a grandmother to beat it into him like Starnes did.

Otis is scratching his way up the bank. His leather-soled cowboy boots slip a couple of times, and he goes to his knees to catch himself. "Oomph!" He's panting and sweating—a confused look on his face like he's lost track of what he's doing and why.

He makes it to the shoulder, straightens up like a bear, rising from all fours, and starts around the car to the driver's side. He doesn't know that Starnes has taken the keys from where he left them in the ignition.

"I'm driving," says Starnes. "You ain't half-awake."

Otis steadies himself with his hand on the hood, then turns and heads back toward the passenger side, legs stiff as stove wood. Starnes gets in, reaches over the dash, shakes a Lucky out of the pack, and lights it while Otis lowers his butt into the seat. Starnes pulls into the road. He clicks on the mike, calls 'em all in.

"Y'all got anything?"

Everybody talks at once. Nobody says shit. "Come on in, then. Everybody that's been on duty over sixteen hours go home. The rest of you meet me at the office in one hour. He's out there. We gon find him."

Starnes turns the car at the next crossroads and heads toward town. He can see two more county cars a quarter-mile ahead of him and the truck pulling the trailer with the dogs in it. He drives for a couple of miles in silence, glances over at Otis. Sure enough, he's fast asleep, his square head bumping the door post, a tobacco stain at the corner of his mouth. Goddamn this running, hiding cop-killer. Goddamn these sleepy, fat-assed deputies and pussy-chasing patrolmen. Starnes might as well be doing the job by himself.

He starts going back over in his mind the places they've been, trying to think of what they've missed. There must be something. What's left to check in town? They were by Rosemont Greene's early this morning after they left the boy's mama's house. Got Rosemont out of bed with a shotgun in his face. Lanky, gray-skinned, like he was cured in diesel smoke. Didn't even blink at the shotgun. Might as well have been a notepad. "Nawsuh, I knew Mr. Darryl, and we allus got along fine." Said it *grieved* him that Mr. Darryl was dead. Grieved for Mr. Darryl's family too. Every word of it was bullshit. Said he didn't know where the sorry-assed nigger was who shot Mr. Darryl and didn't care what happened to him. "He ain't nothin' but trouble, and I don't mess with trouble. Had all I can stand of it."

Rosemont can run his mouth like a jackhammer.

"You gon be in a lot more, Rosemont, that boy shows up around here and you don't tell me about it."

"That boy ain't 'bout to come 'round here. He does, I'll kill him myself."

Starnes pretty much believes Rosemont doesn't know where the boy is. Rosemont's interested in one thing: money. And he don't like any trouble that might interfere with his getting it. He knows Starnes will shut him down and haul his black ass downtown as accessory—doesn't matter how much he's willing to pay. No more making money off white boys. No more making it off colored, either.

Might be a good idea to check back in on him tonight, though. Keep him on the grill.

Starnes downshifts to stop at a T intersection. Oscar Hopewell's store sits directly in front of him across the Tuscaloosa–Meridian highway. Four men on the porch, smoking. He gives them a wave as he makes the turn toward town. One of them hollers something. "Naw," says Starnes under his breath, "We ain't found a damn thing."

He runs his mind over the shacks they visited during the hunt last night and most of today. They went in every one he's ever known about on the river road and a few he didn't know were there. Had one old man on his knees in the yard, peed all over himself. Wife about half his age and children wailing on the porch. What's an old man like that doing with a young wife and a litter of kids? Probably his daughter. Kin don't make no difference. Hump anything they get a mind to.

Might have missed a shack in there somewhere, but he doubts it. Hard to be sure in that second-growth sweet gum and cane. So thick a wild hog couldn't live in there. But a man mean and hard as Rosemont Greene or Raiford Waites could. Build a hut—hide out forever, long as he had food. Cover his scent some way. Ammonia will do it. Ajax. Red Devil Lye. Red pepper'll ruin a dog's nose for a whole day. And this boy is smart enough to know that. If he's in there, it may take some time to find him. They'll run the dogs again tomorrow. They nearly wore them out today and the deputies handling them, too. Had to take Ole Tracker down to the water and bathe him. Slobbering like a cat that drank antifreeze.

Another day, another five days, down on that river, fighting their way through the thickets, tracking a man that might be already gone to god-knows-where. Dogs dragging. Flies, ticks, mosquitoes, moccasins, canebrake rattlers, and not a breath of air. It might kill Otis and Tracker both by this time tomorrow.

He puts the cigarette in the ash tray and sticks a finger down his collar to scratch a prickly itch. Been worrying him for over an hour. Twig caught in his shirt with a briar on it. Got it in that last thicket they had to fight through. He pulls it out, flicks it out the window.

That's why Otis was so hepped up this morning at the killer's momma's house to take the younger brother downtown and beat it out of him. The "eeny, meeny, miney, mo," treatment they call it. "Catch a nigger by the toe." Catch him by some other parts, too. Use a cattle prod the right way, you can get a phone book of names and addresses out of a deaf mute. Show 'em that noose they got hanging in the back cell. It works, nearly every time. But the newspapers got wind of the last time they did that, and next thing you know a bunch of professors over at the college, and some high-and-mighty preachers—Catholics, Lutherans, Episcopals, or whatever they call themselves—held a meeting and signed a paper against him. Called it a "List of Grievances." Gave it to the newspaper. Took it down to the Mayor. Mayor got on the Sheriff. Sheriff raised up off that dirty old sofa in his office by the jail, propped himself on them crutches he uses to do everything—even go to the bathroom—and told Starnes to cut out the hard stuff. Acted like he'd never heard of it before. So-called spinal injury. That Sheriff never had a spine. Brain, either. Just a drunk who can't walk, trying to get disability, claiming it was from that chase out on the bypass. He wrecked a patrol car, but he wadn't hurt a bit in that chase. Starnes was there.

He checks the rearview. He's the last car. The patrolmen have already taken the new bypass to their spread-legged widow in Cottondale. Otis is out cold, head half out the open window. It would fall off and bounce along the asphalt if his neck wadn't so thick.

'Course the man they had in custody that time died, but that doesn't need to happen if you do it right. And it wasn't over a dead deputy then, just a half-starved whore who worked the bus station. You'd have thought she was Cinderella the way the papers carried on over it—"the most brutal murder in years... perhaps a serial killing"—until the man they arrested died. Then the whole tune changed: "Will we ever know now whether he was guilty or innocent?" Starnes don't arrest innocent. Hell, they'd of had a confession if Otis hadn't left him hanging too long.

Otis has slipped down in the seat a couple of notches. Grunts. Pushes himself up to wedge his head back against the door. The good deputies like Darryl move on—go to trade school, even to college—or get killed. Leave the dregs to Starnes. No wonder his job is so hard.

No, he wasn't quite ready to follow Otis's suggestion this morning 'bout hauling folks downtown, but that was over twelve long, hot hours ago. And as the evening light settles across the long rows of new-planted corn and cotton south of town, he's thinking about that kid, Raiford Waites's brother. There was something a shade too calculated in the way he moved this morning, eyes quick and keen as a weasel's. That boy knows something. Or if he doesn't, he soon will. Whip it out of him. He doesn't look like he could take it for long.

Starnes remembers his grandmother whipping him. Tall, raw-skinned woman, arms and wrists strong as a mule's neck, looked like they'd been scrubbed with steel wool and lye soap. Knot on her elbow where she broke it as a child. Gave that extra pop to her swings. Used a folded length of harness strap, sounded like a gun shot, tore up his legs and butt like plowed ground. She'd stand there, spraddle-legged in that ratty old dress and beat him over the scabs from the last time. Cracked a leg bone once hitting him with broom handle when she couldn't find the strap. Reason he limps now. Cut his eye, too, using his daddy's old belt. Buckle wrapped around his face. Never healed right. Claimed she was thrashing the Word of God into him. Had him memorizing Bible verses. And he memorized, too. She taught him that. He memorized 'til his brain hurt. He could fake her on the Hebrew names and stuff—she couldn't spell—but she knew "begat" and "begot," "beseech" and "behold." She'd catch him on something every time, rip his hide anyway.

But she wasn't whipping him over no Bible verses. He knows that now. She was whipping him because Starnes's mama ran off and his Daddy stuck that shotgun in his mouth a year later and blew most of his head off. Right there in the living room while Starnes and his grandmother were at church. She kept him from seeing that. He'll give her that much. He stood out there in the yard, eyes level with the porch floor, January wind blowing off the cotton fields, and listened to her inside the house wailing like that wind, cussing his mama, and smashing furniture. Neighbors came, hauled buckets of water, tracked blood up and down the front steps. He doesn't know what made him do it, but he squatted once to peek under the house, and his daddy's blood was dripping through the floorboards, making little pops in the dust. And every drop told him one thing: the fragile, splintered bottom of his life had just dropped out.

They caught him about half-an-hour later over on Tarrant Town Road, running to God knows where. Took him to stay with kinfolks in Marion 'til after the funeral. His grandmother scrubbed the floor and walls of that living room the whole time he was gone, but when he came home, the stain was still there—a faint shadow on the floor, about the size of a goat skin, that seemed to be alive and still spreading. That's when the beatings started. The sting of those beatings is still in his butt, and that ragged stain still hangs in his mind.

Darryl's blood all over that trailer near Taylorsville, too. Like the two deputies with him had used his body as a floor mop, dragging it down the hallway to get him away from the shooting. He can see Darryl's feet wobbling from side-to-side as he slides, the little white furrows his boot heels plow through the blood-covered linoleum. And his face, maybe trying to look up at Parnell who had him by the uniform shirt, pulling. That surprised look he used to get—almost a grin—when something weird happened that he wasn't quite ready for. Like you'd played a joke on him. Darryl was still a kid in a lot of ways—broad-shouldered, athletic—but still a kid, with a kid's muscles in his arms and thighs and across his stomach. You could see that even through his uniform. Played football in high school—fullback or something. Starnes wishes he'd known him back then, watched him play. But that look on his face—how many times has Starnes seen that—like Darryl was waiting for Starnes to help him understand whatever it was had him confused, straighten it all out, give him the answer. It made Starnes want to reach out and put a hand on his shoulder every time, give him a playful tap on the chin. Actually touched him once in the bathroom of the courthouse. Just a hand on the shoulder and a little praise for the testimony Darryl had just given in the Epson case. Darryl standing there at the urinal. Surprised Starnes that he'd done that—touched another man while he was holding his dick. Never would have done it before. It just seemed natural. He just reached out and did it. Felt the starch in Darryl's shirt and the warm skin underneath. Freckled, probably, just like his face.

A truck loaded with cows has pulled up on his bumper. One of those Daughtrys from that big farm down near Eufaula. Oughta arrest his ass. He glances at the speedometer. Thirty miles an hour. Damn. He thought he was doing 60. Thinking too hard. This Darryl thing, this manhunt, has got a hold on him.

He moves the patrol car toward the side of the road, waves the truck around. He eases off the gas, downshifts gently, and pulls onto the grassy shoulder. Lets it idle in neutral. Takes one more drag off the cigarette, flips the butt out the window onto the road, and leans his forehead against the top of the steering wheel. He didn't cry when his daddy died. He didn't cry when his mama left. And he didn't cry when his grandmama beat the daylights out of him. And he's not going to cry now. But he misses Darryl Culp. Damnit to hell, he was the only thing about this stinking job that made it worthwhile, made it bearable. And by God he will be avenged.

Pick that boy, A.C., up and haul him in. Let his mama and the rest of 'em decide whether to let him get the treatment or give the other brother up. That'll work, and it's exactly where they're headed with this.

*My foot will be dipped in the blood of mine enemies and the tongues of my dogs will do the same.*

His grandmama really liked that one.

## The Town

A late-day breeze stirs the treetops along University Avenue. Shadows from the great oaks around the library stretch across the open field where students build homecoming bonfires in the Fall and play softball between classes in the Spring. All is quiet, save the cooing of pigeons from the library eaves and roller skates of a couple of faculty kids, clicking over cracks in the sidewalks.

Lights are on in the bars and pool halls along the Avenue. The regulars are ordering their first beers, chalking cues. In the fraternity and sorority houses, students clink silverware to their plates and rush upstairs to get ready for dates. Sonny Hucks is on his back stoop, picking his teeth from eating his supper, watching the first cars roll into the Red Elephant lot. In the tree-lined neighborhoods next door, folks put up garden tools, clean fish at the backyard faucet, turn stove knobs to start supper.

Richeboux's mom has put her garden tools in the shed, washed her hands and forearms, clipped in another bobby pin to get the damp hair off her neck, pulled the leftovers from the fridge. Water runs in the tub down the hall. Arnold's already in it, drinking his fourth beer of the day, soaking in his Saturday night bath. They'll eat, watch Arnold's favorites on TV—*Gunsmoke, Dinah Shore, Have Gun Will Travel.* She doesn't try to read anymore on the weekends, not after the last blow-up. Around 11:00 they'll head to bed. He'll want sex. She'll let him have it. She's tired. She'll sleep through the night if the ambulance and police sirens don't wail on University Avenue and Richeboux gets home at a decent hour.

She throws a dish towel over her shoulder, rests the heels of her hands on the sink, and stares out the window into the square block of backyard. The bushes she's carefully planted and tended, patches of grass that need mowing, fade into shadow. Richeboux's old bicycle hangs upside-down from pegs under the shed roof. She thinks briefly of his seventh Christmas, the cold morning out on the sidewalk at their house on Dearing Drive when his daddy helped him learn to ride. Humidity rusts everything in Alabama. She's told him a thousand times to take that bike down to the Salvation Army or the Christmas giveaway project at the fire station.

Everything about Richeboux is left undone—a horse stalled in the starting gate, kicking everything around him. Except that girl he hangs out with. He wants her, Peg can tell, but that gate will shut too. Her and her fancy plans. She's not even pretty—flat chested, tight little rear end. You raise a kid, give him everything you've got, pour your life into him, and he goes running off with a sassy little bitch like that. That's the way it goes. Life's a set-up, especially if you've been left to raise a kid on your own. It leads you on, gives you hope, then slaps you in the face with it.

Things are different in the old mansions downtown and the newer ones, nestled among the elm-shaded streets that swirl about the Tuscaloosa Country Club. It'll be the usual leisurely drive to the Club, cocktails on the terrace overlooking the 18th green, dinner on starched tablecloths with nimble, white-jacketed darkies serving still-bleeding roast beef. A few more drinks over slurry conversation, and they'll wind their way home, drunk or partly drunk, shuck their evening clothes in a hamper for the maid to pick up Monday morning and fall into bed. Sex—maybe. Barely remembered in the morning.

Mem Cohane's parents won't be part of that scene this evening. They cut short her father's birthday celebration so her mom and dad could rush to Birmingham to see Mem's grandmother who's been admitted to the hospital. It's her hip this time, and that's the last straw as far as they are concerned. No more living alone. They'll spend the night in her Mountain Brook mansion and make arrangements tomorrow to bring her to Tuscaloosa to live with them. They wanted Mem to come with them, but it's a battle they didn't feel like fighting. "Why do I have to drive all the way to Birmingham if she's under sedation and moving in with us anyway?" So they agreed: she could remain behind if she found a friend to stay with her. She got on the phone immediately, made arrangements with Sonya Landsberger, and is already headed out the door to pick Sonya up.

"Be careful, Honey," says her mother. Her voice drops as the screen door closes and Mem's footsteps echo down the sidewalk toward the car. Mem's father stands in the foyer wearing the birthday golf shirt Mem just gave him, the keys to his car in his hand. He shakes his head. "She'll be O.K. Sonya's responsible. Mem's a good girl." She's never disappointed them before.

Katherine Kusinski sits in her kitchen across from her husband. The fold-out supper table is laid with china and old silver she brought from Poland, the Irish linen she picked up at a thrift shop in Birmingham. A single candle flickers from the pewter holder at the center of the table. She has on her best dress, unbuttoned down the front—no underwear, no stockings, never stockings. She sips from a tumbler the wine her husband brings from the PX on his trips to Fort Benning, reads poetry by candlelight—the new poets, Plath, Sexton—while he eats with gusto the spaetzle she prepares for them every Saturday night when he's in town.

She glances up occasionally, measuring the pace of his meal. The heat of the candle blurs the lines of his angled jaw and shaved head, the squared shoulders of his uniform jacket. When the meal is over, when she's drunk half the bottle of wine, she will close her book and go to the bedroom, sit on the edge of the bed with her dress open, and turn off the bedside lamp. But before she does, as if to say goodbye to the most secret part of her, she will examine the spidery veins at the tops of her thighs she has noticed for over a year and wonder if the boy noticed them too this morning when they made love.

Her husband will clear the table, place the dishes in the sink, blow out the candle. She will hear the steps in the hallway, look up as the dark form appears in the door. He will move quickly, his fingers encircling her neck, his arm scooping under her legs, throwing her back on the bed. His knees in their rough gabardine will spread her thighs. A quick unzip of his fly. Her arms will splay above her head as he enters her. A quick gasp, a long moan, and it will be over. He will retire to his bedroom, leaving her alone in the panting silence.

Across her backyard, a mile down the railroad tracks in Cherrytown, the smaller liquor houses are running late—may not open at all in respect for the preacher. The funeral parlor has shut its doors. Acee's mom is headed home to bed on the arms of neighbors. Travis has stayed on to help Mr. Alexander with the preacher's casket. They'll move it into the back room where the air is cooler over the concrete slab floor and keep it there 'til tomorrow when they load it and the flowers into the hearse and drive down to Sylacauga where the preacher is from. Young pastor at Rehobeth Church is doing the service. He's kin to the preacher somehow—second cousin, nephew. Travis brings in a couple of galvanized tubs, runs a hose through the window from the spigot outside, and begins filling them with water to keep the flowers fresh for tomorrow's service. Of course, the Ladies of the Lord group from the church will bring new ones. Some of the ones he's watering won't make it. Travis listens to the water thrum against the side of the tub. The funeral home, with its whispered silence, is a natural place for him to work—gives him a place to grieve.

Rosemont's place is closed. First Saturday night in over ten years.

Told 'em it was out of respect for Preacher, but he's got other things on his mind. Right now he's out back behind a shed, talking to Bailey Bridewell while Bailey runs a tune-up and over-haul on Rosemont's spare liquor truck. It's a poor man's cardboard pick-up, '52 Chevy with blue paint faded to white, stains of rust, and a cracked windshield. But under its hood is a rebuilt '56 Cadillac engine with dual carburetors. Got a rebuilt transmission, too. New springs in the back, Jeep-tread tires, weights he can fit on the wheels for traction on miry roads. May have to run a river bottom or two. It'll outrun any pick-up the crackers have got, and it will go places no police car could ever go.

The rest of the crowd from the visitation at the funeral parlor is gathered on porches in swings or rickety chairs. The strains of a hymn rise from one of the porches, sung by a woman in the choir at Preacher's church.

> *I shall not be, I shall not be moved,*
> *I shall not be, I shall not be moved,*
> *Just like a tree, planted by the waters,*
> *I shall not be moved.*

Other women take up the hum. Beyond the chorus, a murmur runs through the neighborhood, a nervous mixture of voices and unspoken thoughts. The men smoke; the women whisper. The older ones dip snuff, spit streams into the yards. The men recognize the worry in each other's eyes, reflexively shoot glances down the road into the darkness.

Out in the county at Ellis's Uncle Woodrow's house, the men who take care of the unpleasant work for the folks downtown are just getting started. Cars and pick-ups rev up, pull out of Woodrow's yard, filled with men, shotguns, baseball bats, pick handles, coils of rope in the trunks. They've got bloodhounds and a pit bull-mix chained in the back of two of the pick-ups. The bloodhounds are illegal for folks other than law enforcement, but Deputy Starnes don't care, long as you chasing colored. Soon as they get out of Woodrow's rutty driveway, they'll be cruising the county roads—spreading it out, looking for cars with dark heads and faces. The shacks along the river have been searched two and three times each. People living in 'em know what will happen if they catch that boy there. They made that pretty plain. So there's nothing to do now but drive and look. Frogs croak from the ditches and creek beds. Crickets call from the fields and grasses. Whippoorwills from the swamps and pine barrens. It's gon be a long night. But you can never tell. The son of a bitch might fall right in their lap.

Down at the jail Chief Deputy Starnes sits with his boots crossed on his desk, waiting. He's got four fresh officers, just came on the night shift, loading up. They're packing in the pump-actions, extra boxes of shells. Night sticks and cuffs in their belts. .38s all loaded. Four other men he calls on from time-to-time when he needs extra help will be there directly. Couple of extra highway patrol cars on the way from Montgomery. Hour or so, they'll be headed for Cherrytown. Gon find Raiford Waites if it takes all night.

## Richeboux

Six beers in ten minutes. He's never done that before, and he's not sure how it all came about. Mem left. He remembers that. He'd wanted a cigarette, started into the Red Elephant, paused in the foyer at the cigarette machine and peered into the dining area through the swinging glass doors. Half the high school was in there, yapping, sucking shakes, shoving in burgers and fries.

Jamie, Ellis, and the others were there in their usual corner booth, Jamie's mouth going a mile-a-minute, laying out the plans for the evening. Ellis next to him, emptying a cup of ice into his face, lips working like a cow nibbling a branch. Ronnie saw Richeboux, rose, grinning from the booth, that look of relief on his face. Then Andre. Richeboux had glanced back down at the cigarette machine. Not enough change, and that was it.

He bolted out the restaurant doors, grabbed a six-pack out of Jamie's trunk, and scurried into the bushes behind the restaurant. He sat, cross-legged in the leaves and chug-a-lugged them, tossing the empties toward the restaurant's overflowing garbage cans. He remembers the last empty banging off the nearest trash can and spinning to a stop in the gravel driveway. Then he got up and started walking.

He comes to a wobbly stop beside the road. Cars zip past. Headlights hit his eyes like flash bulbs. Someone yells from a passing car. He looks over to see a boy from County High, a ballplayer he struck out three times straight last year, leaning out the passenger-side window, giving him the finger. Black hair in ducktails, greasy licks of it blowing across his face. *Get your hair cut, asshole—you might be able to see the ball.* Richeboux staggers toward the curb, catches himself, and lurches back in the direction he was headed.

A quarter of a mile ahead car tires rumble over the railroad tracks, the same Birmingham-to-New Orleans tracks he slipped across this morning on his way to Mrs. Kusinski's. But where is he headed now? Maybe up to the parking lot at the high school. A vague notion he's left something there. If he goes back, hangs out a while, maybe he'll figure out what it is. Sit on the pitcher's mound in the practice field next to the lot, remember the tightened spring of his windup, the spray of sweat as he flung his body forward, the sharp smack of his fastball in the catcher's mitt. That feeling of perfect connection he's not felt in a while.

The sidewalk ends at the railroad crossing. He stops to let a couple of cars pass before he starts across, gets halfway, and stops again to look down the tracks. The twilight is almost gone, but near the bend, half-a-mile away, he can make out the tree line where he crossed this morning, headed to Kusinski's" apartment. She's probably there now, on the couch where they fucked earlier that day, curled in her warm igloo of light. Something about that image drags him down. So posed. So alone. It's the way she was before he got there in the morning and the way she returned to after he left. He came before it was in good, felt it drip out of her. She took over then, gripping him with her arms and legs, pressing him into her body and its smells of overworn dress and unwashed hair, smothering him with the sadness that lurks in every corner of that room. He can still feel it, creeping over him, seeping in like a stain. But it wasn't her sadness that made him cry. It was something inside him that did that. Whatever that is is still in there. And he's not going to find it up at the high school parking lot, remembering the good ole days of baseball.

A car honks behind him. He lurches forward, grabs the pole of the crossing signal, hangs on with both hands. It would be a dim walk down that railroad right-of-way. Blurry spots of light wink through the banks of privet, sweet gum, and cedar along the tracks. It's easy enough to do in the daylight when he comes to visit her. Just take it slowly, one tie at a time. He's got all night.

It feels good to leave the street behind him, the criss-crossing headlight beams of his classmates on the way to picture shows downtown or to the Cottondale Drive-in where everybody goes to make out. Jamie, Ellis, Andre, and Ronnie are probably on the road by now, off to blow up something. What? That old colored man's pile of cans? Probably themselves too. Who gives a shit. He left that behind when he swiped the beer. And with each step he takes down the gloomy right-of-way, he feels more certain that he's never going back.

Pukey bile burns his throat. The effort to swallow it causes him to stagger. His feet drag like they did when he wore the ankle weights Coach Talbert made him wear in the off-season to build up his legs for baseball. Rocks roll and click against the rails. The ties seem to rise off the gravel when he tries to step over. He catches a toe, lurches to keep from tripping. Before him, the right-of-way narrows into its dark tunnel of trees and bushes. Silence builds like it's holding its breath.

*The big black man, down on his knees beside the road. His heart thump-thump-thumping, revving itself to rise and give chase. Thumping and pumping him toward where he finally wound up, face down. He must have fallen face down. He was running all out when Richeboux last saw him.*

That nervous thing is coming, like hooks embedded in his chest pulling him toward her. They dig in when he finally admits he's not turning back, and they get worse the closer he gets. He'd hoped the beer would get him over that. He'd hoped the sinking daylight would wipe out the caught-in-the-glare feeling, too. But that's coming on as well. He's never been here at night before. He's never even seen her at night.

The thought adds to her mystery and power, like creeping up to a rocky den and hearing the low growl inside.

Ahead is the spot where he pulled himself up the bank to her house this morning. He needs to pee, but there's something else brewing way down deep. A tremble runs across his stomach before his guts clench in the big contraction. He tries to turn to the side, hoping for some reason to keep it off the rails and ties. The effort almost tips him across the rail and headfirst down the shoulder of the grade. The beer tastes almost the same coming up as it did going down, but it smells worse and hurts his throat. He leans forward, shaky arms braced on even shakier knees, lets the second and third lurches spatter off the rail. He wags his head, spits the last drip to the ground, and waits a minute to be sure it's over. An ache in his ribs rises toward his brain. It'll be a splitter by morning.

He makes his way down the shoulder of the grade, fumbles at his fly and barely gets his peter out before he starts pissing into the dirt. The sound of his stream spattering the hard red clay tells him how alone he is. But that's O.K. He's still standing, feet planted on solid ground, holding his dick. The rails are real, the creosote ties are real, the moon above. He can take anything —at least for now.

He zips up and uses the slender trunks and bushes to pull himself up the gap to her backyard. There are a few porch lights turned on down the row of duplexes, but the yard of her apartment is even darker than the railroad bed. An aura of light shows through the window of her kitchen door. That would be from her reading lamp in the living room. So she's in there, just as he imagined she would be, with Lawrence, Thoreau, Dickinson—one of the dead people she makes them read in class.

He hacks up a last gob of bile and starts toward the glow of light—walking better now. The puking helped. A buzz hits him as he vaults up the steps to her back stoop. He steadies himself and raps his usual rap with the knuckle of his index finger against the glass of the door. His heart picks up a beat; burpy breath hangs between him and the pane. He sucks air in and out to try to clean things a bit, waits, raps again. A shadow moves. Her silhouette eclipses the light from her reading lamp. And suddenly she's there, her face to the glass. The light over the stoop flicks on. The door jerks open six inches. Her features are shadowed by the edge of the door, but he hears her breathing.

"Richeboux—what are you doing here?"

"I 'on know." He leans forward, rests a forearm on the door frame, expecting her to open the door so he can step in. "I just needed to. After this morning...."

His fingers grip the edge of the door, just above her face. She lowers her head. The hair is pinned into its messy bun. A naked foot that seems larger than life is visible on the linoleum in the wedge of gray light from the stoop—but the sliver of dress above her knee is different from the rumpled dress of the earlier visit. It's fancier—black or navy blue, with white piping. The bottom buttons are undone.

She opens the door farther, raises her face to him. "Richeboux, have you been drinking?"

That mother tone in her voice—it always pisses him off. She teases him with it, but this time it's more like a line drawn between them.

"You can't come in. My husband is home. He's down the hall, sleeping."

Richeboux tightens his grip on the door. That panicky feeling comes over him, like he used to get in her class when she called on him and his mind was drifting—usually to her.

She whispers louder now. "Really, you need to leave. I've got to go."

"Where?"

Her eyes run over him and rise again to meet his. They are both darker and brighter than they were this morning, pupils shimmering like candlelight on water. But the face around them is as blank and unmoving as the barren shore.

"Here, Richeboux. In my house. With my husband." The door

opens a couple more inches so the light can better hit her face. Moths have gathered, whacking at the bulb. One flutters in his hair and messes with his balance. Her gaze is steady, adamant, but he can't stop himself.

"I'm in trouble," he says. He can taste the bile again. His breaths come harder. "I need help."

"Not now, Richeboux. It won't work now."

She pulls the door knob to shut it. He holds on, stops it before it closes, saving his fingers and an inch of opening.

She glances over her shoulder into the shadowy apartment, listens a moment, then turns back to him.

"Please," she whispers. A tone has entered her voice he's never heard—pleading, almost desperate. It occurs to him in the muddle of his brain that she's scared of him—maybe always has been. Maybe that was part of the deal for her from the beginning.

"Who is it?" comes a male voice from down the hall, deep, like a command to "halt!" A door opens. Feet shuffle.

"You see." She almost hisses it.

"But I thought..."

His fingers slip away. The door closes. He slumps forward, rests his forehead on the windowpane. Her hand rises toward the lock, which slides with a worn, supple click. She turns and walks back toward the living room. "Cat," she calls. "After the garbage can again."

He pushes himself from the door, teeters on the edge of the stoop, then leaps to a crouch on the ground, steadying himself with his fingertips. He wants to retch again, feels like a mongrel cat, like she said, slinking around the back-stoop garbage cans amidst the rot, discarded bottles, and cans. He rises slowly and walks from the orb of porch light into the darkness, toward the gap in the hedge that waits like a hole to nowhere. He stops, turns, takes one last look.

She is back at the window, watching him. The glow of her reading lamp is gone; it is all black behind her. Her face flickers in and out of shadow as the giant wings of a Luna moth blot the light from the outside bulb. She flattens a cheek against the glass, where his was a moment before, and he feels the coolness of the pane against his own face. He has the urge to go back to her, fall on his knees on the stoop, search her eyes, her lips for a sign of an opening. He knows it's there, and that's the hell of it.

He whirls and runs toward the hole in the hedge. His legs and feet are working now, jumping giant chasms that open before him in the dark. The face in the window was real, the lonesome sadness still in it. But it is one more thing slipping away into the mumbo-jumbo of this endless day.

# Acee

*"Nigger art,"* said Raiford. *"You're wasting your time."*

Acee sits on his stool and stares at the statue. An ache from his fainting spell stabs behind the eyes, never quite hitting the same spot. He rubs his temples to make it go away, welcomes the breath of evening through the open shed door, feels the lantern he's just lit begin to warm his feet.

"Well," he says, "you called me. What you got to say?"

Tendrils of oily smoke shimmy up the figure's thighs and flanks. Lantern light flickers on the welded joints. The plow-blade heart rests in the middle of the twisted strips of iron and steel, the strands of greening copper that make up the statue's chest. It reflects more of the lantern's light than the other parts, but it's lost the magic it had in his dream at the funeral home. It's just another piece of metal, and it pisses him off. It's like everything else in his life. It leads him on, then vanishes; demands but doesn't give. It's like a great heron, standing with that curious crook in its neck, watching for a fish.

*You have completed me,* the statue said. *Now the real work begins.*

He rises halfway from the stool, bends to fetch the lantern, then plops back down. There is something else, a feeling that somewhere in the light and shadows there is a third presence. He glances about. Nothing new he can see—dirt floor; welding tanks; hose, torch, and goggles; piles of scrap metal making jagged shadows against the bottom boards of the wall. His eyes move to the empty doorway framing the dark shapes of bushes and the limbs of a large pecan tree, hovering over the backyard. Full of leaves now. When he dreamt the statue was moving, the limbs were icy and bare, defining their own sculpture against the morning sky. And he wondered: was it the pattern of the limbs themselves or the jagged blotches of sky between them?

He turns back inside. The interior of the shed seems darker, as if night has slipped in unnoticed. He does another quick survey of the shed's interior. And then he sees it, like the tree limbs against the sky— the exaggerated shadow of the statue itself against the wall. The shadow is full of holes where the glow from the lantern slips through the spaces between the metal, defining chaotic patterns of light and shade. There are even more holes for light than welded parts. He's never seen them before except as openings to insert more iron, copper, and steel. But those spaces are as much a part of the statue as the joined pieces of metal. It's as if some magician, growing quietly within the statue, has enticed him, piece by piece, to create something he had no idea was there.

Acee lifts the lantern, and begins to move it around the statue. Everything changes: the shadow expands and contracts, the splotches of light and shade cast by the lantern mutate into a limitless possibility of shapes, stretch themselves like rubber, shrink into kernels of cinder and gold. He feels his body changing with them, drawn through the statue— the open places and the metal itself—into the infinite playground on the wall.

He lowers the lantern, gives his head a quick shake to let the scattered parts of his brain fall back into place. The sense of another presence returns. He glances toward the door to see Resa, leaning against the door frame, arms folded. Her feet are laced in dirty-white tennis shoes. One ankle is crossed over the other. The fine lines of her shins are golden-brown in the lantern light.

"How long you been standing there?"

"Long enough to wonder if you were going to vanish before my eyes into that sculpture that's got such a hold on you."

"What you think it is?"

Resa gives a long sigh. "I don't know, Acee. But I think you do."

Acee stifles the urge to look back at the statue. His gaze falls instead on the cradle of her stomach and thighs, their promise of movement, and then to her face with its soft plains of flesh, dark eyebrows, and lashes, pupils that do not move.

She pushes herself off the doorframe, nods over her shoulder into the dark. "Rosemont said meet him at nine. It's about that time."

"Yeah," he says.

"Come on. We'll walk together."

Acee shakes his head. "I got to take it from here on my own."

"I'm going, Acee, every step of the way 'til you leave with Raiford."

He shifts the lantern to take her hand, but she's already gone. He steps through the shed door, pauses, and glances back at the statue. The shadow, too, is gone. All that is left is the ghostlike shape, bent in the dark.

# Richeboux

Richeboux's foot catches on a strand of honeysuckle as he leaps from the bank of Mrs. Kusinski's backyard to the tracks. His body lifts, arms pinwheeling, stomach and rib cage anticipating the belly-flop on the oily gravel of the railroad bed. Rocks, sharp as railroad spikes, jab his chest and stomach, knock his breath out down to his bones. He lies for a moment, straining for air, finally rubs a stinging hand over his face. His upper lip is swollen; his forearms are scratched and cut; he's banged a wrist against the edge of a rail. It hurts, and there's a knot rising on it, but he doesn't think it's broken. He pushes himself to all fours, rolls onto his butt, and sits with his arms draped over his knees, hoping he won't puke again.

He gets to his feet and rests with his hands on his thighs, then straightens and looks back down the tracks to the Hackberry Road crossing he left thirty minutes ago. Car lights cross robotically back and forth. Human robots driving.

He flicks his tongue across his lips to test for blood and looks down the tracks in the other direction toward the depot. No lights there. It's a good mile to the next crossing. He's never been on that section of the tracks before, though he used to live across the lumberyard that runs along one side of them.

He takes a deep breath, interlocks his fingers behind his head, stretches from side-to-side, and starts walking. The numbness from the fall is gone. Stinging pain is creeping in. What the hell was he doing there? What did he expect? The real numbness began when the bolt on her back door clicked shut like a circuit being tripped in his brain.

His feet crunch the gravel between the ties. His head hurts, but it's hard to tell whether it is from the beer or the fall. His legs are back mostly. Smells are coming back, too—a whiff of the paper mill upriver drifts in to mix with the stink of his own breath. Behind him, the distant beep of a car horn, back at the crossing. He still needs a cigarette. She used to smoke. Her husband still does. He should have asked her for one. She could have at least done that. He tries to get his mind off it, concentrate on his body, the way his gait is easing and lengthening as he walks, the looseness coming to his arms, the sensation returning to his hands and fingers as if the blood is awakening. His body always comes back—sooner or later. It saves him at times like this. He picks up his pace, feels the tracks begin to curve as they bend around the lumberyard in their run to the station.

He's away from the lights of the houses and parking lots now and into the darkest part of the right-of-way. There are hobos along here, the ones who don't catch a freight and move on. Drunks, mostly. They hang around this section of the track—more abandoned buildings here, more places to hide. He's seen their empty Thunderbird and Manishevitz bottles in the ditch beside the tracks where he's crossed to Mrs. Kusinski's. He's seen them down by the train station, too, loitering around that trashy corner where the dives and low-rate pawn shops are, sleeping on the filthy concrete, staggering about, trying to work up the nerve to cross to the station platform and beg for change. They can get nasty if someone turns them down.

But it's O.K. He'll clear the curve in a minute and be able to see all the way down to the next crossing at 15th Street—lights, traffic, a new opening to somewhere.

But where? That meeting with his father—he's avoided thinking about it all day. The look his father gave him—more than disappointment this time. It was disgust, meted out in the shitty job he offered. The long day of fighting with Mem. Ms. Kusinski's apartment, full of books and husband. The black man—the man who is no more, who was quietly walking home on a Friday evening until some white boys came by and ended everything. *Boom, just like that*—on his knees, then running through the dust; then crash—onto the ground, like Richeboux just did when he came down the bank. Face down in the dirt with its cool, musty smell—like the entrance to a tomb. The two gravediggers in the cemetery when he and Mem stopped to talk, shoveling the new grave. They smelled it. But you don't when you're dead.

He's close to the edge of the lumberyard now. Night has fallen for real. The bushes lining the tops of the banks hang darkly over him. There are huge rats along here. They feed off the junk the hobos leave. When he was a kid, barred owls hunted the corridor at night, picking off fat meals. In his bedroom across the lumberyard, he could hear their whoops when he woke up alone after his sister died and his father left. They were raucous, almost laughing, as if a gang of harpies had moved in. But he took comfort in them. The owls were out there with quick, sure talons and slow-beating wings. They ruled the night.

Ahead of him the thin strips of steel vanish into the dark. Mem will be on those strips, the flanged wheels turning faster and faster, pulling her north toward her future, leaving him here—same streets, same dirt, same rails, same life. She's on the other side of a window, just like Mrs. Kusinski—the window to her mother's Cadillac, her "Most Likely to Succeed" picture in the yearbook, her college acceptances to Wellesley, Vassar, Mount Holyoke, a bunch of others—places he's never heard of and refused to ask where they were. "Up north," someone said. "New England." Another country; another window.

It was there from the start, that first morning in Mrs. Pritchett's homeroom almost two years ago when Mem got up from her desk, walked down the aisle and plopped her butt in Ernie Partlow's seat, the student who sat in front of him who'd been sent to the office for trading dirty pictures. She crossed her legs under her paisley print skirt and rested her forearm on his desk like she owned it. Knees sticking into the aisle, the calf and ankle of one leg entwined around the other. (He never understood how girls could do that; it made his balls hurt to see it.) He tried to keep his eyes on the homework he should have done the night before, but her seat squeaked as her entwined legs flexed and let go of each other then flexed again. He fancied he could hear the soft brush of the skirt's hem on her skin, feel the first magic in that winky smirk—or maybe he fancied that, too, he's seen so much of it since. Before that moment, she'd never said a word to him. For all he could tell, didn't even know he existed. And suddenly she was talking as if they'd been sweethearts since the first grade—what a great game he'd pitched the Friday night before. "Poetry in motion," she'd said with a smile he'd never imagined her face could make. He'd stopped hearing most of what she said after that, but he remembers that she didn't wear perfume like a lot of the girls do, and he remembers her muscles, moving as if working their way out of her skin, the energy in her body—how it ignited his, like when he hit his groove on the pitcher's mound, under the lights with the crowd watching. Except she was the crowd. And maybe she was the groove, too.

She led him straight off a cliff, and he let himself fall, loving every slow tumbling second of it. By the time they walked out of homeroom together, headed for their first classes of the day—his in algebra, which he hated, and hers in French, which she loved—he was reaching for her hand. "Uh-uh. Not yet," she said. It was like hitting the glass with his fingers.

He's about midway through the bend around the lumberyard. The banks of the right-of-way have lowered, almost to track level. They are also narrower, not over six feet on each side between the shoulder and a sagging chain-link fence. He wasn't ready for that—the closed-in feeling. Through the fence to his right, the blocky outlines of lumber stacks loom against the purplish glow from downtown. Farther down the rails, near the 15th Street crossing, the right-of-way widens again and a side track splits off so trains can pass at the station. To get there, he'll have to pass two old, tin-sided buildings that parallel the tracks—machine shops, maybe railroad storage bins. The fence runs right up to the front edge of the first one. Some large-leafed vine—kudzu, poison ivy—has climbed from the fence onto the roof. Across the tracks, behind the fence on the other side, a dim yellow bulb on the front of a shack lights a wide, gravel lot, filled with the hulks of railroad cars and equipment: iron wheels on long, black axles; couplings set on end; rails thrown on top of each other like trees in a windfall. Light from the bulb glints off of them, giving them a skeletal look.

He clears the bend around the lumberyard, and the lights of the 15th Street crossing come into view. He makes them his beacon. There's less traffic there than back at Hackberry Road. But it's later in the evening—must be past nine, maybe headed toward ten o'clock.

A bottle clinks on the gravel, gives a skip, and smashes against the rail at his feet. Shards of glass pepper his shin and ankle. It came from his right front, over toward the tin buildings. He leaps to the other side of the track, crouches, studies the shadows around the buildings and the scraggly line of trees along the right-of-way fence. Nothing moving. The top of the rail feels cold to his palm. His fingers clutch the sooty underside. His breath blows in and out like a lagging engine.

The best thing is to run. He's way too fast for a drunk hobo who can't hit shit with a bottle. The crossing is maybe a football field away. He can cover that distance easy. His legs are ready to pump; his arms ready to start churning. He makes a false start, ducks back, and then pushes off the rail into a sprint, head down, plowing ahead.

The second bottle misses by a couple feet, bounces in the dirt and weeds on the other side of the track, and clanks against the base of the fence. He flinches and drops back into a crouch. That one came from somewhere in front. And then he sees the man, a bloated silhouette, slinking up the side of the grade. The man stops dead-center of the tracks, maybe fifty feet away and bends forward with his arms hanging as if he is waiting to make a tackle or heave another bottle. Or maybe he has a knife. Hard to tell with the whole front of him in shadow.

Richeboux takes a step backward, catches a heel on a tie, and has to move quickly to keep from falling. There's a tremor in his legs, but it's not beer now; it's adrenaline pumping. He could turn and run back down the tracks to the spot he's just left between Mrs. Kusinski's and the A&P lot where he parked this morning for his visit. He could scramble up the bank to the lot and head toward 15th Street where it runs by the high school. But he does not want to go down there again—ever! He backs up a couple of more steps. The man has started forward.

"One more step," says Richeboux, "I'll stomp your goddamn ass."

"You-ain gon stomp nuthin', you little shave-tail piece of shit. Fuck with me, I'll cutcha balls off."

Richeboux checks behind him. Sometimes they work in pairs. Nothing but the lonely rails and darkness. He calculates the chances of a quick sprint forward, a dodge around the man, then slipping past him between the track and the fence. It's a good fifty feet to where the man is weaving along the tracks, and he notices for the first time that between him and the man there's an even narrower place in the right of way where a section of chain-link fence has broken loose from its poles and sagged toward the ground. Directly across the track from the sagging fence is a stack of ties.

The man slurs out a string of words, sways back and forth as he comes, waving an arm front of him as if he's flicking a switchblade. Probably a bluff. But even in his crouch, the man looks big. And drunk as he is, there's something solid about him, something that's not giving way.

Richeboux grabs a handful of rocks and lets the smaller ones slip through his fingers to the ground.

The man halts, shifts a foot forward to keep from pitching onto the track. He straightens unsteadily and peers at Richeboux. The light from the railroad shack glints on what looks like a broken bottle, held by the neck.

The man raises the bottle into the light. "I'll dig ya fuckin' eyes out."

"You got me real scared," says Richeboux.

The man stares at the bottle as if he's checking to be sure it's still there, turns back to Richeboux. "You see this? It'll shred ya peter like a train hit it."

"Get out the way, old man. I'm just headed to 15th Street."

The man lowers the bottle, sticks his head down, and cranes it forward like one of Woodrow's gone-in-the-tooth hounds, sizing up a fight over a scrap of food.

"You ain't headed nowhere til I see some money. Lay it right there onna tracks, then get the hell outta here."

"I ain't got no money."

The man spits to the side of the tracks, wobbles a bit, gives a little laugh as if he's talking to a buddy. "He ain't got no money." He turns back to Richeboux, takes a step backwards to get his balance. "Bullshit! Goddamnmuthafuckin'bullshit."

Richeboux tightens his grip on the rocks. It's all come around again. A great sadness descends. "I ain't got no money," he says. "I ain't got shit."

The man tries to shake something from his head, then starts forward. Richeboux throws the rocks when the man is about thirty feet away. At least a couple of them must have landed, but the man is so drunk, he's numb. Richeboux leaps a few steps back, stoops for more ammunition, grabs the rough wood of a tie that skins his fingers. But he's up again with two more handfuls of rocks. He hurls the first handful. The man keeps coming, cussing under his breath. Richeboux's knees jump with adrenaline. He clenches his fists to stop the shake in his arms and hands. The man is approaching the spot where the sagging fence and stack of ties squeeze the right-of-way. He's let the bastard cut him off. He should have kept running at the man after the second bottle.

He checks behind him again, switches the three remaining rocks to his throwing hand. One is larger than the others, sharp-edged, with the weight of a lug nut. He drops the other two and stares straight at the man's head. He's put baseballs in spaces smaller than that. He could kill the son-of-a-bitch if he calms down and throws it hard enough. "Get back!" His voice is so loud it sounds like someone next to him is yelling.

The man stops, still swaying, still leaning forward. Richeboux takes a breath, settles into his stance. Somewhere toward downtown a car honks. Birds flutter in the vines climbing the shed. Richeboux takes a reflexive glance backward like he would to do to check a runner on base. Another deep breath, waiting for that second between heartbeats. Utter stillness. He winds up and hurls the rock as hard as he can. Even before the end of his pitch, he hears the whap against the man's forehead like a stone hitting dead wood. The man slumps to his knees in the jagged gravel. Behind him, down the track a car passes noiselessly over the 15th Street crossing. "Ohhhhh," he says. He balances for a moment as if about to offer up a prayer, then pitches forward on all fours, shattering the bottle into the rocks beneath his hand.

He collapses onto an elbow, pushes himself back to all fours again.

"Awww," says the man. "I'm a-dyin' here."

Richeboux's hands tighten to fists. He could walk down there, stomp this groaning, blubbering piece of shit into the tracks. "Naw you ain't."

"Yeah, I am. You done killed a pore ole starvin' man. Throwed a spike at me." The man says it as if Richeboux has cheated to win, as if throwing a railroad spike breaks some hobo rule of fair play.

"I ain't even got a spike." Richeboux gazes over the man's back, down the tracks to the crossing. Grab him by the arms, drag him down there and leave him. Someone will see him, call the police. Call an ambulance. "You were gonna cut me with that bottle. What did you expect me to do?"

"Awww, aw, lordy." The man is rolling his head from side to side. "Ain't you ever heard of the Good Samaritan?"

Richeboux kneels, rests a hand on the rail for balance, feels about for a couple of good rocks, larger than the ones he had before. He finds one, big as a hatchet head. He rises and starts forward. It's going to be close, but if he keeps to the shoulder and avoids snagging himself on the sagging fence, he can just slip by. The man tries to look up at him, collapses once again onto an elbow. His thick, matted hair is tangled with twigs and plastered in one spot with what looks like a gob of axle grease. The shoulders are fleshy and rounded under a white shirt so thin it seems worn into the skin. Richeboux is almost past him, ready to turn and sprint toward the lights of the crossing.

Suddenly the man throws his entire body across the rail—no gone-in-the-tooth hound, but quick as a cat. He grabs Richeboux's ankle, the thumb and fingers surprisingly thick and strong. Richeboux tries to jerk free. The man's wrist and forearm are like a tap root. He reaches with his other hand, snatching a handful of jeans. Richeboux goes to one knee. The rock is still in his hand. He can smash it into the man's skull, take care of everything. The man hangs on. Richeboux topples backward down the railroad bed. The back of his head hits the clay. The rock slips from his hand.

"Goddamn you," says the hobo. "Leave a man to die on the tracks."

Richeboux gets to his butt and works his way backward toward the fence, dragging the man after him down the rocky slope of the bed. It's like dragging a dead goat. He makes it across the damp clay and into the weeds beside the tracks, feels his palm scrape a piece of broken glass, his head and shoulders press into the steely pattern of the fence. He begins to kick, jamming his free foot into the man's head and shoulders.

"Help me," says the man. He starts clawing his way up Richeboux's body. "Help me sonofabitch." His fingers hook into Richeboux's belt. Richeboux tries to pry them loose. They are slick with blood. The man's knees and elbows are digging now, coming over the top of him like a wet rat, stinking of rot-gut and months of unwashed flesh.

"Get the hell off me."

Richeboux's braces hard against the fence, takes a wrenching hold on the man's shirt, and manages to roll both of them over. His own knees are scrambling now. He jams the man down beneath him, gets astraddle the stomach, rips the man's fingers from his shirt. He leans forward with all his weight and presses the man's wrists against the ground. The man's arms go limp. Richeboux's own arms shake to his shoulders.

"Oh, Lord," says the man in a gurgling moan. He's heaving, rotating his head back and forth as if trying to shake a lifetime of misery from it.

"Don't you puke on me," says Richeboux. He hears his own breath, halting, desperate. He wants to let go the man's arms, ball his fists, and smash them over and over into the soggy, whimpering face. "I oughta whip hell out of you, you sorry piece of shit."

The man gags on a wad of snot. "You done already done it." He hacks it onto the ground. "I'm mon die rightchere in this ditch."

Richeboux leans harder against the man's wrists. "You gon give up?"

The whimpering starts again, but weaker. He lets the man go, rolls to one knee, and gets to his feet. He steps over the still heaving stomach and walks back to the track, rubs his palm with his thumb where the piece of glass cut him. He sucks the blood, spits, and wipes his hand on his jeans. The man struggles to all fours and falls onto his butt.

Richeboux starts toward the crossing. Behind him the man mumbles about Jesus and the loving word of God until he breaks down into hacking and coughing. When he speaks again, his voice is loud and clear.

"I fought tha war," he says. "Over in Okinawa, Japan. Fighting for 'Merica."

Richeboux keeps walking.

"Killed me a bunch of Japs. Prob'ly more'n a thousand."

*Bullshit. They all fought the war.*

"I seen the shadows. Everywhere." He sucks in and lets out a blubbery breath. "Lord, them shadows. Satan's a-chasing me with 'em."

The old bastard's brains are pickled, but something truly frightened has crept into his voice. Richeboux stops. He's got a couple of rocks in his hand that he must have picked off the railroad bed, though he doesn't remember doing it. He rubs them against each other, glances back.

The man is on his knees, bent forward. His shoulders heave in convulsive sobs. A keening whine comes out of him like lightning running down the rails. Richeboux wants to cover his ears, yell at the man to shut up. Why won't the son-of-a-bitch leave him alone?

The man sucks in a breath. "I'us there," he says. "Right whur it hit after ole Harry dropped the bomb. Chirren, men-an'-women burnt to shadows. Nothing but black spots on the ground." He rests on one arm and starts to scratch about in the dirt. "Not a building, not a tree, not a stone big enough to set on. A spot," he says. "Nothin' but a goddamn spot." He raises his face to Richeboux. Wet cheeks glisten in the dim light.

"Lord, save 'is boy. Don't let him see what I seen."

Richeboux jams his hands in his pockets. Shadows. Hard to see in the darkness. But if you look long enough, they are everywhere. Stacks of lumber in the lumberyard; across the fence in the junkyard—hulks of equipment and piles of rails. Under the eaves of the tin buildings. His own thin shadow, waiting at his feet on the tracks.

And that's it, isn't it? The shadows in the eyes of his dying sister have followed him all his life. And since last night when he threw that egg, a shadow has crept across everything. It's as if the landscape itself is following him, growing darker, pushing him toward a tiny, distant spot.

The man is still praying behind him: "Please Jesus. Put your hand on 'is boy's heart."

Richeboux sticks his hands into his back pockets, throws his head back, stares into the night. Stars signal back at him from the great dome of sky closing down around him. He takes a quick, jerky breath. Then another. The scream begins as a slowly rising moan. It tears from every part of him and hurls itself into the night. His arms rise with it, fingers grabbing at the sky until his lungs ache. He drops forward, hands braced on his thighs.

The air around him feels shattered. The man has gone silent. Richeboux catches his breath, looks at the man. He has his shirttail to his face, dabbing at his forehead where the rock hit.

"Amen," he says. "Amen."

"Amen to what?"

"What you just said."

"It wadn't a prayer."

"Yeah, it was," says the man. "Bout the best prayer I ever heard."

Richeboux is back in the smell now, kneeling in the weeds, holding the man by his shoulder, putting his fingers to the forehead where the dabbing was going on. There's a good-sized lump and a sticky gash covered with grit. The hairs of the eyebrow below it are caked in blood. The man dabs at his wound with his filthy shirt tail. Richeboux's T-shirt is dirty, but it's cleaner than that. He pulls it over his head, bunches the tail of it in his fingers, and starts to dab gently at the wound. The mix of their breath in the close night air has a metallic edge to it—the remains of their mutual fear. He braces the back of the man's head while he presses the cloth to stop the bleeding, goes to the man's wounded hand, cleans it the best he can, wraps it in the T-shirt, and closes the bloody fingers over the cloth to hold it.

The man is dribbling words that make no sense. He doesn't seem to feel the pain. Or maybe he's just used to it. Richeboux stands and looks down at him.

"You ain't gon die."

"Not tonight, I 'on reckon." He looks up at Richeboux, licks his lips as if searching for the last drop of something. "What's yo name, son?"

"Richeboux."

"Richeboux what?"

"Richeboux Branscomb." It has a strange taste to it. He hasn't said his own name in a long time.

"What's yours?"

"Bob."

"Bob what?"

"Bob nuthin'. Quit usin' it long time ago." The man drops his gaze to his bandaged hand.

Richeboux tightens his belt over his naked belly, glances down the track. "You ain't got a cigarette, have you?"

"Ain't found one all day."

He sighs, looks back at the man. "Well, I'm gon be going."

The man nods.

Richeboux reaches into his rear pocket, pulls out his wallet. He's got four dollars left from what he used to buy the beer at Uncle Rose's. At least three belong to Jamie and Ellis. He folds them all and drops them in the man's lap.

"God bless," the man says.

Richeboux starts walking. The pace gets faster, then faster still. And before he knows it, he's running down the track.

## Resa Robinson

The smell of Rosemont's place rises out of the ground at you as soon as you walk in the yard: stale beer, cigarette smoke, and sweet body powder, soured by sweat. Leftovers from the night before, from a thousand nights before—folks drinking, juking, and rubbing up against each other. But tonight it's dark and quiet, like one of those haunted houses you see in the pictures before the thunder booms and lightning strikes.

I've got hold of Acee's hand. Tension running up and down his arm like his blood is on fire.

Rosemont's nowhere in sight when we walk in, just Marcus Futrell, the bartender, sitting in the shadows behind the bar, half-asleep, ashes from his cigarette about to fall in his lap. Acee lets go my hand, raises the globe on the lantern, and blows out the flame.

"Hey, Marcus."

Marcus lifts his eyelids, stares for a minute, tries to pull the cigarette from his lips, and burns his fingers on the end. He jumps off the stool, cussing and wagging his hand. Acee shakes his head. He ain't got time for the likes of Marcus—never has. Marcus takes his burnt finger out of his mouth and points it toward the hallway that runs toward the rear. "Rosemont's in the back. He's been waiting on y'all."

We go down the hall to the shed room Rosemont calls his office but it's mostly a place for his men customers to sleep when they're too drunk to make it home to their wives. He keeps an old fold-out army cot in there with a wool blanket on it so nasty I wouldn't touch it, much less lie on it and try to sleep.

Rosemont is sitting in there smoking with Bailey Bridewell. The last flicker of daylight slips in through the window. Bailey looks like one of those bowlegged bulldogs with the face mashed-in. Doesn't talk much, smells of grease and burnt motor oil. Most you see of him usually is his butt sticking out from under a hood somewhere and his legs so short his feet won't touch the ground. The way he and Rosemont are sitting looks like they've been there a while, not saying much, feeling the darkness ink its way into the room. Rosemont sits like he always does, elbows on his knees, hands hanging from his wrists like they're about to drop off, fingers thin as spider legs holding his cigarette.

Acee reaches for the string on the overhead bulb.

"Leave it off," says Rosemont. He nods to Bailey. Bailey gets up, gives a shy look to me and Acee, and slips on out the door. Rosemont motions toward a couple of cane-bottomed chairs that look like either one of them should have splintered under Bailey's rear end.

Rosemont sits for a minute, looking hard at me, that little crinkle in his eyebrows, the end of his cigarette bright as a bonfire. "What you doing here, girl?"

"You told us at the funeral home to be here by nine."

"You know I wasn't talking to you. Your mama find I got you mixed up in this, she'll be on me like a hornet."

I look him right back. "I'm not leaving Acee 'til he does what he has to do."

Rosemont shakes his head, looks up at Acee like he's waiting on Acee to set me straight. Acee nods toward my purse.

"Let me have one them Kools."

Acee smokes even less than I do, but I guess he's thinking if Rosemont is smoking, he needs one too. I get my pack and give Acee one. He bends to the side, lights up. I can feel from where his elbow is touching me that he's tense as a fiddle string.

Rosemont keeps watching him. He rolls his own cigarettes. The glow is brighter, and they pop when he lights up.

"How you doing, Acee?"

Acee blows out a long breath of smoke. "Where's Raiford?"

"He'll be here when time comes."

"What's that mean?"

"What I just said."

Acee glances around the room like Raiford's hiding in one of the corners.

"That woman bringing him?"

Rosemont flicks an ash into the sand-filled coffee can at his feet. "You ain't got to know all that. You just got to be here when the time comes."

"What you call us down here for then?"

"We'll get to that directly. But right now, there's something I'm gon tell y'all, and you best listen"—he nods toward me—"specially now Resa's got her mind fixed on setting here and ain't gon leave." He leans forward on his elbows, looks up at us, and there's the slightest twitch around his eyes. Maybe it's old age putting in an early visit. Maybe he's just worn out with all the doings. But for the first time in my life I think I see something soft in Rosemont. He helped pay my college and all, but I always thought that was because Mama shamed him into it.

That growly voice of his hasn't changed though, and his pupils are steady as ice. "I been dealing with Deputy Starnes now for over twelve years. I know the copperhead son-of-a-bitch better than any man in this town. And the thing about it is, he's done run out of places to hunt. And that's bad, 'cause it means he's got to look for another way." He pauses a minute, takes a drag, lets his eyes rest on Acee. "Wouldn't surprise me a bit if him and his boys be down here before the night's over. And if they do, they gon be starting with you and me."

His cigarette pops. The rising trail of smoke gets a wiggle in it.

"You understand what I'm saying, Acee?"

Acee's sitting straight in the chair like he's bracing for someone to push it over. He nods his head.

Rosemont's voice is like a mop dragging across the floor. "Now, listen: soon as we finish talking here, I'm gon make myself scarce 'til we start on Raiford's business in the morning. You know what's best, you do so the same." He turns his eyes on me.

"Resa—you hear what I'm saying?"

"I'm taking care of Acee."

Rosemont shakes his head again, then he stops real quick and shoots a look past us at the door to the hallway. I freeze, grab Acee's hand.

Rosemont raises his hand to keep us quiet, glances toward the window, and sits with his hands on his knees and his head cocked. Then he gets up real slowly and eases past us into the hall. I hear the back door creak open. I squeeze Acee's hand, breathe quiet as I can. I can hear Acee's breaths, though. He's staring straight ahead at Rosemont's empty chair.

Pretty soon the back door scrapes shut and Rosemont slides the latch. He walks up the hall and tells Marcus to go on home. Soon as Marcus is out the front door, the latch slides into place there as well. Rosemont comes back to the room with me and Acee, takes the army blanket off the cot, and hangs it from the nails he's got sticking above the window. Except for Acee's cigarette, the room gets dark as a grave.

"That fice dog that follows Bailey around," Rosemont says, "sniffing 'bout the porch, looking for scraps."

He takes his seat, pulls out his paper and tobacco pouch, and rolls another cigarette. By the time he's done licking it, twisting the ends, and lighting it, it feels like it took all day.

"Y'all got a place to hide?"

I rest my hand on Acee's back. The muscles are hard as pine knots.

Rosemont's eyes stay on me like I'm the one with the answer.

"We can go to Sister May's house," I say. "They don't know her. Got no reason to mess with her over this."

Rosemont flips his ash into the coffee can at his feet. I notice for the first time the oiled planks of the floor running straight from Acee's feet to the toes of Rosemont's black, pointy-toed shoes, sticking beyond the rolled cuffs of his overalls. Like the two of them are locked into the same track and I'm just standing beside it watching with the night falling silent and empty outside. The room is so quiet I can hear it ticking. An owl hoots from the woods across the parking lot. I almost jump out of the chair.

Acee clears his throat. "If Starnes is gon be running around the neighborhood, how we gon get Raiford out of here?"

"You ain got to worry 'bout that."

"What you mean I ain't got to worry? I got to drive him, ain't I?"

Sometimes Rosemont's grin doesn't show in his mouth. It stays behind his eyes like he's telling a joke to himself. "Naw, that's changed. Winfred is."

"Winfred, who?"

"Winfred Alexander," he says. "Runs the funeral home. I believe y'all was over there this afternoon."

Acee taps his ash into the palm of his hand. Rosemont sticks out a foot, pushes the quart can across the floor in Acee's direction.

"How come Mr. Alexander's part of this?"

"He got the hearse."

"Where is Raiford gon hide in a hearse?"

"In the casket."

"In the casket."

"Same one you just saw had the preacher in it."

Acee stares at the floor like he's studying it for an answer. He glances at me then back to Rosemont.

Rosemont coughs his cigarette cough. "Yeah, we gon bury Raiford tomorrow at Rehobeth Church over near Sylacauga, where y'all's friend, the preacher, come from." He looks at us with a mocking look. "Y'all still churching every Sunday, ain't you. You heard about Lazarus?"

I see it then. It's like that old thimble trick my grandmother used to do, hiding the button, making us kids guess which thimble it was under, moving them about with hands as quick as a sewing machine. It's Rosemont, straight down the line.

Acee still has that angry tone in his voice. "So what's gon happen once the casket gets to Rehobeth Church?"

Rosemont rests his elbows back on his knees, interlaces his fingers. The nails are warped and have long, dark cracks in them. "That's where you come in. That pick-up out there in the shed that Bailey just put that rebuilt motor in—you gon be driving it."

"Carrying what?"

Rosemont's eyes stay on Acee like he's waiting for the light to go on.

Acee turns to me. I nod. He looks back at Rosemont.

"Preacher's body."

Rosemont's got about a dozen gold teeth. His smile is like a grill on a Cadillac. "Acee, I b'lieve there's a little bit of your daddy left in you yet." He winks at me. "Winfred's gon donate us one of them cheap caskets—ain't no more than a pine box. We putting that in the truck under a load of stable manure with a pipe through the lid where Raiford can get air."

Acee rubs a palm with the thumb of his other hand like he's reading it. "Then switch down at Rehobeth."

Rosemont blows the answer out in a long cloud of smoke: "The living for the dead."

I can hear Acee breathing again.

"Who all knows 'bout this?"

"Me and you. Resa. Winfred cleared it with the preacher's wife. Marcus, much as he knows anything. I imagine Bailey Bridewell got a whiff of it. Course, Raiford. That white lady he runs with.

I rest a hand on Acee's knee. "What if they catch Acee in that truck? It'll be the same as if they catch him here in the neighborhood."

Rosemont shrugs like he's shaking off a chill. "Well, he's better off on the road than he is 'round here. He's leaving at the best time of day. Raiford ain't gon be with him 'til after he leaves the church. That's seventy miles from here."

"There are sheriffs and Klan around Sylacauga just like there are here," I say. "All the way to Georgia, all the way to wherever Acee's going with Raiford in that casket."

"State line," says Rosemont. "Somebody else'll take over there got some Georgia plates." He studies the floor a minute, looks back up at me. "Ain't no scheme foolproof, Resa. This the best I can do. And it's good enough to fool a cracker like Starnes. Meanness ain't smartness."

Acee slides his hand down his thigh and takes hold of mine. "What time?"

"Be here 'round three. Moon be down by then. Take the truck up to Winfred's, pick up Preacher's remains. Winfred'll be there. Head on down to Rehobeth. Wait behind the church. Hearse'll be there by seven. Make the switch. Funeral starts at nine."

Rosemont stands, puts his fists on his hips. "Don't come here for that truck the way you and Resa just come. Take the road down by Hadley's creek and come up through the woods out back. Go back that way now, too."

Acee reaches for the lantern, gets up, and holds his hand out to Rosemont. Rosemont takes Acee's hand, nods toward the lantern. "Don't be thinking 'bout lighting that." He puts a hand on Acee's shoulder and guides him toward the door.

"Now's the time," he says. "This been coming for a long time— way 'fore any of us was born. Y'all go on, now. Stay hid. Something change, I'll get word to you at May's."

He lets go of Acee, puts his arm around my shoulder, and walks us down the hallway. At the back door he undoes the latch, opens the door a crack, and studies the moonlit backyard and parking lot. Then he steps back and nods for us to leave.

"Y'all remember what I said 'bout keeping to the woods."

"There's snakes in there," I say.

Acee nudges me from behind. "Damn the snakes."

I can feel Rosemont's eyes on us all the way across the parking lot.

# D. Sugarman Starnes

Starnes gets in the patrol car, shakes a cigarette from the pack on the dash, and punches in the lighter. The patch of toilet paper on his chin where he nicked himself shaving is still in place, glued by its speck of blood. He starts the engine and heads out of the Sheriff's-Office-and-Jail parking lot onto 21st Avenue.

Five carloads and two pick-up truck loads of men follow. Four of the cars, plus his, are law enforcement—three his men and two highway patrol. The trunks are filled with pump-action shotguns, couple of double barrels, boxes of shells, and four twenty-five-year-old Thompson submachine guns he's never had to use. Borrowed some of that new tear gas stuff from Chief up in Birmingham. Every man in uniform has a heavy metal flashlight, night-stick, and service .38. He doesn't know what the other crowd has, but he's made them leave their sheets and hoods at home. Hasn't got time for that bullshit; doesn't need the hassle he'll get from the papers and the Mayor if word gets out he's led a bunch of Klan into Cherrytown. He's temporarily deputized all of 'em, though he doesn't know of any authority he has to do that. Raise your hands, swear on a Bible—good enough for getting done what needs to be done.

He's got an emergency on his hands, damn it. Needs whatever help he can find.

Otis is in the second car. Starnes has spent about all the time with Otis he can stand. The three men Starnes is hauling are regulars he's known for years except for Tony Taggart, the twenty-year-old he hired last week as a part-time dispatcher, who looks more like fourteen. In fact, something about Tony looks unborn—skinny, with veins that seem to run outside his see-through skin. He's what Starnes imagines a blue baby would look like if it grew up. He doesn't say much, and Starnes has some doubts he's going to work out as a dispatcher or anything else. On the radio he sounds like a hair-lip.

The other two men in Starnes's car act like they're headed for a party. They're nervous is what they are, trying to draw Starnes into the conversation. They want his no-bullshit voice to tell them it's going to be all right, just like he explained it would be five minutes ago when he gave his speech in the jail parking lot: we'll grab the boy we want, be headed back to town in less than an hour.

So it's Shug this and Shug that. "What houses we going to start with, Shug?" "Going back to his mama's house again?" "Hell, Shug, we searched ever plank and board of that place twice already." Starnes nods and grunts. Driving helps him think, work things out. And there's something that needs working out. It's been bothering him like a tick crawling up the back of his neck: a vague feeling that he's overlooked something. His plan's got a blind spot. He's looking for a sinner when a devil is close at hand.

And that devil is Rosemont Greene. Starnes has pretty much written Rosemont off since his visit to Rosemont's place this morning. Rosemont sat there on his bed in his shorts and dirty undershirt and gave Starnes that I-ain't-done-a-thing look, put that face on, coming out of dead sleep with the twin barrels of a twelve gauge in his face. When they come to hassle him about selling beer to white boys and being behind on his protection payments, he hems and haws, shuffles about, won't look you in the eye. This time he looked right at that shotgun—pupils didn't move; eyes didn't blink. Rosemont knows something. Hell, he might be running the whole damn show that's kept Starnes and his men from catching Raiford Waites. 'Cause they would have caught the son-of-a-bitch by now if he wasn't getting help from somewhere.

So Starnes is changing his plans a bit. While the rest of them are finding A.C.—and they'll find him, whatever it takes—and keeping the lid on things in Cherrytown, he might take a few cars down the rutted dirt road from the main part of the colored section, toward Rosemont's place. Search the hell out of it, whether the Saturday night crowd is in there or not, whether Rosemont himself is there. You never know what you'll shake out of a colored crowd when you catch them by surprise.

## Katherine Kusinski

She knew it would come to this months ago, the moment she answered his first knock on her door and saw him standing there, slouched on her front porch with his resentful look barely hiding his need. She could feel the heat. And later, when they brushed elbows at her dining room table as they worked their way through the first chapters of *Moby Dick*, she let her elbow stay there pressed against his, their needs melting into each other. That body, so hard and obedient to her touch. The lust that shimmered though the gray, haunted eyes. She was into the rush of it instantly, letting it take her and him wherever it would go.

She curls herself into her favorite seat. It's O.K., it will all be O.K. The room is still there, the couch, the end she sits on, a nest to her body. That same blanket of light, falling over her and the scattered treasure of books.

A sob breaks in her chest. She drops her feet to the floor and slumps forward, trying to muffle her groans with her forearms. Whatever allowed her to imagine that this wild and unpredictable boy could be some kind of answer to life in this lonely place? She remembers the

Saturdays, sitting where she is now, waiting for his tentative rap on the door, anticipation crawling over her like viper's breath—that titillating fusion of ecstasy and need.

They could have been caught. These things creep out in high school settings almost as if they rise on their own in the adolescent unconscious. Whispers around open lockers, giggles in the halls. She'd be crucified.

She sits upright, wipes her nose and wet cheeks with the back of her hand, and takes a deep breath. He's gone; it's over. Richeboux will never tell. It would be like inviting their truth into the very people he's at war with. He's too proud, too angry, too... honest. He has too much integrity to tell. She's never thought of it before, but that's the best part of him. That, too, added to the attraction. A person to trust, to share hopes and longings with. To share dreams. They did that—she's sure of it—in their own, unspoken way.

The look on his face tonight under the filmy porch light when she told him, "No." The faintest glimmer of panic as if he'd finally leapt for the fantasy she'd been offering and her hand was no longer there. He'd laid his need at her feet. She could have knelt and touched it, placed a hand on his arm, walked him around the yard, listened, maybe even held him close in the shadows. None of that frantic squirming against each other. Just the two of them, alone in the quiet dark. Comfort—deep comfort. Mother. Teacher. Friend.

That's true caring, isn't it? A willingness to give what is needed in whatever form. That's what lies beneath (or above?) the passion in Lawrence's novel, that paragraph she read this morning, the little speech she gave afterward. That's what she was prescribing in her dreamy way.

And that's how she betrayed him. This boy she led on and on to wherever she was or wanted to be—she doesn't even know. She owed him protection; she knows the dangers well enough. But she stood there and didn't move. What a coward! What a failure at her own game. So, what is she going to do now—sit here and let him lurch off into the night?

She pulls her legs under her, begins to pick at a strand of fabric on the frayed arm of the couch. She *cannot* try to see him again. It would be the ultimate act of weakness, selfish to the point of cruelty.

Above the mantel is a worn tapestry of Tristan and Isolde, her only material legacy from her parent's estate. Richeboux's eyes often went there when they sat and talked—or, at least, she talked; he grunted or mumbled. But a couple of times his sulky mood slipped away, as one might absentmindedly take off one's clothes, and he asked about the figures on the wall. He couldn't remember the names even after she told him the story. Romeo and Juliet he called them, after she said the older story was a source for Shakespeare's play. *He* was the one drifting then as he looked at those faded lovers, and he was not drifting toward her. Mem Cohane, most likely. But that didn't bother her. He's young; she's young; the lovers are young—and innocent.

Ah, but Mem—the kind of mind that doesn't have time for innocence. Does her schoolwork effortlessly, as if she's seen it all before. It's mainly a mental exercise for her, no feeling for the stories, the beauty, the passion, the pain. A too-easy life. Too quick a brain. Charging ahead into her cocksure future.

She's seen Richeboux and Mem in the hall, books in hand, or in Mem's case, pressed against her chest, staring at each other, deep in conversation. When she first saw them that way it struck her that Mem looks a bit like she did as a teenager—or at least like she thought of herself. She felt a pang over that, especially the time Richeboux looked up and caught her watching them. They parted with a light squeeze of hands when the bell rang. The figures in the tapestry also appear to be waiting for a bell only they can hear.

She lets her gaze fall back to the couch, the books, the cat. So where is Miss Cohane in Richeboux's hour of need? Perhaps she's the cause of it. There's that pang again. She needs to let that go. But if Mem is the cause, she should at least be a part of the solution.

Her free hand moves to her knee, slips back the hem of her dress, finds the old scar from her father's saber. She caresses the raised line of flesh with her fingertip in a circular motion. It reminds her of faraway times as a child, full even then of yearning. Trails in deeply arched forests, sloping horizons of trimmed grass, towering houses of granite and stained glass. A calmness settles over her. Her toes flex against the coverlet. Her legs anticipate their unwinding. She swallows the lump in her throat left from crying. And before she knows it, she's standing, walking toward the wall-phone in the kitchen. She pauses to listen down the hall. The snoring has followed its usual route to deep sleep. She turns on the kitchen light, finds the phone book in the drawer, opens it, flips through the "Co," and there it is, "Cohane," and, of course, there are two listings: Mr. Adam C. Cohane and Miriam L. "Mem" Cohane. She met the parents once. They're just the kind of doters who'd give a smart, demanding daughter her own phone line.

## Richeboux

A short-circuited streetlight buzzes and flickers over the rails and pavement of the 15th Street crossing. Richeboux halts to catch his breath. The hobo's stink clings to him as if he has piggy-backed the old man down the tracks. He turns to look into the darkness from which he came. The shadowy banks of the right-of-way and silhouettes of the railroad shacks have shrunken against the cinereous glow of the downtown sky. A glimmer of moonlight on the rails. Is that movement he sees—the old man, slinking back to his nest in the weeds to lick his wounds? Or maybe headed off to buy hooch with the four dollars Richeboux gave him—flush his brain of those burned shadows.

A couple of cars pass, a pick-up truck with three guys in it—one of them swigging a beer. The truck is a red, souped-up '49 Chevy, like the truck the guy was driving who yelled at Richeboux and Mem earlier that afternoon. Richeboux touches the place where her fingers lit, bird-like, on his arm, bearing their soft plea: "Please don't—for me." Sometimes she's even whispered it. He watches the truck's tailgate and rear bumper scoot off toward the main drag downtown.

He shakes his head free of Mem and turns up 15th Street. Keep moving forward, away from Mrs. Kusinski's apartment, away from the Red Elephant Grill and high school. Within fifty feet he comes to a graveled drive on his right, sloping down to the entrance to the lumberyard. The double-swing gate is bound shut with a rusted chain and a lock like the ones he's seen on freight cars. It's the weekend, and the saws aren't running. He walks down the incline, hangs his fingers in the chainlink gate, and stares down the mushy, clay and sawdust road that runs through the yard. Blocky shadows from the stacks of lumber give the road a snaggle-toothed look. There used to be a door in the fence at the far end so people could walk through the yard. Aces used that door when he came to visit. But mostly it was maids on their way from the colored section to the society houses downtown. They'd walk through Richeboux's old neighborhood to get there. Folks on his street didn't have maids.

His old house sits at the far end of that road in the darkness beyond the fence. The woman who lives in the house now uses his and Leigh's bedroom for a beauty parlor—or so his mother says, who sees it as a desecration. It's an awful tiny room for a beauty parlor. When he lived there, they could barely fit two single beds in. It was on the driveway side of the house. He used to lie awake in there, listening to his father's pick-up truck leave early in the morning and come home late at night, the same truck his father took him fishing in. Four feet from where he lay, his sister's breaths wheezed like winds through a cave. Sometimes they seemed to stop altogether. He would hold his own breath and wait for hers to start again or at least for some movement from her side of the room. He waited for the sound of that pick-up, too. Some nights a panic set in—that his father wasn't coming home. After his parents started arguing, his father came home later and later. Richeboux conjured all sorts of reasons, but the one he came to rely on most was that his father had been killed, run his truck off a bank, tumbled it over and over until the body flopped out on the ground. Then one night, about a month after his sister died, his father didn't come home. Richeboux can still remember the all-night silence of that driveway, the darkness unbroken by the flash of headlights making the turn, dipping across the sidewalk and into their yard. He longed for the uncertain flutter of his sister's breathing, like a bird, vanished from the room.

He leans into the gate. The chain-link pattern is cool against his forehead, naked chest, and belly. It's all coming back, right down that snaggle-tooth road between the stacks: a huge swelling wave he's been running from his whole life. He can hear the slosh of it, feel the flecks of wind-blown foam hit his cheeks. Soon it'll be up to his knees, its watery fingers creeping up his chest.

He lets go of the fence, sits in the gavel road with his arms on this knees, and lowers his head onto the cradle of his interlaced fingers.

Leigh started it with all that stuff about the Indians she'd gotten from a book their mother read them. There was the seven-foot-tall Choctaw Chief, Tuskaloosa, who fought the Spanish Explorer, Hernando De Soto, and Moundville, the nearby site of an Indian village that vanished long ago. Leigh got it in her head that the Indians were still there, hanging around as spirits. She nagged their mother into taking them to Moundville, though Richeboux could see in his mother's eyes when she finally said, "yes," that she wished she'd never heard of that book.

Acee showed up in the yard the morning of what Richeboux's mother called their "outing," just as they were getting into the car. He stood at the corner of the yard with his hands in his pockets and stared at the car like he'd never seen one before, then turned and walked back toward the lumberyard gate.

Leigh bounced in the front seat. "Let Acee go too!"

Richeboux's mother was halfway in the car. She paused with her hand on the door.

"Acee."

He stopped but didn't turn.

"You want to come with us to Moundville to visit the museum and see the Indian mounds?"

Acee looked back at the car. His eyes were squinched together as if his brain was arguing with itself. He ran his tongue over his lips, looked at his feet as if he was puzzled that they were still there in Richeboux's yard. "I best get on home."

Richeboux leaned out the car window. "Come on Acee. They got mounds over a hundred feet high and Indian bones."

His mother tapped the key on the windshield. "It's O.K., Acee. We'll be back by early afternoon. I reckon you're more Indian than we are."

———————————

It was a clear Spring day. The March wind blew. Leigh danced in it. It blew their mother's hair and wrapped her dress tightly around her legs. Richeboux and Acee raced each other up and down the mounds. From the highest mound, way above the treetops, you could see the Black Warrior River. The four of them stood and watched a sailboat tack back and forth across the wind-whipped surface.

Richeboux's mom held Leigh in her arms to see the boat. Acee stood on tip-toe. He kept glancing at Richeboux's mother, watching her face. "What's that?" he said and pointed at the sailboat. "How come it don't fall over?"

"It's the wind," she said. "They know how to use the wind to lift the sail and push it forward."

Acee stretched his arms out like a bird, turned his face upward, and closed his eyes. The wind blew against him in wider, circling gusts. He tipped backward but caught his balance and held himself as if hovering in the wind. The sun shone on his forehead and cheeks, down the rim of his nose, accentuated the half-moon curve of his closed eyes. Not a muscle moved in his face, but there was a smile nevertheless.

"Acee's flying," said Leigh.

Their mother set Leigh down and opened her arms like Acee's. Richeboux kept his eyes on their mother's empty hands. Then she, too, spread her arms, let her head fall back to look at the sky. The wind whipped her hair and dress. She closed her eyes, and her face opened in a smile Richeboux had not seen for a long time.

Richeboux spread his arms. The four of them were above everything, the grassy plain of the park, cut by its winding driveway; the tall pines along the river; the sparkling water beyond. The spirits were there, just as Leigh had said.

Their mother had made sandwiches and lemonade. When they came down from the high mound, she spread their picnic on one of the wooden tables at the edge of the museum entrance patio near a concrete statue of de Soto, receiving a wooden peace pipe offered by a tall, angular Indian with a sharp face and three feathers hanging down the back of his head.

"Is that Chief Tuskaloosa?" said Leigh.

"I don't know," their mother said. "He's tall enough to be." She walked over to the statue and read the inscription. "It just says 'de Soto,'" she said. "It doesn't give the name of the Indian."

Leigh gave most of her sandwich to Acee and began to skip about the table. "Where are the Indians? I want to see the Indians."

"They're inside," said their mother.

She got up and gathered the picnic leavings to take to the car. "Wait here," she said. "We'll go see them when I get back."

Leigh started whining—"I wanna go in now."

"Hush!" their mother said. "We have to go in together." She looked from one of them to the other. "Understand?"

Acee lowered his head, twiddled his thumbs in his lap.

The guard was a thick little man in a tan shirt and too-short, green trousers. He stood just inside the door as if looking out from a pulpit. A stack of brochures was clutched to his chest. He shook his head as they walked in.

"Unh unh. Not him. Colored day's on Monday."

The glass entrance doors swung shut. Acee backed against them.

"He's with us," Richeboux's mother said. "His mother works for us."

"Can't help it. Coloreds on Monday. That's the rule."

"We like Acee," Leigh said.

"It's just this time," said their mother. "We came all the way down here, and we'll only be a few minutes."

The guard slapped the brochures against his thigh. "Do I have to say it again?"

Their mother's voice took the tone Richeboux had heard her use with his father. "Say whatever you want. But I'd like to know what it's going to hurt for one little colored boy to walk through this museum on a beautiful day like this and walk out?"

"Lady, I been here on Mondays. It's like a bunch of kangaroos got loose." He nodded toward the other customers. "There's old folks in here. We can't have him running loose amongst all these people. Now, I'm gon say it one last time: that boy stays outside!"

Richeboux looked at Acee. His head was bowed like he was hiding. Richeboux whapped him on the shoulder. "Come on," he said. "I don't want to go in this old museum anyway. It stinks in there."

Their mother pushed Richeboux aside, knelt before Acee, and fished a dime and nickel from her purse. "Here," she said. "Take this and go to that vendor cart out there and get a snow cone. We'll be out in a minute."

Acee slipped through the opening between the doors and started across the yard toward the vendor. His fists were rolled in his pockets. His head was bowed. He raised it a couple of times to glance about.

"I'm going with him," Richeboux said.

Leigh ran for the door. "Me, too."

His mother grabbed Leigh's hand. "No, you're not. You badgered me into bringing you down here, and you're going to see it. There's nothing we can do about Acee." She took Richeboux's arm and pushed him and Leigh toward the entrance to the exhibit. The guard shoved a brochure at her. She paused and stared at him. "Get that thing out of my way."

The doorway to the exhibit room was low and cave-like with

the word, "Panorama," over it in letters the color of bright-red lipstick. Richeboux halted just inside the door. The air was heavy and cold and smelled of earth. The room was large, atrium-like with a wraparound balcony and a three-foot stucco railing they would have to peer over to see the exhibit. Other visitors milled about, looked over the railing, pointed and whispered. The custodian, an old lady in a black skirt, white blouse, and lace-up granny shoes, strolled about the balcony with hands clasped behind her back, stopping to answer questions. Leigh pulled back on their mother's hand.

"I don't wanna go."

"Nonsense," said their mother. She picked Leigh up, rested Leigh's rear on her forearm. "You wanted to see the Indians, and here they are."

Richeboux fixed his eyes on the railing. Beyond it there was no floor. He was sure of it. The opening went down, well below the level they were standing on. And whatever was down there gave off the cold, earthy odor of death.

Their mother walked toward the railing. Leigh jerked her head away as soon as she saw what was beyond. "No!" she said. She twisted about in her mother's arms. "No!"

His mother stood frozen at the railing, staring down at the exhibit. Leigh rested her chin on her mother's shoulder and stared back toward the lobby. There were tears in her eyes. Her fists were curled at her neck.

Richeboux forced himself to the edge. And there they were: the bones of over a hundred Indians, scattered in the dust of their uncovered graves. Brows of skulls and rims of burial pottery reflected light from four dirty skylights and the bare bulbs spaced below the balcony railing. In some plots there were small skeletons next to larger ones. The dark eye sockets stared past him at the ceiling. The toothless mouths hung open as if caught in time. He held fast to the railing. It was the loudest silence he'd ever heard.

The custodian passed behind them, patted Leigh on the head.

"It's O.K., honey. They can't hurt you."

She placed herself next to Richeboux at the railing. Her hands were covered in purplish spots, and as she gripped the railing, the flesh on them sagged between her stretched tendons. "They buried favorite belongings with the body, you see, so the person would have them in the afterlife. Graves with more objects than others mean the person was wealthy or, perhaps, a chief."

Leigh's thumb was in her mouth. She began to whimper.

Richeboux's mother looked down the rail at the woman and turned her gaze back to the graves. "It's all so dusty," she said.

"There's no one to clean them," said the custodian. "They'll just lie there, I suppose, until the building crumbles." She drew a deep sigh. "The pottery was beautiful once. There are a few polished pieces in the room off the lobby."

"It's a shame," his mother said.

"I used to fret over it," said the woman. "But my husband says, 'Why get so worked up over a bunch of dead Indians?'"

When they left the room of bones and returned to the lobby it was like leaving the dim past for the sunlit here-and-now. His mother set Leigh down and tried to take her hand. But Leigh was already headed for the glass doors to the outside. And beyond them, in the even brighter sunlight on the patio, stood Acee. His hands were still in his pockets. His eyes looked away as if they'd already left for home.

His mother took Leigh to the bathroom, and Richeboux joined Acee outside.

"It wadn't nothing," he said. "Let's go pee." He headed around the side of the building where there were large bushes.

"I done been," said Acee.

Richeboux wedged himself between two large hollies next to the wall, unzipped and started to pee. And there on the ground, where his stream spattered against the dank earth, lay the wooden peace pipe held by the Indian in the statue. It was broken in half. He thought of picking it up, but it had pee all over it. When he finished, he kicked it under the largest holly, and went back to the patio.

Acee stood where Richeboux had left him. His arms were crossed. And the look on his face was the same one Richeboux had just seen through the glass doors of the museum. Over Acee's shoulder, the stone Indian bowed toward de Soto with his empty, offering hands.

———————

Richeboux rises slowly, brushes the gravel from his jeans. Down 15th Street, police sirens wail, headed his way. He tenses, ready to crouch in the driveway. But the cars turn. Their sirens begin to fade. He slouches his shoulder against the gate. Even if he could get it open, the one at the other end is locked. Maids take the bus now.

The police sirens trail off toward the far side of the colored section. The light above the railroad crossing gives a final "pop" and dies. The glow from the downtown lights, beyond the trees of his old neighborhood, diffuses into the light of the moon. He gives the gate a final shake, turns to head up the incline to the main road.

Even before the gate's hinges stop rattling, the owl's shadow passes over him, and glides down the road between the stacks. The broad gray wings are spread in perfect horizontal. The talons hang like trailing hooks. The wings flap. The talons open. The landing is soft and certain. The wing tips clamp downward into the sawdust of the road as if hiding the business below, making the catch dead certain. The bird balances on its wings, attacks with its beak, works its feet into the prey. Then suddenly the movement stops. For the shortest second, the owl's head turns Richeboux's way with its pitiless beak, the all-knowing amber eyes. The feet shift again; the great wings spread, begin their slow, powerful beat. The bird lifts off, hauling the rat by its spine. Its drooping tail and dangling feet barely clear the top of one of the stacks of lumber.

Soaring above everything like him, his mother, Leigh, and Acee on top of that mound, watching the sailboat cut though the glittering water. Like the passage Mrs. Kusinski read to him this morning.

*The finely breathing wind..., the yellow sun sinking in crimson.*
*To her it was so beautiful... she wanted to gather the glowing*
*peaks to her breast and die.*

He turns and walks back up the incline to 15th Street. Not a car
in sight. He crosses the road to where a path dips from the shoulder,
crosses a ditch, and leads toward a patch of woods. Beyond that is
Cherrytown, where it began this time last night, near the spot where
Acee's journey to his house used to begin. He starts walking. His arms
are as strong as the owl's talons. His legs are loose. His body is back.

## Rosemont Greene

Can't stand bib overalls. Never could. Wore them the whole time I was growing up, picking cotton not more than five miles from here. Quit 'em soon as I got me enough money to buy some real clothes—gabardine slacks and shoes you can hide a razor in. Low-cut shoes too, so you can get that razor out quick enough to use it. But I done climbed back in my overalls tonight. It's crawling-in-the-dirt time.

Been setting here in this patch of woods across the back parking lot of the store now for over two hours. Butt so cold it's done ached all up in my bones. Chigger-bugs and ticks crawling up my legs. Gnats and mosquitoes buzzing like hornets. You know they gon hit when you hear that *Zzzzzzit!* in your ear. Like somebody done run a mill saw through your head. And right there 'cross the road, hanging over the shed room window of my store, is that old army blanket I keep up for privacy. If I'd been paying attention to myself instead of trying to get Raiford Waites's butt down my liquor cellar in the field behind the store, I'd have brought it out here to scrooch up under. At least keep the mosquitoes off.

Can't sneak over and get it now. Too damn close to when Starnes liable to show up.

I may be done got too old for this shit.

I reach around and take the army .45 out my back pocket. Heavy as pig iron. Done 'bout wore a groove in my hip. I lay it in front of me next to the flashlight. Thing of it is, if Starnes's boys come on foot, I ain't sure I can hear 'em. Night-jars and crickets down in the field behind the store act like they trying to out-sing each other. Bullfrogs in the swamp sound like Louis Armstrong on a cracked trumpet.

It's dark down here when the place ain't running and the lights ain't on. Them two black oaks in the front yard pretty much block out the moon. Starnes and his boys got any sense, that's exactly where they gon be. More I set here though, more I wonder: maybe his boys had enough for a while. Resting up for tomorrow. They been down in that bottom land along the river for the last twenty-four hours, hauling their butts through canebreaks and swamp water, sliding their balls and dicks over logs big as a tractor tire, banging toes and shins on them knobby cypress knees. Following them bellering, soapy-mouthed hounds. Makes me grin, just thinking 'bout it.

I done time in the dirt and leaves before—lots of it. Run the swamps and canebreaks with bloodhounds chasing me. Course, couple of times in my younger days it was some woman's husband. I wadn't but sixteen then. Could have run to Africa and back, jumped over the moon. But after that it was bloodhounds or shepherd police dogs. And I admit, I was scared some of them times. You get right lonely busting your way through the woods and briars by yourself. I done had enough of that shit.

I remember the stories my grandma told 'bout slaves trying to escape during slavery times. Ones that got caught—they hauled back all tore up, arms broke, heads busted open. Had what she called, "a gone-for-dead look." She'd set there, talking, voice getting lower and lower, kind of glancing about like she was afraid somebody was listening, them old, bony fingers picking at a scrap of yarn in her lap. "Then they'd call us all out to watch the beating," she said. "Most pitiful sights I ever seen."

I done 'bout convinced myself Starnes ain't coming, and I ain't had a smoke since I been out here. I work my way back into the thicket, fish a new-rolled butt from the bib of my overalls, and light up. Hold it down near the ground when I ain't taking a draw, and think things over.

The plan we got oughta work. Long as we get past Starnes. Long as Raiford stays hid in his hole. Long as Acee gets himself down here and do what he's supposed to do. That's what's got me worried. Acee's nervous as a horse 'round a rattlesnake, and Raiford's more like the snake itself—hotheaded like his daddy, Delentha, was. Got hot with me when I put him in that liquor cellar. Looked back up at me from the bottom of the ladder. Afro hairdo matted on his head. All that running and hiding like a animal done made him look like one.

"Gimme a gun," he said. "I lost mine in the swamp."

"You ain't gon need no gun, you stay in this hole."

"I might not stay in this hole."

"Live like a dog for a few hours," I said, "or get shot, skinned, and gutted like a deer." I threw him down a pack of cigarettes and some matches. He was still staring at me when I shut the trap door.

And Acee. It was clear as sunlight through that shed room window when we had our talk with Miss Leone: he don't want no part of this. Her trying to pin him down with them ice-pick eyes. Acee ducking and dodging all over the room. It was there tonight, too, when he come down to the store with Resa. Set there all fidgety, feet shuffling about, tapping the floor, like they might just pick up and leave on their own, no matter what his head and shoulders gon do. Had that out-of-breath sound in his voice. Got to be hardness in there somewhere—he's Delentha's son and Raiford's brother. But the preacher might have done ruined that—"summoned forth" (that's how he'd say it) the softness in Acee. And ain't no doubt: it's done got worse since the preacher died. That's what Resa's so hung up on. She was protecting it tonight, pushing back 'gainst me at every step. Shoulda made her leave and made Acee set there and look me in the eye. Put some hardness back in him.

I take one more draw on my cigarette, crush it out in the leaves. Slug-slime all over my fingers. Stay here long enough, I'll slime up myself. I start to crawl on back to where I left the flashlight, kinda bobcat style, and that's when I hear it. I freeze with one paw off the ground.

Car engines, humming up the hill through the trees. Tires thumping over the ruts in the road. Oil pans scraping along the dirt.

I switch from bobcat back to down-on-my-belly, like a alligator. Sure 'nuff, couple of them black and white Fords come coasting into the yard. Done turned their engines off. Whip antennas swishing from the bumpy ride. Bubbles on top look like thumbs been hit with a hammer. I can't tell how many deputies are inside. The first car eases up under one of them oaks. Then, 'fore I know it, the second one cuts on its engine and headlights and comes tearing past me into the back lot, doing one of them slide-in-the-gravel, bootlegger turns. Puts its grill within two feet of my store's back stoop.

Men all shapes and sizes pour out. Hard to see 'em in those tan and gray uniforms through the dust, but I count five. Got their guns out, night sticks and billy clubs swinging. Headlights shine off their backsides as that big, flat-topped deputy, Otis, leads them up the steps. Been known Otis a long time—no more brains than a bent nail. I grab a good hold on the .45 and scoot farther back in the bushes.

'Round front, more car doors slamming. Boots tramping up the stairs and on the porch. Both bunches of 'em—front and back— jerk screen doors off hinges, kick in the wooden ones. Door knobs and hardware fly every whichaway. They commence to thrash about inside, hollering, slamming doors, turning over furniture. Liquor glasses smash against the bar and floor.

Then from somewhere in the middle of that ruckus, the Devil starts to speak like he's shouting from the jaws of Hell. "Rosemont Greene, hear me! The wrath of God has descended on you. Woe to those who hide their deeds in the dark. You got Raiford Waites, you better give him to us. Don't, in the morning this place'll look like the walls of Jericho. And you'll look like you been thrown in the lion's den."

Starnes is eat up with anger like a corpse is eat up with worms.

But when he starts quoting Scripture, you know for sure the monster done took over.

One of the bastards picks up a chair in my shed-room and busts out the window. Pure meanness. Glass, sash, mullions come spraying out in the yard, along with the blanket I use to cover it. "Whoeee!" they say. Like they having a party. A couple of deputies come stomping out the back door, down the steps, shining flashlights all under the house, even up in the trees, then head for the sheds and outbuildings. I ain't seen no dogs yet, and that's a damn good thing. 'Cause they'd track Raiford down 'cross that field to the cellar. And they'd already been done found my ass laying here with my belly in the dirt.

The two men with the flashlights sneak up to the pick-up Bailey Bridewell fixed up for Acee, peek into the cab and bed, and move on.

I take a breath, tell myself it's gon be alright. They ain't gon go running 'round searching the woods at night without no dogs. Besides, Starnes's got the whole neighborhood to search. And he done tore my store up so bad, there ain't nowhere around here left to look. Except the place where the treasure's hid.

"Tear up the floor boards if you have to," says Starnes. "There's liquor stored here somewhere. Son of a bitch might be there."

Starnes kicks the back door aside, rips what's left of the screen door off its hinges, throws it into the yard, and comes prancing out on the stoop with his fists on his hips. Got that whip handle in one hand. Cigarette dangling from his lips like he's somebody out the wild west. Commences to look about the back yard. I could hit that son-of-a-bitch right between the eyes if I had the .30-30 I keep buried under the house. They've probably already found the sawed-off twelve-gauge pump and .38 I keep behind the bar. Liquor-running guns. Got one of them Savage "over-and-unders" in there, too. .22 rifle barrel laying on top of a .410 shotgun. Best squirrel gun I ever had. Took it off Bailey for a gambling debt. Keep it in a slit in my mattress for backup, just in case.

Otis stomps through the back door and locks his butt in place next to Starnes. Sure enough, he's got the twelve-gauge in his hand like he's gon squeeze it in two. They whisper back and forth a minute. Then Otis heads back inside, starts yelling orders. When Otis gets worked up, he squeaks like a furnace door.

The two men with the flashlights walk toward the back stoop, poking each other, joking and jabbering. Starnes flips his cigarette in the dirt at their feet. "Come on, we leaving. He ain't here."

"Where to?" says the skinny one. Mouth dripping snuff. Got a growth on his jaw big as a puff-ball mushroom.

"Back up the hill," says Starnes. "Find that smart ass son of a bitch, A.C., or whatever his name is."

He turns, goes back in the house. Deputies come pouring out both ends of the store. Got a whole case of Falstaff and a couple bottles of liquor apiece, some of it my best 'shine I have special made. Ferment it with yeast—not a drop of sheep shit in it. All that liquor wouldn't have been in there if I didn't have to make room for a cot and drink-case table in my cellar for Raiford. Give him a lantern, too, and I'm hoping that somewhere behind those wild eyes of his, he's got enough sense not to light it.

The two deputies been searching out back start arguing with Otis at the patrol car about going in for their share.

"Get it and get back," he says. "Shug's ready to go."

The engine starts on the Ford out front. It backs out the shadows of the oaks and sits with its lights shining smack in my direction. Starnes is driving. Got his elbow out the window, staring up at the store where two or three deputies still grabbing at the liquor over the bar. Couple of bottles break. Starnes jerks up the emergency brake, gets out, slams the door, starts toward the front steps.

"Parnell, you and Tossie, get the hell out of there and get in the car."

Deputy with the mushroom jaw scoots on out the back. Got a bottle of white liquor in each hand. Jumps in the car with Otis. The other one comes out the front, clambers down the steps, and makes to dodge past Starnes toward the car. He's got a bottle under one arm and one in each hand. Starnes grabs the back of the man's shirt, steps directly in front of him, and smashes one of them bottles with his whip handle. He jerks another bottle out the man's other hand and throws in the yard. Then he puts his face right up under the man's nose until the third bottle drops from under the man's arm. Well, at least that's two bottles that ain't broken.

"Now, get your ass in the car!" Starnes says.

The man runs toward the car, hand dripping blood, trying to get a bandana around it.

Otis pulls his car 'round to the front and waits for Starnes's car to lead the way. Starnes's standing with the car door open and one foot on the running board still cussing the deputy he caught with the bottles. Directly he steps back, slams the car door, raises that whip handle and brings it down on the roof of his car like a pistol shot. Then he walks over to Otis's car and does the same.

"Everyone of you sons-of-bitches got a ounce of liquor on you, better get it out of your hands. *Now!*"

Bottles and beer cans come flying out the car windows. Couple of bottles hit together and break. Beer cans spewing everywhere. And I'm thinking: well, there's about ten more bottles saved, and if this shit keeps up, I'm liable to drink one myself.

Starnes kicks a couple of beer cans aside and gets in his car. He pulls ahead of Otis, and starts up the road. I watch the taillights bob and shimmy out of sight 'fore I get up to my butt, fish out another smoke. I light it, and look over at the store.

They done wrecked it: windows broke, doors tore off, not to mention all the stock they busted. Probably drank some of it, too. Take me a month to get back in business. I ain't a praying man, but I'm asking Somebody that ain't here on the ground with me to please let that juke box still work. Thing cost me over two-hundred dollars. I think about easing out of my hiding place to go take a look, but when Starnes leaves a place, it's like some nasty, ghost part of him stays behind—like he done left a cobra in the yard. I can almost smell it, squirming and sliding about, flicking that forked tongue, waiting for a sign of movement.

I smoke a while to calm down. Night sounds start to creep back in. Crickets and nightjars. Old bullfrog makes the ground shake. All that noise. Yet and still, when you by yourself in the woods at night, there's a kind of quietness under it all. Breeze rustling the trees. Birds fluttering. Varmints sneaking about. It always makes me feel peaceful, like whatever's coming down around you, everything's gon be alright.

But something won't settle tonight. It's that cobra feeling again. Them police cars: they shoulda been up to the main road by now. But they ain't. They're setting on idle not more than halfway up my driveway. And there can't be but one reason for that. The son of a bitch is letting men out to sneak back on foot. I scrunch myself farther back in the thicket and check to be sure that extra clip of .45 bullets is still in my pocket.

## Mem Cohane

Mem places the receiver in its cradle and rocks forward with the heels of her hands on the edge of the bed. Mrs. Kusinski—of all people! She glances over her shoulder at the alarm clock on the matching bedside table. It's too far in shadow to read, but it must be at least ten.

"Katherine," she'd called herself. Their English teacher. What in the name of God possessed Richeboux to go running off to her? She tutored him last year, or was it the year before? Or both. Anyway, that ended a long time ago, once he was off the team.

Through the open window, her friend Sonya's voice wafts up from the patio below, dripping with traces of the gin/sherry mix Mem poured for them earlier as they sat by the pool. Sonya is trying to sing along with songs from her pink Zenith transistor radio. She fumbles at the dial, switching stations, finds sudden blasts of music and joins in, out-of-tune and off-key. Mem chose the sherry and gin because those bottles were already half empty and her parents were less likely to notice. But she shouldn't have mixed them. Big mistake.

"My parents or yours?," Sonya yells over Martha and the Vandella's *Heat Wave.*

"Neither," Mem says. "Turn it down! I'll tell you in a minute."

It all makes sense, sort of: Richeboux drunk and upset. Mrs. K didn't say it was over Mem, but what else could it be? When his feelings get loose, they crash about like they're lost in the dark. She can't stop herself from playing with them, prodding them here and there. Sooner or later the game changes to hide-and-seek, with her creeping closer and him slinking further into the shadows. It's exciting thinking about slipping into those shadows with him. But that's over now. She all but dropped the "goodbye" word when they parted at the Red Elephant. She's never let it go that far before, though she's played around with it. That thing, whatever it is, that makes her push it with Richeboux. And this time something fell over the edge. She felt it in every step as she flew up the stairs to answer the phone.

Dampness from her swim suit has seeped into the bedspread. Her first two-piece, which her mother says is at least a size too small. She turns off the bedside lamp and gets up to head back to the patio. She, too, is a little woozy from the gin and sherry. "Shit," she whispers, and plops back on the bed.

Why didn't he just do the usual and go off and get drunk with his stupid friends? Is Mrs. K some kind of guardian angel just because she helped him pass English—her own stupid course? He could use a guardian angel with a witchy–bitchy mother like Mrs. Branscomb. But not *Kath*-er-ine, "Kooky Kusinski," the kids call her. She reminds Mem of one of those haughty, swishy actresses her parents like, Joan Crawford or Vivien Leigh, playing her own made-up role. "Literature is life; life is passion"—every day at the beginning of class, before she stretches and purrs herself into her never never land of poetry and make-believe. Butt against the chalk tray, head back and chin up, the high heel dropping to the floor, instep rubbing the calf of her other leg. Nylon on nylon. It's a neat trick. The guys grin and whisper. Mem's even practiced it herself in front of her parent's full-length mirror. If she used it right, it would make Richeboux jealous, maybe get a rise out of him. She'd need stockings and high heels to pull it off, though, both of which she hates.

And the dreamy trance—Mem is not the trancy type.

But tonight Mrs. K's voice was different—a "woman-to-woman" thing, as if they were equals. Like, we're adults here, he's in trouble, and we've got to help him. "Mem," she said (not "Miss Cohane" anymore), "Mem, he really needs you now. Do you think you can find him?" How does she know what Richeboux needs? That's Mem's job, and she's an expert at it. And how exactly did Mrs. K put it: "he *really needs* you now"; or was it more like, "he really needs *you* now." As opposed to whom? There wasn't any of that Mr. Branscomb stuff, either. It was Richeboux this and Richeboux that. She almost whispered it.

"Come on, Mem! Iss that new singer I want youta hear. She sings that new kina music—like Folk, but iss not."

"In a minute!"

Joan Baez—*Lily of the West? Barbara Allen?* Mem's way ahead of Sonya on the music scene.

Sonya says Mrs. K's got the hots for the boys in her class. Sonya doesn't know squat about sex, but she can sniff it out like a weasel. Of course Richeboux *is* good-looking—she wouldn't date anybody who isn't. And she's heard that breathless crowd of junior-class teeny-boppers whispering about him in the hall. "A real man," one of them said. He's more like a twelve-year-old when he's around her. He doesn't care a thing about Mrs. K's wonderful world of literature, and she sure doesn't know a thing about sports. So, what would they talk about? It's all bullshit, and she's not going to think about it anymore.

Mem sticks her feet straight out from the bed and points her toes, feels the stretch of her perfectly tanned legs, which she can't appreciate fully in the dim light. When she and Richeboux go parking, down by the river, he begins sometimes by putting her legs across his thighs, stretching them out along the seat, bending over them, and rubbing his fingertips in a circular motion on her knees as if he's admiring finely turned wood. It always catches her by surprise, sends tingles everywhere, and she wonders where his urge to do that comes from. She loves watching the back of his neck bent over her, the way the moonlight through the car window outlines the stretched tendons, the overlaying swatches of hair brushing the frayed collar of his T-shirt. She counts seconds to see how long she can resist putting her fingers there.

She rubs her hands down the muscles in her thighs, stifles the itch to slide a palm between them, work a finger under the suit, take care of what Richeboux would be taking care of if they were out together, parked in one of the usual places.

Unh, unh. That's all done and over with. She bounces her legs off the edge of the bed, releases a sigh.

Why didn't Mrs. K just invite him in? She has a husband of some kind. Where was he during the tutoring sessions?

Mem rises from the bed, runs a finger under her bathing suit bottom to re-cover her rear end, pulls it out, and lets it pop. So what is she supposed to do: drive around town looking for him, walk up and down the streets and boulevards, calling—"Riiiche-boux!"

She starts toward the door to the hallway, stops, and turns reflexively toward the mirror over her dresser. She can barely make her image out in the dark, but ruffles her damp hair anyway and admires the silhouette she makes with her arms cocked behind her head. Kim Novak did it somewhere.

At the top of the stairs, she pokes her head out the window. "Sonya, turn it down!" Sonya is splayed out on the chaise lounge, her head flopped to the side. She drank about two-thirds of the gin/sherry mix. "The neighbors will start complaining," Mem whispers to herself. Not a word to Sonya about this Kusinski thing. It would give her burrowing little mind something to dig for.

At the bottom of the stairs she stops, absentmindedly clicks on the air-conditioning, and heads to the kitchen. Richeboux says drinking lots of water is the best way to avoid a hangover.

"Are you comin' er not?" yells Sonya from the patio.

"Getting water."

"Bring me some. I'm thirsty."

Mem reaches in the cabinet for another glass.

"Alka-Seltzer, too. I think I'm gonna barf."

Mem slams the glass down on the counter. This afternoon with Richeboux in the cemetery, the back of his head frozen in place across the hood of the car when she asked him about the colored preacher, Resa's and Acee's friend. She felt like grabbing him by the ears before he finally looked at her. The same old excuse he and his buddies use for everything they get into: "County High." Bull crap. They blame everything on County High because County High is full of rednecks.

But it wasn't County High this time. *He was there!*

A tiny pain, lodged in the pit of her stomach starts to spread. At the very least he knows who did it—Ellis, Jamie, some other idiot in their bunch. Or some entirely different idiot from some entirely different bunch. Richeboux is worthless as a liar, and he certainly can't lie to her.

She spreads her fingers on the countertop. The charm bracelet with Richeboux's charm on it clinks against the Formica. Why doesn't he listen to her? She knew something like this was going to happen.

So, is that why he went to Mrs. Kusinski's? He's scared, he needs advice? A small bubble of regret bursts in her brain. It could have been her if she'd been more careful at the Red Elephant.

She fills Sonya's glass, fumbles for a pack of Alka-Seltzer in the drawer next to the sink under tape, gauze, iodine, asprin, and a jumble of prescription bottles her mother keeps for every ailment she can imagine, then turns and heads out through the dining room and the sun porch toward the patio. Bugs zip through the muggy air and plop onto the surface of the bottom-lit pool. The backs of Sonya's roly-poly shoulders are pressed into the wrought-iron grill of the chaise lounge. Cigarette smoke curls around wings of coal-black hair, which she cuts and dyes to look like Liz Taylor's in *Cat on a Hot Tin Roof.* A flush of anger overtakes Mem. She tucks the Alka-Seltzer pack into the top of her swim suit, pictures Sonya at their all-girl, spend-the-night parties, calling everybody "Big Daddy." "Awwww, Big Daddy." So stupid. Boobs aren't everything.

Sonya's calves rest across the wrought-iron coffee table. She spreads her red-nailed, double-jointed toes open and shut. Claims the exercise calms her nerves. Maybe Liz does it, too.

"Ju bring it?"

"Yeah." Mem waves the water under her nose.

"No, the Alka-Seltzer."

"I guess we're out."

Sonya pushes herself up to sitting and reaches for the glass. Mem pulls it away.

"Give it!" Sonya says.

Mem eases the glass toward her. Sonya snatches it, spilling half of it on her legs.

"You're mean," she says, brushing the water off her legs with her free hand. "Who wassit onna phone?"

"None of your business."

"I bet it 'uz Richeboux, and you're not tellin."

Mem reaches for a cigarette from the pack of Kools next to Sonya's leg, lights it, and puffs out a mouthful of chlorine-tasting smoke. She stifles a cough. "It was Mrs. Kusinski."

Sonya raises herself off the seat and tucks her legs under her as if to get a better view. "Oh my God! You won the English prize."

Mem takes a long puff—feels dizzy.

"No. It's about Richeboux. She used to tutor him."

"Mmm. Ver-ry interesting."

Mem shoots her a not-one-step-further look. Sonya slumps back, seems to want to say something, but either can't form it in her brain or get it to her lips. Mem glances at the liquor mix remaining in the glass on the table, thinks of tossing it into the pool. Maybe she should just leave. Take her mother's car and drive, whether she looks for Richeboux or not. Let Sonya sit and stew, do her best to cover if Mem's parents call, which her mother will almost certainly do.

"So, what about Mrs. K and Richeboux?"

"She wants me to help her get in touch with him is all. Something about credits to graduate."

Sonya grabs her cigarette from the ashtray. The inch-long ash plops onto her leg. "Ouch!" She brushes it off, looks up at Mem with peeking-animal eyes.

"I thought y'all broke up."

"Here!" Mem tosses the Alka-Seltzer into Sonya's lap, crushes out her cigarette, and reaches to turn down the radio. The phone in her bedroom rings again.

She makes another dash up the stairs, counting the rings, which grow more insistent with every step. She grabs the receiver, even more out of breath than the last time.

"Richeboux?"

"No, Mem—it's Resa."

"Resa?"

Mem lets herself down on the wet spot, takes a deep breath. *She should have called first.* She could have done that instead of wasting time with Sonya. "Oh, I'm so glad you called. It was so good to see you today. How are you doing?"

"We're not doing so well."

Mem twirls her wrist, wrapping the black phone cord tightly around her finger.

"What's wrong?"

Resa seems to be putting her hand over the receiver to talk with someone in the room with her, probably her boyfriend. Mem glances at the bedside lamp. Decides not to turn it on.

"Mem, things are real bad down here. The sheriff and a bunch of his men are all over the neighborhood, dragging people out their houses. They hit Acee's uncle in the head, knocked him off the porch at Acee's house. They say he's hurt real bad."

Beyond her bedroom window, the darkness is stained greenish-yellow by lights from the pool. The distant hum of an air-conditioner mixes with the muffled music of Sonya's radio—something by Danny and the Belmonts.

"Is the boy—I mean the man—they're after, is he there?"

"No. I'm with my cousin May at her house. Acee is hiding out back. I just know they're looking for him to make him tell where Raiford is."

"Oh." She pivots a foot back and forth over the soft piles of rug. "Can't you and Acee just leave?"

For a moment there is no answer. It sounds like Resa has dropped the hand holding the receiver to her lap.

"Mem, we can't *just leave*. We can't go running around in the woods with nowhere to go, hoping the Sheriff won't find us."

Once again the receiver Resa is holding seems to drop away. Mem strains to listen. Sniffles. Gasps of breath. Muffled sobs. They come like blows to Mem's chest. She's off balance, fumbling for the first time in her life.

"Mem, it's real bad down here. It's...." The words dissolve into a tremulous moan.

Mem feels the stillness in the hallway beyond her bedroom door. She twists the cord until the flesh of her fingers swells. "You want me to come get you all or something?"

Resa's voice is moist and breathy. "Yeah, that's it. I know it's a lot to ask, but they will kill Acee if they find him. I just know it." She sniffs, wipes her nose. "I was thinking maybe you and that boy you were with—Bo, Acee calls him—he used to be Acee's friend. Y'all are white...." Another pause, another shuddery breath. "Anyway, there's a spot we can meet down a dirt road about a mile from here where it crosses the railroad track. It's in the woods. Cops won't be there. Least not yet."

Mem rises slowly to her feet. Across the bed, through the window, the shadowy boughs of oaks on her front lawn sway against the glow of the street lamp she sees every night as she goes to sleep. She feels naked and exposed, reaches to straighten the elastic on her suit again. It *is* a size too small.

"The road is called Canaan. Used to run to a small church. You can't find it, but I expect your boyfriend can. It's off the road to Rose's. He's probably been there. White boys go down there from Rose's to hang around and drink."

Her parents will die if they find out she's gone into the colored section at night—all the stupid stuff they've got in their heads about what goes on there: drinking, dancing, wild music, and other unimaginable things, a power that seduces you into a dark side of life. Even if she lucks up and finds Richeboux to go with her. In fact they'd hate that even worse. They'd probably have him arrested.

"I.... Resa, I don't even know where Richeboux is. We had a fight today."

Resa is sniffling back tears. "Can't you find somebody else?

The image flashes into Mem's mind of a *LIFE Magazine* picture, a couple of months ago, a colored woman at a civil rights march, white, turban-like wrap on her head, tears pouring down her cheeks as if they ran from her heart. Mem sees Resa's face now, head bowed, tears dripping onto the phone.

"Come to my Aunt May's house," Resa says. "I'll take you where we need to go."

Mem takes a deep breath. "How do I get there? Better tell me real slow."

———

She's into a Sunday dress—she does not know why she grabbed that one—and tennis shoes. She bounds down the stairs, yelling to Sonya, trying to remember where she put her mother's car keys.

Richeboux—he should be here now. She should have held on to him until... when? Well, at least until she didn't need him anymore.

Sonya slouches against the doorframe between the dining room and kitchen, Alka-Seltzer glass dangling from her hand.

"Mem. *Where* are you going?"

Mem finds her purse. The car keys are under it. "It's Richeboux.

He's in trouble. If my parents call, tell them I'm asleep, tell them I got the cramps and went to bed."

"But Me-em!"

"Are you my friend or not?"

Sonya's head tilts backward. She catches it, flops it forward, and gives it a waggy shake. "I can't lie!"

"Yes, you can, Sonya! You can smoke cigarettes and drink stolen sherry on their patio, and you can tell them whatever I need you to." Mem pauses halfway through the door to the garage and gives her a sharp, blazing stare. "You better, Sonya, if you ever want to see me again."

Sonya slides down the doorframe onto her butt in the archway, one leg splayed in front of her. She manages to set the glass on the floor. Mem slams the door between the kitchen and garage. The Cadillac sits before her like a docked yacht.

## Rosemont Greene

Damn! Might-near perfect plan. And that gimp-legged son-of-a-bitch is 'bout to mess it up. Starnes ain't no smarter now than he was yesterday or day before, but older he gets, more devil there is in him. Should of reckoned on that.

So what the hell I'm gon do now?

When I was in the penitentiary, I done lot of time in solitary. Some days it felt like if I stayed there another minute, I'd bust open. I had to get a-hold of myself. So I'd set real still and rub the ends of my cut-off fingers with my thumb—sort of round and round over each of 'em. Something about stirring up that extra feeling on my fingers unworried my nerves, and pretty soon my mind was settled enough to think.

I look down at my hands now. They up to the same thing. And it's a good thing, too. 'Cause I got some heavy thinking to do.

Could try to get word to Acee. But I done sent Marcus home long time ago, and ain't nobody to carry it but me. Still I could slip down through the woods to the path by Hadley's Creek and work my way up to May's house. But that's counting on Acee being where he and Resa said he'd be, and it's hard to be sure with Starnes's men hopping 'bout all over the place. And if I leave here, I got to leave Raiford down there in that hole by himself. And how long is that gon last?

So, maybe just set here and wait it out. My feet and me get to arguing over that. There's something in a man that don't like setting still when somebody done jumped a step on you. I let my feet win for a minute, stand up to look about and listen. Can't hear nothing from up the driveway. The cars done gone. If Starnes dropped some men there, maybe they're waiting just like me. Or maybe they ain't in the driveway a'tall. Maybe they're sneaking 'round behind me through the woods.

I set back down, start back to rubbing my fingers. Last thing I need is to go running about Cherrytown, trying to find Acee. It's a good four hours before he's due down here to get that truck. Most likely, Starnes be gone by then. And the men he's done let out up the road be gone with him. But now, that thing he said 'bout the walls of Jericho—I don't know 'bout that. Worked up as he is, he might take a crazy notion to burn me out. And then there ain't but one thing left to do. Everything I own is in that store, including the cash I got stashed in that tin box up the chimney. Me and this .45 gon have to go to work.

Got me so disturbed I done pulled out another smoke without thinking. Something else besides Starnes has got me nervous. There's him and his boys up the hill toward Cherrytown and Raiford in the other direction, down 'cross the field. And I'm setting smack in the middle. All the noise Starnes's men made tearing up the store, Raiford's bound to heard it. Now, the question is: is he gon set there like I told him to, or is he gon get a crazy notion in *his* head. Raiford and Starnes got one thing in common: they angry men, and when men get angried up as much as they are, they don't think straight. Raiford come out that hole and get to running loose 'round here, what plan I got left is right out the window. Then folks gon start getting killed for sure.

Them cars been gone now over ten minutes, and ain't a deputy showed up yet. Maybe Starnes didn't let no men out a'tall, just switched drivers or something. I crawl on back in my hiding place, rest my back against a big sweet gum, and light up my smoke. Got lots of set-and-wait time 'fore Acee shows up to get that truck. Might as well play it cool like Marcus is always saying. Get a little sleep, keep my ears perked up the hill for Starnes's men.

Ain't been more'n a minute, and sure 'nuff here they come, cussing and stumbling down the road. Sounds like a couple of 'em. They keep coming, bitching 'bout Starnes making 'em set in the woods all night and watch a empty house. The one doing most of the cussing, first one in the yard. Big, sloped-shouldered man. Old as I am. Huffing and puffing like he just pulled a wagon up a hill. Starnes done strapped one of them old army radios on his back, 'bout the size of a case of beer and made of solid steel.

"Damn this thing," he says. He squirms it off his back and sets it on the ground. Then he pulls out his old peter, scrooches up to the bushes at the edge of the yard, and lets it rip—playing with it to see how high he can make it go.

Second man no more than a shadow slipping out the woods. Stands there in the moonlight like if it hits him long enough, he'll come back to life. Scrawny-assed little cracker. Skin has a blue-moon shade to it like he's been weaned too early. Now, you talk 'bout nervous. I can see him shaking from thirty yards away. Got one hand on his gun and the other holding his belt, like, if he lets it go, his whole body gon slide to the ground.

I start to relax a bit. Starnes done reached way down in the bag for these two. I could slit either one of them crackers's throats without the other one knowing it.

I'm thinking 'bout crawling back to my smoking place behind the sweet gum when I hear something moving in the other direction—down 'cross the field where the liquor cellar is. And I'm cussing Starnes again. 'Cause if he's sending men from all sides, he's done figured out that this place is where the action gon be. And if that's true, somebody got to think up a whole new plan mighty damn quick.

I'm back to the belly crawl again, straining to see 'cross the parking lot to the shed where the truck is and down into the field toward the liquor cellar. Still as a ice pond. But I can hear the night breathing. I done set my .45 down somewhere, and I feel about in the leaves 'til I find it. Then I see a man's outline. He's half in shadow, got his back pressed up against the truck shed. Directly he darts out and comes loping 'cross the field and into the lot. Back bent low, swinging his arms, hands near 'bout touching the ground. Light on his feet as I used to be. And I know soon as the moonlight hits that bushy hair that he ain't no deputy.

Goddamn Raiford Waites! Goddamn him to hell.

# Richeboux

The moonlit path to Cherrytown is a narrow strip of clay, packed nearly to stone from years of maids walking to work and colored men and boys headed to their shifts at the lumberyard. Tall weeds rise on either side. The shadows from the woods between him and Cherrytown feel alive like the darkness before he met the hobo on the railroad track.

He's halfway down the shoulder of the grade when tires squeal down 15th Street toward the high school. A metallic green Cadillac, like the one Mem's mother owns, careens through the brightly lit intersection onto Loop Road, the same road he and his buddies took last night to Cherrytown, and the same one he and Mem took this afternoon to Uncle Rose's. Fins and pointy, rocket-shaped taillights identical to the ones that slipped past him in the Red Elephant Grill parking lot earlier.

The taillights disappear behind the bushes on the corner across from the high school. The tires squeal a couple seconds more down Loop Road. Couldn't be her. Before he took her there this afternoon, he's pretty sure she'd never been to Cherrytown. On the other hand, how many cars like that are there in this town? 'Course he doesn't hang around the Country Club's parking lot.

He squats, rests his elbows on his knees, laces his fingers together.

*What the fuck difference does it make?* Yet an ache hangs in the air between him and those vanishing taillights. Streaks of red into the night.

He steadies himself, takes the next few steps down the grade and onto the Cherrytown path. Even if there are other cars in town like the one he just saw, how many of them would be driven by someone who never uses her turn signal?

## Mem Cohane

In Mem's rearview mirror the cop's spread-eagle silhouette stands like an iron statue forged in the flashing light from his cruiser. The revolving beam sweeps the intersection of the entrance to Cherrytown, ignites her car's interior in bursts of red. She's never been told what to do by a cop before.

"This whole area is closed. Now get that thing turned around and get the hell out of here."

She can still feel the cop's breath-like fingers on her neck, his flashlight beam on the five inches of knee below her skirt hem, smell the nicotine-stained hand resting next to her on the Cadillac's windowsill. Beyond his thin waist and broad shoulders, beyond the cruiser itself, way back in the neighborhood, people were shouting, dogs barking. A siren wailed and died. Doors slammed.

She takes it slowly. Her hands are shaking. The sleeping monster of defeat places a heavy hand on her shoulder. She chokes back a sob. She cannot fail. She's got to find a way. Behind her shouts still come from the neighborhood, a bullhorn, a whistle. The Cadillac seems too big for her to drive. She slows further. She needs a place to turn, to get out of sight, before she's back to the main drag and away from Cherrytown altogether.

To her right just ahead and across the road from the flagpole in front of Druid, the colored high school, stands the old ice house her parents used to go to when she was a toddler, before they got their Frigidaire. A worn and broken concrete platform runs down the front, and a narrow driveway slips around the far side toward the back. She checks the rearview. The cop leans with his back to her, his gut pressed against the cruiser, talking on the radio.

She cuts her headlights, and makes the turn, easing the Cadillac along the gravel drive and down the dark corridor between the brick side of the ice house and a bush-covered fence. Branches of cedar and Ligustrum scrape the side of the car. She cringes at the sound, imagines the puzzled look on her father's face as he rubs his fingers down whitish streaks on the doors and fins in the morning.

Behind the ice house she turns the headlights back on and brakes at the entrance to a dirt lot full of mud holes, each one dark and deep enough to take half of a wheel. A pale ice truck sits with its rear bumper against a loading dock off the back. She eases ahead, dodging the mud holes, and pulls face-in to a rusty chainlink fence on the far side. She pushes in the headlights knob and cuts the motor. It's dark back here. The moonlight is not getting through. Dead-quiet except for the far-off crackle of the cop's radio.

Richeboux should be here. It pisses her off that he's not. As she drove over here from her house, she watched for him—a glimpse in the headlights of the familiar hunched shoulders, hands jammed in jean pockets, plodding along the road. O.K.—maybe it's partly her fault, but it feels like a betrayal.

She gets out of the car and slumps against it, adjusts her eyes to the empty desolation of the lot. Can she really do this, make her way on foot, smack through the middle of Cherrytown at night? She's got the directions from Resa, but what if she still can't find the house? What if she goes to the wrong one? Sure, she made friends with Resa at Y Camp in D.C. and hung out with Lamont and Trenton, the two colored boys. But this is different. There are juke joints and liquor houses in this area, and unlike this afternoon when she was bubbly with excitement over going to Uncle Rose's with Richeboux, she does not want to see what goes on in them. Not now, anyway.

About thirty feet down the fence, under overhanging honeysuckle, a gate is slightly ajar. She tries to pull it open enough to let herself through. It is knitted in vines. She puts her whole body into it, and finally moves it enough to get by. The moonlight seems brighter on the other side as if she's stepped into a twilight zone creepier than the darkness she's left behind. She is in the backyard of what appears to be an abandoned house. Its windows are boarded. If she crosses the weedy yard to the next street and turns right, it should take her to Bartlett Avenue, the one she was trying to turn onto when the cop stopped her. From there she can cut left and head two blocks down to the next T intersection and turn right onto the street where Resa's Aunt May lives. That street does not have a number or name.

She moves carefully across a yard of rusty old stoves, automobile parts, discarded soup cans. Crickets chirp. Tree frogs whirr and click as if counting her steps. The sole of her tennis shoe slips on a rounded bottle and twists her ankle. She stops, tests it gingerly, and moves on. On either side of the abandoned house, other houses, small and in need of paint, are jammed in close. No lights, but a suggestion of people sitting and waiting beyond the clapboard walls, listening to the dark. As she draws closer, a meager glow reflects in the window of one of the houses—an oil lamp burning low on a kitchen table.

She makes it to the dirt road in front of the houses. It's as empty as a road through a ghost town. She heads down it toward Bartlett, walking fast. She could run, but that might bring attention. The iron-man cop might be off his radio by now. He would have a clear view down Bartlett to its intersection with the road she is on. She stays as close to the ditch as she can. The daytime world she saw earlier when she and Richeboux went to Rosemont's has retreated into a world of secrets and shadows.

She crosses the road as she approaches the intersection with Bartlett, crouches behind a perfectly trimmed hedge, and peers down the block toward the police car. The red light still blinks dull orange against the tree leaves on the side of the road. She leans further and sees the cop, leaning with his butt against the car. He's got his flashlight out, looking at a magazine—maybe that *Playboy* thing Richeboux and his buddies swap and drool over. She could probably make it the two blocks to Resa's aunt's road without the cop prying his eyes from the centerfold and swinging around to see her. But what if he does? Would he shoot her? Her other choice is to double back on the road she's just taken and cut through more yards until she comes out onto Resa's aunt's street. There are no streetlights down there, and it's three blocks from where he's standing. She turns in her crouch, looks back at the street she's just come up.

Which houses to pick to slip between? Which yards?

She makes her way slowly, reversing steps when she has to, working her way around snaggle-toothed fences, sagging porches, clucking chicken coops, and tire swings. A large dog barks somewhere down the block. Farther away another answers. Within five minutes, she's on the road that leads to Resa's aunt's house. On the other side of it are newly planted rows of cotton, so long and straight they seem pulled by the moon. She moves down the road quickly, eases up to the intersection with Bartlett, squats a moment by the ditch, and gets ready for her dash across.

A car door slams back at the intersection where the cop is. A starter grinds. The engine roars to life. Tires spin and throw gravel. Headlights leap down the road in her direction.

The car tears through its gears. The engine strains as if trying to lift the car from the road. She falls onto her butt, catches herself with her hands, whirls and scrambles into the nearest yard, seeking bushes, shadows, fence lines, wherever she can find to hide. A strange, whiny sound seems to follow her that she realizes is coming from her throat.

The car's headlights beam past, across the intersection, lighting the cotton field. Brakes squeal and lock. Sliding tires grind into the gravel and dirt. She backs slowly across the dirt yard, ready to turn and run for it.

But the car whirls through the turn onto Resa's aunt's street and speeds off in the direction she herself is heading. Mem squats, steadies herself with the tips of her fingers. Tremors run through her arms. Though the cop has left, she feels exposed. She glances over her shoulder at the house of the yard she's borrowed to hide in. All dark. The taillights of the police car fade up the road through a thickening cloud of dust. In her cheeks and eyes, the pressure of welling tears. Richeboux! Why couldn't he have been there when she looked for him on the way over? She needs that smell of dust and dirt about him. It turns her on when they make out, pulls her deeper into the places he lives. She draws a quick breath and jams her tongue against the roof of her mouth.

*Well, he's not. And that's that.*

She pushes herself to her feet, and steps out of the yard onto the road. The red glimmer of the police car taillights disappears into the night.

But in the distance, in the direction the cop is heading: gunshots? doors slamming? Men yelling, for sure. A trembling comes to her legs. She starts them moving, slowly at first then picking up speed until she is at a full run through the settling dust, down the road toward the house she hopes is where Resa told her it would be.

# Rosemont Greene

I tell you what: I come within a inch of shooting the motherfucker myself. Busting out the cellar like a wild man after all I done for him. I had that .45 raised, following him right down the sight. Voice in my head says, "Hold on there, Rosemont! You 'bout to blow away a black man for trying to save himself, same as you would do." I lower the pistol, shake my head. *Got white people all over my ass. Don't need colored too.*

Have to grind my teeth to keep from hollering at him, though. Grab hold of my ankles to keep my feet from running 'cross the lot to the store and dragging his sorry ass back.

I sneak a glance back at the deputies messing around in the front yard, then watch Raiford take the back steps two-at-a-time, dodge around the broken door, and scoot on inside. I'll say this, the son-of-a-bitch can move. And what for: liquor? cigarettes? I gave him some of those. He better not be looking for no gun. But one way or the other, I got to get Raiford out of there 'fore one of them cops hears him.

The old deputy zips up, joins the nervous, skinny one under the oak trees, and starts cussing about why he has to do the dip-shit work while Starnes and the rest of 'em are up where the action is. He's growling and coughing, talking through his cigarette.

I'm back to the alligator, working my way toward the low end of the thicket away from the cops. Puts me closer to the store, less ground to cover. Dampness from the leaves and moss done soaked all the way through to my spine. Gnats all in my hair, down my shirt collar. Mosquitoes following me every inch of the way. Hard to swat with a .45 in your hand. I get to my place, roll on my back with the gun resting on my chest and take a breath. I can hear Raiford moving about inside the store, taking it slow, feeling his way. He's been in there enough to know where things are, so I'm hoping like hell he ain't gon kick something or stumble on it. But the cops done made such a mess of it, it must be like picking his way through a junkyard.

'Round front, the cops still yapping—mostly the old one. "Old Shug's bad eye got that fear-o-God light in it tonight. When that light comes on, Oooo-wee! Look out!"

I get up to one knee, and click off the safety on the .45. If I'm gon do it, ain't no better time than now.

I'm in my bent-over lope, maybe four steps into the lot, when Raiford's see-in-the-dark radar gives out. Big crash in my bedroom off the back of the store. Sound of the stuff I keep by the bed—alarm clock, flashlight, snuff cans—bouncing off the walls, rolling 'round on the floor. And I know right then he's done turned over my mattress, looking for that .410 over-and-under.

I drop to one knee, and I admit: for the first time tonight I done lost track of the next move. I turn to head back to the bushes. But my feet ain't persuaded 'bout that direction either.

The old deputy commences to yelling: "Gotdamn, gotdamn!" The skinny one comes sliding out from under the shadow of the oak trees. He's got hold of his pistol with both hands, pointed at the ground like he's gon blow a hole in it. Moves like a robot running on electricity. Stops, jerks his head about, ducks, jerks some more, then starts backing up the road, leading to Cherrytown. The old man is running in reverse, too, grabbing for his pistol with one hand, fumbling for his radio mike with the other. Either they ain't seen me, or they too scared to admit it.

Another big crash comes from inside the store. Raiford ain't even trying to stay quiet anymore. I reckon he's done got the gun and is looking in the drawer for the bullets and shells.

I whip back 'round and make my run for the store.

"There he goes!" yells the skinny one.

The radio crackles and bleeps. The old deputy yells and stammers into it like he hollering down a well —"Sh-Sh-Shug, we found the son-of-a-bitch. He's right here back of the liquor house."

Broken glass all under my feet where they done busted out the shed room window. I slam my back against the siding under the shadow of the roof, ease up to the window, tap on what's left of the glass with my gun barrel.

"Raiford, you gone crazy? You hear them police 'round front? Get the hell out of there!"

Inside the store is quiet as a cat watching a rat hole. The old cop's gone back to hollering: "Get on around back, Tony. Head him off. Naw, stay here, wait for Shug. Naw, go on—easy, real easy."

I poke my head above the windowsill. "Raiford. Come on out the back and head for the woods down by Hadley's Creek. I'll be right behind you."

Raiford commences thrashing about inside, fighting his way through all the mess to get out the back door.

Bam! First shot comes through a front window and whaps a inside wall. Now they done got started, they can't stop. Pow, pow, pow, pow! Glass breaking all over the front of the store. Bullets zinging. Boards splintering.

Raiford's inside cussing 'bout something he done tripped over. I lean my shoulder harder into the siding. I got that naked-in-the-back-feeling like I used to get in my running days—right there, smack between the shoulder blades.

I whirl around, and sure 'nuff, there he is. The skinny one, named Tony, is edging sideways 'round the corner of the house, taking it one step at a time. He's got that .38 waving all over the place—back of the store, parking lot, woods, sky. He'd have the moon covered too if he could draw a bead on it. Shaking like he's having a fit.

Bam! Another shot comes from 'round front. More breaking glass. And I'm thinking: when this thing gets over, me and Marcus gon have to patch up every bit of this shit. And when you working with Marcus, you basically working alone.

And here comes Raiford, jumping out the back door, light-footed as a fox. He's got that Savage .22/.410 over-and-under broke open, jamming a bullet and shell in, cramming other bullets and shells into his shirt pocket. Rounds of both kinds dropping from his hands onto the stoop.

Tony finally remembers what his pistol's for. First shot misses the whole house. But now he's got his finger working, he don't stop. I duck and flinch with every one. Bullets whack the siding, rip a couple of holes in the tin roof.

Raiford slips sideways on the stoop to get himself out the moonlight under the shadow of the roof. Drops to one knee. A loose .410 shell roles off the edge of the stoop to the ground.

Tony standing there with his mouth open and his gun hand hanging at his side like his arm's broke. I guess shooting up the night and not hitting nothing done made him more scared than he was before. Directly he raises the pistol and looks at it like he ain't sure what it is and how it got there. Then he looks up at me and Raiford. Then he looks back at the pistol. Then his hands go to scrambling, trying to reload. Fingers shaking. Bullets dropping every whichaway. Whining like a old hound I used to have, scared of the thunder.

I'm looking back and forth from Tony to Raiford so fast I done got dizzy. A edge of moonlight runs 'cross of Raiford's face, lights up that Afro like he's got a ball of fire on his head. He snaps shut the over-and-under, raises his head, takes in me, Tony, and the whole parking lot.

"Naw, you don't!" I say. I stick the .45 in my pocket and wave my hands. "Ain't you got no sense? Run 'fore that cracker quits shaking and learns to shoot."

Tony done finally got loaded. The cylinder snaps shut. The whining stops. Next bullet clips the tin overhang above Raiford's head.

Around front the other cop still blasting away at the front of the store.

Raiford sets his foot, shifts his weight onto one knee, and raises the butt of the gun to his shoulder. He takes his time, like he's got all day. Rests his cheek against the stock, kind of feels the wood in it. I'm steady in the nerves, but I ain't never seen nobody cool as Raiford. Muscles move like they're made out of motor oil. Got one eye squinted, the other one aiming down that barrel like the look alone gon kill whatever it's pointing at.

Tony's next shot whizzes past my nose and smashes a pane in my bedroom window not four feet from Raiford's head. Raiford don't flinch.

But I do, 'cause I done had enough. I step out from the shadow of the shed roof and get smack between 'em. Something telling me the whole time it's crazy, but something's got to be done, and I'm the only one in the neighborhood got sense enough to do it.

I turn and look at Tony. Sweat running down his face. Adam's apple working up and down like a piston. Shaking's done turned into more like a chill.

I look him dead in the eye. "Put that thing back in that holster and get out of here 'fore you blow your own foot off and they have to drag you out."

He wipes a palm on the seat of his pants then puts it back on the handle of that .38. I notice his trouser leg then. He done peed all down it.

I turn to Raiford, nod down toward the woods.

"Go on and git! I'll take care of him."

Tony starts shuffling sideways back toward the corner of the store. Trying to keep his gun on me best he's able. I'm glancing back and forth between him and Raiford again. The barrels of that .22/.410 following Tony with every step.

I shift 'round to stay between 'em.

Raiford's eye ticking like a watch hand. "Get out the way, ole man."

"So, you gon shoot me, now?" I say. I raise my hands in the air. "Go on, then! Kill me. Kill 'til the killing's done."

# Resa Robinson

Resa's fingers twist the hem of her skirt, then press it out on her leg. It's been half an hour since she hung up the phone. Mem should have been here by now. White people get confused when they drive in the colored section, stare straight ahead, keep their hands locked on the steering wheel, try to imagine it away. Next thing you know, they've got a wheel in a ditch or taken a wrong turn.

Across the dark room, May sits on the couch like an African queen. Except for the hour or so in her garden every morning, this couch is where she spends her time, smoking the small cigars she likes with the plastic holder on the end, receiving visitors like messengers to the court. As a child, Resa used to picture what May would look like with her hair knitted in jewels and sea shells and pulled tight from her temples, mirth and wisdom shining out through the quiet, ageless eyes. But May doesn't need a crown. Her massive immobility says it all.

The cigar smoke stings Resa's nose and eyes. She wishes May hadn't given up dipping.

May taps an ash into the tray all but hidden in her lap. "He's all right, Baby. They ain't got no reason in the world to come looking here."

Through May's open window come sounds of sirens, yelling, and doors banging over on Cherry Street, three blocks away.

"They don't need a reason. All they got to do is guess."

Outside, sitting in the dark behind May's backyard shed under mats of Ligustrum and honeysuckle, Acee is waiting. She gave him her cigarettes, but he's probably not smoking. A different version of Acee set in after they left Rosemont's—hardness in his jaw, quickness in his walk, eyes focused on nothing but what was in his head—a man who knows what's got to be done and aims to do it. More like Rosemont would be. Or Raiford. She taps a fingernail on the table next to her. No, not Raiford; it's all Acee now.

She won't risk going out to Acee again until Mem comes. *If* Mem comes.

Acee's folks are on Cherry Street where all the noise is. Preacher's folks, too. She prays he won't decide to go over there, swerve down that road of guilt his mother and Travis have laid out for him.

Down the street toward Bartlett, a car turns onto May's road, the sound of its engine gunning louder and louder as it heads in their direction. Mem! A rush of gratitude, a flash of anger: can she be that stupid, this rich white girl, to come barreling into Cherrytown this time of night with police all over the neighborhood? Maybe she found her boyfriend along the road somewhere, and he's the one driving.

She leaps to the nearest front window, pulls back the curtain. A black-and-white police car shoots past, heading toward the turn that leads down to Rosemont's. Dust swirls into May's yard, rolls over the cotton rows across the road. They've caught Raiford? Arresting Rosemont? Everything she's feared is starting to happen. If they get Raiford, will they leave Acee alone or will they look for him even harder, call him an accomplice or something?

"Set down, Baby. Ain't a thing you can do."

Resa drops the curtain, stands for a moment at the window. Shots—one, two, then a bunch of them. No doubt where they are coming from. Beyond the last house on the road May lives on, beyond the edge of the cotton field where the woods begin, there is only one place to go—the road to Rosemont's.

She turns and starts her sprint across the living room toward the kitchen. "I got to warn Acee."

"'Bout what?" May says it like a command, reaches for Resa's wrist as she passes. It is as if the earth, itself, has grabbed her.

"Didn't you hear that shooting?"

"Folks shoot down at Rosemont's all the time. Don't mean a damn thing."

Resa twists her arm to pull free. May holds for a moment, lets her go.

Resa crosses her arms and squeezes them into her ribs below her breasts. She wants to bend forward, let her back sag, let the tears come. But she cannot do that. Not now.

Beyond the front door, a rubber sole squeaks on the paint of May's concrete stoop, followed by a light tapping. Resa looks at May. A winding band of smoke rises from May's lips and into her wide nostrils. She blows it out through her nose and mouth, nods toward the door.

Resa rises to her feet. "Who is it?"

The mantel clock in May's bedroom bongs the half-hour. Resa can almost hear the wheels turn.

"Who is it?"

A whisper comes from outside. "Resa? I'm looking for Resa Robinson."

Resa lunges for the door, jerks the latch, and pulls Mem inside.

The hug is tighter even than when they said goodbye at Y Camp, but it ends abruptly.

"I'll get Acee," she says. "Where's the car?"

## Rosemont Greene

When a man as steady as Raiford Waites draws a bead on you and the only thing moving is his trigger finger, you know you 'bout to get shot. The only thing you can do if you're out in the open is look him right back. And the whole time I'm doing it, I'm saying to myself: them same eyes that are squinting down that sight at you now are the same ones used to light up when him and his brother came down to the store when they was boys and you gave them candy. But there ain't no candy tonight. Ain't no light either. Them eyes got a stone-dead look, like their only purpose in the world is to hold that bead and kill whatever's in it.

"Well," I say, "what you waiting for?"

Tony behind me kind of whimpering, sliding his feet cross the gravel toward the corner of the store that I'm pretty sure he's wishing real hard he'd never left in the first place. And I'm wondering: is he trying to point that .38 at Raiford or at my back. 'Cause, way he's been shooting, if he's aiming at Raiford, he's more likely to hit me.

I bow my head. This is one hell of a way to go—standing right here in my own back lot next to my own store I done bought and paid for, shot by somebody I 'bout helped raise or by some cracker deputy sheriff so scared he done wet his pants. And I ain't even gon know which one did it.

Up the hill toward Cherrytown, sirens howling, headed this way.

I look back at Raiford. He ain't moved a hair, but the figure 8 shape of that gun muzzle is pointed about a inch to the left of my head, which tells me Tony still sliding in that direction.

By now the old-man deputy done edged his way down the side of the house, staying hid, and yelling at Tony, "Where's he at? Is he inside?"

Tony mumbles something. I glance back to see if I'm 'bout to have two pistols aiming at my back, when I see the old man's hand reach out, grab hold of Tony's shirt, and jerk him back behind the corner of the store.

Sirens getting louder. At least one or two done left the main road, turning down the road to the store.

"Raiford," I nod toward the woods. "This is your last chance." I lower my arms and hold them straight out, palms up, like I'm catching raindrops.

I been in tight spots before where a man's been put to a decision 'bout living and dying and if dying, how he's gon do it. Raiford's still exactly like he was before, braced on one knee, gun steady, eyes sighted down the barrel, finger on the trigger. And the muzzle's done moved squarely back on me. But something has changed. And what that is is that he ain't done it, and 'cause he ain't, he knows and I know that the time for doing it has passed.

His cheek eases up off the stock. He lowers the tip of the gun barrel. He's still got that squint in his eyes, but its more like he's trying to puzzle out where he is and how he got here. He sets the butt of the stock on the stoop and holds onto the barrels with both hands like they're a crutch for a one-legged man. Then he commences to look about like he's lost something.

The deputies are still back 'round the corner, arguing over what they're gon do next. The sirens keep getting closer.

I lower my arms. "Raiford! What you gon do?"

He stands up, looks down at the gun he's holding in one hand, looks back at me.

"Nothing," he says.

Police cars tear into the front yard, sirens wailing, red lights lighting up the woods and treetops like they done caught fire. Couple cars stop around front. 'Bout three more come wheeling 'round the house, sliding in the gravel. One near 'bout knocks me over. They rock and roll to a stop, doors opening, folks yelling, pumping shells in the twelve-gauges. Dust so thick you can't see. I turn to face in their direction, hear Raiford's gun clatter onto the boards of the stoop.

Soon as the spotlight hits me I raise my hands. At least ten cops are leaning 'cross car roofs and hoods, pointing their guns at Raiford and me. Third time tonight somebody done drawn a bead on me. You generally don't survive one.

Starnes is on the bullhorn, yelling in that burnt-out voice of his. "On your knees! Keep them hands up where I can see 'em."

Soon as my knees hit the ground, I feel the weight of that .45 sag in my hind pocket. My right hand wants to grab it and throw it on the ground, but my brain jerks my hand right back up to the sky. Might die anyway, but ain't no sense in committing suicide.

"Cuff 'em!" yells Starnes.

Four cops move out from behind the cars and head in my direction.

When a beating is coming, ain't a thing you can do but get ready for it. I learned that the hard way. I know as well that if you move too fast to cover up, you may get shot instead of beat. So I wait 'til the first metal-toed boot busts a rib 'fore I double over and get in my beating position—knees up to my chest, hands behind my head, wrists and forearms trying to cover my face and ears.

Don't do much good. They all over me, kicking, stomping, trying to jerk my hands loose. They kick the .45 loose from my pocket. "Look at this!" one of 'em hollers. "Oughta shoot him with it." He jams the muzzle into my temple. That's number four, and I know I'm a dead man for sure this time. Starnes come busting in over me. "Get that gun away! I'm gon take this son-of-a-bitch alive."

They pull my wrists behind my back, clamp the cuffs on. The kicks and stomps keep coming. One catches me behind the ear, and I see that light fading, just like the old days. And I ask myself the same question: is this it, or am I gon see that light again? When that starts to happen, parts of you seem to leave one at a time. It's like your body vanishes before your mind does. You can't feel what they're doing to you. You can't hear what they're saying. But you can hear what's going on in other places. And over by the stoop where they got Raiford, it sounds like horses kicking out their stalls.

# Richeboux

Richeboux has wandered off the path. The ground grows soggier; branches hang lower and thicker. The air has a green-gray smell of rot and muddy bottoms. Bullfrogs harrumph, harrumph. Cricket frogs whir like playing cards he used to clip to the spokes of his bicycle. A foot slips on the slimy under-leaves. He struggles to get his balance. Somewhere to his right a whippoorwill's call whistles through his brain.

He's descended a good twenty feet since he left the 15th Street crossing. The creek between him and Cherrytown couldn't be more than fifty feet ahead, but there's the swamp, or bog, or whatever. Wetness seeps through the canvas of his tennis shoes, oozes around his feet. He takes a couple of steps backward. The whippoorwill stops. The cricket frogs sink into underwater silence. And then he hears it, up the hill, beyond the woods across the creek, distant sounds of sirens and pistol shots smacking the air.

He backs up a couple more steps, eases off to his left, and works his way to solid ground under a grove of old pines. Moonlight lies on fallen needles in fractured patterns of black and bronze.

The gunshots and sirens have stopped up the hill, but shouts ricochet through the trees. Car doors slam; engines rev. The sounds are farther away than he first thought, over by Uncle Rose's place, not the center of Cherrytown. Finally arresting folks, shutting the joint down. It's been coming a long time.

He takes a seat, drapes his arms over his knees, lets his head droop. Pine needles prick bare skin where his blue jeans have ridden down his ass. Mosquitoes buzz in his ear. He slaps one, feels the blood on his fingertip, waves his hand around his head to ward off the gathering swarm. What the hell is he doing here? Everything that has happened tonight seems to have led to this spot.

At least a dozen mosquitoes are on him—back, shoulders, eyes, and neck. He stands, smacking at himself, flailing the air. He shouldn't have given the T-shirt away, but they'll bite through that too when they're mean enough. He stops flailing, blows a mosquito off his nose. The noises over toward Rose's have stopped. A brazen cricket frog reclaims the stage. A couple more join in, then the whole chorus.

He shakes his arms and shoulders and walks toward the creek, looking for an easy place to cross. He's thirsty as hell—has been for a long time—and before he knows it, he's into a squat. It's nasty water—runs through at least a dozen culverts coming into Tuscaloosa. He dips his hand and draws the water to his mouth. It tastes like sulphur and burnt lemons. He dips again, and again, then goes to his knees and scoops the water in sweeping gulps. He splashes it on his neck and head, and over his shoulders, feels it run down the channel of his spine.

He's still on all fours with both hands sinking into the mushy bottom of the creek when he hears more sounds from up the hill. He raises his head, shakes the water from his ears. The sounds are low and steady—the turning of at least a dozen engines. His coach once told them about sitting in a foxhole in the snow in France, listening to German tanks rolling through the trees in his direction. Like a force from hell, he said, breaking through the crust of the earth. The sounds up the hill are big V-8s: Fords, Chevys, pick-up trucks with ragged mufflers, and something about them—their number, their all running together—brings a touch of the terror his coach felt in France. They cruise to the center of Cherrytown. Engines die. Doors slam.

*What the hell?* He sits back into a squat. The mosquitoes keep coming. The sound of a bullhorn crackles through the trees, splitting into squawks and blurts he can't decipher.

It's there, whatever it is, at about the same place where things began last night. That's how it works: you can face up to whatever is splitting you in half in the light of day, or the roads will join on their own in the night's desolate landscape. He knew that the second he threw the egg.

Just upstream from where he sits, a small waterfall splashes against a rim of rocks. Moonlight glints in the current as if schools of minnows are running in it. He reaches toward the waterfall, then stops, drops his hand, and curls his index finger into the soft red mud under the bank. He digs out a good fingertip full, holds it up before him in the moonlight, and begins the first line of war paint, like his sister did when they played Indian, down the center of his nose.

## Rosemont Greene

I stick my head out the window to watch 'em drag Raiford to the police car 'til Otis slaps his fat fingers 'round my forehead and shoves me back in. Jams the tip of his nightstick under my nose.

"You want some more of this?"

I shake my head.

"Then set in there and don't move."

He reaches through the other door and rolls my window up. I ever do get out this shit, Otis gon wake up one morning and find himself dead.

But I can tell from what little I seen that Raiford's in bad shape. Arm hanging loose, blood running down his face and out his mouth. Limping when he tries to walk. Thought maybe he was dead at first.

Starnes is standing in the middle of it all, pointing that whip handle. "Put him here... put him there!" Eyes beaded up like a hog-nose snake.

I lean back against the seat, shut my eyes. One of them 'bout closed anyway. I try to get comfortable, but it ain't easy. Arms cuffed behind my back. Every time I go to rest one way, something pulls another, starts a whole new pain. I 'spect a rib or two is broke and maybe a wrist. Feel it swelling against the cuff. Lip cut; blood in my hair; shirt barely hanging on. You colored and mess with the police, you might as well get used to it. Naw, that ain't quite right: you better learn how to stand it. 'Cause it ain't gon get no better down at the jail, even if we get there 'fore some of this crowd get out the ropes and chains. Raiford's a dead man, and he's probably done took me with him. *Don't nobody control Raiford but Raiford*—what I told the Preacher. Well, he done controlled it, alright. He's done controlled us both into hell.

I finally work myself sideways on the seat, let my head down against the back. Feel a little rest come for the first time since it all started. Cars starting their motors, revving 'em. Otis gets in the driver's door. Smells like a cow got in the car. Sweat running all down his face and neck, soaked his uniform. I sit up, watch that deputy, Knob-face, with the cancer on his jaw, get in the passenger side. He turns his ugly head and grins at me. That cancer don't move, and the side of his face it's on don't move much, either.

"You gon die, boy."

"Who gon kill me!"

He turns back to the front. "You'll find out soon enough." He nudges Otis like he's done told him a joke. Otis pushes him away and starts the car.

We follow Starnes up the road. Must be five more cars behind us. Raiford's back there somewhere, laid out on a back seat. I stretch 'round to look out the back to see if they gon set my store on fire. No flames yet; may be coming back for that. Knob-face running his mouth 'bout how he captured the "fugitive." "I was the first on the porch. I'm the one took him down." Ain't no way a scrawny-ass cracker like him could take down Raiford. Must have been a dozen of 'em. There was nearly that many on me.

We sway and swaggle up the road. Every time that car jerks, it's like a ice pick jabbing up under my ribs. We make the turn on the street that runs by May's house. It rides smoother, and I rest a bit easier. Be out of Cherrytown soon, off the dirt roads, and headed down the hard surface to the jail. But before I know it, Starnes runs right on past the main road out of Cherrytown and heads over toward Cherry Street. Everybody else follows. Ain't a house light on or a soul in sight. Like driving through a graveyard. Minute later, we pull to a stop on Cherry Street, 'bout as close to the center of Cherrytown as you can get. This ain't no place to be lynching nobody, and I'm wondering what that fool got up his sleeve now.

Starnes gets out, starts directing traffic. Pretty soon he got cars lined up, head-to-tail along the ditch beside the road except his car and the last one in line. He's got his car turned 'round in the center of the road, facing down the road and the last car in the center of the road facing his. Light up Cherry Street like a dance floor.

Starnes walks up to the car I'm setting in, carrying that bullhorn of his. Says to Otis, "Get out and follow me."

Otis gets out. Knob-face does, too. "Stay here," says Otis. "Don't take your eyes off him. He's as mean a bastard as you ever saw." He looks about. "You, too, Tony. Come over here and help Tossie keep an eye on Mister Rosemont Greene." Tony sort of walking sideways, I reckon to hide where he peed on himself.

Otis trots off after Starnes. Knob-face gets out the car, rests against it with his elbows on the roof, then bends down and leans in the front window. Got his hand on the stock of that .38, that same grin 'cross his face. "I don't need no help with a smart-ass like you. Just try something and see what happens." Didn't have these cuffs on, wouldn't take much to jerk that gun out his belt and stick it up under his chin. Tony comes creeping up and stands 'bout two feet away from the car behind Knob-face with his hand on his pistol. Still shaking like he's got a tic or something. Skinny as a hound. I decide to name him Blue Tick.

'Bout then I get an idea what Starnes is up to, and sore as I am, I can't help but shake my head. Starnes ain't a stupid man, but when a man gets angried up like Starnes over that deputy, he liable to do stupid things. And bringing Raiford and me back into Cherrytown to make some kind of show over it is down-in-the-dirt stupid. Ain't nobody from Cherrytown had the nerve to fight back yet—nobody except Raiford—but there's some around here been working up to it for a long time.

"Get him out," says Starnes. "Lean him against the car. Otis, I want you and two men on that boy at all times."

I hear the door open couple of cars behind me, deputies grabbing at Raiford, jerking him out.

"Get your honky hands off me," he says. Sounds like he's talking through rubber. I hear the door shut. They slam his body up 'side the car.

I can't see Raiford for the cars, but I can see Starnes, marching up and down in the middle of the road in front of where they got Raiford, swinging that bad leg, slapping his whip handle against it like if he hits it enough it'll start working normal. Pretty soon he stops his pacing, casts his eyes up and down the street, raises the bullhorn.

"You people come on out your houses. There's something out here you need to see."

He drops the bullhorn. Raises it again. "Don't make me have to come in and getcha. Some of the boys out here ain't gon take that kindly."

I look farther down Cherry Street past the last police car setting with its lights on, shining up the road toward Starnes. Some of them crackers was down at the store done got out their pick-ups, hanging 'round the back of the last police car like they're afraid to get too close to Starnes less he turns and runs 'em off. Bloodhounds in the back of the pick-ups yowling their heads off. Yard dogs 'round the neighborhood answering back.

Pretty soon the first porch lights come on, then some others. Screen doors start to open. Some of 'em been jerked off the hinges. Windows broken. Post knocked out on old lady Haskell's porch, roof caved in. Starnes is pacing again, tapping that gimpy leg. People mostly out their houses now, keeping to the shadows of their yards. Raiford and Acee's mama, Sister Waites, out in Preacher's yard moaning and crying. Preacher's wife and others holding on to her.

"Shut that woman up," says Starnes. "And shut them dogs up, too."

Past the top of Starnes's car, 'bout halfway down the block, Elton Brown and that hotheaded bunch he hangs with standing beside the road. Must be a dozen. Got their arms crossed, staring at Starnes.

"Get that boy out here where they can see him," says Starnes. "From both sides of the street."

The deputies drag Raiford to the middle of the road, close to Starnes, couple of car lengths from where I'm setting. He ain't even trying to stand no more. Toes leave drag marks 'cross the gravel. His mama wailing again. "Lawd, oh Lawd. Have mercy, have mercy." People murmuring, starting to move about. Glaring at Starnes, I look straight at his back, slam my fists against the window. Seeing what he done to Raiford makes me want to put a axe blade right between his scarecrow shoulders.

Knob-face moves 'round front of the car to the road side. Stands spraddle-legged, facing me with his hand on his gun like a cowboy. "Jest try it," he says. Blue Tick still on the ditch side of the car; head twitching like he's having a fit.

Otis and his boys pull Raiford up between 'em. He kind of hangs there, head flopped over to one side, while they turn him 'round real slow-like in the middle of the road. But I get a good look at his face in the headlights, and I know, beat up as he is, life's flickering in Raiford still. Burns brighter in folks like him. Did from the start. It don't go out easy, no matter what they do to him. Sometimes that's good. But sometimes it can make bad things a whole lot worse.

Starnes raises the bullhorn again. "Y'all take a good look at this boy. This is what happens when you kill a police officer, a good man, trying to do his duty. Good as ever walked the ground in this county. Liked the colored. Treated y'all right. And this boy shot him down like a dog. He's in the hands of the law now. He's gon reap what he sowed."

Elton Brown and his bunch have eased out in the street. And they've eased out of somewhere else, too—the shadow across your life from years of, "step aside, nigger," "no colored," "back of the line," "back of the bus"—all them tear-down-your-soul feelings. That shadow is gone from their faces. Yelling at Starnes, arms hanging loose at their sides, moving down the road in our direction.

The air starts to get that crackly feeling, like electric currents are running through it. Knew a man once, cuffed from behind, worked himself free. Backbone like a snake. Slid his butt through his arms. I'm too old for that. But I've kicked police car doors open before—locked and unlocked. Just have to hit 'em hard enough.

Starnes ain't paying no attention to Elton's bunch. But Blue Tick is. He's facing 'em, backing up. Hands still on that pistol grip, head jerking all over the place. He looks over at Starnes, mouth opening and shutting like it's got hinges on it. But his voice won't work.

They got Raiford turned back 'round now, facing across the road where they started. Starnes raises the bullhorn again, starts yelling his bullshit 'bout wrath of God this and wrath of God that. "You have allowed the Devil to slip amongst you, and the wrath of God shall pour like water upon your head." My 'pinion, wrath been pouring on Cherrytown over a hundred years. But it ain't the wrath of God.

Blue Tick finally gets his voice and starts yelling sure 'nuff, pointing up the ditch he's standing by. I figure he still trying to warn Starnes 'bout Elton's bunch 'til I look where he's pointing and see that white boy, just sauntering down the road beside the ditch. He passes right by Elton's group. They stop and look at him like a ape just walked by. He keeps on coming, 'round the back of Starnes's car. Wild looking. Got his shirt off and his body all painted up in red mud. "Chief T" wrote 'cross his chest; mud down his arms and nose; 'cross his cheekbones. Hair wild-looking like he's been rolling in the dirt. Red taillights shining on him attest Starnes's prophecy: Devil himself done walked up.

## Resa-Acee-Mem

Mem leads. They run, crouching forward, down the road from May's house to Bartlett. The air is chalky with dust; smells of car exhaust, and gunpowder. It coats their lungs and clothes. Behind them, yells and sirens come from the woods down by Rosemont's place. To their left on Cherry Street, doors slam, a woman wails in the night. Dogs bay all over the neighborhood.

Acee stops, shakes his head, and rises to full height. "I ain't doing this. I *can't* do it."

Resa lurches, grabs his arm in both hands. "Acee, they'll be here any minute."

He jerks free, stands and listens, trying to pick through the noise: which houses are being searched; who's being beaten, shot, dragged to a patrol car.

Twenty feet ahead, Mem drops to a knee then to all fours. "Resa, Acee, come on!"

Resa wraps Acee in her arms, puts her mouth to his ear. "Come on, Baby. Nothing you can do. You got to save yourself." She gives him a hard squeeze. "And me." She unwraps her arms, and takes his hand. Her pull is gentle at first. He stands with his face turned toward the noise on Cherry Street and lets his arm stretch from the shoulder. She takes his wrist in both hands and yanks. He staggers forward, gets his balance, and by the time he does, they are running again.

The three of them make it to Bartlett and crouch in the shadows while Mem checks down the road to be sure there's no cop car at the intersection where she was stopped before. The street is empty and dark, made even darker by the lights on Cherry Street, visible above the rooftops and through the trees. The shouts from Cherry Street are muffled, less frequent. Resa squeezes Acee's hand. His body is as tight as his metal sculpture.

"We'll make it," she whispers.

"Let's go," hisses Mem. She sprints across Bartlett. Resa pulls Acee across the road. They wind their way among the darkened houses and weed-filled lots. A gathering of crows croaks and stirs in a treetop, shaking the branches.

The Cadillac waits in the moonlight. Resa and Acee press their backs against the honeysuckle-covered fence as Mem fumbles with the key at the driver's side door, trying to make her hands, wrists, and fingers work in sync. She drops them to her side, takes a deep breath, and tries again. The door opens. She finds the trunk key, runs back and pops the latch. The lid yawns open.

Acee looks at Resa. "I can't do that."

"Acee, please. Don't stop now. We got to get out of here."

"I ain't riding in no trunk."

"Baby, just 'til we get out of town. I'll get in with you."

"No! I can't do it."

He turns toward the gate they've just come through. Resa grabs his arm, whispers to Mem. "You got some kind of blanket? We'll lie on the back seat."

Mem grabs the blanket her mom used to cover the back seat with when she took their old cocker spaniel to the vet, shuts the trunk lid, and opens the back door. Resa slips in, lies on the seat. Acee follows, letting himself down into her arms. Resa kisses his temple, looks up at Mem as she and Acee work their bodies together, fitting tighter and tighter into the soft wedge of the seat. Mem's fingers grip the top of the door. She watches until the movement stops. Resa's eyes are still on her as she holds out her hand for the blanket. Mem shakes out the dog hair, tosses it in, shuts the door, runs to the driver's side.

She takes it slow out of the ice house parking lot and driveway. The intersection where the cop stopped her is empty. She turns right and heads out of the neighborhood with her foot light on the pedal. When they make it through the turn onto Loop Road, she gives it the gas.

Resa rests a hand on her shoulder. "Mem, take it easy. They'll stop us for speeding."

The car comes to too quick a halt at the intersection with 15th Street. The stoplight flashes incandescent red across the hood and interior of the car. A street-spraying truck passes before them across the intersection, washing the gutters on their side of the street. The huge, rounded tank with its black letters, *City of Tuscaloosa*, changes from white to the color of watery blood and back to white under the flashing light. Mem looks both ways. To her right, beyond where the city truck is headed, a lone car sits dead center of the A&P lot across 15th Street from the high school. A Ford, like the cops drive, but no bubble on top. She turns left and heads downtown.

"Mem, where are we going?"

"I don't know. Maybe my church."

"Your church? What church?"

"First Presbyterian. It might be open."

"Mem, we can't go there. It's less than two blocks from the police station."

Headlights approach and pass. A tire catches on the edge of a curb. Mem jerks the wheel. Acee's forearm slams the back of the front seat to keep him from rolling onto the floor. The front tires squeal as they straighten in the lane.

"Well, we can't go to my house. A friend is there. She'll blab all over town. My parents might come home, too."

"Honey, we've got to go somewhere, and it's got to be away from here."

Mem rocks back and forth on the seat, cradling the steering wheel as if the circle of plastic and chrome holds a secret answer to their predicament. Before them, a block down the road, is the intersection with the ramp leading up to the bypass. Next to it stands a large white sign with black lettering and an arrow pointing up the ramp: BIRMINGHAM. The car is halfway past the up-ramp when Mem hits the brakes. The Cadillac screeches to a stop in the middle of the road.

"Oh, god," says Resa. "It's them."

"No!" says Mem. "I'm getting us out of here."

She jerks the lever into reverse. Rear tires squeal. She jams the brakes again, throws the lever into "Drive," and they are off up the ramp.

"Damn," says Acee in a loud whisper. "Slow the fuck down."

"Honey, please," says Resa. "We got to take it slow wherever we're going."

Mem levels off at sixty as they hit the elevated section of the bypass. Four lanes of road open before her. Her grip on the steering wheel relaxes. She falls back against the seat. The tires hum on the new concrete.

"We're on the bypass," says Resa, as if confirming it to herself as well as Mem and Acee. She tightens her hold on Acee. "It's O.K., Baby, there was nothing you could do."

As the overpass begins its northward sweep toward Birmingham, it rises and banks to the right over the woods and swamp between 15th Street and Cherrytown. Through the open driver's side window, Mem can see the lit porches of Cherry Street. Cop cars sit in the road, one with its doors open. A small group of men, too dark to distinguish, talk and gesture in the street. Further down the bypass where it straightens through the turn and drops again to ground level, there is a gathering of lights at a spot among the trees—Resa's Uncle Rosemont's place, lit with headlight beams and red lights, flashing from the roofs of police cars. Mem switches to the right lane, stays in it until they are near the outskirts of Tuscaloosa.

Resa and Acee shift in the back seat. He pushes the blanket to the floor. "I can't stand that heat. It's got fleas in it."

Resa raises herself to a half sitting position against the back door and pulls his head onto her lap. "Stay down, Baby."

A large sign reading "Bessemer and Birmingham," flashes by on the right. Resa watches through the rear window as the back of it recedes, turns and again, rests a hand on Mem's shoulder.

"Mem, how much money you got?"

"Whatever's in my purse."

"I got an aunt in D.C. May's sister, Maxine. She's quarrelsome and stingy, but she'll put us up if May tells her to. If we had the money, we could catch the bus from Birmingham. There's one that leaves around five-thirty or six a.m. I took it to Y Camp last summer."

Mem stretches across the seat. The Cadillac wobbles in the lane. She pops open the glove compartment. The envelope with her mother's stash of "emergency" bills is exactly where it's supposed to be.

## Rosemont Greene

Blue Tick grabbing at his pistol, squalling at the white boy like a calf caught in a barb-wire fence. "Get back! Get back! This is police business." He's scrambling backwards, and next thing, he done hit a culvert and fell butt-first in the ditch. Feet poking in the air.

Starnes hears him this time and turns to look. The white boy keeps coming, cuts through the gap between where I'm setting and Starnes's car. I see then—he's one of the white boys comes to the store for beer. There this very afternoon with the white girl Resa knew. He comes to a halt in the center of the road about a dozen feet from Starnes. The police holding Raiford let him drop to his knees, but they keep a grip on the hand cuffs, which twist his arms way up his back. I know that trick. It'll pretty near kill you.

Couple more cracker cars come tearing up, slam to a halt with the others down there past the last police car. They hop out with pistols, shotguns, bats, tire irons, start up the road. Ain't one of 'em under two-hundred pounds. Crackers already there fall in behind. Got a pit bull with 'em, practically foaming at the mouth. All along the road, folks watching, start to edge in a little closer. Elton Brown's group done come to a dead halt.

Starnes sees Elton for the first time. "Get the hell back," he says. "Get your asses off this road."

"Our road much as yours," says Elton.

The white boy is still standing there, got his arms crossed like he's done finally got to where he was going and it's just like he thought it would be. Some of the deputies and highway patrol that's been standing by their cars, start to bunch toward the middle of the road, edging toward Starnes and Raiford. They got billy clubs out, hands on their guns.

Starnes turns toward the white boy, cocks his head like he's studying it all out. Been through it before, knows how to handle it. But the whip handle has quit tapping. That squint is back in his eyes and that nervous twitch is yanking at the skin around the bad one.

"Take him to the hospital," says the boy. "His brother used to be a friend of mine."

Starnes wraps his fingertips 'round the narrow end of the whip handle and bends it into a loop in his hand. "Who the hell are you?"

The boy's eyes are lit like he's just walked out of a war. He lets 'em wander over the whole crowd then back at Starnes.

"Chief," he says.

"Chief?

"Chief Tuskaloosa." The boy runs his finger 'cross his chest under the mud letters.

Starnes spits the dust off his lips. "You're drunk. You're one of those punks goes down to Rosemont's for beer."

"Naw," says the white boy. "I'm sober now. I used to be a pitcher."

Starnes is looking about, trying to add it all up. Down the road past Raiford and the deputies holding him, the other officers are in a line across the road like they're blocking an escape. Pack of crackers still moving up behind 'em. Still got that foamy-mouthed dog on a leash. Hounds chained in the back of the pick-ups start baying again; yard dogs all over the neighborhood yelping right back. Sounds like a fifty-dog coon hunt. Starnes nods toward the crackers. "Keep them boys out of this!" A couple of the patrol turn, hold out their arms, start walking like they're herding chickens. Crackers start to argue, shaking guns and ball bats.

'Bout now I'm wondering where Blue Tick is. I ain't seen him get out the ditch, and I'm thinking, scared as he is, he might have done crawled under the car. I jerk 'round and look out the back. He's done slipped up between the car I'm in and the one behind it. Holding that .38 in both hands, watching that white boy like they're the only two left in the street. This time he ain't shaking. And right then I know he's the most dangerous man there.

Starnes looks back at the white boy. "I don't care who you are, you're interfering. Get out of here 'fore I arrest you, too."

"That's what I come for," says the white boy. "I killed him. Right here in this road last night." He points directly at the dirt 'round Starnes's feet where they say Preacher Gryce died.

Starnes looks about at the people in their yards, the police cars all jammed in beside the road. Even looks at me, pressed up to the window. There's a lost look in his face I've never seen before, like he's done dropped a keg of gasoline and is watching it spread 'round his feet. He turns toward Otis and a couple other deputies. "What the hell's he talking about?" Back to the white boy, fists on his hips. "Are you loose from the loony bin over at Bryce's?"

"Naw," says Otis. "He ain't no chief, either. Used to pitch up at the high school. He was their ace 'til he beaned that boy from Montgomery, daddy's on the Highway Commission."

"I didn't mean to," says the white boy. The light in his eyes vanishes. Tears start. "I just did it. I didn't know any better." He starts walking toward Starnes with his wrists out like he wants Starnes to slap the cuffs on. Starnes takes a step back, then two more. The white boy is still coming, tears mixed with the mud, running down his cheeks. Starnes keeps backing, smack into Otis, standing there with his mouth open. Otis slams into one of the deputies holding Raiford. The deputy starts to fall. And that's when Raiford breaks loose. Better to die here in the road with his people watching, I reckon, than get beat to death at the jail. He can't make no time, though. He's all hunkered over, dragging a leg. Folks in their yards bow their heads; some turn 'em away. They start a moaning sound like it's coming up out the ground.

It's done got to me, too. I'm itching all over, got my face up to the glass.

"Cracker sons of bitches. Let that boy alone!"

Damn the white man! I could get out this car, I'd die right there in the road beside Raiford.

Raiford ain't made ten steps before he falls face down, gets up, slides a few steps, falls again. By then the cops all over him, billy clubs and flashlights rising and falling like they're hammering nails.

"Have mercy!" Preacher's wife's yelling. "Have mercy!" Me and Elton's bunch are yelling too. Couple of rocks come flying. One hits the hood of the car I'm setting in. Sister Waites wailing like she pulling the heavens down.

That white boy moves almost fast as I do.

"Get off him!" he hollers. He jumps right in the middle of it, grabbing police by their shirts and arms, pulling 'em off Raiford. He gets a flashlight 'side his head, goes down, gets right back up. By then I'm believing Starnes is right: that boy *is* crazy. He's swinging and flailing ever whichaway.

He clears some ground, too. Every one of them police he knocks down quits beating Raiford and turns on him. He starts backing away, feeling his way toward the edge of the ditch.

"Get around behind him!" yells Starnes. "Cut him off from them people and them houses."

Four, five police jump the ditch and ease 'round behind. They got a circle on him now. Otis's fat ass anchoring 'bout half of it. The boy stops at the ditch's edge, smack in the middle of the circle, like a bobcat amongst a pack of hounds. Raiford lying in the dirt not more than twenty-feet away. 'Bout then, Blue Tick moves out from behind the car I'm in and eases up to the rear of the circle. Points that pistol directly at the white boy's head.

Starnes peeks out the corner his eye and whirls about. "Tony, put that gun down!" He glares at Blue Tick 'til Blue Tick lowers the pistol, turns and nods back toward the white boy. "Otis, you and a couple of others get some cuffs on."

The white boy sticks out his wrists again. Otis and another one grab him under his arms; highway patrolman clicks on the cuffs. Otis gives the boy a jerk, and they start him toward a patrol car. That brightness is back on his face like he's seeing the rapture.

They pass by Raiford lying in the road, bleeding, or what's left of him. "No!" hollers the white boy. He slams his body into Otis, then slams the other way and jerks free. He drops to his knees right there in Raiford's blood and bows his head like he's praying. Otis looks over at Starnes. Starnes standing there with his mouth open, shaking his head. Everybody else is pretty much frozen. Then the white boy raises up and grabs at the air with his manacled hands. "Shadows," he says. He gives a big heave in his chest, bends down toward where his own shadow is falling 'cross Raiford. "Black spots on the pavement."

"Get his ass up," says Starnes.

"Shadows," screams the boy. He falls over Raiford on all fours, scratching at the dirt. Then he raises up with two handfuls of it and flings it in the air. "Turning people into shadows!"

Barrel of Blue Tick's .38 jumps a good foot in his hands. The white boy's head slams back. He don't even get his arms down, just falls lengthwise 'cross Raiford's body, face bouncing on the road.

Everything is still as a ice pond. One more rock from Elton's crowd, already been thrown, lands a couple yards from Starnes. He's standing like a man been knocked in the head. I look back at them two lying 'cross each other in the road, and I know Raiford is dead, sure as that bullet hole is between the white boy's eyes.

I sort of come to myself then. I been kicking at the door with my feet, even cracked a window. I look around to see if anybody's headed my way with a billy club. They're all standing with their mouths open, staring at them two dead boys. The deputies peek up at Starnes, then back at the bodies, then peek 'round at each other like they're hoping Starnes can raise them boys like Lazarus from the dead. I lie back 'gainst the far-side door, take a breath, and wonder what the hell's gon happen next.

Starnes finally gets his brain to working, walks up to Blue Tick, jerks the pistol out his hand and smacks him 'side the head with it. Boy drops like he done fell out his clothes. Starnes gives him a kick. Blue Tick doubles over, whining, holding his belly.

"Tony, I oughta kill your ass." Starnes draws in a deep breath, leans forward and screams it. "Every goddamn, stupid son of a bitch in the county gets hired by the Sheriff's Department." He stands over the boy a while. Then he clicks open the pistol cylinder, turns the pistol upside down, and empties out the bullets. They fall on Blue Tick like rain.

## Acee

The white girl hits the brakes. The Cadillac screeches to a halt on the highway just past the weedy lot of an old gas station. A single bulb burns over the rusted-out screen door. A dusty, outdoor phone booth sits on one side of the cinder block building.

Acee leans forward with his arms on the back of Mem's seat. "Unh unh! We got to keep going. Things get out of hand in Cherrytown, every cop in the state will be headed this way."

Resa runs her hand up Acee's back, gives his shoulder a squeeze. "Acee if we're going to D.C., I've got to call May and get her to call Maxine. We have to have a place to stay."

Three lanes over a Pontiac GTO convertible flashes by in the meager light from the filling station. White kids in the back yell at each other, headed toward Tuscaloosa. More headlights are up the road, a quarter mile or so behind it.

Mem throws up her hands. "What do y'all want me to do?"

"Drive!" says Acee.

"Pull into that gas station," says Resa. "And get us out of sight of the road. I'll make the call."

"Aw naw," says Acee. "This is gon mess us up."

Mem backs in and pulls around to the side of the building out of the light from the front and comes to a stop under some pines shading the moon.

"Cut off the lights," says Acee, "and leave that motor on."

Old cans and bottles, hidden under the pine straw, crunch beneath the car tires. The top hinges of the booth's folding door have been torn loose. The door sags across the entrance. "Good pussy—dial 90125" is painted in drippy white letters across the milky glass.

"Damn," says Acee. "That phone ain't gon work, and we pop a tire, we ain't got time to change it."

"It doesn't take long," says Mem. "I even know where the jack is."

Acee stares at her perfectly cut hair, the placid assurance in her squared shoulders, the side of a face that has never admitted doubt.

"You ain't never changed a tire in your life."

"Easy, Baby," says Resa. "I'll be right back." She's out of the car in a flash, steps over the sagging door and into the booth.

Mem stares straight ahead, shoulders raised, both hands on the wheel. Acee falls back in the seat. On the highway, two motorcycles roar by, tassels whipping from the ends of their handlebars. The headlights of a fast-moving trailer truck sweep across the filling station lot, blinking a negative of Mem's head. Here he is, a black boy, sitting in a rich white man's car in the middle of the night in some lonely, deserted place with the man's daughter—about the same age he is. They've got the chauffeur thing all turned around. But it wouldn't matter anyway: if they get caught by the wrong people, he could wind up at the bottom of a river with chains around his neck.

Behind the glass, Resa's fuzzy silhouette bends into the receiver as if trying to hear.

"See?" says Mem. "It's working."

"Roll down these windows," Acee says.

Resa's voice rises and falls in indecipherable bursts. She rubs her forehead with her spread thumb and fingers, slumps with her forearm braced against the glass. Finally she straightens, drops the hand holding the receiver to her side. In a sudden flurry, she tries to return the receiver to its cradle, whacks it against the side of the booth, and leaves it dangling on its cord. When she steps across the broken door, her shoulders are slumped inward toward her chest. Tears stream down her cheeks.

"Oh no," says Mem. Acee straightens in his seat.

Resa leans forward with her palms on the ledge of the passenger-side window and looks at Acee.

"He's dead."

"Who?"

"Raiford."

It is as if a silent bomb has emptied the space around him. "Naw!" he says. His hands lock on the back of the front seat. He stares at them and then up at her, the brimming eyes, the wet cheeks, and clenched jaw. He releases his grip and falls back in his seat.

"The police killed him in the same spot where Preacher died last night. Beat him to death."

Everything—Resa's tear-streaked face, the shaggy oval of Mem's head, the rearview mirror, the muted lights from the dash—melt and run together. The swirling colors fade in and out, resume their shapes, fade again. Numbness congeals in his flesh and skin. His head starts to spin. Or maybe it's the car. Maybe both.

"Acee!" says Resa. "Look at me!"

He grabs the rim of the back seat to brace himself, falls back, starts to yell curses and kick. His feet slam over and over into the back of the passenger's seat until something inside the seat gives.

"Stop," moans Resa. "Stop, please." She is bent forward, her arms folded across her stomach.

Mem is out of the car, running around the front, grabbing for Resa. "Oh, Resa, no." They fall together, and even above his own sobs, Acee can hear the squeak of their bodies sliding down the polished car door to the ground.

He drops his face into his hands, letting it out, then chugging like a crippled engine to a stop. He drapes his wrists over his knees. Resa and

Mem are back on their feet, holding each other, watching him.

"I'll kill 'em," he says. "I'll go back and kill 'em all."

Resa breaks from Mem, reaches in and massages his neck and shoulder. "Yeah, Baby. But right now, we got to get out of here. We got to get out of this state. If we don't we'll wind up same as Raiford."

Mem starts around the car. "Resa's right." Her eyes are clear, her face set in a new firmness. She lurches for the car door handle as if it's her last chance to escape the panic that has finally grabbed her.

Resa climbs in next to Acee, pulls him to her. Warm, wet breath fills the tiny space between them. "I'm so sorry, Baby. I'm so sorry."

He wipes his eyes. They drive five miles before his throat relaxes enough to speak.

"What did May say?"

"The police were yelling, beating on doors, pushing people around. They knocked Travis off the porch at your house. Hurt his head. Mr. Alexander got his hearse and took him to the hospital. They arrested Rosemont down at his place. Took him to jail."

"Uncle Rose?" says Mem. "How can they arrest Uncle Rose?"

Resa stares at Mem. "He's black," she says. "And after they'd taken Rosemont off, some of them went back down to his liquor store and set it on fire. May says it's burning now." Resa draws a breath. "That Starnes is evil. And those crackers that follow him around with guns and liquor."

"Yeah." Acee rests his head on the back of the seat. "That's the way it is and the way it's always been. So what?"

The white girl's face takes on a grave-like hue in the light of the dash. Silence hangs among the three of them like a spiderweb.

The Cadillac seems elevated, a capsule floating through the empty darkness, its air conditioning sealing them from the hot, sticky night. Acee inhales deeply, feels the catch in his breath, presses his knee against Resa's. Loneliness rises from the floorboards and leather upholstery, takes a seat beside him, and crosses its legs as if it plans to stay.

He clears his throat. "Anybody else hurt?"

"Some white boy."

The thumps of tires across a swollen tar joint in the concrete highway come barely noticed through the car's giant springs.

"White boy?"

"Yeah. May said he walked right in the middle of it, tried to help."

"Help who?"

"Raiford, I guess. They killed him next to Raiford in the road. Shot him in the head."

"What the hell was some white boy doing walking into Cherrytown?"

The "Entering Jefferson County" sign flies past the car windows. The white girl's head jerks toward it then back to the road.

"I don't know," Resa says. "He had his chest and face painted like an Indian."

The brakes lock. Acee and Resa slam into the back of the front seat. The Cadillac buckles in the road, squeals sideways, and comes to a rocking halt with the headlights facing across the opposite lanes. Acee flops back in the seat, shakes his head, and helps Resa off the floor.

"What the hell!"

"It was him!" Mem screams. "It was *him*." She pounds her fist on the steering wheel.

"Who?" says Resa.

"Richeboux!"

Resa touches her shoulder. "Mem. It couldn't have been. He didn't have any reason to be there."

"He paints his face!" she said. "On the ball team when he was pitching. He's Chief Tuscaloosa."

Bo and the Indians. When Acee and Bo played cowboys and Indians as kids, Bo wanted to be an Indian. Braver. Better fighters, he said. He liked taking his shirt off, smearing on war paint from his sister's finger-paints. After the day Bo's mother took him and Acee and Bo's sister to Moundville, it got real serious. "Acee, you shoulda seen those bones," Bo said. "Bones of real Indians. Especially the skulls, round and shiny, where Leigh says their spirits live. I wanted to give those bones bows and arrows. I wanted 'em to walk out of there."

But this morning when he saw Bo at Rosemont's, the Indians were gone. And so was Acee's old playmate, the boy whose cloudy features skulked under shadows of sadness until his grin finally broke free. The second time they met in the lumberyard, there was Bo, standing by a stack of lumber, that grin pealing away from his tooth as he watched Acee draw closer. *Hey, Acee. Beat you to the top!*

But the white boy who leaned across the car seat this morning to say, "Hello," wasn't hidden by shadows. He was caught in the middle of something squeezing him tighter and tighter. Acee knows that feeling. It comes from all sides like a circular vise. Bo's quick, animal eyes were glazed over. "Come on," he'd said to Mem. "We gotta get out of here."

The Cadillac is blocking all of one northbound lane. Its rear tail fins stick halfway across the other. Mem shakes the steering wheel as if she will pull it out. "No!" she screams. "No, no, no!"

Resa puts a hand on her shoulder. "Honey. It can't be. It's got to be one of those university students working with Raiford."

A turquoise '57 Chevy, headed toward Birmingham, slows to ease around. It has two men in it. Acee pulls Resa down in the seat.

"Mem, please. Don't let them try to help," says Resa.

The Chevy's engine idles alongside. The driver yells through his open window.

"What's happening, darlin'? You all right?"

Mem wipes her eyes, cracks her window. "Yes," she says. "I had to dodge a dog."

The men whisper, chuckle. The second man speaks. "Did you miss it?"

"Yes."

"Well," says the driver. "There ain't nothing to cry over then, is it? Which way you going, darlin'? You got that figured out yet?"

"Birmingham. I'm turning now."

"You gon need a tugboat to turn that thing around. Charlie here says he'll be glad to give you some inside help?"

The Chevy's passenger side door opens.

"No!" she says. "I'm fine."

"Says she don't want it, Charlie."

Charlie is halfway around the rear of the car. "She ain't seen it, yet."

"Please," Mem says. "Please." The tears start all over. She lowers her head in a halting sob.

"Come on, Charlie," says the driver. "We done upset this lady enough. Let's go."

Charlie gets back in the Chevy, leans across the seat to yell out the driver's side window. "You missing a hell of a chance. Take care of them tears in a minute."

The car peels rubber as it takes off. Mem begins to sob again.

Resa wraps her arms around Mem's shoulders. "Thank god! You did good, Honey. But we've got to get back on the road. Cops will come. Somebody else will stop to investigate."

Mem backs, turns the car, backs again, and straightens into one of the northbound lanes. She leans forward, arms wrapped around the steering wheel, taking in slow, deep breaths. The car picks up speed as the landscape rises slowly toward the low, iron-filled ridges that run through the heart of Birmingham. The speedometer needle arcs beyond the limit. Then she floors it. The Cadillac sways back on its springs and stays there. Seventy, eighty, ninety. The needle trembles toward 120 mph, its last number. Rosemont once said a well-tuned Cadillac will do way better than that.

At the crest of every hill, the car lifts skyward on its springs. A quarter mile ahead are taillights. The Cadillac is closing fast.

"Stop it!" yells Acee. "You'll catch up to those two crackers that hassled us back there. Besides, you gon draw every cop in the state."

Mem taps the brakes, begins to sob again. By the time she reaches the top of the next hill, they are down to forty, then thirty.

She glances back at them. Her eyes are swollen, her face is soaked in tears. The edges of her hair are pasted to her cheeks.

"I'm sorry," she says.

Acee nudges Mem with his knuckle. "It don't matter. We got to stop anyway. We got to go back."

"To where?" says Resa.

"Tuscaloosa."

Mem pulls the car to a stop on the shoulder.

"Acee, look at me," says Resa. "We cannot go back."

"We ain't got a choice. Mama's back there. Travis. All those people. Raiford's and Preacher's bodies." He nods toward Mem. "Bo, or whoever." He slips his hand into Resa's. "I've got to go."

Another car slows in the lane to their left. One driver. He cranes his head for a good look before he resumes speed.

Resa shakes her head. "See? You ready for that the rest of your life?" She bends toward Mem with a breathy whisper, "Keep going," sinks back in her seat and crosses her arms. "That's it!"

At the fading edge of the headlight beams, a farm road dips off the shoulder and through an open, wooden gate, barely hanging on its hinges.

"There," Acee says. "Pull down that road. I got to think."

"About what?" says Resa. "Acee, listen to me. Starnes's men, the Klan, some of those night riders—*sooner or later they will kill you!* You got talent, Acee. You've got a chance. You'll throw it away if you go back to Tuscaloosa."

Mem eases the car over the edge of the highway and down the shoulder. The rear bumper hits as the car bounces at the bottom. They rattle across the cattle guard and head up the rutted road. The car sways in the ruts, jerking the steering wheel back and forth.

"Take it easy," Acee says. "Car's too wide for the tracks. Ride the center and side."

Resa sits with her arms crossed, face set, staring out the window.

The moony night slips by.

Mem pulls to a halt behind a grove of trees on a grassy rise bright with moonlight. She rolls down the windows, and cuts the engine. Acee gets out and starts walking.

"Where you going?" says Resa.

"I don't know," he says.

The ground feels good beneath his feet. So does the stretch of muscles in his calves and thighs. Tufts of weed cast shadows in the sunken tracks of the road. He stops, kneels and puts his hand to the bare ground. The cooling clay draws out a measure of his sorrow. A breeze brushes his forehead, stirs the grassy night. Moonlight soothes the landscape around him. He starts walking again, lets his arms swing, feels the rhythm of that old song his mama used to sing.

> *That little black train's a-comin'*
> *It's comin' 'round the bend,*
> *It'll take you home to Jesus,*
> *Where you can find a friend.*
>
> *God loves all the children,*
> *And children love our Lord.*
> *He's got that train a-waitin',*
> *If you just climb on board.*

He walks ten yards more and stops. A small creek zig-zags toward him, then bends southward toward the main road. He imagines the red clay banks in the daytime: hanging tufts of Bahaia and orchard grass, the worn-down places where cows lumber, drink, and squirt shit. White man's cows. White man's land. Even in the moonlight.

It's Raiford's back he keeps seeing, walking away on the day of their baptism through the parked cars and on down the road after he stalked from the river with Preacher's voice thundering behind him: "God ain't through with you yet." Their mama on the bank, crying and pleading. The other people with her, frozen in place, watching. And Raiford kept going, right through them, shaking the water off like it had snakes in it. The same Raiford who took over after their daddy left and became not only Acee's big brother but his best friend. The one who took up for him in the neighborhood and held his hand as they walked through the lumberyard to meet Bo. That back—he knows it now. It had the same shape, the same insolent swagger their daddy's had. Last time Acee saw his daddy, he was walking out the door.

When Raiford walked out of that baptismal river, he took Acee's last hope for comfort with him. And when Acee's turn came for the baptism, he'd just let it happen, gave himself over to Preacher's big hands, let them push him down. The cold water closed about him. The sky faded and was gone. The big hands came again, tightening under his armpits, lifting him from the dark, sandy murk, bursting him into the sunlight and cool April air. They set him on his feet in the water and shoved him gently toward the bank. The people were cheering and smiling, waiting with open arms. But a goneness infected the whole scene. It lay before him along the surface of the water as he made his way to shore, away from Preacher, anchored behind him in the current. Raiford was not there, and the fact was—and Acee knew it even then—Raiford had been leaving Acee, their mama, and the whole neighborhood for a long time.

Now gone for good. A sob swells in his chest like a wave that began way out to sea. He clenches his teeth, lets the force of it come, breathing it in and out. And Preacher, too—gone for good. Those big hands folded one-over-the-other in the coffin. Raiford and Preacher pulled the ends of the high wire that held him weightless at his baptism, and he's been dangling from it ever since.

"*Oh Lord, call this young man. He's got the spirit; give him the will.*"

"*What you gon do now, brother—keep pretending or follow me to the next step?*"

Truth is, that tension is gone, washed away in the current that's taking them all. You can't separate them anymore—what Preacher was doing and Raiford was doing. Time won't allow it. What's coming next is already here: Martin King, Rosa Parks, that preacher in Birmingham. It will take Preacher's patience and courage and Raiford's *im*patience and courage. And he doesn't have either combination.

A quarter-mile away on the paved road, a logging truck works through its gears. Further toward Tuscaloosa a siren wails. Acee glances back up the dirt road. The women are slumped against the car, hugging each other. There's a carnality in the way they grab each other and hold. Their immediate descent into body. It gives off a magnet-like heat, makes him want to run away and be held at the same time.

He knows nothing about D.C. other than rumors that filter back from people who've moved up there: not perfect, but better; you've at least got a chance. But chance at what—more Red Elephant Grills to fry burgers in, except the owner's skin is the same color as his? Janitor work in some government building?

But back in Tuscaloosa, Starnes and his men. Resa's right: they'll be watching him, particularly if he takes up Preacher's work. It'll be a life like Raiford's and Rosemont's—dodging and weaving, watched by Starnes every day for an excuse to lock him away.

There is something else back there in Tuscaloosa. His sculpture, waiting in the shed behind his house, and so is its shadow on the shed wall. It used to be all about the metal—melting it under the hissing flame, joining the pieces of it in into shapes he did not know were there until he and the torch made them happen. But now there's the whole new world of shadow and light—the sky, seen through those icy tree branches beyond the shed door, the kaleidoscope of shapes his sculpture made on the shed wall from the swinging yellow light of his lantern.

*Artist's hands*, said Preacher. *Careful in their work.*

It *is* a whole new world. It's packed with action, misery, promise, and change. And he's standing right on the edge of it.

The white girl has moved away from the trunk. She stands with her legs spread and arms folded, staring toward the pasture as if the blame lies out there and if she stares long and hard enough, she'll find it. That look of gazing forward, stamping her foot at the present, demanding the future. She loved Bo. She thinks she loves him and Resa. But in the end, she'll be like all the other "I-like-the-colored" white people. She'll leave—leave him and Resa, leave the fading memories of Bo, leave Tuscaloosa—and vanish into her sunlit life. Probably headed for some fancy college up North. Come September, she'll be standing at the depot with her parents, all dressed up in the latest college fashion. It will be colored men like him hauling her trunk to the baggage car. And he'll know every one of them.

But he'll hand her this: she's got guts. And you can bet your ass that whatever her future is, she'll take it on her own terms.

Beyond the pine-crested ridge before him, there is a smoky red glow—the steel mills of Bessemer and Birmingham. Iron and fire. Run all night. Streets and neighborhoods around them turned a gray-brown from years of settling smoke and soot. Streets where colored people live. Those people will be there in the morning like they are every morning when the sun comes up through the rusty haze, the women fixing breakfast, the men on the morning shift eating, grabbing lunch sacks, getting ready to plod down those streets toward the yards and buildings where the smokestacks are. "Mules," they used to call 'em—the rich white men who worked 'em back in the prisoner-lease days. *Get a good mule, work him into the ground.* Make some real money. It won't be long now before the harness is on, the sweat starting to run. The sun is headed their way, moving westward across the ocean, gleaming off the estuaries, fields, and forested land. Its first rays are already lighting the rooftops in D.C.

"Acee." Resa clears her throat and tries again. "Acee." She's still leaning against the Cadillac, fingers spread on the metal, face still in shadow. "Where are we going?"

The question hangs between them in the cool night air.

"I don't know." He turns toward her, opens his arms with his palms up. "Where you wanna go?"

"With you."

A cloud's shadow moves across the pasture. Behind it, the land looks even brighter than before. On the far side of the pasture, cows are bedded down for the night, dark lumps against the moonlit field except for those under the shadow of a huge oak. He's not noticed them before.

He starts back up the twin tracks of the road toward the car. It feels good to be moving. He wants to keep moving, somewhere in the direction of the rising sun.

## Rosemont Greene

Nastiest jail cell I ever been in. Cockroaches running 'round big enough to put a saddle on. Slop bucket in the corner ain't been emptied for over a week, and I'm lying on a mattress smells like a team of mules emptied their bladders on it. Speaking of which, I ain't emptied mine since they drug my broke-up ass in here over six hours ago.

And there's that thing hanging from the ceiling over my head. I been studying it since the early morning light come slipping in through the window bars. Started with a leak, I reckon, spread to a three-foot-wide hole where the plaster done cracked and fell off the lattice. One of Starnes's dumb-ass deputies tacked rotten boards criss-cross of the hole. Left rusty nails hanging out every whichaway. Couple of the boards done already popped loose, and I'm asking myself: if that mess of shit falls, can I flip out the way fast enough to keep from getting more beat up than I already am? And I ain't sure 'bout the answer 'cause there ain't no part of me that feels like it's gon flip anywhere.

I reckon that groaning noise I been hearing is me. Ain't nobody else in here.

And they done made a mess out of me. Lips all swole up, face feels like a nest of hornets stung it. Got to be a couple of ribs broken. Every time I gag it's like somebody swinging a axe in my chest. Head busted. Wrists all cut up from where they yanked the cuffs to drag me in here. And on top of all that my bladder's 'bout to bust wide open. Eight-foot-wide cell, bunks on both walls, and they put the bucket in a corner where there ain't a thing to hold onto but your own peter. I ease myself back against the wall, counseling to myself: *one step at a time, Rosemont. One step at a time.*

If I'm gon make it to that bucket, I got to crank my mind down to inches. Move a finger; move a hand; move a toe; move a foot. Rest between. I finally work my way to a setting-up position, drape my arm over one of the chains suspending my bunk from the wall, and let the arm hang for balance. I set for a minute to rest myself. Must be a hundred flies buzzing over the slop bucket. Sound like airplanes. Some of them Blue Bottle flies big enough to carry the whole bucket off.

Times like this, you got to work your mind like a lug wrench: tighten down on that need to pee. Tighten that pain away. Get the body locked in so the brain wheels can start turning. And I got to get mine rolling down the road. Starnes don't hardly sleep, and it ain't gon be long 'fore he'll come sidling in here wanting to tell me 'bout all the charges he's gon lay on. And when that time comes, I got to have a plan. And it better be good.

Cigarette pack on the mattress next to where my head was laying. Jailer gave it to me last night 'fore he shut the lights out. Saggy ole grandmama's face. Claimed he used to preach.

"Ain't but one in it," he said when he tossed in the pack. "Starnes finds out I give it to you, he'll fire me. Have to go back to preaching."

Never could stand filter cigarettes. Like trying to smoke Kotex.

"Much obliged," I said.

He threw in some matches, mumbled something 'bout, "pray to Jesus," and shuffled off down the hall. Big metal door clanged shut. I listened to them keys turn the lock. Must have taken a whole minute.

I fish out the cigarette, bite off the filter. Finally get a match struck on the edge of the bunk, draw in real slow. Last thing I want to do now is cough.

I look over at my other hand, resting 'cross of the chain. Sure 'nough—thumb at it again, rubbing the stub ends of my fingers. And I know the wheels are turning. Just set quiet and let 'em spin.

And the first thing comes to mind is the picture of them two bodies lying in the road, one cross of the other, one white, one black, and red leaking out from both of 'em. "What a shame," Preacher's wife was crying, hands to her face. "What a shame."

The white boy was taller. His body laid 'cross Raiford's so you couldn't see much of Raiford—just a leg sticking out on one side, shoulders on the other, and the bloody side of his head where somebody's boot tore a ear loose. *Shame*, Ludy said. Well it *was* a shame, but it was a damn sight more than that. "Shame" is what colored call it when there ain't nothing they can do to stop it and they're scared to call it something else. It was a lynching, what it was—a damn murder. That beat-up body lying in the road, same little boy who used to come to my store for candy, Acee trailing along behind him. Hell, I gave Raiford his first beer. Mama got word of it, come down there carrying a parasol. Said if I did it again, she'd bust my head open.

But that white boy—I ain't never seen a white person—man or boy—act that way toward a colored man. The way he threw out his shackled arms and fell 'cross Raiford made it look like he was trying to protect Raiford from something. But that something had done already happened. And there's a white boy, just as dead as Raiford, lying at Starnes's feet in the middle of a road in Cherrytown. Now, I heard of a lot of lynchings, and one thing I know for sure: white folks don't usually die in 'em—especially folks 'round here local.

Thumb is working my stubs good now. I can feel the tingle moving up my arm.

And right there is the key: that white body lying dead in the middle of Cherrytown. Raiford being dead don't mean a thing—not to Starnes, not to the newspapers, or them white folks running everything downtown: just another colored boy got himself killed trying to act like a man. And if that body laying 'cross Raiford had been black, well it might have raised some questions 'bout how come two black men got shot and beat to death in the same spot. But after a week passed, wouldn't amount to a drop of pee in that bucket over there.

But that other body was white. And that boy wadn't dead in anybody's mind 'fore Starnes's man killed him. It was alive for a whole bunch of folks who must have known him—mama, daddy, teachers, the white girl with him when he come down to the store yesterday to buy beer, that bunch of cracker-heads he was riding with when one of 'em threw the egg at Gryce. And now that boy—that mama's son—is dead as Raiford, shot through the forehead, right out there in the road, lit up in Starnes's headlights like a picture show. Everybody standing 'round with their mouths open: Starnes and his deputies; them white men in their trucks with their shotguns, tire irons, and ball bats; the State Highway Patrol; and near 'bout every colored person in Cherrytown. They seen that boy, all painted up, walk up to Starnes calm as you please and stick his wrists out to be arrested. He might of been crazy and he's probably from some cracker family that don't amount to much, but the fact remains: he was white. And there ain't a damn thing Starnes can do to change that. You could see it on his face: standing there like the Holy Ghost done dropped dead at his feet.

Can't let myself grin. Crack every scab on my face. I take another one of those slow, easy drags. Strarnes done got his ass in a fix, and he knows it. When he looked down at that boy in the road, he could hear the hobgoblins coming: newspaper reporters asking questions, that bunch of ministers and them professors up at the University raising a ruckus, Mayor and Sheriff running around, trying to throw the blame anywhere but on themselves. Boy's parents, if he got any, setting front and center in a picture on the front page of the newspaper under a big headline: "Ex-High School Pitching Ace Slain in Cherrytown." Probably make the Birmingham and Montgomery papers, too.

Here's what Starnes got to do: he can hunker down, get the network going, work up the story for the white witnesses 'bout what happened last night. They all on his side. They'll say whatever he tells 'em to.

And here's what he can't do: he can't make up no story for the colored that seen what happened to that boy. They most definitely ain't on his side, and they're mad as hell. Only one person can take care of that problem for Starnes, and that man is setting right where I'm setting now. And that's the ace I'm gon play to get my ass out of here.

Shit in this cigarette tastes like it was scraped off the warehouse floor. I b'lieve they put dog hair in it. I shift my butt to take some weight off my bad side, hang a little tighter to the chain.

So that's the deal, and that's what Starnes is gon do, that and let me walk out of here, or crawl if I have to, 'fore the next sun sets.

And then I got my own problem: how'm I gon keep *my* peoples' mouths shut? 'Course, it'll get out sooner or later, but I got to buy Starnes a good six-to-nine months or he'll have my ass back in here on some charge he's done cooked up. Some of the folks will do what I tell 'em to. Some'll listen to what I say 'cause they don't want no more trouble. And some'll listen 'cause they know it's what Preacher Gryce would counsel if he was around. If I can find Acee, get him on my side, they'll listen to him, too, 'cause they done got it in their heads he's the Second Coming of the Lord. But I seen those faces out there along that road last night, and some of them done got so mad they don't care anymore. Some of 'em—Elton and his bunch, four or five more—done jumped the fence onto Raiford's track, ready to take up where he left off. They'll be hollering 'bout Sheriff Starnes to anybody who'll listen.

I got to get ahead of that. And what that means is, much as I been trying to stay shy of it, I'm gon have to join in and take over. Got to get things going in the right direction. Got to be the hand that turns the wheel. And the best way for me to do that is do what I'm best at: planning, talking, and making money to help things along. I been practicing all three my whole life.

Soon as I get out of here, I'm gon call a meeting. Gon show 'em how to play it cool, make all that swole-up anger work for 'em. You got to start quiet and slow, talk to people—preacher's folks, the lay-lowers, the go-'bout-my-own-business folks. Get 'em on your side, build up a following like Gryce was trying to do. And it's got to be wide enough and deep enough that when the time comes, white folks can't throw it off on "a few bad niggers." Like, "most of them know their place. It's the trouble-makers stirring things up." Gryce was right 'bout one thing: this freedom thing is spreading. We got to keep it spreading. Right time come, touch the fire to the gasoline.

Damn if I ain't near 'bout talked myself into the civil rights business.

I push off the wall, stick what's left of the Marlboro in my lips, and brace both hands to get to my feet. Aw, Lord! They must have busted at least four, five ribs. I hold to the bunk chain to steady myself, breathe slow and easy.

I'm gon tell you one thing, though: time I get out of here, that store of mine better still be standing. If it ain't I know where Starnes lives—old farm house used to belong to his family, way out in the county. His wife left him ten years ago, and he's been living there alone ever since. One of those dead cold nights in January, when he's walking from his shed back to the house, toting an armload of firewood, he ain't gon make it. He's got that Adam's apple sticks out like a Studebaker grill. Hard to cut through, but a good enough razor man with a sharp enough razor can slice it like a cantaloupe. And that man is standing right here, getting ready to take that first step toward the bucket.

June 2012

# Acee

Acee Waites sits on a porch overlooking the sea, facing westward. A salty breeze flaps the dish towels he has hung to dry on the line above his head. Toward the horizon, the ocean shrugs and throws itself at the base of cliffs below where he sits. The waves boom and fade, waiting on the next boom to come. In that hissing silence, he feels the emptiness of the house behind him. The metal sculptures he created as reflectors and prisms for his variegated gardens of color and light—all he has left from his life's work as an artist—stand in sentient silence in his garage-studio up the hill. They have not spoken to him since Resa died three years ago, leaving him only the memories of their winding journey together, beginning in that defining moonlight beside the highway to Birmingham. Those memories toll like bells in his brain—the shots and sirens, the screeching police cars; his wailing, bent-necked mother; Raiford beaten to death; the people of his old neighborhood mourning the dead, awaiting Acee's return with their nervous, hopeful eyes.

And Preacher, with his giant hands in which Acee felt so small as a boy and even as a young man. All that praying together in the study behind the church, Acee's knees grinding the floor through the white-folks' hand-me-down rug. The love and expectation in every look Preacher bestowed on him. Somehow, as strong as the expectations were, it was the love that finally made the difference. That's what made the decision for Acee in the moonlight on the dirt road near the highway to get back in the car with the white girl and Resa and keep going to Birmingham and beyond. Preacher gave Acee the welding torch and scrap iron, got him started on that first statue of the tall, bent figure with his arms reaching out, which Acee now knows was Preacher himself. That statue and the infinite array of shadows it cast on the rough shed wall opened Acee to the magic of his own imagination and the possibilities of another life. It gave him permission to do what he needed to do. And Preacher did it without even knowing it. Or, perhaps he did know it. Preacher did not shy from the unlimited possibilities of love.

That first sculpture is on some scrap heap in Alabama now, or maybe part of a boiler plant in a place like Preacher used to work in. Dead, like all those people in his past are dead. Except Resa. Somehow she is still here. They grew old together. He feels her in every part of him, sees her movement in every roll of the sea, hears her whisper in the swish of the waves against the shore.

And Bo, the white boy. Every month or so, Bo rises like a moon in Acee's mind and brings with him the same moonlit question: has he forgiven Bo? The white boy who threw the egg at Preacher, goading him to run himself to death in his own neighborhood in front of his own house. The white boy whose face years before, streaked with his sister's finger-paints, would light into a grin when he and Acee met in the lumberyard. The white boy who looked at him across the car seat when they met down at Rosemont's, denying all of that, or afraid to admit it.

Beyond the cliff top, gulls squawk and circle. It is high tide. Waves riding the swells crash at the base, slosh among the rocks, and release the briny smell of the sea. The sun reddens and sinks toward the water. The towels hanging about his head flap more slowly. He's noticed it more and more lately: moments like these where time seems to pause and hold its breath.

Bo was there in the end. Acee and Resa heard all about it from May even before it became a legend in Cherrytown: a white boy trying to save a black man from a lynching. Once again playing Indian—face and chest streaked with red mud, fighting out the end of the blood war he started. But when Acee thinks about it, maybe that egg had to be thrown. And when it was thrown—by a white boy in Cherrytown—it for sure had to hit a black man, and maybe that had to be Preacher. Maybe the black man needed to be a special man, a leader in his community, a man of genuine goodness, who in spite of that felt the historic shame of that crack against his skull and the yolk dripping down his neck, found his years of lost anger, and gave chase. The Raiford part in us all. Maybe all those things had to happen, just in that order, and had been waiting to happen for a long time. And the white boy—maybe he had to be special, too, in his own way. Not a Kluxer, not a hater of black men, but a boy with a not-quite-dead spark of humanity who once had a black playmate. A white boy who, by hurling the egg that knocked Preacher to his knees, stirred the black community to rise to its feet, and helped some of them, including Acee, start walking.

The sun melts slowly into the water. The waves seem to come slower and heavier below the cliffs, hiss for a longer time on the beach. "Hush," they seem to say. "Hush." He'll drift off in a minute—that ten minutes or so he catches every day before he goes in to make his supper. And soon he will hear, as always, the trickle of water in that creek, running through the pasture beside the old Birmingham road, and see beyond the treetops, the frozen brightness of the moon. And he will feel again the distance between him and Resa, standing by the car with the white girl, waiting for him to make up his mind as to what they will do. He will know that the decision to leave Tuscaloosa was made even before he turned toward her and started walking up the road, even before they met Mem and sneaked their way out of Cherrytown. Because when Preacher died, Acee began the search for *himself*, found the light and shadow of what he was meant to be, and discovered in some vague corner of his heart that Resa loved him for it. And at that moment, he was already gone.

# Acknowledgments

Well, it's tempting to just say all writers since *The Dream of the Rood* and all writing teachers on the eastern seaboard. But I'll try to narrow it down.

Many very generous and talented people helped me write this novel. It's difficult to define categories such as teachers of writing and writers who read my work and advised.

I have had terrific writing teachers: Georgann Eubanks, Lee Smith, Laurel Goldman, and numerous writer/teachers at Bob Boyer's excellent New York State Summer Writers Institute at Skidmore College, many of whom are our most celebrated writers. Both Lee and Laurel read parts of the manuscript and offered encouragement and suggestions. Members of Laurel's writing class (Mia Bray, Alex Charns, Linda Finigan, Alice Kaplan, Mary Moore, Kathleen O'Keefe, and Martha Pentecost) also helped—especially Mary Moore and Linda Finigan, two exceptional writers and critics—who read the manuscript in its entirety and bucked me up during dark days when I was ready to commit the whole project to the fire.

Other writers helped immensely with the progress of this work. Chief among them is Craig Nova, who not only read the manuscript and offered detailed critique, but has served as good friend, morale-booster, and backbone-supplier through this entire process. Craig is not only a preeminent American novelist and teacher of writers, he is a life-long and exceptionally keen student of the writing craft. And craft is what he taught me more than anything—the meaning of and practice of it. That plus attitude, which is to say—how to treasure the beauty and tolerate the absurdity of the writing life.

Another dear friend and icon among American writers, Elizabeth Spencer, indulged out-loud readings of chapters in our writing group and read parts of the manuscript. Elizabeth is one of those astounding Southern women (perhaps men, too) whose genteel nature enhances and sharpens the genius that is already there. Her word is gold. Her observations were always quick, polite, and dead on the mark.

And once again, Lee Smith—one of America's most talented and certainly its most exuberant story-tellers. I have found much generosity of spirit among writers, but I doubt there is another writer in America who has offered more encouragement and help to aspiring writers than Lee. She is one of the most positive and supportive people I know. I never leave talking with her without a bounce in my step and new determination.

In addition to Laurel Goldman's writing group, I am privileged to be a member of two other groups of talented writers and kind people who have patiently listened to and read parts of this novel and offered helpful, often crucial critique. The members of these groups who have helped with the novel are—in addition to Elizabeth Spencer—Laurence Avery, Maudi Benz, Cece Conway, Michael Cornett, Lucy Daniels, David Fruenfelder, Billie Hinton, Marjorie Hudson, David Lange, Jennifer Lange, Terri Lange, Lew Lipsitz, Spencie Love, Dorette Snover, Jack Raper, Elizabeth Robinson, and Tom Wolf.

Two good friends who graciously read all or parts of the manuscript and offered helpful suggestions are Jo Ann Boozer Ray and the multi-talented Sharon Swanson.

Members of my family—all keen and passionate observers of the human condition—have assisted this effort immensely by listening to chapter readings and offering critiques. My son, Will Bennett, fiction-writer and playwright, read the manuscript in pieces at various times and as a whole at the end. He is an exceptionally gifted writer/critic/

editor, and his suggestions and advice encouraged and guided me at crucial moments along the lonely writing-way. My daughter, Purcie Bennett, astute reader and listener, heard parts of the story and also provided needed encouragement and advice. My wife, Betsy Bennett, to whom this book is dedicated and who is a lifetime student of almost everything, including literature, read the manuscript at least twice in addition to listening to readings of individual chapters. Her help has been invaluable, not only as adviser but as life-partner. None of this would have happened without her.

And last but not least, Molly Tinsley, who possesses in spades what I've learned (the hard way) are the skills of an exceptional editor of fiction: literary talent, deep knowledge of the craft of writing, patience, "people skills," self-confidence, and persistence. Her help on this novel improved it in countless ways.

**Walter Bennett** is a writer and former lawyer, judge, and law professor who lives in Chapel Hill, North Carolina. He has published essays and short fiction in both print and online journals, plus numerous articles on the legal profession and one highly acclaimed book: *The Lawyer's Myth: Reviving Ideals in the Legal Profession* (University of Chicago Press, 2001). He is a native of Tuscaloosa, Alabama.

## Other Recent Offerings From Fuze Publishing:

*The Gift of El Tio* by Larry Buchanan and Karen Gans

*Nobody Knows the Spanish I Speak* by Mark Saunders

*Entering the Blue Stone* by Molly Best Tinsley

*Satan's Chamber* by Karetta Hubbard and Molly Best Tinsley

*The Mother Daughter Show* by Natalie Wexler

*Black Wings* by Kathleen Jabs

Available at www.fuzepublishing.com